Seeing the whisky bot
half, I lunged for it, wra
around the glass neck. As
sharp, broken end and thru

Abruptly, he skidded to a halt and ~~g
back away, putting his hands up in surrender. "I won t
hurt you."

Backing up further, I edged over to the front door.

"Please," he said softly, "I won't hurt you."

As I looked into his pleading eyes, my stance
softened. Why was I running? This was what I'd been
looking for. Another survivor. Another human being.

I just hadn't counted on it being so terrifying.

Hands still in the air, he edged past me like I was
some frightened animal caught in headlights and made
his way over to the front door. He twisted the handle
quickly and then used his foot to kick it wide open.

"You can leave whenever you want," he said, "But,
please…just…stay. Talk to me. Please."

I looked out into the storm. The rain outside
seemed to be falling even harder, relentlessly smashing
into the veranda decking with deafening thuds. When I
glanced back at him, my fear ebbed away a little more.

Watching him closely, I lowered my arm and
dropped the bottle. "I'll stay," I said.

As the World Falls Down

by

Katy Nicholas

Cities in Dust, Book One

As the World Falls Down

The Wild Rose Press, Inc.
PO Box 708
Adams Basin, NY 14410-0708
Visit us at www.thewildrosepress.com

Publishing History
First Mainstream Paranormal Edition, 2019
Print ISBN 978-1-5092-2867-6
Digital ISBN 978-1-5092-2868-3

Cities in Dust, Book One
Published in the United States of America

Acknowledgments

Special thanks to the following people;
My long-suffering friends, for putting up with my
eccentricities, and for reading every version of this
book, countless times—Amanda, Vicky, Rosie, and
Sheila.
Authors Rich Shifman and Jesse Frankel,
for their endless support and advice.
My (too big to name everyone) family,
for always being there for me.
And, lastly, big hugs to my dog Skylar.

Prologue

Before…

As the sun rose, I woke with a start, my nightclothes drenched in sweat, my heart pounding rapidly.

I only knew the dream had been terrifying but remembered nothing of it.

The battery-powered alarm clock atop my bedside cabinet informed me it was five A.M.

It wasn't quite time for me to get up, but with the remnant adrenalin of the nightmare coursing through me, there was no point trying to go back to sleep. Rising wearily, I stretched my arms wide, my spine cracking as though I hadn't moved in days. After a brief massage of my neck muscles to soothe the painful crick, I made my bed and dressed quickly.

Before leaving the room, I reached into the top drawer of the cabinet and retrieved a small white envelope with the name 'Rebecca' written neatly across it. My fingers traced the lettering as a wave of sadness caused my heartbeat to falter. I swallowed down my emotion and clutched the letter close to my chest.

You can do this, I told myself, repetitively chanting it like a mantra in my head.

Taking one last glance around my bedroom, I shut the door as quietly as I could, then crept across the lounge and into the kitchen.

The remnants of our last meal together were still on the dining table, so I set the letter down against a wine bottle where I was sure she would find it.

Rebecca.

On tiptoes, I crept back into the lounge and toward Rebecca's bedroom. The door was ajar enough for me to poke my head through the gap and look in on her. She was soundly asleep, so swaddled up in her duvet, all I could see were the long tendrils of her dark hair spread out over her pillow.

I blew her a silent kiss. "Goodbye, Rebecca."

Outside, the sun rose higher into a cloud-strewn, pink and orange sky. As the rays broke through the clouds and touched my skin, I tilted my head back and closed my eyes, savoring the warmth.

The twittering of a sparrow brought me out of my reverie. The little bird sat on the thickest branch of a nearby apple tree, flexing its mottled black and brown feathers as it chirped and sang. It gave me a brief glance before it took off and flew southwards, to the ocean.

I planned to head that way myself. It'd been so long since I'd seen the sea that the thought of being able to watch the waves crash onto the shore filled me with a sense of elation. Still, it wasn't quite enough to subdue the guilt welling in the pit of my stomach.

As I made my way around to the garage to collect my backpack and bike, the worries and doubts began to circulate in my mind again. My hand hovered uncertainly over the door for a few seconds before I took a deep breath and twisted the handle.

You can do this.

I conjured up an image of the ocean and closed my eyes, trying to recall the sounds of the tide coming ashore—the roaring whoosh of the surf, and the clank of rolling pebbles as the sea dragged them into its belly.

Like the irresistible song of a siren, it called to me. Pulled me. Whispered to me.

"Find us."

Chapter One

After…

It was probably June, but the days and months were something I'd long lost track of. The weather was hot but not intolerably so. Summers in the southwest of England rarely saw temperatures climb past the balmy eighties.

A slight breeze touched my cheek and flooded my senses with the familiar scent of wet earth and moss. Petrichor—that's what they called it—the scent produced by rain when it falls onto dry soil. I couldn't remember how I knew that.

I'd been caught earlier in a sudden torrential downpour that drenched me before I could find shelter. Although mostly dry again, the seams of my denim shorts had begun to irritate my thighs.

Weary and uncomfortable, I scanned my surroundings for somewhere to camp for the night, but the ground here was too uneven and overgrown.

My supplies were lashed onto the back of my pushbike, which I more often pushed rather than rode. Cycling up and down the country roads had taken its toll on my untrained muscles, not to mention all the water I gulped down to rehydrate myself.

Today, it'd become painfully obvious that getting to the city would take a lot longer than I'd anticipated and forced me to question my decision to leave in the first place. The promise I'd made to Rebecca—not to be away too long—already looked set to be broken. Unless, of course, I went back home now.

Whenever I thought of my aunt, a little voice in the back of my mind—*her voice*—begged me to return, but my stubborn streak spurred me onwards. This was something I had to do, and that was all there was to it.

I grunted despondently as another steep hill loomed in the distance, pitted with potholes so cavernous they'd become ponds from the last rainstorm. With some skillful maneuvers on my part, I managed to steer the bike around them without falling in.

It certainly hadn't taken the roads long to fall apart after the apocalypse. Roughly four-and-a-half years on, nature had made easy work of ripping the tarmac asunder, and all she needed to do now was swallow up the remnants.

Here, in the countryside, the bramble had reclaimed the terrain with a vengeance. Mostly, I trod it down as I went, but occasionally the little bastard thorns latched on and sank into my socks, gouging my flesh and leaving my gray-white knitted knee-highs dotted with fresh spots of red.

Welcome to the end of the world. The apocalypse. The end times. The closing credits. The last scene of a bad B-movie to which I'd been given a front-row seat.

At nineteen, I'd watched the swift death of the human race as seven-and-a-half billion people had succumbed to a plague unlike any other.

That was it — a virus. Quick and quiet with hardly any time to become hysterical and hoard tinned goods.

And four months was all it took.

Maybe it was better that way, rather than a long,

strung-out demise. Kinder even.

Time had passed in a blur since then. My Aunt Rebecca had religiously kept track of time in the beginning, but after a while, she'd stopped marking down each sunrise. She'd told me that she didn't need to know anymore, and I couldn't give her a good enough reason to keep putting the big red X's on the calendar day after day after day. In any case, with our seasons so far out of whack, thanks to global warming, Rebecca relied on her intuition for tasks like planting and harvesting. It generally worked out okay.

We still marked the traditional anniversaries as we'd always done—such as birthdays and Christmas—just not on any pre-determined date. Instead, we celebrated whenever my aunt decided we would, based on her best-guess approximation of the real date, and more importantly, her mood. Having once scavenged a box of party plates and candles, she'd declared it my birthday, despite being nowhere near cold enough to have been March. She'd also constructed a glitter-covered banner which read 'Happy birthday Halley!' which she'd re-used every year since.

I wasn't even sure our lackluster attempts at celebrations could even be called *celebrations* at all because they were never much different than any other day, except for using it as an excuse to over-eat tinned puddings and consume far too much alcohol. Still, on those days, Rebecca seemed happier, and so I participated in the revelry even though I saw little point in it.

A breath caught in my chest at the familiar pang of guilt that'd plagued me since leaving home. My poor Aunt Rebecca left all alone. Would she start counting the sunrises again until I got back?

Stop it!

Resolutely, I pushed the stirrings of remorse to the back of my mind and gripped the bicycle handlebars tightly, starting up the hill with renewed determination. This lasted all of five minutes until I began to sweat so fiercely my eyes stung, forcing me to let the bike crash to the ground as I vigorously wiped my face with the hem of my vest.

"Damn it!"

It took a few moments—and a tangent of swear words—but I eventually managed to collect myself enough to continue. Upon reaching the summit, I chucked the bike down again and collapsed starfish-like onto the only bit of bramble-free grass on the roadside, panting hard until my heart stopped racing and resumed a normal rhythm.

Water. I needed water, but my supply had run low. I'd caught some in the last downpour, but only a large mug full at best. Desperate, I reached into my bag and gulped down the entire bottle like I wouldn't regret it later when I started to die of thirst. Then I lay in the grass for a good half an hour, cursing my impulsivity, before I got back on my feet and started off again.

In the distance, there were a few abandoned cars parked outside of an old petrol station. Most of the old fuel stations had little shops inside stocked with basic essentials. Some of them had been thoroughly looted, while others, especially those out here in the country, hadn't been touched at all.

Most of the inner-city petrol stations had been commandeered and manned by the army toward the end, allocating fuel only to key personnel and *not* to the general public, who just wanted to get as far away from the madness as possible. The other stations, like this one, were drained and then locked up, shutters down securely, waiting for it all to blow over. If lucky, I might find something to drink and eat inside.

By the time I reached the parked cars, the need for hydration again made my tongue so dry it tasted like sawdust in my mouth. The first vehicle I approached was a large red MPV, covered in dust and wrapped tightly in some bindweed that'd crept over from a nearby hedgerow. It now covered half the forecourt. I wiped the grime off the middle section of the driver's side window with the bottom of my vest and peered inside. Seeing no human remains, I pulled the weed strands away from the door and wrestled it open. Thankfully it was unlocked, not that I hadn't become accustomed to smashing the occasional window every now and then if need be. I simply didn't have the energy for vandalism.

Rooting through the car, my efforts were rewarded with half a pack of chewing gum and a still-sealed carton of children's orange cordial. Triumphantly, I shook the drink up and pierced the foil hole with the attached straw, sucking the liquid down before I had a chance to decide whether it tasted all right or not. It constantly surprised me what remained edible years after it was deemed out-of-date.

Unfortunately, the other two cars on the forecourt yielded nothing but an empty plastic water bottle and a clear sandwich bag of something green and moldy.

My interest shifted onto the kiosk building behind the forecourt. Despite the anterior door being locked up tight with shutters and chains, the goods entrance around back had only been covered with a sheet of plywood and secured with two padlocked hasp and staple locks. For such eventualities, I'd packed a crowbar in my rucksack. When the hasp hinge finally tore away from the wood, I quickly gained access, immediately finding myself in a small, dank storeroom. The shelves were mostly empty apart from a few basic brand tinned goods and bottles of pop. The main shop, however, yielded nothing. The shelves were utterly barren of anything aside from dust and dried-out insect carcasses.

Deciding to call it quits for today, I unrolled my sleeping bag and spread it out on the storeroom floor, where I feasted on watery spaghetti hoops and rice pudding. With my belly full and suitably rehydrated, I retrieved a map from my backpack and marked off my progress with a red pen.

By following the coast and sticking to back roads, I'd reach Bristol in just over a week at this pace. While the motorways and highways were a faster route, such places were better avoided. The main roads served as mass graveyards now, cluttered with thousands of stationary vehicles, the skeletal inhabitants forever stuck in gridlocked traffic as they'd made futile attempts to escape or get home to the people they loved.

Such scenes had been described to me in horrific detail by my aunt, intent on sheltering me from it all by making sure I never wanted to venture from our little village. It hadn't worked. Ironically, seeing it for myself may well have dissuaded me from this quest.

Or not.

The voice in my head, urging me to look for other survivors, would only have gotten louder and louder if

I'd continued to ignore it. There had to be someone else alive out there somewhere.

Surely, Rebecca and I couldn't be the only ones left?

As night fell, I lay on top of my sleeping bag, in the darkness, listening to the sound of distant thunder. Somewhere, a storm raged, but here it stayed dry and hot as I struggled to fall asleep.

****

The next day began dismal and gray, the swollen clouds spitting out rain at unpredictable intervals. Occasionally, lightning flashed overhead, followed by a low rumble of thunder but nothing violent enough to send me running for cover. The wind had picked up significantly, but I found it refreshing after the humidity of the past few days, although I could feel my cheeks starting to burn from the battering.

It wasn't long before I reached a little village.

Quaint, pastel-colored cottages encapsulated a harbor littered with the wrecked hulls of fishing boats still moored to the quayside with rusted chains.

I walked past, imagining what it might have looked like before the world ended. The image I conjured in my mind was so vivid I could almost smell the fishy whiff of the day's catch slowly festering on the barrows.

In the summer, this place would have been a tourist trap, besieged with beach-loving families in search of a patch of sand to lay their towels and eat their fast-melting ice creams. I half-expected to hear the cries of overtired children, pestering their parents for a replacement cone after letting the first one liquefy and slop to the ground. I envisaged couples walking hand in hand down the promenade, laughing, and sharing a pot of whelks or crab sticks.

At the end of the row of cottages, I came upon a souvenir shop, its big, wood-framed windows covered in a layer of dirt so thick it obscured my view of the tacky curios which undoubtedly lined the shelves.

Curious, I set my bike aside and pushed hard on the big brass handle of the door, which creaked open after a few shoves, albeit grudgingly. Suddenly disturbed by my presence, a cloud of dust particles swam about in front of me, causing me to cough and cover my mouth. Excessive dust often meant that a corpse or two had decomposed close by, but there were none I could see in the immediate vicinity. I'd simply have to be mindful when I walked around, to avoid tripping over them— they posed no other threat to me. This was no zombie apocalypse, after all.

Leaving footprints in my wake that sent dust bunnies swirling into the air, I roamed up and down the aisles, examining the treasures and trailing a line in the settled dust on each shelf with my index finger. After a while, my eyes fell upon a small wooden box, decorated with tiny white shells and little plastic seahorses. I picked it up and gently blew the cobwebs from it, opening the lid tentatively. Blue velvet lined the inside, and under the lid, a little oval mirror had been glued haphazardly to the fabric. Upon seeing my own altered eyes in the reflection, I quickly snapped the lid shut again.

The virus had left me with a strange, red ring around my ice blue irises, serving as a constant reminder that I should be dead, like virtually everyone else who'd become infected. Whether immune or just plain lucky, my aunt hadn't caught it. Sometimes, though, I wasn't sure Rebecca considered us the lucky ones at all.

My knuckles whitened around the little box before I threw it hard against another shelf of knickknacks, smashing it into several pieces and sending a half-dozen lighthouse statues crashing to the floor. About to make an abrupt exit, I suddenly caught sight of a long, oval mirror on the far wall. I walked over to it and traced the top corners of the wooden frame with my fingers, admiring the delicately carved little starfish that lined the edge, their spindly arms reaching out to hold the mirror glass in place. I moved in front of it to see my reflection—something I'd rarely done since the end of the world. Not that I'd spent much time gazing into mirrors before the apocalypse either.

Growing up, I'd always been a little self-conscious. Curvier and shorter than most of the other girls in high school—and somewhat introverted—I preferred to blend in rather than stand out. I'd never thought of myself as particularly pretty either, although my one and only friend Lizzie had often told me how gorgeous I was whenever I'd criticized my appearance.

"You're beautiful, and I love you!" She'd told me, during one, dull science lesson at school. The teacher had gone home ill, leaving a disinterested prefect in charge of the class, who'd disappeared off to the toilet block for a smoke every fifteen minutes or so. Largely unsupervised, Lizzie and I had chatted idly for the next hour.

"I'd die for your ass!" she'd confessed, a little too loudly, prompting a group of boys on the opposite table to snicker and wolf whistle. Lizzie had flipped them her middle finger and continued talking. "And, your lips! They're so kissable!" With that, she'd pouted like a fish and planted a sloppy peck on my mouth. I'd laughed so hard I'd barely managed to catch my breath.

I missed Lizzie most of all.

As I looked at my reflection now, the image staring back surprised me. My appearance differed a little from how I remembered it. I'd thinned out quite a bit around my waist and thighs, while my hips and chest had remained ample. My dark brown hair, which I'd tied into a loose ponytail, was much curlier and longer than it'd ever been and flecked with the same sun-bleached, auburn highlights I'd always admired in my aunt's hair. Had this not been the end of the world, my appearance would've provided me with a decent confidence boost.

Such was the irony of my near-solitary existence now.

With an angry grunt, I quickly left the shop, managing to ride my bike on and off where the ground stayed flat and less overgrown. By late evening, I'd passed through a few more sea-side villages much the same as this one, and skirted around a major town.

Upon discovering another empty, unlocked car abandoned at the roadside, I sat in the back seat, dining on a tin of baked beans and then an expired cereal bar that tasted of cherry-flavored cardboard.

I fell asleep before dark, but bad dreams kept me from sleeping for more than a few hours at a time. Since leaving home, I'd had the same recurring nightmare over and over, the details of which quickly faded from memory as soon as I woke up. All I remembered of it was...*red*. A dull carroty red and a strange feeling of familiarity.

I put it down to anxiety, not wanting to think too much on it, and tried to get a few more hours of shut-eye. Unfortunately, try as I might, sleep alluded me. At the sound of birds singing a pre-dawn chorus, I reluctantly got up and recommenced my journey.

The morning was hazy and damp. A thick sea mist-swathed the ground, and I struggled to see beyond a few meters in front of me. It began to thin a little as the sun rose higher but still obscured anything at a distance, aside from a church spire poking out from one of the rolling banks of fog. I headed toward it, passing by a boarded-up pub which had probably closed for business long before the end of the world.

The floundering pre-apocalypse economy had been ruthless in its destruction of the humble local watering hole, favoring large chains with two-for-one cocktails instead. My mind conjured up images of Sunday worshippers, hurriedly pouring out of the church and straight into the pub for a quick pint. They'd be home before two P.M though, to put their feet up and watch football, with a steaming roast dinner sat on their laps.

Absently, I drifted through the gates of the churchyard, just managing to find the stone path that weaved up to the church. It was surrounded on either side by moss-enveloped gravestones of various heights and shapes. Most of them were pre-war, leaning too far back or too far forward for me to read the inscriptions. The only thing keeping them upright now was the long grass and the twisting ivy threads.

The church doors were slightly ajar, encircled by two stone angels forming an arched threshold. I slipped through the gap in the heavy wooden doors and tip-toed inside. Enough sunlight beamed in through the highest leadlight windows to illuminate the aisle as I walked down it, pulling at the encroaching ivy that wrapped around the long wooden pews nearest the entrance.

So much colder inside than out, I shivered and smoothed down the rising hairs on my arms. My footsteps echoed on the stone floor as I approached the alter, my sense of smell suddenly overpowered by the scent of musty old books and beeswax polish, still lingering in the air after all this time. By the altar, I stopped and gazed up at the tall, arched, stained-glass window behind it. It was mostly unbroken apart from a small section in the middle where a tree branch had come through, just above the head of an angel with golden hair and orange wings. The colors reflected onto the white stone walls all around me, projected out by the slivers of sunlight managing to penetrate through the fog outside.

Dazzling.

Eventually, I tore my attention away and turned around to leave.

A little scream escaped from my throat as my eyes fell upon the two silent figures watching me from the front pew. A startled pigeon bolted from one of the ceiling beams above me and flew over my head, causing me to shriek once more and duck down beside the altar.

With my heart racing at light speed, I slowly straightened and stepped away from the skeletal voyeurs. The two long-dead parishioners remained still as I sidled past, their heads bowed against each other at the temples, eyes closed. A deep chill rattled my bones at the sight of the tormented expressions on their withered, leathery faces.

They'd died in anguish, and yet the scene before me was also one of serenity and tenderness. Strangely, I envied them, huddled together in a place they found comfort in, frozen in a loving embrace until they finally became dust.

It was their *togetherness* I envied most of all.

Heaving a sigh, I left them to their peaceful repose, making sure to push the wooden doors closed, sealing their makeshift tomb as I exited the church.

****

Before…

My mother died shortly after I turned fourteen. Back then, I'd been allowed to walk home from school by myself without the constant, overbearing presence of my stepfather.

We lived in a small, two-bedroom flat in what used to be an old Victorian house, divided into three units over three floors. Our rooms were on the top floor and once belonged to my grandmother, who'd passed away when I was two years old, six months after my grandfather.

As for my father, his name was Samuel, and he had chosen not to be a part of my life. According to my mother, this was for the best.

For the longest time, it'd been just the two of us— my mother and me. Two years ago, however, my mother had married Andrew after a brief whirlwind romance.

He'd been all right at first, charming and generous, and understanding of my mother's occasional bouts of sadness and melancholy. He'd soon shown us his true colors though, unable to keep his real personality locked away forever. Andrew was prone to either being silent or angry, spending most of his time tinkering with a guitar that he couldn't play to save his life, and only speaking to my mother when he wanted to criticize her or control her.

They constantly argued over trivial things and issues that existed only in Andrew's twisted mind. If my mother were late home for any reason, he'd accuse her of being unfaithful. If she didn't answer his phone calls immediately, he'd berate her for being inconsiderate. Living up to his expectations proved impossible.

After one particularly aggressive rant about how my mother never made him a priority, Andrew had announced that he intended to move out. Months on, I saw little evidence of him trying to find somewhere else to live.

He'd recently got some administrative job working evenings in a call center, which meant he'd be around more, much to my dissatisfaction.

I began taking the long route home from school to minimize the amount of time I had to spend in his presence. Some days, he'd go to the pub after lunch, and then we'd only see him briefly for dinner before he left for work, still slightly inebriated.

Those were good days.

His car wasn't on the driveway when I got home, and I breathed a sigh of relief as I put my key in the door to the communal entrance. I hurried up the stairs, eager to watch some television before he got home and moaned about the noise or my choice of program. Unlocking our front door, I quickly hung up my coat and school bag in the hall and then skipped down the hall to the living room.

"Mum?" I called out. I got no reply, but it wasn't unusual as she often went to the supermarket before dinner.

Planting myself down on the sofa in front of the television, I retrieved the remote from between two couch cushions and flicked idly through the channels in search of something to watch. I settled on a pop music channel and vegetated for over an hour before my empty stomach began to launch a revolt against me. Checking the time, I knew Andrew would be back any minute, expecting dinner to be on the table.

Where was my mother?

I hauled myself up of the sofa and went into the kitchen, flipping on the switch of the kettle and delving through the biscuit tin for a cookie. Once the kettle had boiled, I made myself a tea and then absently rechecked the time by my watch.

Maybe her bus was running late?

After gulping down the tea and then several glasses of cordial to stave off my hunger pangs, I headed to the bathroom. As I reached out for the handle and stepped forward, the sole of my right foot made contact with something warm and wet. The carpet where I stood was thoroughly soaked, leaving the coffee-colored pile a few shades darker than it should have been. I lifted my foot, pulling off my wet sock to examine it. The water had an unusual color to it, and it had stained the white cotton an orange-yellowish shade.

I pulled on the door handle only to find it locked. "Mum?"

After no reply, I banged on the door and called out a few more times, my voice becoming more frantic each time I shouted for my mother.

Andrew suddenly appeared in the hallway then, breathless and unsteady from climbing the stairs in his intoxicated state. He strode over to me and shoved me out of the way.

"Natalie!" he shouted. "Open the door!"

He pounded so hard on the door I heard it crack against the frame. Despite his short and scrawny appearance, Andrew was strong. He charged the door, shoulder first and it swung open, the wood around the lock splintering off with a crunch.

"Stay there!" he barked at me.

He went into the bathroom, his trainers splashing on the water-logged lino. He froze as he turned toward the bathtub, his face draining to an ashen pallor. He stood still for a moment, staring, breathing heavily. I walked forward, and he thrust out a hand to stop me.

"Stay there, Halley!"

My mother had named me after a comet because right up until my birth, she'd been terrified of my arrival, but then I'd turned out to be the most beautiful thing she'd ever seen.

That's what she'd said.

Andrew pulled his mobile phone out of his pocket and dialed the emergency services, asking for an ambulance. I blinked, not knowing what to do, my head swimming with panic.

Now that the door was open, I heard the sound of a tap running, and from the way the water moved across the floor, the bathtub had overflowed.

Why hadn't she turned it off? Had she fallen asleep? Had something happened? Why did she need an ambulance?

I couldn't think properly. My thoughts were

scattering in different directions. I looked down at the floor of the bathroom, at the water gathering around Andrew's feet, which had strange, floating veins of red swirling about within it.

Blood. It was blood.

Chapter Two

After...

It had been four days since I'd left Rebecca. Each town and village I passed through appeared much the same, all of them empty, overgrown, and devoid of any trace living human beings had ever walked the streets.

The occasional cat or dog crossed my path, scruffy and thin, no longer spoiled by human owners. Since the apocalypse, they'd resorted to scavenging on rodents and insects. Sometimes, they picked at the bones of corpses too.

Grimacing at the thought, I reminded myself that we all did what we had to do to survive. Except, I needed to do more than just *survive*.

My aunt never wavered in her conviction that we were all that remained of the human race—in the reachable vicinity, at least. In her time looting the southwest, not another living person ever crossed her path—not one.

"It's just you and me, my sweet girl," she'd said.

For a time, I'd accepted her truth, but in the end, I needed to see it with my own two eyes, especially before resigning myself to the grim reality of living the remainder of my existence at the cottage. Rebecca had always brushed off my most predominant fear—if I didn't find another living person, I would end up alone, sooner or later. Rebecca was already in her fifties, and although she was in good health, there were no doctors or hospitals to rely on anymore if she became seriously ill. This fear always lingered in the back of my mind, however hard I tried not to think about it.

The closest city was Bristol—my aunt had never traveled up that far, leaving it an unexplored possibility. I reasoned most survivors would have stayed in—or at least close by to—the more developed, urban areas, within easy reach of food and other supplies, especially since there were no running cars anymore. To me, it made sense, even though my aunt and I still lived out in the country, miles from any major metropolis. She loved her cottage and had no intention of abandoning it any time soon.

I'd also aimed for Bristol because it was somewhere I could get to on two wheels without wandering too far from home. A reachable destination. A target.

My aunt hadn't wanted me to leave. In the end, though, she'd reluctantly agreed to let me go. In fear of her changing her mind, I'd snuck away early one morning while she slept. Not an act to be proud of, but what choice did I have? We all did what we had to do to survive, right? Rebecca included.

When I turned onto a little side street, the high-pitched mew of a cat startled me. It gave another yowl as it stretched and rolled around in the middle of the road, exposing its pinkish belly to the hot sun. It lifted its head slightly at my presence but didn't move from its spot. In the days before the apocalypse, I would've stopped to pet it and give its ears a good scratch, but hunger had driven most of them feral now. Any affection I showed this kitty would most likely leave me with multiple claw marks and a nasty bite wound. Even as I passed by, allowing a generous space between us, the scowling tabby eyed me with such a look of disdain it left me feeling distinctly intimidated. Thankfully, it let me pass through its territory unharmed.

A little while later, I came upon an injured bird—a jackdaw, flapping about in the long grass, trying to fly but unable to lift its left wing properly. The black feathers on its chest glistened with spots of fresh blood, and I figured it must've come up against a hungry animal recently. Maybe even the menacing tabby from earlier.

My eyes darted about, looking for predators. As a precaution, I pulled the crowbar out of my rucksack and steered my bike one-handed, ready to swing at anything that tried to eat me. I could take down a fox, but anything else would probably be more difficult. I saw nothing, and I heard nothing apart from the flap-flap of the unfortunate jackdaw.

I lowered the bike down next to the bird and tried to examine it, despite its frenzied hopping to get away from me. Blood seeped from several small, deep puncture wounds in its skin. The wing hung at an odd angle, definitely broken. Eyes wild with fear at my proximity, it squawked loudly and made another attempt at retreat, but in its disorientated state, it only managed to gyrate in a circle. The kindest thing would be to put it out of its misery before it got picked off by another animal, or it died of dehydration or shock. I let it go and stood up, considering my moral obligations. I didn't want to kill it. Neither should it suffer.

If my aunt were here, she'd have no problem

wringing its neck. We kept birds at home and trapped rabbits, but Rebecca was the only one to do the culling, and it never seemed to bother her.

My turn.

I waited silently for the bird to take a break from its frantic flapping, my heartbeat resounding in my ears as I aimed the crowbar and steadied my jittery grip. Somehow, using a blunt object seemed less distasteful than doing it with my bare hands.

The metal rod came down heavily on the jackdaw's head with a thump. I swung it twice to be sure. It was definitely dead by the second blow.

For lack of a shovel, I used the crowbar to carve out a shallow grave in a soft patch of earth and then buried its lifeless body, covering the area with a few rocks to stop it from being unearthed by some wild animal later. Noticing a few smudges of blood on my vest, I suddenly felt very unclean.

Retrieving my bike from where it lay, I steered it toward the sound of the ocean. Earlier, I'd seen a few signposts at the roadside pointing the way to a beach, and so I made my way down through the narrow streets, eventually coming out onto a crescent of luxurious, new-built, beach-front homes. Mostly unoccupied, only a few had cars parked in the driveways. I ducked into an alley between two villas and followed it until I ended up on a wide concrete promenade. I parked my bike against the seawall and freed my rucksack from the frame.

Once at the shoreline, I stripped down to my underwear and then pulled a bar of soap and a washcloth from my bag. The bird's blood didn't scrub from my vest very easily and left a yellow stain on the white material. It would have to do. I could've just thrown it away, but it seemed wasteful to me. With the vest laid out on the pebbles to dry, I took the opportunity to go for a swim and scrub myself clean too. I kept my underwear on—not that there was anyone here to see my naked body should I have chosen to skinny dip.

Maybe my choice to be modest reflected my hope that I wasn't alone.

The sea was incredibly cold despite the day's heat, but I soon became acclimatized and comfortable enough to float in the water and bask in the sunshine for a while. It wasn't as relaxing as it should have been; I kept thinking about how I'd bashed the jackdaw's head in with the crowbar. It made me feel dirty all over again.

****

Against my better judgment, I took the path through the woods instead of attempting to fight my way through the bramble overtaking the adjacent lane. The thick layer of decomposing leaf mold on the copse floor had kept the weeds at bay, making it the preferable route. As soon as I entered the woods, though, my instincts told me it was a bad idea.

Pushing my bike along as rapidly as possible with my attention fixed firmly on the path ahead, I tried hard to ignore the eerie creaking of the trees as they shifted with the breeze.

The moment I heard the loud snap of a twig behind me, I instantly wished I'd trusted my instincts. The hairs on the back of my neck rose suddenly and sent a cold chill down my spine as I slowly turned around. My eyes darted about to the shaded areas between the trees, scanning the shadows for any sign of movement, but I struggled to see anything clearly in the fading, late-afternoon light. Just when I thought I'd imagined it, a brief flash of something gray appeared in my peripheral vision.

As slowly and as quietly as possible, I leaned my bike against the nearest tree trunk and slipped my hand into my rucksack, searching for my crowbar.

It wasn't there. Shit. I must've left it on the ground next to where I'd buried the bird.

I attempted to steady my breathing. For all I knew, it was merely a wood pigeon stalking me through the scrub—certainly no reason to panic. Still, as a precaution, I slid my backpack onto my shoulders in case I needed to run. If the ground hadn't been so uneven and strewn with roots, it would have been faster to ride my bike. As it was, I had no choice but to rely on my own two legs to carry me safely out of the woods.

Another loud crack to my right made me turn sharply. I strained my ears to listen for further noises, but I could barely hear anything over the sound of my thundering heartbeat. As I backed up, a protruding root caught my ankle, sending me into a backward tumble. My bottom took most of the impact, and I managed to refrain from crying out when I hit the ground, landing in a patch of stinging nettles. Rapidly, I scrabbled back onto my feet, and put my back to a thick oak tree while I caught my breath, hissing from the burning rash forming on my upper thighs.

My mind spun, trying to rationalize my predicament. What could be out there? A dog, maybe. Or a boar. Either of those creatures, driven by hunger or fear, could quite easily kill me if I couldn't outrun them.

I scanned the undergrowth for something I could defend myself with—a heavy branch or a sharp stick. A few meters ahead of me, I spied a rock about the size of my hand. Moving away from the protective shielding of the tree, I inched forward to pick it up, but I instantly stiffened when, out of the corner of my eye, my pursuer made a move. There it was—a large gray shape about twenty meters away, between two giant ferns.

Blinking, I twisted my head. It was no boar, and certainly *not* a dog. The bulk of the animal was massive, and it stared directly at me with its bright yellow eyes.

A wolf.

Mostly a murky-gray mass of fur, it had a much darker patch of steely, almost black, coloring across its face which only served to bring out its big-eyed, piercing glare.

Of all the challenges I thought I'd have to face on this journey, never for a moment did I consider falling foul of a wolf. Why would I? They weren't native to Britain, having been hunted to extinction several hundred years ago, and therefore it—or perhaps its wolf parents—must've escaped from a zoo at some point during the apocalypse. Probably when the power went off for good, rendering useless the electrified fences keeping it captive.

As the wolf ran its pink tongue over its sharp teeth, I began side-stepping carefully through the wood to put as much distance between myself and the wolf as possible. But, for every step away I took, it padded closer toward me.

Maybe it was just curious because it didn't look particularly malnourished, although hard to tell under all its fur.

I continued to creep away, hoping to find the road again—and possibly somewhere to hide. Out here in the open, I was too exposed.

The wolf matched my pace, putting one enormous paw in front of the other, slinking over the ground with ease while I struggled to keep my footing.

Our ominous dance was suddenly interrupted by the sound of birds taking flight from a tree to my right. The wolf paused and looked up, watching the startled pigeons flap skyward.

Impulsively, I wheeled around and ran as fast as I'd ever run in my life, leaping over any obstacle in my path and using my forearms to shield me from the overhanging branches that tried to smack me in the face.

As I tore through the underbrush, my ankle became hooked on a coiling thread of bramble, and I pitched forward, sliding across the ground on my stomach. For a second, I lay there dazed until a low guttural snarl caused my blood to run cold. I dug my fingernails into the mud, scraping up a mixture of stones and leaf mold into my fist, and with one vigorous movement, I rolled onto my back, launching the dirt in the direction of the wolf. Its gray bulk drew back, giving me a fleeting moment to get back on my feet.

It snarled again, a dribble of saliva seeping down from its lower jaw. I slowly lifted my foot free of the bramble that tripped me and shuffled back.

On the ground beside me lay a fallen branch, discolored and dying but still appended to other thinner branches, making its form somewhat fork-like. In seconds, my hand wrapped around the wood, knuckles white with compression as I thrust it back and forth at my pursuer.

The wolf balked, reversing a few paces back into a thicket. With all the strength I could muster, I threw the branch like a javelin at the creature and ran again, faster than ever, fuelled by another surge of adrenaline.

Finally, the trees became much sparser, giving way to a sizeable playing field. I bolted immediately for a wooden castle structure in the center of a large playground. It was raised off the ground by a few meters, the inside of its highest tower only accessible by ladder.

The grass around the asphalt section of the park was long and slippery, but I managed to cut across it rapidly without skidding over. Upon reaching the wooden ladder, I scrabbled upwards, skipping over every other rung until I could pull myself up into the tower. I didn't know if wolves could climb ladders, but I probably stood a better chance in here than I did outside.

Gasping for breath and shaking uncontrollably, I crawled to the other side of the hexagonal room to one of the little porthole windows facing out to the direction I'd come from. My eyes searched the surrounding area up to the tree line.

The wolf was nowhere to be seen.

Sweating and panting, I slumped down to the floor, feeling relieved. Still, to be sure the creature hadn't followed me, I repeatedly peered out of the porthole and scanned the park until it was too dark to see any more. The castle turret would have to serve as my shelter for the night now because there was no way in hell I was climbing down until daylight. Pulling my sleeping bag from my rucksack, I wrapped myself up in it and curled up on the floor, resting my head uncomfortably on the hardwood planks.

That night, residual adrenaline and an overstimulated flight or fight response kept me awake. From the direction of the woods, I heard the distant howl of wolves—more than one—as a full moon rose to its zenith. They sounded far enough away from me not to pose an imminent threat, and so I relaxed a little.

Oddly, the sound of the baying wolves comforted me. The wolf wasn't alone. He—or she—had a family. A pack.

Human or otherwise, no one should have to be alone forever.

****

Before…

I remembered the funeral with painful clarity.

The wake took place in our small, two-bedroom flat, which now contained hardly any evidence of my mother ever having lived here at all. Only one small, framed picture of her remained—a photo taken of her on the day she'd married Andrew, two years previous. She looked beautiful, her dark hair curled and pinned atop her head, intertwined with various little flowers and jewels. She was smiling too—something she did less and less of in the years that followed.

Not many people attended the funeral. My mother had slowly lost contact with her close friends after marrying Andrew, as he hadn't liked them. Her only friends were Andrew's friends, and they came and went like the tide. Our family was small, just my Aunt

Rebecca and me now.

Some of our neighbors from the flats below came with offerings of home-baked cakes and casseroles lest we starve now my mother wasn't around to cook anymore.

My stepfather told everyone she'd died from an undiagnosed heart condition. He'd googled a more satisfactory cause of death so he wouldn't have to tell people his wife had slit her wrists in the bathtub.

After a while, he seemed to believe his version of events over the truth, which was preferable to thinking too deeply about why she'd done it.

Why? I thought about it all the time. Was it because of him? Or something I'd done?

Maybe it *was* better to believe she'd suffered a heart attack.

Andrew had been quick to donate everything she'd ever owned to charity and purge our home of any painful reminders of her. It seemed a strange way to deal with grief, but later, I would come to understand why.

He was angry at her.

She'd abandoned him. She'd taken control from him. She'd made a decision without him and rendered him powerless. It was a feeling he was both unfamiliar with and infuriated by. He wasn't the only one feeling angry. For making her life so miserable, my hatred of Andrew grew exponentially. But, of course, I said nothing and kept my emotions locked firmly away.

My aunt Rebecca had arranged mostly everything while Andrew relished the role of the devastated widower, crying when it seemed appropriate to do so and pretending to be comforted by the sorrowful reassurances of people he couldn't care less about. As the day wore on, his narcissistic attention-seeking turned to irritability, and everyone soon left, telling themselves he was just sad and tired.

Poor Andrew.

Rebecca poured him a whiskey and sat with him at the kitchen table, as close as she could manage to be next to a man she loathed. As usual, I stayed out of his way, in my room with the door ajar so I could still eavesdrop on their conversation.

My aunt and my mother were so alike they could have been twins, though my Aunt was almost a decade older than my mother.

Rebecca was tall and slim with long, curly, brown hair that fell effortlessly to her elbows and swished around when she walked. My mother had preferred her own hair a little shorter and usually tied it up in a ponytail because Andrew liked it that way.

The irate look on his face suggested to me that he found Rebecca's presence unsettling—probably, at least in part, because of the close sisterly resemblance—and he only made eye contact with her when absolutely necessary.

My aunt exchanged pleasantries with him first, asking him how he was coping, asking him when he planned on going back to work. She touched his hand in a gesture of tender affection, but I knew she would rather not be anywhere near him.

Rebecca made no secret of her disapproval of Andrew, although she only shared such views with my mother and I. Around Andrew, she maintained an air of politeness, not wanting to become one of the people he slyly exiled from my mother's life.

"Why don't you let me take Halley home with me?"

He swallowed down the caramel-colored liquid in the glass he nursed and then poured himself another.

He wasn't a particularly handsome man, although he seemed to attract a lot of female attention. His features were dark, making him look almost Mediterranean with his raven hair and thick, black eyebrows. He wasn't overly tall either, barely reaching Rebecca's shoulder when they stood side by side. For such an unremarkable man, he still somehow managed to maintain an air of intimidation and superiority.

To Andrew, everyone constituted a value. If he deemed a person as an asset, he became their best friend, but if he found them to be a liability or a threat, he would cast them aside without a second thought. Every move he made was a calculated effort to get whatever he could from people, be it adoration or financial gain. It was no coincidence this flat had belonged, unmortgaged, to my mother.

Andrew took another drink, swilling the whiskey around in his mouth before swallowing it.

"Take Halley with you, huh?"

My aunt forced another sympathetic smile. "It's what Natalie would have wanted."

Andrew chuckled and leaned back in his chair. "No, I don't think so. Thank you for the offer, Rebecca, but you aren't needed."

He'd phrased it to be deliberately unkind because he'd been insulted by the insinuation he might need help.

Rebecca glowered at him, clenching her jaw in angry frustration. "It would give you some space."

Andrew shook his head. "I said I didn't need your help."

He finished his drink and stood, forcefully kicking the chair back against the wall. He picked up the whiskey, drinking the last few dregs straight from the bottle and, when empty, slammed it down on the worktop, wiping his mouth with the back of his hand.

Andrew licked his thin lips. "You should leave now."

As I peered at Rebecca through the narrow gap between my door and the frame, her expression turned from frustration to fear, clearly rattled by his sudden display of authority. Her breath grew quick, but she kept her composure as she stood and started toward my bedroom.

Andrew quickly stepped in front of her, blocking her path.

"I just want to say goodbye," Rebecca said, her voice a little strained.

My stepfather didn't move. "I'll pass the message on. The door's behind you."

My aunt blinked and glared at him. He met her gaze like a predator guarding his territory. She continued to stare him down, her jaw twitching as she ground her teeth together. Eventually, though, she turned away from him. "Fine. If that's what you want."

He sneered. "It is."

My heart sank. Placing my hands together like we'd done at primary school during the Christmas church services, I muttered a quick prayer.

Please, God, make Andrew let me go. Please let me live with Rebecca.

I couldn't understand why he wanted to keep me

around anyway—except for the small amount of government assistance he received to help feed and clothe me. Surely, I would be in his way here—a liability.

Sighing heavily, Rebecca glanced toward my bedroom door and mouthed a silent "Sorry."

Moments later, the front door slammed shut, and she was gone.

After that day, the only contact I had with Rebecca was when we spoke over the phone. She would call me once a week on a Friday evening after Andrew left for work.

It would be four years before I saw her again.

Chapter Three

After…

The days melted away, indistinct from one another. I walked. I ate. I slept.

By the seventh day, I utterly missed my bike. The weight of my backpack on my shoulders made my spine ache, and the canvas straps rubbed painfully against my skin.

Now and then, I imagined my bike, abandoned against the old oak tree in the woods, doomed to a rusty death. It was strange how, in the absence of human beings, I'd become so emotionally attached to an object. Not that I'd ever been particularly attached to many humans.

I still had about a hundred and sixty kilometers to cover—another four or five days of walking. The heat hadn't helped, tiring me out quickly and slowing me down. Soon, I would have to veer away from the sea and head north to reach the city, but for now, I still followed the edge of the southwest, which had grown distinctly more perpendicular and hillier as I approached the Jurassic coastline. In the distance, the land tapered up and up, forming craggy, white bluffs that dipped and rose in uneven waves.

I started climbing in a slow and labored manner, hampered by the long grass underfoot and the intoxicating heat making the ground shimmer. My skin burned despite my regular routine of smothering myself in sun lotion, although it'd probably lost most of its potency over time.

On several occasions, I slipped on the rocky terrain underfoot, falling to my knees, which were now bruised and grass-stained. The last time I tripped, I ended up stumbling into a rabbit hole, twisting my ankle. Swearing repeatedly and loudly, I dug my right shoe out from a muddy mass of roots and bunny dung.

Now, I was covered in sweat *and* filth.

The weather began to turn just as I headed down a steep decline from one of the highest elevations. The sun had disappeared behind some purple-gray clouds, and I didn't need a weather forecast to tell me a heavy rain was coming. Still, I lingered on the cliff edge, staring out to sea, the salty air blowing my hair in all directions.

Exhausted and sore, I looked down at the base of the cliffs for somewhere to rest and shelter from the oncoming storm.

Directly below lay a small stretch of woodland. Tall trees waved back and forth like they were slow dancing to the sound of the waves crashing on the beach beyond.

Something caught my eye then—a glint in amongst the swaying firs. I peered at an area by the edge of the woods, but it wasn't until a more substantial gust of wind bent the trees enough to reveal a large, wooden structure. The glint seemed to be coming from the roof, but I couldn't quite make out what reflected the sporadic sunbursts—a skylight possibly, or a chimney cowl.

I headed away from the cliff edge, searching for a

road down to the bottom, and quickened my pace when I caught sight of some cars.

Six, dust-shrouded vehicles were parked neatly in two rows on a large patch of flattened dirt. In front of them, a metal sign hung from an old wooden telephone pole, informing me this was a private car park for residents of 'Siren Bay.' To the side of the parking area was a narrow road, sloping and meandering downwards until it disappeared into the tree line.

When a few spots of rain touched my face, I began to sprint.

The road seemed to go on forever, down and down, sometimes becoming so steep I struggled not to slip. By the time I reached the bottom, the rain fell harder, although the trees provided some shelter from the deluge.

Here, the path widened a little to reveal a row of mobile homes, each with its own picket-fenced slice of garden overwhelmed by bramble and ivy. I scanned each one for shelter potential. They all appeared sturdy apart from an older model that'd fallen foul of an uprooted tree. The metal chassis folded in half from the impact. I could have my pick, providing I could fight my way through the overgrowth to the front door.

Still, I was curious about the wooden building I'd seen, so I pressed on.

I soon came to another little path through the wood with the words 'private property' stamped into a metal arch above the ingress.

A flash of lightning tore across the sky above me, causing me to duck instinctively. Usually, I enjoyed watching a good storm—as long as I wasn't outside in it, in woodland and surrounded by nature's own lightning rods.

Quickly, I followed the path until the gravel track gave way to a decked area with steps leading up to a well-weathered wooden cabin. There, I halted for a moment to appraise the wooden structure. Despite its faded, slightly ramshackle appearance, it looked sturdy. Cozy even. A veranda encased the outside of the cabin, the rain hitting the wood decking so hard it sounded like someone letting off fireworks.

Taking care not to slip on the wet boards, I made my way to the front door, which was protected from the weather by a large, blue-striped awning. I slipped my rucksack off, my spine cracking as I stretched out and rolled my shoulders, hoping to ease the tension building in my tender muscles.

Elated to have found somewhere dry to rest, it took me a while to notice the terracotta pots lined up against the balustrade around the veranda. A variety of plants grew in each of the containers: rosemary, thyme, traffic-light peppers, and tomatoes, to name only a few. Reaching out to one bushy plant, in particular, I plucked one of the soft green leaves from the stem. My fingers rolled the sprig about until the scent of fresh mint permeated the air around me.

These plants were all well-cared for, free of weeds and pests, and tended to—recently.

I let the leaf fall to the floor as the realization dawned on me.

There had to be someone here.

Someone alive.

"Hello!" I shouted and began pounding on the front door.

Lightning ripped through the sky overhead again,

causing my heart to beat faster than it already was. The thunder following the flash roared so violently it rattled the whole structure.

Alarmed, I gripped the door handle and yanked on it, but it refused to budge. Balling my hands into fists, I pounded again—harder and with more determination.

Hearing no response, I ran around to the side of the cabin, skidding on a puddle and banging my hip on the balustrade. Cursing, I stumbled over to the side door and tried to pull the handle down. Again, it refused to move. My fists made contact with the frosted glass pane as I knocked so hard against the door my knuckles cracked.

"Hello!" I shrieked, but my cry was drowned out by another crash of thunder.

Growling, I skirted around to the back of the cabin.

A wave of relief swept through me when I discovered one of the windows slightly ajar. I slipped my fingers into the gap and pulled the window open as far as it would go.

"Is anybody here?" I screamed, straining my ears for a reply.

Nothing.

After a moment of fleeting hesitation, I grabbed hold of the window and lifted myself up enough to be able to kneel on the sill. As I managed to get one foot onto the frame, I slipped on the wet UPVC and tumbled into the cabin. My body slammed onto the floor with such a thump it couldn't have gone unheard. Luckily, I landed on my side rather than on my head, though it still took me a few moments to gather myself.

I was in a bedroom. The sheets on the bed were disheveled and creased. Items of clothing were strewn everywhere or in crumpled heaps on the floor. Several stacks of books had been piled up against the walls, in between the furniture. I stepped over the debris and crept into the dark corridor ahead of me. I passed by two more rooms as I slowly moved forward, mindful of what I might find.

I shouted out again but still no response.

At the end of the corridor was an open living area with a kitchenette and a lounge-diner. As I slinked into the kitchen, my feet skidded on a puddle of brownish liquid pooled on the linoleum. The musty stench of stale beer wafted into my nostrils when I kicked a collection of cans out of my way. They were all empty apart from the one that'd spilled out in front of the doorway. Rubbish was scattered everywhere, along with used tins of food stacked up in unsteady towers on the worktops, just waiting to topple over.

I moved carefully into the lounge, my eyes darting about curiously until my gaze rested upon something that made my blood run cold.

On a small sofa, covered by a large quilt, was a shape resembling a human body.

Creeping closer, I gripped one corner of the blanket and pulled it down to reveal the form underneath.

It was a man, his face a ghostly shade of gray, turning into a blueish tint around his lips. His arm hung limply beside him, an empty bottle of pills lying on the carpet, inches from his fingers.

Please, do not be dead. Please.

"No," I whimpered as I rushed forward and put the palm of my hand on his cheek. He was still a little warm. My hand went to the side of his neck, and for a few seconds, a faint pulse fluttered against my fingertips.

"Wake up!"

I shook him vigorously, but he remained motionless.

With nothing to lose and a vague idea of how to perform resuscitation, I leaned forward and pressed my mouth against his.

The moment our lips connected, a surge of static rushed over my body, leaving me momentarily stunned.

Shaking it off, I took a deep, steadying breath and blew air into his mouth, over and over. I doubted I was doing it correctly, but carried on, watching his chest rise and fall a little each time.

After several minutes, I stopped. It wasn't working.

Out of nowhere, my mind conjured up the image of my mother's blood as it had swirled around in the water spilling from the bathtub on the day she'd died. It prompted a swell of anger to form in the pit of my stomach and rise into my chest.

Spying a mostly full bottle of whiskey on the side table next to the sofa, I grabbed it and poured the amber liquid over his face. I then slapped him so hard my hand stung.

After a brief pause, I hit him again. Harder.

"Wake up!"

Nothing. Nothing at all.

Balling my hands into fists, I brought them down hard onto his chest and then pummeled faster until my arms throbbed from the action.

Still nothing.

Defeated, I sank to the floor and sat with my head in my hands, a hot tear rolling down my cheek.

I was too late.

With my head bowed, I cried quietly, my emotions alternating between despair and rage. Absently, my hand reached out for the—now empty—whiskey bottle. With all the strength I possessed, I threw the bottle against the wall. The resounding *boom* on the wood echoed throughout the cabin, shaking the timbers. The sound reverberated in my ears for a few moments and then dissipated, leaving nothing but the *thump-thump* of the rain falling onto the roof above.

I almost didn't hear the *crackle* of breath that left his lips as his diaphragm twitched.

My head snapped up. I waited for the longest time, saying a thousand silent prayers in my head, hoping it wasn't just my imagination.

It caught me off guard when his chest suddenly jerked, and I scampered back on my hands until I crashed into the wall behind me. His chest heaved again as he sucked air into his lungs. He rolled onto his side, coughing, and vomited up the contents of the pill bottle. He retched and gagged while he struggled to breathe, but eventually, with his stomach finally empty, his chest began to rise and fall more evenly. Seemingly exhausted, he rolled onto his back again and began to sob.

My heart broke at the sight of this poor, dejected soul, but the shock rendered me immobile. All I could do was watch him as he sat up slowly and wiped the moisture from his damp cheeks, the right one now sporting an angry, red welt in the shape of my hand.

He was older than me, mid-thirties, maybe. The lower half of his oval face sported a thick layer of dark stubble, one day away from becoming a full beard. His hair was a deep brown color, almost black, with unkempt waves falling over his weary and bloodshot eyes. The sight of the familiar red ring around his amber irises caused me to let out a sharp gasp.

He was a survivor, like me.

As his hand went out for his missing bottle of whiskey, his eyes fell upon mine, and he froze abruptly.

For what felt like an age, he simply stared at me. My heart raced wildly. As the panic enveloped me, I impulsively scrabbled to my feet and bolted toward the open window in the bedroom.

"Wait!" I heard him shout out as I ran down the hall.

I stumbled across his bedroom to the window, hearing his footsteps pound on the floor as he came after me. I started to climb onto the frame, but his hands went around my waist and lifted me away. I kicked back, and he lost his grip on me long enough for me to break away and run back into the sitting area.

Seeing the whiskey bottle on the floor, smashed in half, I lunged for it, wrapping my trembling fingers around the glass neck. As he ran toward me, I lifted the sharp, broken end and thrust it in his direction.

Abruptly, he skidded to a halt and began to slowly back away, putting his hands up in surrender. "I won't hurt you."

Backing up further, I edged over to the front door.

"Please," he said softly, "I won't hurt you."

As I looked into his pleading eyes, my stance softened. Why was I running? This was what I'd been looking for. Another survivor. Another human being.

I just hadn't counted on it being so terrifying.

Hands still in the air, he edged past me like I was some frightened animal caught in headlights and made his way over to the front door. He twisted the handle quickly and then used his foot to kick it wide open.

"You can leave whenever you want," he said, "But, please…just…stay. Talk to me. Please."

I looked out into the storm. The rain outside seemed to be falling even harder, relentlessly smashing into the veranda decking with deafening thuds. When I glanced back at him, my fear ebbed away a little more.

Watching him closely, I lowered my arm and dropped the bottle. "I'll stay," I said.

****

The man hurriedly cleared a space in the kitchen for us to sit. Underneath piles of dog-eared magazines were a couple of tatty, leather bar stools which he dusted off before motioning for me to sit on one.

"Sorry," he mumbled.

Every time I glanced into his sad eyes, my gut wrenched unpleasantly, and I wasn't sure what to say to a man who'd just downed a pill-whiskey cocktail with the intent to kill himself.

"My name is Nate," he stammered.

I gave him a half-smile. "Halley."

He was obviously uneasy in my presence, and I wondered how long it'd been since he'd seen another human being.

"Halley. Halley. Halley," he muttered, repeating my name to himself as though he was trying to make sure he remembered it. "Like the comet?"

I nodded.

He stared at me for a few unnerving moments and then ruffled his unruly hair. "Do you want anything to drink?"

"Please."

"Tea? Or coffee?" he asked, "Or vodka?"

He gave me the faintest of smiles, and for reasons I couldn't pin down, my heart jolted in response.

"Tea," I replied.

He stood and dug a kettle out from beneath a pile of dirty crockery. I watched him plug it in like it was an everyday occurrence before I realized what he'd done.

"You have electricity?" I asked, confused.

The power stations had been purposefully shut down to avoid a nuclear meltdown, given the dwindling personnel numbers. There was simply no one left alive to run them. With no electricity in over four years, it'd been a while since I'd last plugged anything in.

He pointed upwards. "Solar panels on the roof."

That explained the glint of light I'd seen from the clifftop.

He reached into an overhead cupboard and produced a box of tea bags. My joy began to bubble over.

"And—" I snatched the box from him and surveyed the packaging intently, "Tea bags!"

My aunt and I had been reduced to herbal brews very early on in the apocalypse. When a crisis occurred, we Brits drank tea. It stood to reason that supplies of tea bags dried up quickly when the virus hit. The coffee disappeared not long after.

A little embarrassed at my response, I handed him back the box.

Our fingers touched for a brief second, and I felt an electric surge snake down my arm and spread out over my entire body. A few static particles burst against the skin on the back of my hand, and I hissed at the sudden pinching pain they inflicted.

He must have felt something too because he recoiled quickly, flexing his fingers with a frown as he studied his hand.

"How did you find me?" he asked, after a few moments. "Did you see the messages I left?"

With a frown, I shook my head. "No, I didn't see any messages."

He looked fairly dejected by my admission. "I left messages," he murmured. "So that people would come here."

A little lost for words, I began to bite anxiously on my bottom lip. "Sorry."

I'd always found social encounters awkward and challenging, keeping my circle of friends small and relying on my friend Lizzie to lead the way in social situations. Waitressing, though, had forced me to act a little friendlier and be more outgoing. Happy customers left bigger tips.

Eager not to say or do the wrong thing, I glanced around the room, searching for clues on what to talk to him about.

The brown leather sofa that Nate had been laying on sat next to a wooden side table, carved with intricate depictions of elephants and giraffes traversing the Serengeti. The tabletop itself was cluttered with so many bottles of beer and empty crisp packets I could hardly see the matching lamp with its zebra print shade. In geographical contrast, the center of the living area was covered by a huge oriental rug, so vast it hid most of the beige carpet beneath it.

The cabin may well have once belonged to avid travelers.

Above the sofa hung a large canvas portrait of a

sailboat, and either side of it were several framed photographs, but I sat too far away to see any detail.

"How did you find this place?" I asked.

"It's my parents' place," he replied and then cast his glance floorward. "*Was* their place," he added, sadly.

Instantly, I winced. Talking about his dead parents was bound to upset him. I wasn't good at this.

He handed me my tea and went into the sitting area, lifting one of the framed photos from the wall. Behind it, a dark patch of wood marked its place—clearly, it'd hung there for years. He handed me the picture but seemed to avoid looking at it himself.

The photo had been taken here, just in front of the cabin on the beach. A middle-aged man and a woman stood with a young man in his early twenties. He handsome with dark wavy hair and a mischievous, but beautiful, smile.

"Taken about fifteen years ago," Nate said, focusing intently on my face.

"This is you?"

"Yeh."

My eyes flicked back and forth between the young man in the photo and the one who stood before me. Physically, Nate hadn't changed much. Maybe his shoulders were a little broader and more muscular now. He looked more like his mother.

"They were wanderers at heart, traveling to the furthest reaches of the globe. But when dad suffered a heart attack, they decided to put down roots," he said. "They wanted to be 'off the grid' here as much as possible. When everything went to hell, I knew where I had to come."

"So, it's only you here?" I asked but regretted it immediately.

He looked at me sadly. "Yes. Just me," he mumbled, "For the last four and a half years."

Alone, for all that time. What must that have been like? I wanted to console him, but I didn't know how. What could I possibly say?

"I'm so sorry," I whispered.

He nodded and shied away from me, raising his trembling hands to cover his face. His shoulders began to shake, his breathing fast and sharp as he sobbed again.

I slid off the stool and tentatively put my hand on his back, my heart breaking for him. It took me by surprise when he turned and put his arms around me in an almost crushing embrace, his chin burying into the side of my neck as he wept while his fingertips dug into my shoulder blades. He held me so close that I could hear the rapid thuds of his heartbeat, racing to a rhythm matching my own. Neither of us spoke for what felt like an age, but eventually, I pulled away from him and took several steps back.

This was…intense.

"I need some air," I stammered.

Nate blinked and cleared his throat. "Me too."

The storm had moved away from the bay, so we went outside.

The air was clearer, although the clouds still hung gray and heavy in the sky. We leaned over the balustrade and looked out across the beach to the ocean, the waves crashing onto the sand with a resounding *roar*, leaving puddles of seafoam in their wake. Seagulls padded along the wet sand, *squawking* loudly while foraging for washed-up sea creatures.

A mixture of different emotions welled uncomfortably in the pit of my stomach. I was relieved to have found someone, but unsure of what to make of him—this forsaken man who'd spent nearly half a decade alone like some castaway, waiting for someone to come.

I thanked my lucky stars Rebecca hadn't caught the virus and died, leaving me alone. I couldn't even begin to imagine what struggles Nate had faced here with no one to help him or encourage him. It wasn't so hard to see why he'd lost hope after so long.

Breaking the silence, I sighed longingly and then turned to face him. "It's so beautiful here."

Trying to read him proved difficult because his somber expression gave very little away. He stayed close to me though, his hand lightly brushing against mine as I gripped the top beam of the banister.

"Yes, it is," he replied. "But it isn't enough."

As selfish as it made me feel to admit it, my existence back at the cottage hadn't been enough for me either, each day passing the same as the next, with little deviation. Rebecca appeared content to carry on this way, but I certainly wasn't.

He sighed and faced me squarely. "I looked for people," he said. "I drove from place to place until the fuel went bad. I left messages on walls and bridges for people to see, to tell them where I was. No one came."

My mouth dropped open to speak, but no words came out.

"Still," he mumbled, "I shouldn't have done what I did. With the pills."

With a nervous gulp, I began to gnaw on my

bottom lip again. "I can't imagine what it's been like for you, here on your own."

Nate looked straight into my eyes then. "No," he said miserably. "I wouldn't want you to imagine it at all."

His eyes pierced mine with an intensity unfamiliar to me. No one had ever looked at me this way before. Part of me desperately wanted to turn away, but at the same time, I found myself transfixed.

"Will you stay here the night?" he asked, after a while, finally shifting his gaze from me, "I can make up the bed in the spare room for you?"

In all honesty, I hadn't thought that far ahead.

"There's a rainwater tank out the back, and there's more than enough water for a hot shower if you want one," he added.

He had me at 'hot shower.' The words almost made me giddy.

Nate's appearance might've resembled a vagabond, but I certainly wasn't looking my best either. Sore and filthy, my hair was a matted, greasy mess, and my clothes were dirty and wet, chafing painfully against my flesh.

"I would love a shower," I blurted out. In the back of my mind, however, I wondered if I should be accepting such an offer from a man I'd just met. But what choice did I have? Plus, I *really* wanted a hot shower.

He beckoned for me to follow him to a large bathroom located next to one of the bedrooms. The shower cubicle was separate from the bathtub— which was being used to store clear plastic boxes stacked on top of one another, marked with labels like 'shampoo' and 'soap.' The walls were half wood-paneled and half-papered in a cream, floral design. Despite the clutter, it was clean and smelled of lavender.

"Use anything you need." He retrieved my backpack from where I'd thrown it under the awning and dropped it down just inside the door, before closing it shut.

I shrank at the sight of my reflection when it appeared suddenly in the full-length, brass mirror hanging on the back of the bathroom door. The past few days of sleeping rough combined with the changeable weather had left my eyes bloodshot and my eyelids sore and swollen. My hair had knotted itself into several nests and somehow ensnared multiple clumps of foliage, now twisted up in my wayward curls.

After pulling out the looser bits of leaf and twig, my eyes flicked quickly over the rest of my body. The sight of my mud-smeared legs and bramble-scratched shins made me grimace. Embarrassingly, I couldn't remember the last time I'd shaved my legs, either—not that anyone could see the hair under the layers of grime and dried blood.

With a huff, I peeled off my clothes and discarded them onto the checkered black-and-white lino. I then rifled through the plastic boxes in the bathtub for some soap and shampoo, discovering some shaving foam and a razor in my search.

The shower was blissfully hot, and I languished in it for several minutes, semi-comatose from sheer ecstasy. Eventually, I started scrubbing, hissing through my teeth whenever I passed the washcloth over a raw blister where the rucksack straps had rubbed.

By the time I'd finished making myself respectable

for civilized society, the shower tray looked like someone had hosed off a muddy dog. I did my best to clean up and then dried myself with the towel Nate left for me.

A few minutes later, I changed into my last clean pair of shorts and a thin-strapped vest top, and rather than putting my malodorous trainers back on, I went barefoot.

Nate was in the small bedroom opposite, changing the sheets on a single divan bed. The lingering cloud of dust in the air gave me the impression this room hadn't been occupied in a long time. He looked up when I entered the room, his eyes scanning me from head to toe.

"You're bleeding," he said.

As I looked down, a thin dribble of fresh blood trickled from an angry welt on my collarbone.

"That looks sore." He disappeared into the bathroom for a minute and then reappeared with a first-aid kit. He opened it up and took out several bits and pieces, then dabbed at the blood on my chest with cotton wool before gently applying antiseptic cream and a plaster. Flutters of exhilaration rose in my chest as he brushed my damp hair aside to tend to another one of my sores. Every time his fingertips touched my bare skin, I felt a slight buzz from the contact.

After applying the final dressing, he smiled. "Are you hungry? I can make us something to eat?"

"Starving."

He nodded but looked a little embarrassed. "Just let me clean up first. You can rest in here awhile if you like?"

Before I could reply, he turned away and headed

back down the corridor.

There was no denying how exhausted I felt. The freshly made bed looked divinely inviting, and despite the soothing warmth of the shower, my thigh and calf muscles still ached. Surely it wouldn't hurt to lay down for a moment or two?

I crawled onto the mattress and curled up on my side. The cotton sheets were cool against my skin and smelled of the same sweet lavender scent as the bathroom. After the last week of sleeping on the hard ground or laying across the back seats of cars, this was pure nirvana.

My eyes closed momentarily, and it took a lot of effort to force them open again. I didn't think it was a good idea to fall asleep and leave myself so...vulnerable. Before the virus, I'd never have done anything like this—accept an invitation to sleep in a strange place by a man I hardly knew. But the world was a very different place now.

Needs must when the devil drives, as my aunt often said.

And anyway, finding a survivor who also happened to be a depraved pervert would be terribly bad luck.

My eyelids dropped again, and this time, it was enough to pull me down into a deep sleep.

****

Before...

In my mother's absence, I took on all the chores she'd been responsible for. For the last three years, I'd no other option than to get out of bed just after six AM and make a start on the housework. Now I attended college, my homework had doubled, but I still managed to stay on top of it by studying while Andrew was at work. He left the flat at five PM and didn't usually come home until just after midnight, which meant I'd seven blissful hours to myself.

While I'd rather have walked alone to college, Andrew insisted I wake him in the morning so he could drive me—even though, at eight-thirty AM, he grumbled about it and thundered about like a bear with a sore head.

To anyone looking at us from the outside, he was the dedicated, hardworking stepfather, but behind closed doors, he was an aggressive, controlling, drunk. Lately, however, he'd been a little easier to live with, but only because he'd found himself a shiny new girlfriend to focus on.

Her name was Lisa, and she was twenty-three. For the last few months, whenever Andrew took an evening off work, Lisa would drop by our flat. They couldn't be seen out in public together because she was married. In fact, three of Andrew's most recent relationships had been with married women. He seemed to enjoy the challenge of obtaining the unobtainable. The trouble was, once he got what he wanted, the allure waned, and he quickly lost interest.

With Lisa around, Andrew acted like the caring, considerate, sympathetic human being he always claimed to be. While it nauseated me to my core, life became a little more bearable for me. So convincing was this show of congeniality, I almost believed it myself, thinking maybe Andrew had changed because of his feelings for Lisa. Of course, it was an illusion. As the weeks passed, he struggled to keep up the pretense, and little slivers of his true personality began to slough out.

They started to argue about Lisa leaving her husband—Andrew wanted her to end the marriage as soon as possible and move in with us, but Lisa thought it far too soon.

Fast losing his control of the situation, Andrew resorted to more desperate measures.

It began small. He'd send Lisa anonymous flowers and gifts, knowing her husband would be home to see them delivered. Andrew phoned her late at night, and if she didn't pick up, he'd sent her a hundred texts about how much he loved her and wanted them to be together—again, when her husband would be home to hear her mobile buzz continuously, well into the early hours of the morning.

Lisa, like me, wasn't allowed to switch her phone off either. To ignore Andrew was one of the worst things a person could do because then he'd rant on about how inconsiderate and disrespectful it was and how worried he'd been. The arguments always ended the same way—with Lisa apologizing. Then I'd have to listen to them 'make up.'

Sometimes, Lisa would sleep over when her husband was away for work. A few times, I'd gotten out of bed during the night to get a drink of water, only to find Lisa in the kitchen with an ice pack pressed to her backside, or sometimes, to her wrists. We never spoke to each other on those occasions, just exchanged awkward glances, both of us pretending everything was peachy.

One morning, however, Andrew's misdeeds finally caught up with him.

It was his enraged hollering that woke me from a rare Sunday morning lie-in.

Out of concern for Lisa, I got up quickly and went into the lounge. She stood by the window, her gaze directed down at our driveway, lines of glistening tears spilling down her red cheeks. Out in the hall, a door slammed, and the sound of Andrew's heavy footsteps echoed on the communal staircase.

Not wanting to make my presence known, I crept into the kitchen and leaned over the sink to peer out the window.

Andrew's car was in the driveway, the front windscreen shattered with both wing mirrors dangling limply against the chassis. But this wasn't the worst of it. A thick layer of white paint covered the car, obscuring most of the shiny red paintwork he'd painstakingly cleaned and polished yesterday.

Andrew only stayed outside long enough to utter a string of profanities and kick the front bumper before storming back into the building.

"Have you seen what your fucking husband has done to my car?"

Lisa, not used to seeing her perfect boyfriend quite so livid, flattened herself against the wall. "What did you expect?"

Andrew stiffened and flared his nostrils. "What did you say?"

When Lisa didn't reply, he lunged forward and forcefully grabbed hold of her arms. "This is your fault! You should have been honest with him."

"Well," she muttered, sadly, "He knows now."

Andrew's upper lip curled into a snarl. "Who's going to pay for my fucking car?"

Lisa glared at him for a few seconds before pulling herself free from his grip. She rushed into the kitchen and reached into her handbag, which hung on the back of one of the dining chairs, and retrieved a cigarette and lighter. An uneasy feeling gnawed at my stomach as I watched her struggle to light the thin white stick with trembling fingers.

"Did you hear me?" Andrew yelled as he strode into the kitchen and slapped the lighter out of her hand.

A look of disbelief registered on her face. "I'll pay for the repairs to your shitty car, okay?"

But it wasn't okay because Lisa didn't know the *real* Andrew.

She wasn't expecting the hard crack of his knuckles against her cheek or to hear her hair splitting as he grabbed her ponytail and yanked her head back.

"Don't ever speak to me like that again!"

Impulsively, I jumped forward and tried to wedge myself between them—if I didn't, Lisa would end up with more than a black eye.

"Dad!" I managed to choke out.

He'd made me call him 'dad' as part of his doting stepfather act, but the word sat like acid on my tongue.

"She's not worth it! She'll call the police and get you into trouble. You don't want that, do you?"

My mother used to try and pacify him in the same way. "She's not worth it," I repeated softly.

Andrew's eyes flickered between us for a minute before he let go of Lisa and let her drop to the floor. "Get out!" he spat.

Lisa wheezed as she got to her feet, using the dining chair to help her stand. She slung her handbag over her shoulder and scurried, head down, to the hall.

"Oh, and Lisa?" Andrew called after her. "You forget about this, and I'll forget about my car, yeh?"

Lisa only stopped for a moment to give an emphatic nod before charging toward the front door.

Andrew pulled up a chair and slumped down onto it, examining his red knuckles with a hiss. "Get me some ice, would you?"

With an obedient nod, I fetched him an ice pack, wrapping it in a towel and placing it gently onto his hand.

"I'll do that. Get me a smoke. And a whiskey."

With any luck, he'd drink himself into a stupor and pass out for the next few hours. Rather than pour him a glass, I handed him the entire bottle and a tumbler of ice cubes, along with a cigarette, which I lit for him, his right hand too swollen to use.

"You're right," Andrew said, a wisp of smoke fanning out from the corner of his mouth. "She wasn't worth it."

He seemed to be calming down. "You're smart for seventeen, Halley. Your mother wasn't smart. I guess you must have got it from your real dad, huh?"

An unusual statement for him to make, I was used to him putting my mother down, trying to bait me into an argument, but this insult began with a compliment. He gestured for me to sit and took another drag on his cigarette before offering it to me.

"No, thanks."

He chuckled. "You can't be a good girl all the time."

Reluctantly, to appease him, I drew in a sort breath of nicotine and handed the cigarette back to him, stifling the urge to cough.

"You called me dad earlier. Don't call me that anymore," he said. "I'm not your father. Call me

Andrew from now on."

He quickly knocked back three shots of whiskey in succession and then stubbed his cigarette out in the empty glass.

"Always such a good girl." He leaned across the table and pinched my chin in between his thumb and forefinger. My stomach knotted as his eyes darkened. A false smile spread across his lips. "Not like your mother."

Another dig at her memory.

After a few more seconds of unpleasant eye contact, Andrew stood up, clutching the whiskey bottle in his left hand and dragging it across the table. "I'm going to lie down."

When he'd gone, I let out a relieved breath and rushed to the kitchen sink. I let the water run until it was scorching hot and then splashed my face, eager to wash away the taint from Andrew's touch.

Whatever new game he'd started playing, I wanted no part of it.

Chapter Four

After...

By the time I woke up, the sun had almost set, the last rays of a golden and pink sundown streaming in through the window.

Several hours must've passed while I slept.

Disorientated, I sat up. The bedroom door was closed, and a fleece blanket covered me. I hadn't heard Nate come in at all, but my backpack had been placed down beside the bed, and a bottle of water now sat on the bedside table.

My tongue felt like sandpaper as it rolled over my dry lips. I reached eagerly for the bottle, gulping down every last drop of water.

As I slid off the bed and opened the door, I heard the shower running. For a moment, I hesitated, not knowing if I should stay in the room or venture out. Would Nate think I'd been snooping around if he came out of the bathroom and found me in the lounge? Would he be angry?

I growled. Why was this so hard?

Shaking off my apprehension, I headed down the hall and into the kitchen. Nate had done an impressive amount of cleaning while I'd slumbered. The place was tidy and smelled strongly of bleach, and the sitting area carpet had been purged of all traces of vomit. All the windows and doors were wide open, and a strong breeze blew through, puffing up the curtains and causing them to billow out wildly.

Wandering out onto the deck, I lifted my hands to shield my eyes from the last remnants of the sun as it began to disappear into the ocean.

The view was incredibly breath-taking.

The tree line gave way to a few grassy sand dunes, and further out the golden beach stretched alongside a choppy, blue ocean. The cliffs beyond wrapped around the little bay from end to end as if capturing it in a protective embrace.

I leaned over the wooden rail and breathed in the salty air, the sound of the sea in my ears, a light rain spattering on my skin.

My thoughts turned to Nate and what he'd said about it not being enough.

Paradise was a lonely place with no one to share it with.

"Hey."

My heart leaped out of my chest when he appeared beside me.

"Christ," I puffed, hand on heart. "You—"

I went to tell him that he'd scared the living daylights out of me, but my train of thought suddenly derailed at the sight of his bare chest. He was athletically built, and the contours of his torso muscles were easily discernible under his smooth skin, especially when he moved. I told myself to stop staring, but it was hard not to, being the first male I'd laid eyes on in years. Well, a living one, at least.

Quickly forcing my gaze onto his freshly shaven face, I smiled awkwardly. He looked more like the young man in the photo now, just a little older and sadder.

Nate's mouth twitched into a brief, sheepish grin. "I thought I'd let you sleep awhile."

"Thanks," I mumbled.

"Food?"

"Please."

I'd learned to ignore the pangs of hunger while on my travels, living off packets of dried soups and pasta, often only eating once a day before settling down for the night. No wonder I looked so awful. Expired, processed crap wasn't exactly nutrient-dense.

"I'll cook us something," he replied and went back inside.

Curious, I followed him.

The cupboards in the kitchen were jam-packed, filled with jars and tins—more or less the same essentials my aunt stored in her garage back home. The cooking area wasn't spacious enough for two people, and not wanting to get in the way, I found somewhere else to sit where I could still watch him, fascinated by the sight of another human being carrying out such a mundane task.

A little oak bookcase sat in the corner of the room by the kitchen. I kneeled next to it on the carpet and observed his actions until he caught me staring. I quickly turned my attention to the contents of the bookcase, glancing over the various titles, my interest piqued. It seemed we shared similar reading tastes, and I was impressed to see my favorite fantasy authors among his collection. There was also a half-dozen books on growing food and several medical-type journals.

I slid one of the books out to examine it; a thick,

weighty hardback with a detailed drawing of a human heart on the front cover. My fingers flipped over a few well-read pages before slotting it back onto the shelf.

"What did you do for a living, before the virus?"

Nate looked up briefly from his culinary creation. "Junior doctor."

My eyebrows rose. "Something useful then?"

He shrugged, taking a moment to reply. "Not these days it isn't."

"You don't look old enough to be a doctor."

He paused, staring at the pot of bubbling water on the hob. "I was thirty when the virus hit."

His jaw tightened, and his knuckles whitened around the saucepan handle. It was almost like he was holding back the urge to punch something.

I understood because I was angry too.

He took a deep breath and re-focused on his task. I had no idea what he was cooking up, but I was too hungry to care.

"What about you?" he asked after a while.

"Nothing useful," I replied.

He put a t-shirt on before serving up dinner, which consisted of noodles with various vegetables in sauce. Simple, yet it tasted divine. It was an effort to stop myself from wolfing it down too fast.

A long noodle wriggled up into my pursed lips. "This is so good."

His shoulders twitched in response, saying nothing.

With the art of conversation now apparently lost to him, I did most of the talking while we ate, wittering on nervously and at great length. It took a while, but he eventually began to respond more animatedly.

"Your aunt survived the virus as well?" he asked

when I paused briefly to slurp up another noodle.

"She never caught it."

"That's...do you know how lucky that is?" His tone was a jumble of disbelief and envy.

My head bowed as a pang of guilt twisted my gut.

He frowned, noting my discomfort. "Sorry. I didn't mean to...lucky is the wrong word," he stammered. "I—It's good you weren't alone."

Feeling a little awkward, I resumed my nervous chattering, purposefully steering the talk away from the virus and all things apocalyptic. Nate appeared keen to hear about Rebecca's cottage situated just outside of Liskeard in south Cornwall, and he asked about our life there, all the while wearing an expression on his face indicating he was just as fascinated about me as I was about him. He was also curious about what fruit and vegetables we'd managed to grow there, being slightly more sub-tropical than Dorset.

Eventually, the end of the world reared its ugly head once more as I explained about my need to search for other survivors and how I'd followed the coast with plans on heading to Bristol.

He gave a slow nod. "And that's how you ended up here." It was more of a statement than a question. His expression turned pensive. Whatever was on his mind, it held his attention more than I did, so we ate the rest of the meal in silence. It had almost grown uncomfortable, but when our bowls were empty, he suddenly asked me if I wanted to see the garden.

"I'd love to."

In the phase between twilight and night, I wondered how I'd be able to see much, but an array of solar lamps now shone brightly, lighting the way. As he led me around to the back of the cabin, he explained that his parents had installed the solar panels and the water tank to be as ecologically conscious and self-reliant as possible. They'd also designed a vegetable garden for all seasons and grew more than enough food to sustain them. Surplus edibles were sold off at the local farmer's market or donated to the nearest food bank. His admiration and love for his parents was evident in the way his expression brightened when he spoke about them.

The garden was an extended, narrow area that weaved in and out of the tree line. It began behind the cabin and spanned down to the other caravans I'd seen earlier. Its position and the way it merged with the woodland around it had made it impossible to see from the clifftop. From down here, though, it was impressive in its organization and beauty.

There were two brick outbuildings directly behind the cabin with a lean-to greenhouse connected to one of them and a chicken coup attached to the other. A variety of wooden planters, of different shapes and sizes, had been placed strategically to either catch the sun or use the shade from a nearby tree. Anything not visually pleasing—like the water tank—was hidden away behind trellises of wisteria or feathery ferns.

"After I recovered from the virus, I came home," Nate said. "I'd hoped they'd still be here. Alive, I mean. But I was a few days too late."

A little way off into the woodland, two wooden crosses had been stuck into the ground, each grave outline marked by a ring of pebbles. It must've been utterly harrowing for him to have to bury his parents.

He moved the conversation on swiftly. "I had no

idea about growing food or how to keep chickens. The first couple of years were a bit of a disaster, but I got the hang of it eventually."

I smiled. "It's wonderful."

His mouth twitched with the slightest of grins, but it soon fell. "I planned for more people, though. I really thought they would come."

Finding the right words to offer him comfort proved impossible. His experiences during the last four and a half years didn't compare to my own. Although I could empathize with his pain, I doubted I'd ever truly comprehend the depths of his desperation. I certainly hadn't been able to with my mother.

We left the garden, but rather than go back inside the cabin, we walked along the beach.

The sky was a beautiful shade of indigo, but not yet dark enough or clear enough to see the stars. A slither of moonlight was peeking out from behind a looming storm cloud, and out across the sea, lightning flashed and forked.

In the ever-dimming light, I found myself watching Nate. I studied his face, now able to make out the faint dimples on his cheeks and the slight indent on his chin, previously hidden beneath his beard.

When we reached the center of the bay, we stopped to watch the impressive display engendered by the storm, although my eyes flickered back to him frequently.

It was so strange to stand next to another human being after all this time—one that wasn't my aunt, at least. I felt drawn to him in a way I couldn't quite explain, although it was probably because he was the only person of the opposite sex I'd seen in a very long time.

Unintentionally, my hand brushed up against his, and the hairs on my arm bristled in response, feeling a brief pop of static once again. It had to be caused by the storm. It'd been raging on and off for most of the day, leaving an oppressive heaviness in the air.

He turned to me. "Beautiful and terrifying at the same time, isn't it?"

His question caught me off guard. "Huh?"

"The lightning," he clarified.

The flashes reflected in his eyes as he spoke, and I quickly became lost in them.

"It's getting closer," I pointed out.

He continued to look at me, instead of the storm. When our fingertips brushed together again, he took hold of my hand and gripped it tightly.

"Are you real, Halley?"

My breath caught in my chest because I'd been about to ask him the same thing. Nothing felt real.

"Yes."

It was all I could say.

****

Before…

Lizzie Stone had been my best friend since our first awkward day of high school.

Neither of us had known anyone else and had clung to each other, bound by shared feelings of bewilderment and fear.

We now attended the same college as well, although we'd chosen to study different subjects. It unfortunately meant we could only meet up at lunchtime, but we made the most of it, chatting about Lizzie's colorful social life and her plans to travel after college. My plans were less ambitious; I only wanted to be free of Andrew.

A few weeks from my eighteenth birthday, Lizzie suggested we skive the afternoon off and go to the pub so she could introduce me to her new love interest and his friend.

As he'd driven me to college that morning, my stepfather had told me that he'd be going into work a few hours early—again—and wouldn't be around to pick me up like he usually did. They were making people redundant at the insurance company where he worked, and it was the first time I'd ever seen him genuinely worried about something. He'd started drinking more, chasing his whiskey down with a few shots of vodka as soon as he returned homework.

As a result, I saw even less of Andrew—a blessing since his mood had taken a significant downturn. I made sure I did nothing to aggravate him and stayed out of his way, biding my time until I could leave home and never have to see him again. As I turned eighteen, I'd be able to move out and rent somewhere. I'd already been scouring the internet for student rooms in the local area, as well as jobs I could work around college. Rebecca had also offered me a room at her cottage in Cornwall. For the first time ever, I had options.

"One drink," Lizzie begged me, pulling me into the pub, which stank of stale beer and chip fat.

"Fine."

We sat at a table and waited for Lizzie's new friends to turn up. The man behind the bar eyed us suspiciously while buffing pint glasses, but didn't ask for I.D. Finally, the boys arrived and joined us at the table.

"What's your poison?" the tallest one asked. He was Lizzie's new boyfriend—Sean. They'd met last month at a nightclub when Lizzie was out celebrating her birthday. He was twenty-one and worked as a bouncer.

Lizzie swooned at him. "Vodka and coke."

"Just coke," I said. "Thanks."

Lizzie did most of the talking but brought me into the conversation as often as she could. I managed to make enough of a contribution to not appear socially inept.

At half-past four, my mobile rang. Glaring down at the screen, I realized I had eight missed calls from Andrew. With all the noise in the pub, I hadn't heard it ring.

Immediately panicked, I hurried outside to answer it.

"Where are you?" My stepfather's voice sounded stern and angry.

My heart thumped. "Still at college."

"Don't lie!" came his sharp response. "I waited for you! When you didn't show up, I went into the office. They said you hadn't signed in this afternoon."

There was no point in denying it. "Sorry, Andrew," I said. "I went out with Lizzie."

"You could've just told me that!" he snapped. "I'll come and pick you up. Where are you?"

There was no way I could tell him I'd been to a pub. "The cinema."

It wasn't far away, and I could make it there before he could.

After saying a very quick goodbye to Lizzie, I sprinted to the main high-street and then down to the end of town where the cinema was. I made it there a full five minutes before Andrew's car screeched up onto the curb.

We drove home in silence, but I could tell by the way he erratically steered the car and by the smell of alcohol on his breath that he'd already been drinking heavily. I didn't need to ask him why he was home early either—he'd been laid off.

Once the car was stationary on the drive outside the flat, I opened the passenger door. Andrew suddenly leaned across me and quickly shut it again.

"Lizzie is a bad influence," he said. "You need to stay away from her."

With no intention of indulging him in an argument, I nodded and did my best to look sorry.

"You don't want to end up like your mother at eighteen, do you?"

Alone with a new-born baby, was what he meant.

I shook my head, keeping my eyes focused straight ahead. "No, Andrew."

It wasn't like I hadn't heard this lecture before from him. Once, a few months after my mother's funeral, Andrew had seen Lizzie's older brother hug me at the school gates. As soon as we'd gotten home, he'd called me a 'slag' and punched me in the ribs.

"I'm all you have now, Halley," he continued, "I'll always look after you."

"Thank you," I said flatly.

As he placed a hand on my thigh and squeezed it gently, my heart stopped beating, and my blood turned to ice. All I wanted to do now was get out of the car and as far from him as possible.

I tried to open the car door again, but he dug his

fingernails into the flesh just above my knee. I hissed, and he released his grip. But then his hand went under my skirt and around to my inner thigh.

Don't let him do this. Don't let him do this.

It was as though I'd suddenly turned to stone and detached from my body. I couldn't move, or speak, or scream.

Don't let him do this. *Run.* Don't let him do this.

He used his free hand to grab my face, forcing me to look at him as he leaned forward and laid a sloppy kiss on my lips.

His stale breath filled my nostrils. "See? We can be friends."

As he went in for another kiss, his hand slid further up my thigh until his fingers made contact with my underwear. With his dry lips pressed forcefully against mine, he moved his hand up and down slowly between my legs.

Run. Don't let him do this. Run.

My limbs felt as though they didn't belong to me, and all I could do was sit there, paralyzed by my fear.

Suddenly, Andrew broke away from me. "Let's go inside."

He climbed awkwardly out of the car and stumbled across the driveway, while I remained in the car, desperately willing my body to move. My head began to clear a little as I thought of my mother. How could she have left me with someone like him? Had she known what he was capable of? What else had Andrew done to her?

Somehow, my fear switched to anger, and I could move again.

My hands were shaking so violently it took me a

few moments to pull the handle, but finally, I scrambled out of the car and onto the driveway.

Andrew had reached the communal entrance but was fumbling through his pockets for his keys. With his attention diverted, I ran.

I ran, and I didn't look back. I ran until I couldn't breathe, and my chest burned. I ran until I eventually found an alley to hide in, where I vomited until my stomach was empty and my head thundered so loudly that I couldn't think straight.

Lizzie.

I pulled my phone out of my jacket pocket and dialed her number, praying she would hear my call.

Thankfully, she answered quickly. "What's up?" From the noise in the background, she was still in the pub.

"Lizzie," I stammered. "Please, come and get me."

I didn't need to see her face to know she'd started to panic. Her voice became urgent and demanding. "What happened? Where are you?"

Wherever I'd ended up, I didn't recognize the area, so I gave her the name of the nearest street. "Hurry Lizzie, before he finds me."

She turned up less than ten minutes later, with her boyfriend, in his transit van. She slid out of the vehicle before it had even stopped moving, throwing her arms around me the second she reached the alley.

"What the hell happened?"

I couldn't bring myself to tell Lizzie the truth. "He—he hit me."

She hissed through gritted teeth. "Again?"

Unable to look her in the eye, I just turned away and nodded.

Lizzie took me back to her place and asked her parents if I could stay with them for a few weeks. She'd told them Andrew had kicked me out of the flat—it was another one of those stories that fell off the tongue easier than the truth.

Her parents didn't seem too surprised, having already heard all about Andrew from Lizzie.

That night, he called my phone a couple of times but didn't come looking for me, although he knew where Lizzie lived.

He clearly expected that, like my mother, I'd come back, and we'd carry on as if nothing had ever happened. But I'd never forget. As much as I tried to scrub and scour him away, Andrew lingered constantly in the back of my mind.

I knew then that I needed to be as far away from him as possible, so I took up Rebecca's offer to live with her. She picked me up a few days after my eighteenth birthday but didn't ask what Andrew had done to make me run away, not that I'd tell her the truth either.

Saying goodbye to Lizzie was hard, but she promised to visit me soon.

Once I got settled into my aunt's little cottage, I felt an enormous sense of relief, enough to convince me I'd made the right decision to leave it all behind.

I thought I'd never have to see Andrew again, but I was wrong. There'd be one last time.

Chapter Five

After…

That night, my sleep was sound and dreamless. I heard Nate get up a little after dawn, but I lingered in bed awhile longer. Wrapped comfortably in a soft quilt, I dozed until the smell of fried eggs wafted into my room. I dressed quickly and used the bathroom before following my nose.

In the kitchen, Nate was busy making a banquet for breakfast: eggs, tomatoes, mushrooms, and potato hash. My stomach growled longingly in response.

"Smells amazing," I said, announcing my arrival as I didn't think he'd heard me come in.

He flipped an egg. "Sleep well?"

I nodded. "Very well." I actually couldn't remember the last time I'd had such a decent night's sleep.

He smiled broadly. For the first time, there was no tinge of sadness behind it. He looked much better today too. A healthy pinkish tone had returned to his cheeks, and his eyes were brighter. He really was incredibly attractive, and the thought instantly made me blush.

"You need a hand?"

He shook his head. "No, go sit outside, and I'll bring it out when it's ready."

"Outside?"

"You'll see," Nate grinned.

I did as instructed.

On the beach, he'd set up a small plastic table and chairs, and a parasol. An assortment of condiments and a jug of freshly squeezed orange juice had already been placed on the table. I poured myself a small glass and sat down, feeling the heat of the rising sun on my back. It would be another hot day.

It wasn't long before Nate appeared with our breakfast.

"I could get used to this," I told him as I started eating.

He chuckled. "Sometimes it's nice to pretend the world didn't end, right?"

Right here, right now, it was very easy to pretend.

Something had changed in him since yesterday, as if the dark cloud hanging over his head had lifted a little. The conversation flowed effortlessly, and it was almost like a bubble had formed around us that the outside world couldn't penetrate. It'd been only Rebecca and me for so long that sitting next to Nate felt surreal, and almost like the apocalypse had never happened. *Almost*.

After finishing breakfast, we sat back and basked in the heat, watching the tide go out as the sun climbed the cloudless sky.

"Can I show you something?" Nate asked suddenly.

I cocked my head and frowned. "What?"

"It's about an hour's walk from here," he replied.

The thought of more walking didn't exactly fill me with joy, but I was intrigued. Before we set off, Nate grabbed several bottles of water from a shelf inside one of the outbuildings and dropped them into a small backpack.

We ended up walking to the other side of the cove, where the sand was littered with large boulders. Thankfully, the beach here was partly shaded by the cliffs above. We chatted as we walked, Nate doing most of the talking this time. He told me how his parents had sold their big house in London so he could study to be a doctor without accumulating a mass of student debt. His parents, meanwhile, had purchased the land at 'Siren Bay' so they could finally follow their dream of living self-sufficient by the sea, renting caravans to holidaymakers for an income.

The talk was light at first, but eventually, the subject of the apocalypse inevitably resurfaced.

"I'd been working in a hospital in Bristol when people started getting sick. It was chaos," he said. "I got infected about six weeks after the outbreak, but I survived. I knew it was unusual. We'd admitted thousands of people with the virus and only one person survived. No one else made it."

He clenched his jaw and cast his glance toward the ocean. "The army burned all the bodies in a park nearby."

After his last revelation, the mood changed to a more somber one.

We walked the rest of the way in silence.

The beach slowly became rockier the further we went, and I had to find sandy patches to step onto to avoid sharp stones. When a sharp pebble dug into my heel, I uttered a few mild curse words, lamenting my choice to go without shoes.

Nate finally slowed and stopped when we reached a sea-groin. The walk made me a little breathless, and I panted rapidly until my pulse steadied, downing an entire bottle of water as soon as Nate handed it to me. After making sure I was suitably refreshed, he bent down to a cluster of boulders and motioned for me to come over. Dodging a crab carcass, I knelt beside him.

The stones were covered in hundreds of iridescent spirals. He brushed some moss from one of the larger spirals and took my hand, guiding it over the surface of the structure. I felt a little crackle of static once more as his skin touched mine—odd since there were no looming storm clouds to blame this time.

My fingers traced around the features of the helicoid. "What are they?"

Nate released my hand. "Ammonites."

I examined the swirls, astonished by the spectral color show each one displayed.

"Beautiful," I said, under my breath, quite fixated on the rocks.

"They've been here for about sixty-five-million years," he added, his expression dejected. "I come here to remind myself that life was here before us, and it'll be here again after."

"We're not done for yet, Nate." Given the bleakness of our current situation, it was all I could think of to say. And I did truly believe it.

Nate gave me a smile and a spark reignited in his dark eyes. "I hope you're right."

I sighed. "So do I."

For the rest of the day, we explored the coastline. Nate lit a fire late afternoon and cooked up a shoal of sprats he'd discovered trapped in a rock pool. They didn't look particularly appetizing, but they were palatable. It often surprised me what hunger motivated me to eat nowadays that I wouldn't have touched pre-apocalypse.

As the sun began to set, we started back to the cabin. I walked in the sea, my sore feet soothed by the cool water. Nate rolled up the hem of his jeans and did the same.

The motion of the tide made it difficult to walk in a straight line, and I unintentionally waded in deeper as we ambled along. Losing sight of the bottom, my foot caught on a clump of seaweed that hooked itself around my right ankle and caused me to stumble forward. I swore as Nate lunged to catch me, but he missed, and my body ended up completely submerged. As I lifted my head out of the water, coughing and spluttering, I noticed the bemused smirk on Nate's face and shot him a fierce glare.

He simply laughed. "Are you okay?"

I shivered. "No. It's bloody freezing!"

He snorted, biting back the smile on his lips as he lifted me out the water, leaving him soaked to the waist.

My teeth chattered. "Thanks."

Once back inside the cabin, I hurried to the bathroom to remove my wet clothes and dry off. Wrapping a towel around my body, I peeked my head out of the door.

"Um, Nate?"

He'd gone straight to his room to change.

"Yeh?" he replied from the other side of his bedroom door.

"I don't have any clean clothes left. Do you have something I could borrow?"

There was a pause before he answered me. "Sure."

I heard him opening and closing a few drawers

before his bedroom door opened and he handed me one of his t-shirts.

"We can do some laundry tomorrow," he said and then headed back down the hall to the kitchen.

As I pulled the t-shirt on over my head and smoothed it down, I realized just how short it was. While baggy on me, the seam barely reached my mid-thighs. Nervously yanking on the back hem, I shuffled reluctantly down the hall and into the kitchen.

"Don't you have anything of your mum's?"

"Not anymore—" Nate stopped abruptly when he saw me. After gawking for a few seconds, he quickly dodged behind one of the kitchen counters.

"Wine?" he stammered, reaching up into one of the cupboards.

I made sure the t-shirt was tucked in firmly under my thighs as I slid onto one of the stools. "Everything all right?"

He shifted uncomfortably. "Yes. It's just been a *really* long time since a beautiful woman has worn one of my t-shirts."

My cheeks grew hot, and I let out a nervous laugh. "Beautiful? It *has* been a long time."

His expression grew serious. "Sorry. I didn't mean to make you feel uncomfortable."

"No, it's fine," I muttered, swallowing down my embarrassment with a painful gulp. "Thank you."

No one had ever told me I was beautiful before— except for Lizzie, but that didn't count—and it gave me a little buzz to hear Nate say it.

He poured us both a large glass of red wine without so much as a glance in my direction. After quickly downing his, and then one more, he finally looked at me. "Do you mind if we play a game?"

"What game?"

"Monopoly," he grinned. "It's no fun on your own."

Inwardly, I groaned. My aunt and I played board games most nights to stave off the tedium of the apocalypse. It'd soon become more of a chore rather than an enjoyable pastime. However, since Nate hadn't been afforded such opportunities, it was only right I indulge him. Plus, the idea of a new opponent to crush with my superior skills filled me with a rush of maniacal glee.

"Sure. But you should know, I show no mercy."

Nate narrowed his eyes and set his jaw. "Neither do I."

He set up the game on the table in the sitting room, and we played it for several hours before he conceded he was losing.

"You should've bought Mayfair when you had the chance," I snickered, feeling a little lightheaded from consuming my third—maybe fourth—glass of wine rather too quickly. I took the last of his cash with a villainous squeal of laughter.

He grunted in mock anger when I waved the paper money under his nose in a show of taunting smugness.

"I used to be better at this," he said. "My mum used to make us play this game every bloody Christmas. I hated it, but I always won."

"Then why did you want to play?" I asked him, slurring my words.

He shrugged. "I missed it. Isn't that stupid?"

"No. Not at all," I replied, throwing my dice haphazardly across the table. They rolled over the board and dropped onto the floor.

"Oops." I briefly forgot how short the t-shirt was as I leaned over to retrieve the dice. Thankfully, when I sat back upright, I saw Nate had averted his eyes. After lobbing the dice again, my index finger pushed the little pewter ship on six spaces.

"You know what I miss? I miss being able to look up pointless crap on the internet," I muttered as the room began to spin. "Your turn."

Nate chuckled at me. He threw the dice and then hissed when it landed on one of my properties. "Guess I'd better strip my assets, then."

"Promises, promises," I teased, instantly wishing I hadn't said it. What the hell was I thinking?

Nate raised his eyebrows and hid a smirk, but he didn't respond. When I reached out for my wine glass again, he moved it away to the end of the table and gave me a wry smile. "I think you've had enough to drink."

I waved a finger at him. "Don't tell me what to do!"

He shook his head, holding his hands up. "Just a suggestion, is all."

As I leaned to retrieve my drink, I yawned and slumped back, dizzily. "Okay, you're right. I should go to bed."

"Agreed."

Awkwardly, I clamored to my feet but immediately swayed unsteadily as the room spun away from me. Nate stood quickly and propped me up against his hip. As he half-carried, half-dragged me down the hall to my room, I giggled uncontrollably.

"I think I've had a little bit too much to drink,

Nate."

"No, shit."

When he finally managed to maneuver me over to the bed, he plonked me down at the foot end and then pushed me onto my back. When his hands went around my waist, a surge of panic twisted in my chest.

No.

I flinched and kicked out, my heel slamming hard into his shin. "Get off of me!"

He quickly released me and stepped back. I scrabbled backward until my head cracked against the wooden bedstead, leaving me dazed.

"Halley!" Nate moved toward me again, his hands going straight to the throbbing bump just above my ear. "Stay still," he barked after I flinched again. His fingertips brushed gently over the bruised area, and then he looked closely into each one of my eyes. "You'll be okay. I think."

Before I could respond, he quickly lifted my legs and pulled the quilt out from beneath my rump. He then covered my body with it, gently tucking the edges in under the mattress.

I blinked wildly until my vision cleared enough to see the distressed expression on his face. I'd massively misjudged his intentions.

"S—sorry," I mumbled. "I thought you were going to—"

He cut me off. "I would *never* do that." His tone was more hurt than angry. "Goodnight, Halley."

With that, he left the room, firmly closing the door behind him.

****

Early the next morning, I awoke to hear Nate

clanking pans about in the kitchen. Mortified by my behavior, I considered hiding in my room, but eventually plucked up the courage to face him. Slinking down the hall, I stopped and lingered gingerly in the kitchen doorway.

He turned to me and smiled. "Morning. How's your head?"

"Fine. How's your leg?" I asked, gesturing to where I'd kicked him.

He faked a limp as he crossed the kitchen to fry some eggs. "Fine."

I rolled my eyes and chuckled. "I'm really sorry. I made such an idiot of myself when you were only trying to help."

He shrugged. "I wasn't thinking straight, either. You don't have to apologize, Halley. You barely know me—your reaction was understandable."

Now I felt even worse. This was Andrew's fault and nothing to do with Nate.

I shook my head. "I know you'd never take advantage like that."

He shot me a stern look as he flipped an egg onto a plate already loaded with fried tomatoes and courgette slices sprinkled with herbs. My nose detected the aromatic scent of Thyme and Basil as it wafted over to me.

"I wouldn't," he said, handing me my breakfast. "You're safe, I promise."

Exhaling heavily, I smiled and thanked him for the food. It did seem like he genuinely wasn't bothered about me assaulting him, but it didn't stop me feeling guilty.

Having fallen behind on a list of mounting chores,

he ate quickly and then headed out back after giving me a bucket of soapy water to wash my dirty clothes in. I offered to do his laundry too, but he declined, saying he'd do it later. When everything was clean and hung out to dry, I joined him in the garden to see if I could do anything to help.

"You can feed the chickens if you want."

Happy to assist, I poured fresh food into their feeders and refilled their water dispensers. It didn't take very long though, and I was soon twiddling my thumbs, unable to do much else wearing only a t-shirt. As soon as I had a pair of shorts dry enough to wear, I set about giving the coup and enclosure a good wash down and spruce—something I'd often done for my aunt's chickens at home. As I scrubbed the concrete section of their run, I spoke to them, asking the curious hens to move whenever they ventured too close and got in the way. Nate chuckled at me from time to time as he busied himself in the vegetable garden, pulling up potatoes and carrots from their rooted spots in the dirt.

I felt quite at home here in this little surreal pocket of heaven by the sea. But, what about Rebecca? I'd have to go home soon. What then? Why couldn't she have just come with me as I'd asked? She *chose* to stay behind. So why did I feel so guilty? It wasn't like I was going to stay here forever, although I easily could: hot showers, electricity, the beach. And Nate. There was nowhere else I wanted to be right now, and I certainly didn't want to think about leaving.

"We have a few chickens at home," I told him. "I called them Kim, Khloe, and Kourtney."

He laughed.

"I felt bad when we ate Khloe," I snickered.

He wiped at the sweat running down his face and then came to lean on the chicken enclosure. "Why didn't your aunt come with you?"

I shrugged. "I don't know. She tried looking for people, to begin with, but it got harder to go further from home when the car stopped running."

"Yeh, same."

Petrol and diesel, as it happened, began to degrade after about three months, and was totally useless after six months. All journeys from that point on were made on foot or by bicycle.

I set the broom aside and leaned back against the enclosure fence. "Rebecca was convinced it was just us."

Nate sighed. "In the end, that's what I believed too."

I touched his arm through the mesh barrier. "I refused to believe it. I was sure there *had* to be someone else out there, and I was right. I still think there are *even more* people out there somewhere. In Europe or America, maybe here too. What if there are people alive way up North? Or in London?"

He gave a slow nod. "I don't know. Even if we had a running car, I'd be like looking for a needle in a haystack. Believe me, I tried."

"Well," I grinned. "*You* weren't so hard to find."

He glared at me. "It was luck. Astoundingly *good* luck. Especially since you never even saw any of my messages. This place doesn't exactly stick out."

"Well, I guess that's why it's called *Siren Bay*. It must've called to me."

Nate laughed. "You know, I always wondered whether I should've picked a more obvious location to stay in. Like Bristol or Southampton or London. But I knew this place was my best chance of survival." His eyes flashed with sadness then. "Besides, I really thought people would see the messages I left."

I shrugged again. "Maybe it *is* just us then."

He looked down at the ground and spoke so softly I could hardly hear him. "I wouldn't mind that."

My face burned. "I'm sure I'll start to get on your nerves soon enough. You'll be wishing for alone time again before you know it."

"I doubt that, Halley."

I smirked. "You don't know me."

He frowned and looked back up at me. "Yeh, well, that's the odd thing—I feel like I *do* know you."

"What do you mean?" I asked as I opened the gate of the chicken run and slid out before the hens could follow me.

He rubbed his eyes wearily. "I don't know," he said. "It's hard to describe."

Truth be told, there was *something* about him that felt familiar to me too, although I was certain we hadn't met prior to the apocalypse. "Maybe we met in a past life."

"Not a big believer in past lives."

I pursed my lips thoughtfully. "I don't know what I believe in anymore."

He finally smiled. "Me either."

Bad recollections of the past now pushed aside, I offered to make us something to eat while Nate carried on with the chores. I went into one of the outbuildings where the excess food was stored to see if anything in there would inspire me. After perusing the shelves for a few minutes, I located some spices and a tin of tomatoes and carried them back to the kitchen. This evening, we'd dine on vegetable chili with rice.

At home, after the apocalypse, cooking became my responsibility. At first, with no fresh ingredients available, I made simple meals, but we quickly grew sick of hot dogs and tinned spaghetti, and it wasn't long before Rebecca decided to plant a vegetable garden. She also managed to snag us some chickens which had been roaming around on one of the nearby farms. They should've all been gobbled up by hungry, wild animals by that point, but—as my aunt could testify—these ones were particularly feisty, and fast runners too. Besides, the lazy foxes had begun to favor the towns and cities, scavenging on the dead.

As it happened, cooking for my stepfather day in day out had taught me a thing or two about making tasty meals—if I served up something he didn't like, it'd go straight in the bin, and then I'd have to cook him something else from scratch. Even if what I cooked was what he'd asked for in the first place. My aunt wasn't so critical, allowing my confidence to grow, and I quickly became more creative with our dinners. My flavorsome, spice-infused vegetable chili was one of Rebecca's favorites. Hopefully, Nate would like it too.

When ready, I scooped it out into bowls and carried them outside on a tray, along with some drinks. I sat cross-legged on a little wooden bench and watched Nate finish up his current chore—a leaky water butt which proved a pig to fix, judging by the continuous stream of swearing I'd heard.

"This is good. Really good," Nate said, after hungrily spooning the chili into his mouth.

I smiled. "Thanks."

"Secret family recipe?"

"No. Mum wasn't much of a cook." And, boy, did Andrew chastise her for it.

"You don't talk about your life much," Nate said. "Before the virus, I mean."

"Not much to tell. My mum died when I was fourteen," I answered, staring straight ahead.

"Sorry."

I mechanically uttered my well-practiced response. "It was her heart."

"And then you went to live with your aunt?" he inquired.

He'd spoken a lot about his life before the end of the world, while I'd said very little about my own existence before the apocalypse.

"I lived with my step-father until I was eighteen. Then I left. We didn't get on."

Nate nodded, watching my face closely. He must've noted my obvious discomfort because he didn't press me any further. He licked his lips and wiped a smudge of chili sauce from his chin. "Well, I could get used to someone else cooking once and a while."

I beamed. "I guess I'll have to stay a bit longer then."

****

Before…

I'd managed to get a job waitressing at a café in town so I could give my aunt some money for letting me stay with her. She said it wasn't necessary and that I should just focus on college, but I knew money was tight and wanted to ease the burden a little. Luckily, I'd been able to transfer to the 'Indian Queens sixth form college' to finish up my psychology course.

On the days I wasn't at school, I worked from early morning until early evening, four days a week, which included the weekend. My boss let me catch up on college work during the quiet period between lunch and dinner as long as all the cleaning and any other jobs had been done. I'd get home at around seven-thirty most nights, cook dinner, then fall asleep on the couch well before ten PM. It was exhausting, but I didn't care—my life was finally my own.

Sometimes, I hardly saw Rebecca. She worked full time, managing a small food outlet in a motorway services, six days a week with Sundays off. We'd chat over dinner, but she'd always go straight to bed after, leaving me to my devices. Everything was so different from how it'd been living with my stepfather, who'd gone out of his way to be an ever-present influence in my life.

Unfortunately, as the saying goes, 'all good things must come to an end.'

A few months ago, the boss—a woman in her fifties who insisted I call her Lorna—had fixed a small television to the wall behind the bar. It served mainly as background noise, showing the twenty-four-hour news channel all day long unless Lorna's son switched it over to one of the music stations when she wasn't looking. However, one rainy day in November, we all found ourselves glued to an unfolding news story.

We'd only had one customer come in for breakfast so far, an elderly man—a regular—who always ordered coffee and a bacon sandwich while he sat for two hours reading the paper. Even he took notice of the grim-faced anchor-man reading the news that morning.

"John. F. Kennedy airport in New York has been

closed for forty-eight hours while officials from I.D.R.I.S investigate reports that over a dozen people are seriously ill in hospital after a flight from Tokyo was granted permission to make an emergency landing. Three passengers took sick during the flight and were rushed to hospital shortly after landing. We have now received reports that several other people have become unwell, including gate staff who had not been on the flight. A statement from I.D.R.I.S is imminent."

"Not again," Lorna muttered as she wiped down the vinyl stools by the bar.

There'd been a few serious outbreaks in recent years—an Ebola crisis in South America that killed over a thousand people, an overly vicious strain of the flu in Europe, leaving hundreds dead, and a measles epidemic in Australia that claimed the lives of fifty children. A new, global agency by the name of I.D.R.I.S (International Disaster Response and Infection Stratagem) had been created for the sole purpose of dealing with it all, rather than leave it to the overburdened local authorities. Airport closures were rare, though.

Lorna huffed and spritzed the air with anti-bacterial spray. "They always over-react."

I shrugged, feeling somewhat uneasy.

Our one and only customer grunted and shook his head. "Better safe than sorry, no?"

Lorna wrinkled her nose and carried on disinfecting the bar area, scrubbing meticulously at the veneer worktop. She checked her watch for the third time in as many minutes—Jamie was late again. Nothing new there.

He strolled in half an hour later, a coat thrown

casually over his shoulder and dressed in ripped jeans that Lorna had repeatedly asked him not to wear at work. She probably would've fired him by now if he wasn't her son.

"You're late," she snapped.

"I overslept." He gave her a wry smile and ruffled his platinum blond hair, winking at me with big blue eyes as strolled into the kitchen. Jamie enjoyed staging little rebellions against her, but he never did anything too consequential. He wasn't stupid.

Technically, I was his girlfriend, although we'd only gone out twice so far—once to the cinema and once to the local pub where he'd introduced me to his bandmates. He played the drums and drank shots of neat vodka between sets. Jamie described his style as 'indie' and spent hours bleaching his hair to the gray-white he preferred. But, despite his epic level of cool and devil-may-care attitude, my initial attraction to him was waning fast.

At least once a day, he'd do something to get my blood boiling. He'd be rude to a customer who didn't deserve it or get snarky with one of the other waitresses if they got an order wrong. His attitude sucked. But, away from work, he became an entirely different person; funny, friendly, and attentive. For this reason, and because I was lonely, I'd agreed to a third date.

"It's not just New York," he said as he re-appeared, tying an apron around his waist. "My mate's in Sweden. He says there are loads of people out there with it."

Lorna frowned. "Then why isn't it on the news?"

"I don't know," he answered, a little offishly. "I only spoke to him for a minute. His girlfriend is sick, and they were on their way to the hospital."

"I'm sure she'll be fine," I replied, not knowing then how very wrong I was.

All good things must come to an end...

A week later, I went into work as usual only to find a sign on the front door that read, 'Closed due to staff illness.' No one had called me, and so I tried several times to get hold of Jamie, but he didn't answer. In the end, I left a message on his voicemail, asking if he was okay.

That night, I'd just started dropping off to sleep when my mobile rang with an unknown number.

"Is this Halley?" It was a man's voice, deep and gruff. "This is Stewart. I'm Lorna's husband. I'm sorry, she asked me to call you as she's not doing too well."

I swallowed anxiously. "Is she sick?"

The voice cracked. "Yes." There was a pause. "I'm sorry, Halley, but we lost Jamie this afternoon. Lorna thought you should know."

He hung up.

I stood frozen with the phone to my ear, hoping this was a bad dream.

It wasn't.

Chapter Six

After…

For the rest of the afternoon, I helped with whatever I could. Nate and I bantered back and forth on a variety of subjects, most of which were no longer relevant: reality television, the former government, favorite movies. Despite our eleven-year age gap and different backgrounds, we had a lot more in common than I expected. He also made me laugh, and it was all too easy to forget about the bad stuff when I was around him.

It didn't take me long to realize I was falling for him, even though it seemed ridiculous—how could I feel this strongly about someone I'd only known for a few days? Still, the butterflies in my chest refused to quit their incessant fluttering, a feeling that was quite alien to me.

Sure, in high school I'd developed the occasional crush from time to time, but the closest I'd come to feeling anything more than that was with Jamie. We'd bantered and indulged in a little flirting for a few weeks, and then he'd asked me out to see some weird indie movie at the cinema. After the movie, we'd shared the briefest of goodnight kisses.

For our second date, he'd invited me to watch his band play at a local pub. Afterward, we'd grabbed a takeaway to eat in his car and listened to his favorite rock playlist on the stereo. This time, the goodnight kiss lasted a full minute.

Had the world not ended a few days later, things might've gone further between us. Or not. I'd never been completely comfortable being alone with Jamie, even though I trusted him. Even though I knew he wasn't like Andrew.

What about Nate? Did I trust him? His chivalry last night was enough to convince me his intentions were good but, even before that—from the moment I'd arrived here—I'd felt *safe*. It made no sense.

"Halley?"

"Yes?"

He chuckled. "Lost you for a minute there."

"Sorry. I was miles away."

He suggested we call it a day on the chores, so we downed tools and went inside to clean up. My clothes had completely dried, and so I gave him back his t-shirt before showering. I changed into a short halter dress— not an overly practical outfit for riding a bike, I'd quickly discovered. Being lightweight, I'd packed it, but the low-cut neckline had left my breasts exposed to the sun, and I'd ended up with a crimson chest for three days.

When I wandered back into the lounge, Nate was fiddling around with an old record player. He glanced up at me and then gave me a wry smile.

"You look beautiful."

"Thanks," I stammered.

He told me to pick out some music from a box of records while he showered. I leafed through the collection, only recognizing about half of the artists. It must've belonged to his parents because it consisted mostly of rock music from the seventies and eighties—unless it was Nate who harbored a secret penchant for power ballads and guitar solos.

In the end, I selected at random and carefully slid a record by the 'Blind Temple Lions' out of its dust cover and gently placed it onto the turntable before setting the needle down. The speaker hissed before a sudden blast of electro-rock rattled the turntable.

When Nate returned, he'd put on a pair of smart, black chinos along with a fitted white shirt.

He motioned to my dress and grinned. "I felt under-dressed."

I laughed nervously, trying not to gawk. "Are we going to dinner? I hope you made reservations because I think there'll be a long wait."

He shrugged, smirking. "Damn, I forgot. We could go dancing?"

"No!" I said sternly, with a vigorous shake of my head. He stuck out his bottom lip and held his hand out to me.

"Fine," I relented, letting him pull me up from the floor. "But I can't dance."

He twirled me around and then pulled me into him quickly, putting a hand on my waist. "Me either."

He really couldn't. In between having to dodge his clumsy feet to save my bare toes, I laughed so hard I almost cried. We paused mid-album to catch our breaths and rehydrate, first with water and then with a couple of wines. Blaming the quick tempo for his dire sense of rhythm, he changed the record to something more mellow.

As we slow-danced, the gap between our swaying bodies gradually closed as though we'd become magnetized. I stared up at him and found myself transfixed. It was only when his hand tightened around mine and he leaned in toward me, did I realize we'd stopped moving. A moment later, his lips met mine with urgent, yet tender kisses.

Just as I'd begun to kiss him back and match his fervor, he pulled away abruptly, a look of contrition on his face.

"I shouldn't have done that."

My heart raced so fast. I couldn't speak. Had I found the words to tell him I wanted this too, things might've gone differently. Instead, his sad eyes searched mine for a moment before he hastily switched off the record player.

"It's late," he muttered. "I'm tired."

I reeled a little. "Nate—" was all I managed to say before he cut me off.

"Goodnight, Halley."

He quickly left the room, marched up the hall, and slammed his bedroom door, making me jump.

Waiting for my nerves to steady, I stood alone in the lounge for a few minutes. I could still taste him on my lips. My insides felt hollow like my soul had been torn out. Why had he stopped? Because of last night? Because of my stupid reaction?

Confused and frustrated, I went to bed and curled up under the quilt, pulling the fabric up over my head so I could cocoon myself away from the world. Hugging myself tightly, I laid there in the dark void until I finally fell asleep.

****

My night was unsettled.

Every time I woke up, I kept ruminating about

what'd happened with Nate and replaying the kiss over and over in my head.

Needing to clear my thoughts, I got up just before sunrise and walked down to the beach. For a while, I sat on the sand, digging my feet in and lifting them out to watch the golden particles pour off my skin and back onto the ground. When the sun finally came up, I wandered further along the bay to watch a group of seagulls catch fish. When I lifted my head back and closed my eyes to bask in the sunlight, my thoughts drifted quickly back to Nate. In fact, he was starting to be the *only* thing I thought about.

We had a connection; it was undeniable. And, for me, it was something that went beyond *physical* attraction. I felt *pulled* to him. Even now, there was a growing ache inside me because we weren't together. But, did he feel the same way? Or, had I finally lost the bloody plot? I hoped it wasn't the latter.

None the wiser, with my mind still spinning, I headed back to the cabin. Nate would likely be up by now, and probably wondering where the hell I'd gone.

In the distance, the wooden building shimmered in the morning's rising heat. Though still too far away to see him, I knew instantly that Nate was there watching me. As I got closer, I spied him standing on the veranda, leaning over the balustrade. He didn't take his eyes off me as I approached, and there was an odd expression on his face I couldn't quite place. It was something like concern, only angrier.

"Morning," I said quickly.

"Where did you go?" His voice was gruff, irate.

Something in his tone made me feel cornered. "For a walk. I couldn't sleep," I stammered.

His expression softened a little. "I thought you'd left."

My heart dropped. Giving him a reassuring smile, I joined Nate on the veranda and took hold of his hand. He just looked at me, downcast and miserable.

"What's wrong?"

He shook his head. "I didn't sleep well. I didn't sleep at all, actually. When I got up, and you weren't here—" he swallowed and glanced away, breaking the intense stare he'd been giving me. "I thought I'd frightened you away. Or that you were never really here in the first place. I know how crazy that sounds."

It wasn't crazy at all. "Still real."

"Sorry," he muttered, and squeezed my hand. "About last night."

I wasn't sorry, but I wouldn't tell him that. "What do you mean? It was fun."

"I shouldn't have done that. *Kissed you*, I mean. Not after—"

"It wasn't *that* bad," I laughed, cutting him off. It broke the tension a little.

He gave me a sheepish grin. "Thanks."

I motioned for us to go inside, and then I headed straight to the kitchen. "I'll make breakfast."

"Go for it." With that, he stretched out his arms and plonked himself down on the couch, swinging his feet up to rest on the table.

Through no fault of my own, breakfast ended up a disaster. Mid-omelet, the entire cabin lost power. Nate spent the next few hours with his head in a metal box attached to the back of the cabin, under the veranda. With intermittent use of swear words, he explained that one of the solar grid batteries had fried and he didn't have a replacement.

"I'll have to walk to the industrial estate just outside of Bridport. It's about twenty kilometers. I should've gotten another one last time I went, but the batteries are so bloody heavy," Nate said, unhappily.

"Can I come with you?" Not that I'd any desire to walk a forty-kilometer round trip in this heat, but I didn't want to be alone, or away from him.

"Was hoping you would," he grinned.

We quickly ate some cold, tinned beans and then packed a rucksack with some provisions, which Nate insisted he carried. I wore an empty rucksack, which we'd later use for the battery. We set off mid-afternoon, which wasn't ideal because the sun shone in the sky at full strength and I knew my pale skin would burn quickly. Before leaving, I located a bottle of factor fifty suntan lotion from the bathroom and smothered myself in it, and then slipped it into the pocket of my denim shorts so I could reapply it later. Still, Nate noticed a few spots I'd missed on my back where my flesh was turning red. After watching me attempt to bend my arm into the required angle to cover a strip of skin just above my bra strap, he took the bottle from me and rubbed the lotion into my skin himself. The feeling of his hands on my skin left me exhilarated. Nate, however, looked downright uncomfortable.

"Thank you, doctor," I said.

He smiled wryly. "It's been a long time since someone called me that."

As we walked, he began to tell me more about his life before the virus and how much he loved being able to help people. He'd planned to specialize in neurology.

"You're really smart, aren't you?" I said.

He laughed. "Yep."

I shot him an exaggerated eye roll. "And so humble."

I now understood that his darkest moment had been born from more than loneliness and despair—he'd lost his purpose. There were still things I wanted to know about him that he hadn't divulged—he'd never mentioned a wife or any kids. In case it brought up bad memories, I'd not asked for fear of upsetting him. He'd spoken openly so far about his life before the apocalypse, and it didn't appear to bother him when he talked about his parents. If anything, he seemed to enjoy speaking about them as though it kept his memories alive.

Conversely, I preferred not to talk about my past, having no desire to freshen my recollection of certain memories. Although, not talking about those events hadn't made me forget about them either, and I still remembered all the bad things with a persistent vividness.

I decided to throw caution to the wind. "So, before, were you married or—"

Not only was he very attractive but also clever and resourceful. And a doctor. He was exactly the kind of man my aunt would approve of. Surely someone had snapped him up.

Nate shook his head. "No."

For some reason, his answer made me feel relieved.

"How comes?" I pressed him, as we made our way into a large asphalt car park.

The tarmac was devoid of vehicles aside from a battened-down burger van and a corroded, forklift truck piled high with timbers. There were a few overturned shipping trolleys dotted about among the parking bays, having broken away from their orderly queues outside the storefront.

"I was in a few long-term relationships, but they didn't work out," he answered in a flat tone.

"Why not?"

Nate turned to me with a shrug. "My career was always my first priority." After a few seconds of reflection, he sighed. "I wish I'd done things a little differently."

He led us around the store to the back, down a road marked 'Deliveries Only.' Having looted from here before, he'd already broken the lock and left a crowbar behind a group of large, recycling bins. He stopped in front of a loading bay secured by a massive metal shutter and used the crowbar to lever it up from the floor. Once there was a gap big enough for us to duck under, we went inside. Much cooler in here, it was a relief to be out of the oppressive heat.

Nate stopped, leaning against another discarded forklift while he wiped the sweat from his forehead. He slid the backpack off his shoulders and took a swig of water out of one of the bottles we'd brought.

I continued to pry. "What would you change if you could go back?"

He took a deep breath. "Had a family."

I sighed heavily. It wasn't something I'd thought much about before the virus. At nineteen, I'd only just started to live my life without being under Andrew's overbearing shadow. Having my own family had been the last thing on my mind. Now, even if I wanted children, it was impossible.

In their quest to find a cure, the first known survivors were studied by I.D.R.I.S. From those investigations, they'd learned the virus had made the survivors infertile.

The men. The women. All of us.

Not that I needed any confirmation, but after recovering from the virus, my periods stopped coming. Even if there were more survivors somewhere on planet Earth, there'd be no repopulation of the species. This was our swan song.

Nate cleared his throat, jarring me from my depressive reverie. "A few years before the virus, I met someone. She worked at the hospital with me. It got pretty serious. I asked her to marry me. She turned me down."

I raised my eyebrows. "Oh?"

He made his way into the main store and gestured for me to follow him. "We started arguing all the time. She said I was always at the hospital, and I never put her first. She was right," he said. "Truth was, I didn't love her. Not the way she wanted me to."

He gave me a downcast look. "We separated, but then she found out she was pregnant."

His last statement hit me like a punch in the gut.

I followed him as he meandered down an aisle dedicated to self-sufficiency. Among an array of solar panels, he located the correct battery and hauled it down from a dusty shelf above his head. It was slightly larger than a car battery and just about fit into the backpack.

"What happened?" I asked when it seemed like he wasn't going to finish telling me his story.

He hauled the bag up and slid the straps onto his

shoulders. "She told me she wasn't ready to be a parent. Not with me, anyway." His eyes darkened. "If I'd just reassured her—" he broke off, shaking his head. "I didn't even try to stop her."

Seeing his miserable expression, I instantly felt bad for making him talk about it.

He cast me a deflated look. "Anyway, such things are impossible now. The virus saw to that," he said. "Well, *that* and the fact my online dating profile hasn't seen much activity recently."

My mouth fell open and a laugh tumbled out before I managed to squeeze my lips together, hiding a smile.

He sighed deeply, rubbing at the fresh stubble on his jawline. "Not much point in dwelling on it, it's not like they'd be here now, is it? Probably saved me a lot of heartache in the long run."

"That's really depressing, Nate."

He half-grinned. "You think?"

I went and stood next to him in the aisle and gave him a reassuring nudge. He nudged me back, his smile a little more visible. He then handed me the rucksack of supplies, much lighter now we'd drunk half the water.

"What about you?" Nate asked. "Anyone special in your life?"

"Christ, no! I've never even had a proper boyfriend," I blurted, instantly wishing I could turn back time and not say it. There'd be questions I didn't want to answer.

He raised an eyebrow. "What?"

Feeling my cheeks burn with embarrassment, I looked away. "After I went to live with Rebecca, I dated this guy at work-—well, it was two dates—we kissed twice and that was it. He died a few weeks later of the virus."

His mouth dropped open, and he shook his head. "That's terrible. I'm so sorry."

I shrugged. "It's okay."

It took him a few seconds longer than I expected for the truth to dawn on him. "Let me get this straight. You've never—"

I cut him off. "No, I've never."

"Never?"

The glare I shot him was distinctly irate. "No!"

His expression stayed blank until he finally chuckled, and a smirk spread across his lips. "And I thought *my* story was bloody depressing."

Half-amused, half-mortified, I punched him playfully in the arm a few times.

"Halley," he said, after feigning injury from my attack, his voice adopting a more serious tone. "It's not something you should feel emb—"

Groaning, I threw my head back. "*Do not* finish that sentence!" I'd heard it all before from my friend Lizzie.

He laughed again and held his hands up. "Fine. It's just a bit…surprising."

My response was a little sharp. "I've just never trusted anyone enough to be close with them… in *that* way."

He stopped abruptly in front of the loading bay shutters and turned to face me. "Why not?"

If I'd learned anything about Nate in our short time together, it was that he wasn't the sort of person to let such a statement go over his head. Because he cared. Because he fixed people—or, at least, he used to.

Perhaps it *was* time someone else knew what

Andrew had done to me.

"I just—" I stopped, not knowing how to say it.

This was why I'd never told another soul before. Not my best friend. Not my aunt, Rebecca. No one. My silence allowed me to pretend it never happened, but it was always there, under the surface and waiting to be remembered.

"My step-father. His name was Andrew," I began, my voice so quiet it was almost a whisper. "He didn't like my friends, and he rarely let me go out by myself. He certainly wouldn't have approved of me having a boyfriend. I just stayed out of his way, kept my head down, and tried not to make him angry. I hated him. As soon as I turned eighteen, I planned to move out, so I just waited."

Nate gave me one of his intense stares, but I found it impossible to look him in the eye as I spoke.

"I think Andrew knew I was going to leave. He needed to find some new way to control me," I said, taking a steadying breath.

Nate's expression became grave. "What happened? Did he hit you?"

"Once or twice, when he was drunk," I replied solemnly. "But, that's not the worst thing he ever did."

A lump caught in my throat, and I ground my teeth together in an attempt to remain composed. When I finally managed to lift my eyes and look at Nate, a shadow of revulsion crossed his face.

"Oh, Halley." He lifted his hand to touch my arm but withdrew it almost immediately.

This was exactly what I didn't want. He'd probably treat me differently from now on, afraid to go anywhere near me for fear of frightening away the damaged little virgin. But I *wanted* to be close to him. I *wanted* him to touch me. I *wanted* to be intimate with him, even though I'd always dreaded such things. I just couldn't work out why being with Nate had made me feel so differently. And why now?

When I spoke again, my tone was as emotionless as I could make it, pretending like it didn't affect me anymore. "I managed to get away from him before—" The thought of what might've happened put an abrupt stop to my narrative.

As we stood there in silence, the space between us suddenly became a vast chasm. Almost involuntarily, I stepped forward and wrapped my arms around Nate. He stiffened briefly, but then his hands gently brushed against my spine.

"I won't ever do anything to hurt you, Halley. Ever."

"I know, Nate." I leaned back to smile at him. "And, I'm okay. Really, I am."

It was mostly the truth.

****

Before…

By December, the stir-craziness set in.

Rebecca busied herself in the garage, repainting the walls and organizing the food and sundries she'd stockpiled over the last few days.

After noticing she'd been to the supermarket three times in one day, I questioned her intentions. "Do you think it'll get worse?"

Rebecca hadn't ever been one to sugar-coat the truth, but her troubled expression told me she doubted her own words. "No, I'm sure it'll be fine, Halley. Better safe than sorry, though?"

Not the first time I'd heard those words since this all began.

Knowing she'd be preoccupied for most of the day, I decided to venture into town.

The buses were still running, albeit a reduced service, so I donned my government-issue flu mask and slipped on a pair of sterile gloves. Without these articles, I wouldn't be allowed to travel on public transport or enter any stores that sold food. The government was adamant that we carry on with business as usual—they had it all under control.

The bus driver barely acknowledged me as I stepped onto the bus. A sudden spritz of moisture hissed from a small device above the driver's compartment and showered me with droplets of anti-bacterial cleanser. It smelled of chlorine veiled by a sweet vanilla aroma.

There were only five other people on the bus, all hiding behind their masks and huddling into their winter coats, staring blankly out of the windows like long-forgotten ghosts, yearning to be seen.

When the bus pulled into the station, everyone hurried off without saying a word. I got off last and thanked the driver, who gave me a quick nod in response.

Over half the shops in the high-street were closed, but the bigger chain stores were still open for business. A long queue had formed outside of the post office, and an even lengthier snake of people had lined up outside the local coffee shop. I supposed in times of crisis people desperately needed their pumpkin spiced lattes. *My* chosen destination, however, was Tomlin's books.

Although only a small, second-hand bookseller, I

knew Mr. Tomlin's doors would be open because the man hardly ever went home. The shop was his life, open from early morning till late evening, seven days a week, hosting poetry readings and open mic nights at the weekends.

A bell rang above the door as I entered, and Mr. Tomlin appeared immediately to give me a wave.

He was a man in his mid-sixties with a wild mass of silvery-gray hair and a fondness for brightly colored tunics. There was usually an e-cigarette vaporizer in his hand and a thick cloud of smoke trailing in his wake. He wasn't wearing a mask.

"Morning. Or is it afternoon?" he said. Before I could answer his question, he disappeared into the back room.

After half an hour of perusing the shelves for a new book to read, I settled on a classic by one of my favorite horror authors and took it to the counter, ringing the brass service bell beside the till.

"Mr. Tomlin?" I called when he failed to re-appear.

I made my way over to the backroom, assuming he hadn't heard me and poked my head around the door.

Mr. Tomlin was kneeled on the floor, doubled over and gasping for breath.

"Don't come any closer!" he snapped. "Call an ambulance."

I pulled my mobile phone from my jacket pocket and dialed 999.

"Hello. We are currently experiencing a high volume of calls—" The line cut out and left a low continuous tone resounding in my ear.

"I'll get help," I promised him, and ran from the shop, out into the street.

A few stores down, I spotted two men in green camouflage uniforms—an army patrol. They were everywhere now, mostly to keep the peace and stop looters.

"Hey!" I yelled, sprinting toward them. "Please, you have to help me! There's a man in the bookstore, and he's sick. I tried to ring for an ambul—"

"Where?" One of the men demanded.

"Tomlin's," I responded, flustered.

"Anyone else in there?"

I shook my head.

He pulled a walkie-talkie from one of the pockets of his cargo trousers. "Need a secure closure at Tomlin's bookshop. Over."

"Thank you, Miss," the other soldier said. "You should go home now."

"But—"

He walked past me and up to the storefront of the bookshop. After taking a brief look inside, he closed the door.

"Is someone coming to help?" I asked.

His reply was flat and rehearsed. "We have the situation under control. A team will be along shortly to provide assistance."

"Will he be all right?"

The soldier gave me an irate glower. "Go home," he snapped. "And stay there."

I backed away, nodding my head vigorously in acquiescence.

From further down the street, secreted in a small gap between a bakery and a haberdashery, I spied on the two men. Eventually, a third soldier appeared, carrying a large black duffle bag from which he produced a set of tools. In a matter of minutes, he'd secured and locked the shop door and stuffed some kind of cement-like substance into the keyhole. Lastly, he taped a sign to the glass window—Biohazard. Do not enter.

Having sealed Mr. Tomlin inside, the soldier gave his comrades a quick salute and then hurried away. The two remaining men lingered awhile before recommencing their patrol.

I realized then that I still had the horror novel in my hand, having run from Tomlin's without paying for it. Taking a five-pound note from my purse, I walked back to the bookshop and slipped the money under the door. A fruitless gesture, given that the owner was most likely dead.

Back at the bus station, as I waited patiently for my ride home, a man in overalls began to hang Christmas lights from the ceiling of the ticket kiosk, whistling absently as he stapled the wire in place.

What was it they always said on television?

Keep calm and carry on.

Business as usual.

Nothing to see here.

I wondered how long it'd be before the harsh reality finally sank in.

Chapter Seven

After…

We left the builder's merchants and started our journey back to the cabin. As the afternoon dissolved away, our conversation stuck to much lighter topics. By early evening, we were about an hour from home and following the coast back along to 'Siren bay' when I suggested we take a swim in the man-made sea-pool I'd spotted from the road. Nate didn't object. His t-shirt was so damp it was almost see-through, and his cheeks were a tender crimson shade.

We headed down a steep thoroughfare lined with palms and overgrown purple-flowering Rhododendrons until the road made a sharp turn onto a wide promenade. The sea pool was directly behind a small, dilapidated funfair-come-arcade.

There was something about abandoned fairgrounds that unsettled me. As a child, I'd watched a rather harrowing documentary on the Pripyat Amusement park after the Chernobyl disaster. One image in particular still haunted me—a scientist in a hazmat suit posing next to a well-rusted Ferris Wheel, its bright yellow carriages squeaking in the wind as though someone still sat inside. This place wasn't so different, with its faded merry-go-round of sun-bleached horses and dilapidated, russet-railed rollercoasters, their empty cars awaiting thrill-seekers that would never come.

I grabbed Nate's hand reflexively and pulled a face that conveyed my apprehension.

He shot me an amused smirk. "It reminds me of that film with the clown who—"

"Shut up!" I snapped, cutting him off abruptly, but smiling too. He just laughed.

We practically sprinted through the park to the pool, which was a few meters below ground level, accessible by a set of well-weathered concrete steps. The pool was cut off from the rest of the ocean by a rectangular stony wall, lined with blue mosaic tiles, most of which had cracked and broken apart.

"You first," he said. "It looks cold."

"Fine." It was a relief to slide the backpack off my shoulders. "Turn around then."

Nate put his back to me while I took off my vest and shorts, leaving my underwear on. Sitting down on the edge of the pool, I dipped my legs in, immediately recoiling a little from the water temperature.

"I'm turning around," he announced, leaving me with no other choice other than to just plunge in. I sucked in a gulp of salty air upon contact with the bracing seawater and shivered violently. Composing myself as quickly as possible, I turned around to see him strip down to his boxers. He caught me watching and frowned reproachfully, although it was followed by a mischievous grin.

"Sorry." I covered my eyes with my hand, although I could still see him through the cracks between my fingers.

He sniggered and shook his head. "No, you're not."

As he dropped himself down into the water, I laughed at the look of shock on his face.

"Christ, that's cold."

"Wimp." I teased. "All those hot showers have made you soft."

At the cottage, we washed out of basins of rainwater, only ever warm if we went to the hassle of boiling it first, which was never worth it. By the time we'd boiled enough to make a shallow bath's worth, the water would be lukewarm at best.

He sighed. "Believe me, I've taken my fair share of cold showers."

"Why would you have a cold shower on purpose?"

"It's been a long, lonely four-and-a-half years, Halley," he chuckled.

It took me much longer than it should've done to work out what he was alluding to, and when the answer finally dawned on me my cheeks grew embarrassingly hot.

"Oh, I see."

With a grin, I closed my eyes and tipped my head back in the cool water, lolling in the last few minutes of the day's sunshine. When I cracked my eyes open again, the sky had turned to a dazzling shade of pink.

"How does it do that?" I asked Nate.

"Huh?"

He'd swum to the corner of the pool and was relaxing with his arms stretched out across the edge.

"The colors in the sky," I repeated. "How does it go from blue to pink?"

"It's called scattering. Molecules in the atmosphere change the direction of light—" he stopped, noting my confused expression. "It's magic. Magic makes the sky pretty."

I laughed and paddled over to him, aiming a

playful splash in his direction. He balked a little from the impact of the water on his bare chest and then gave me a half-hearted, empty smile.

"What's up?"

His reply was flat. "Nothing."

"Are you sure?"

He shrugged. "I've just been thinking about how brave you are."

I snorted. "I'm really not."

"But you are. You left home, not knowing what *or who* you might find."

"That's not bravery," I chuckled. "Stupidity, maybe. Desperation, definitely."

Nate shook his head. "Stop being so hard on yourself. I owe you my life."

He was right. I *did* need to stop being so self-critical, and if I hadn't left the cottage, he'd be dead right now.

"You went out into the world *alone*. That's braver than you could possibly know."

I sighed. "Maybe."

His expression became downcast. "I need you to be honest with me, Halley. If being alone with me makes you feel uncomfortable, I can sleep in one of the other caravans—"

"What?"

"I want you to feel safe at the cabin."

I growled. "For Christ's sake, Nate! I'm not afraid to be alone with you."

He didn't look convinced, so I paddled closer and practically pinned him to the corner of the pool to prove my point. "At first, I was a little wary. But not anymore. I trust you."

It was a few moments before he smiled. To break the tension further, I slapped a wave of water toward him again and backed away, pre-empting retaliation. He wiped his face with a hiss and then launched himself forward, grabbing hold of my shoulders to dunk me under. In seconds it became a full-scale war. The sound of our laughter—and my screeching—echoed out across the bay, scaring off the nearby seagulls.

Weariness finally forced us to call a truce and start back toward home.

****

Before…

For over a week, my Aunt and I confined ourselves to the cottage.

We stayed glued to the television as events unfolded, despite it being the same string of news on repeat, unless something new developed. It was like watching the aftermath of a car crash—watching it would do you no good, but it was impossible not to look.

The death toll was nearing the half-billion mark, and every day some different government official would promise us the infection was under control, yet still more and more people succumbed. High ranking politicians were spirited away to emergency bunkers, but it did no good because the virus was everywhere, air-born, and resilient to every drug they countered it with.

Every so often, they fed us a crumb of hope.

"Santino Martinez, the first known survivor of the virus, was flown to a secure location in Europe yesterday. The seventeen-year-old from Mexico City is in a stable condition, and officials from I.D.R.I.S believe he'll be the key to an imminent vaccination. Meanwhile, a survivor from New Orleans, Adam Walker, has also made a full recovery. A statement from Mr. Walker's brother is expected later today."

Rebecca shifted uncomfortably on the sofa next to me. "Never been one to pray," she said, "But, maybe we should."

I looked at her. "You can if you want."

"I just thought it might help."

"Help who?" I snapped.

Rebecca shrugged and rose from the sofa. "I don't know."

With that, she rushed to her bedroom and slammed the door shut.

I hadn't meant to be so curt, but the last time I'd prayed was after my mother's funeral, and it had done me no good whatsoever. People all over the world were probably saying prayers right this very moment, and yet the news only got worse. Still, Rebecca didn't deserve to be on the receiving end of my bad attitude.

Annoyed with myself, I turned the volume down on the television and sought out a distraction in the form of college coursework. I kept telling myself everything would be back to near-normal in no time, however hard to believe that was. My psychology teacher had once told the class that human beings were remarkably good at adapting after a crisis. The show always went on, sooner or later.

A few hours before midnight, there was a statement from Kevin Walker.

"My brother Adam is doing well. He is being cared for by an excellent team of doctors from I.D.R.I.S and will be helping them in any way he can as he recovers.

Thank you all for your kind words of support."

There were tears in his eyes as he spoke. However, the press immediately turned their attention to the white-coated man who stood next to Kevin Walker.

"How many people have survived now?" one reporter demanded.

The doctor shook his head. "I'm afraid I don't know."

A man in a suit and tie with an I.D badge emblazoned with the I.D.R.I.S logo suddenly stepped out in front of the media crowd and leaned into the microphone. "We are currently aware of three survivors here in the United States and one in South America. All four of those individuals have been moved to a state-of-the-art research facility in Sweden. We *will* find a cure."

Four survivors. Only four.

"Is it true the virus causes infertility?" the same reporter demanded.

The man's expression grew taut as though he'd prefer not to answer this particular question. "Initial reports from our laboratory in the U.K have found reproductive function to be affected, yes. This isn't unusual for such an aggressive contagion. Even measles and mumps can lead to infertility."

"Are these issues reversible?" It was a different reporter this time.

"Preliminary assessments indicate the problem is permanent."

"How can you be sure an anti-virus won't cause the same issues?"

"Any vaccine will be thoroughly tested," he responded irately.

"But, with respect, given the limited time frame, how can you—"

"We will know more when further in-depth tests are conducted!" he barked and then added, "That's all at this time."

The I.D.R.I.S spokesperson quickly headed back inside the hospital before the press could direct any more questions his way. The media crowd roared like an angry mob as the camera feed cut back to the newsroom.

The news anchor looked down the camera with a stern expression. "More on this story, later. Now, over to Maria for the weather."

It almost made me laugh. Like anyone gave a shit about whether it'd rain tomorrow or not.

I stayed tuned for more information on Adam Walker, but he was never mentioned again by any officials, although the media continued to question his health and whereabouts.

What became of him was anyone's guess.

Chapter Eight

After…

By the time we returned to the cabin, the night sky was dark and moonless, splashed with thousands of twinkling lights and the faint smudges of faraway galaxies. Unhindered by light pollution, the magnificent spectacle of the universe spread out across the deep blue yonder, observed only by the few remaining humans inhabiting planet Earth.

It made me feel somewhat insignificant. Nate and I were simply two people stuck on a tiny planet, spinning around in a vast universe. Our brief tenancy of Earth—and our extinction—would go totally unnoticed. Perhaps some other dominant species would come along eventually, and hopefully, they'd do a better job than mankind did.

We headed round the back to the solar grid, but it was too dark to fix it now, even under bright torchlight. Nate dumped our rucksacks into one of the outbuildings, and then we walked back around to the front door.

Despite the glow of a few solar lights dotted along the deck of the cabin, I could barely see a thing. In the darkness—and because I'd been staring upward—I lost my footing, tripping over a loose wooden board and banging my knee hard on the balustrade. I yelped and swore. Fortunately, Nate caught me, wrapping me firmly in his arms.

"Halley! Are you okay?" he asked, although he snickered.

"I'm fine," I told him, ignoring the throbbing pain in my leg.

In the dim light, I could just about make out his eyes, burning into mine.

He made no move to release me, the pull toward him more overwhelming than ever as we stood pressed up against one another.

I couldn't do this anymore. It hurt me to want him so much.

But did *he* want *me*? I feared his rejection, knowing it would kill me to hear he didn't feel the same way, but the thought of fighting it any longer left me emotionally drained. All I wanted to do was give in.

So, I did.

Rising up on my toes, I pushed my lips gently against his. For the briefest of moments, I was sure he was going to kiss me back, but instead, he let me go and stepped away.

Humiliated, I turned my back to him.

He didn't want me.

Utterly dejected, I rushed back into the cabin. I wanted to go to bed, crawl under the covers and forget this ever happened.

Except, he came after me and grabbed my arm. "Halley."

"Leave me alone. I'm tired, and I want to sleep." My voice came out as a hoarse whisper as I tried to pry his fingers from my wrist, but he hooked his arm firmly around my waist and pulled me toward him. My fists pushed hard into his chest in an effort to break away, but it was no use.

"Just let me go," I begged.

"We need to talk about this."

He was right, but I was in no state to engage in sensible conversation with him.

Again, I tried to wriggle out of his grip. "I'm tired, Nate. Let's forget this ever happened. Please."

"Halley, I—" he started, but I cut him off.

"It's fine, Nate." My voice cracked. "I get it. You don't want me."

He gave me a despairing look. "*Don't want you*?" he whispered. "Of course, *I want you*, Halley. It's all I can think about."

His hands went to my face, and he tilted his head down until our foreheads touched. "I just can't do *this*."

I slid my hands around his neck. "Why not?"

He sighed heavily. "Because I can't, Halley. I can't lose anyone else I care about. If we cross this line, I won't be able to let you go. Ever."

"Then don't."

"You'll leave me."

"I won't. Where you go, I go."

Nate shuddered and drew in a deep, labored breath. "That's not what I mean," he rasped. "I'm afraid you'll die like everyone else."

I swallowed down the urge to cry.

What could I say? I couldn't promise him anything. It'd be a lie to tell him everything was going to be okay. There were no guarantees, especially in this new world we found ourselves in.

Still, it was no way to live.

There was only one thing I knew for certain. "I want you, Nate."

He closed his eyes and kissed my forehead. "I want you, too."

His words sent a wave of crackling static over my entire body. Leaning forward, I kissed him again—lightly, almost *not* a kiss. He didn't back away though this time. His lips lingered over mine for the longest time until he suddenly kissed me back, hard and hungry.

"*Fuck it,*" he growled.

His kisses became ravenous then, demanding more and more until my head spun. When I finally managed to push him back a little to catch my breath, my fingers found the button on his jeans.

Abruptly, he pulled away, a look of hesitation on his face. "Wait. Wait. Are you sure you want this?"

In response, I yanked the zipper down and let my hands slide into his shorts, caressing the bare flesh of his hips. "Nate, I don't think I've ever wanted anything more in my life."

His eyes flashed with desire, and he lifted me up, grabbing my thighs so my legs wrapped around his waist. He carried me into his bedroom and set me down on his bed, his lips only leaving mine for a second as he pulled my vest top off over my head.

In kind, I roughly pulled off his t-shirt and ran my fingers down the muscular contours of his abdomen. His skin was hot and damp with sweat. His hands went around to my back to unhook my bra, and then he gently slid the straps down off my shoulders and tossed it to one side. Semi-naked and utterly exposed, my heart raced with a mixture of anxiety and excitement.

Nate kept his eyes locked with mine. "If you aren't ready, we don't have to—"

I cut him off with an intense kiss and then lay back on the bed, pulling him down on top of me. He groaned when his bare chest became tightly pressed up against my breasts.

"I know we don't have to, but I *want* to," I whispered as his lips moved to my neck and then onto the bony protrusion of my collar bone. From there, he leisurely made his way down my body, and I inhaled sharply the second his tongue found my nipple. He lingered there a while before letting his tongue trail to my stomach and then gave me a wicked grin before unbuttoning my shorts and sliding them off, along with my underwear.

I gulped, feeling a fresh wave of anxiety rising in my chest. As his eyes moved over my body, he let out a deep breath before diverting his kisses to my inner thighs.

Any nervousness building up in me, instantly diminished when his tongue flicked a spot between my legs.

"Oh my—" I began, too blissed out to finish the statement.

The feeling only intensified when his fingers brushed against my sensitive skin and moved slowly upwards. I felt a brief pinch between my hips, and I whimpered, but the pain eased quickly.

He snapped his head up to look at me. "Is this okay?"

"Yes." It was more than okay.

His brows knitted together with concern. "We can stop anytime."

When he felt I was ready, he quickly kicked off his jeans and then leaned over me, gently parting my legs a little more so he could lay between them.

"Are you *sure* about this?" he asked me again.

With a playful roll of my eyes, I gently grabbed the hair on the back of his head and pulled his face close to mine, letting my tongue flutter against his.

Slowly, still a little hesitantly, he pushed himself inside me.

I stifled a gasp, feeling the same sting between my hips as before, although this time it wasn't as painful.

Nate stilled himself awhile until he began to move rhythmically and deliberately, carefully monitoring my responses to what he did. I quickly lost myself in the way he made me feel as my hips burned with a pleasurable ache that steadily spread over my entire body.

This wasn't at all what I'd expected. I'd always thought my first time would be awkward and uncomfortable but being this close with Nate was somehow both liberating and exquisitely all-encompassing. I'd never be able to get enough of him.

He slowed himself and stopped a few times, not wanting to end things too soon. He was struggling to keep his composure—four-and-a-half years was a long time to go without intimate contact.

As soon as he started moving again, I grabbed hold of his hips and arched my back, so we'd be even closer to one another. When I began to cry out, he quickened his pace, and it wasn't long before a surge of adrenaline flooded over my body in divine electric waves, leaving me in a blissful state of disorientation.

Nate gave one more slow, deliberate movement and then groaned, breathing hard. I held onto him as tightly as I could, feeling his heart beating rapidly against my chest. He buried his head in my neck, kissing me in tender, leisurely, intervals.

"Halley? Was that…did I hurt you?"

He looked at me, genuinely worried.

"No…well, a little, but it wasn't bad," I whispered, lifting a hand to stroke his hair.

He gave me a relieved nod, and then a deliciously wicked smile formed on his lips. He began kissing my neck again, and a little moan escaped from my mouth.

Clearly, this wasn't over yet.

****

As my eyes flickered open, my hand reached out for Nate but found only his pillow.

For one horrible moment, I thought last night had been a dream, but the remnant tingle of static from his touch still lingered on every inch of my skin. Unable to summon the will to move, I laid in his bed for the longest time, my mind on nothing else but what'd happened last night. It all felt so unreal.

Eventually, I disentangled my legs from the thin sheet ensnaring me and shimmied to the end of the bed. After hunting around for my clothes, which had mysteriously vanished, I went to the wooden chest of drawers in the corner of the room and pulled out one of Nate's t-shirts to wear, hoping he wouldn't mind.

My first port of call was to the bathroom to freshen up. The sound of the shower running had been completely drowned out by the sound of heavy rain pummeling the cabin roof, and as I slipped in through the door, I was startled to see Nate—wet and exposed—behind the glass enclosure. Despite the events of last night, I averted my eyes just as he turned around and saw me.

"Sorry."

He opened the enclosure door. "Morning."

"You're awake. I didn't hear you get up," I said, lifting my eyes a little.

He grinned. "I don't recall getting any sleep."

My cheeks suddenly warmed as I shot him a coy smile.

"I got up early to fix the solar grid," he explained. "Figured we'd need a shower. There's room enough for two in here, by the way."

There was a sharp tug at my solar plexus then, and I realized my need for him hadn't eased off at all. If anything, it was worse. As he beckoned me toward him, I pulled the t-shirt off over my head and stepped into the shower obediently. Even with the fierce torrent of water beating down onto my skin, I felt the familiar buzz of electricity as he placed his hand on my lower back and drew me close.

"Do you feel that?"

His lips went to my neck. "Yes."

"What is it?"

"No idea," he muttered, his hands sliding down to my thighs.

"But, it's weird, right?"

"Yep." He lifted me up and pushed me back against the glass wall, kissing me with such fervency my lips ached. I promptly lost my train of thought.

I guessed we'd talk about it later, whatever it was.

****

Hunger finally forced us apart, sometime after midday. Nate quickly fried up some omelets as I opened the front door and flopped down on the sitting room carpet, letting the breeze cool me off.

A few times, I caught him watching me as though he expected me to vanish at any minute. Sometimes, I feared he might suddenly disappear too. Nate had the ability to make me forgot all about the end of the world. When we were together, there was nothing but the two of us, and everything else just blurred into insignificance.

There was no point in denying it to myself. I was completely in love with him.

He joined me on the carpet, and we ate quickly, watching the rain fall onto the veranda. After seeing him yawn a half-dozen times, I shuffled closer to him and laid a gentle kiss on his cheek.

"Sorry, am I keeping you up?"

He sniggered. "Yes."

There was definitely some innuendo implied in his answer.

"We can go back to bed for a bit if you like. To sleep, I mean."

Another yawn. "I think I might need to."

We headed back to his bedroom, where I quickly helped Nate change the sheets that had become twisted up and sweat-soaked during our sessions of abandon. He flaked down on the bed, pulling me with him, and we kissed a little before fatigue saw him pass out. With my head on his chest, lulled by the rhythmic beat of his heart, it wasn't long before sleep took me too.

This time I remembered my nightmare. It felt familiar as though I'd had this dream before—or something similar, at least.

The second my eyes open, I know where I am.

I see my bookcase first, at the end of my bed. All my books are gone except for one title that sits alone on the top shelf. Throwing my blankets aside, I crawl down the mattress, my hand reaching for the lonely book. It is 'Alice's Adventures in Wonderland.'

Suddenly, I'm blinded by the morning sun as it streams in through the window. When my vision clears, the book is gone. Confused, I get up and peer outside.

A wasteland of orange-red sand greets me, below a muted blue sky.

Where the hell is this place?

I leave my room in a hurry to find Rebecca, but instead of stepping out into the lounge, I am now barefoot on the strange sand. As I take in my surroundings, my breath catches. Thousands of skeletal remnants lie on the ground, their bones protruding half-in and half-out of the sand, all crawling away from me like I'm the enemy who burned the skin from their flesh as they tried to escape.

I try to walk forward, but the bones are everywhere and gouge my feet until they bleed. The tiny patch of dirt where I stand is the only part of the wasteland that isn't beset with corpses.

There is nowhere to go.

Something tickles the skin on my toes, and I look down to see tendrils of lush green grass rising up through the red grit. It starts to fan out, covering the carcasses and sucking them down into the ground like they were never there. The vegetation spreads across the terrain like a tidal wave, sprouting flowers and sapling trees in its wake.

Mesmerized, I barely hear the noise behind me and, it isn't until it whispers again, that I turn around.

A human-shaped shadow stands before me. It floats closer and closer until it envelops my body, and I can no longer breathe.

Clutching my throat and gasping for air, my knees give way and I fall to the ground. The grass rises around me. I begin to sink. My fingernails dig into the dirt as I am dragged down and down, the sunlight diminishing the deeper I descend.

A voice in my head tells me not to struggle, but I continue to resist until my body is too weak to fight anymore. With my last ounce of strength, I cross my arms over my chest and close my eyes. But the end doesn't come. Still, the voice in my head whispers to me.

"This isn't how it ends," it says. "We are waiting for you."

It is the sudden warmth on my face that wakes me. When my eyes open again, my body is back on the grass, as though I am Alice on the riverbank, waking from her dream of Wonderland.

"We are waiting," the voice murmurs again. "For both of you."

****

Before…

Three billion people gone in two-and-a-half months.

It was January, cold and wet.

The news was much of the same, with random snippets of other events inserted in between the usual horror. Elderly people were dying because they hadn't received their yearly flu jabs. A church in Wales had become a cat sanctuary. There was a mass-suicide of over two-thousand people in Berlin, and some C-list celebrity had married their fiancé on his deathbed.

The news anchors changed daily, and today's

events were being read out by a former soap star in an animal print dress with huge, gold-hooped earrings that swung about whenever she moved her head.

Most of the time, it was like watching a surreal, avant-garde student film.

A dwindling throng of journalists still camped out at key locations, waiting to be the first to break any major news. I.D.R.I.S was yet to come good on their promise of a vaccine, and as the world went to shit, the people wanted to know why.

After days of no updates, a representative from I.D.R.I.S finally rolled up to Downing Street and stood, side by side, with the acting prime minister—a man whose name I kept forgetting because he'd only taken up the role last week.

"Thank you for your patience," the prime minister said, from behind his flu mask. He stared down at the cameras with a look of cool superiority in his eyes. "There has been a delay in delivering the vaccine, but rest assured, it is only a matter of days before the first inoculations begin."

His manner seemed genuine, but it didn't necessarily mean it was the truth. He was clearly reading from a pre-prepared script.

The reporters started with their questions. The representative answered most of the questions with the same non-committal responses.

"Can you tell us how many survivors there are now?"

"I don't have that information to hand."

"What about the infertility issues?"

"I'm only here to discuss the vaccine."

"We heard there was a survivor in Bristol. Can you

update us on their condition? Where are they now?"

"I have no information on that at this time."

One reporter stepped forward, somewhat aggressively. "I've been told by a reliable source that some people in the U.S are immune to the virus. Has anyone here been found to be immune?"

The I.D.R.I.S rep nodded. "It's not something I've been made aware of, but with any virus, there are always a small number of people resistant to it."

I blinked at the television screen. Maybe my aunt and I were immune. Maybe we wouldn't catch the virus at all.

The same reporter asked another question before anyone else could get a word in. "Is it true there is no vaccine because it isn't a virus?"

Not a virus? What the hell did that mean?

"That's ridiculous," came the response from the rep. His eyes flickered about wildly over the crowd. "We're doing everything we can to get a vaccine out to the people. We ask you to have faith—"

The cottage was suddenly plunged into a dark silence—the second power outage today. I got up and went into the kitchen, where Rebecca was mopping the floor. The whole cottage stunk of bleach now as my aunt sanitized every surface at least twice a day. I didn't say anything about how pointless it was because it gave her something to do and allowed her to believe she had a modicum of control over what happened to us.

She also prayed several times a day, in her bedroom, usually with the door wide open so I could hear. She prayed, asking over and over that we be kept safe from the virus. But, if the news was anything to go by, no one was safe from the virus, no matter how much they bleached, boiled, and locked themselves away. The virus was everywhere.

But my aunt and I hadn't caught it so far. Maybe we *were* immune. Or, if not, all we had to do was stay alive for a little while longer until they found a vaccine.

For the first time in months, I felt hopeful.

Chapter Nine

After…

The days faded into weeks, and before I knew it, almost two months had passed by.

Nate, as it happened, kept track of time dutifully—it was late August.

Still, I found myself too swept up in our idyllic bubble to care about much else, although Rebecca frequently crossed my mind. It was selfish of me not to have gone home already, and I knew she would be worried. The truth was, for the first time in my life, I was truly happy. It made me reluctant to want to be anywhere else.

Being with Nate was so very easy. We spent our days lazing on the beach or taking walks along the bay in the rain. We did chores when we needed to but rarely spent any time apart. We made love as often as we liked, wherever we wanted. The need for each other was just as intense as it was in the beginning.

After a week of bad weather, the roof on one of the outbuildings began to leak. Having just returned from a supply run to the builder's merchants on the industrial estate, we set about replacing the felt. Nate did most of the hard work while I passed him tools and distracted him every so often with a kiss.

The weather had grown hot again after the storms of heavy rain, leaving me with a cracking headache, and so I climbed down from the roof and went to fetch us drinks. I returned minutes later, holding two tall tumblers of water in each hand. Nate shot me a smile and then shuffled over to the ladder. As if in slow motion, he miss-stepped and fell backward off the roof, hitting the floor hard with a sickening thud.

A scream ripped from my lungs, and the glasses slipped from my hands, shattering on the ground beneath me. "Nate!"

I ran to him, skidding down onto my knees by his limp body and taking his head in my hands.

"Nate!"

A few seconds passed by in what seemed like an eternity before he opened his eyes and choked in some air. A flood of relief washed over me. I kissed his cheeks while he coughed and wheezed.

"For Christ's sake," I snapped, "You could've been killed!"

He coughed and grinned. "It's your fault! You keep distracting me."

My hand went out to give him a playful slap, but he grabbed my wrist and pulled me down on top of him. He kissed me urgently, although he was still a little breathless. I thought about resisting, on principle, but it was useless.

Swiftly, he rolled me over on to my back and pinned me to the ground, wincing in pain ever so slightly.

"I may have bruised a rib," he grimaced, ignoring my indignant glare by pressing his lips against my neck.

I sighed longingly. "This is exactly why nothing gets done."

****

It took me a good five minutes to hunt down my underwear from wherever Nate threw them after undressing me. He gave me a wry smile while pulling his jeans back on and then ruffled the dirt out of his hair. I narrowed an eye and pursed my lips to hide my smirk. As I pulled my dress back on over my head, he came up behind me and locked his arms around my waist.

"I love you."

His statement caught me off guard. He hadn't said it before, and my heart skipped several beats.

"Do you?" I asked coolly and leaned back against his chest.

He spun me around to face him. "Yes. I thought it was obvious."

"Then don't die," I replied.

Probably not the response he was looking for because he looked a little downcast.

He tightened his grasp on me. "Tell me you love me."

"Maybe later."

Nate didn't really *need* me to say it. He *knew* I loved him. He *knew* I was as hopelessly and blissfully entangled in this as he was.

He laughed. "I'll just have to withhold certain benefits till then."

"You wouldn't."

A low, mournful groan rolled from his throat in mock-annoyance. "No, I wouldn't."

I shot him a seductive smile and leaned close to his ear. "I love you."

He continued to hold me captive for a little longer, stroking my hair as I rested my head on his chest, but eventually, we reluctantly detached from one another so he could finish his work on the roof.

The pounding in my head hadn't eased despite drinking several pints of water and loading up on painkillers, so I ran a cloth under some water and applied to it to my forehead, and then flopped down on the pink velvet chaise-lounge in the bedroom. Positioned beneath the window, I could easily keep an eye on Nate from here without causing him further distraction.

A storm front rolled in about an hour later, bringing a strong wind and lowering the temperature considerably. Luckily, Nate finished repairing the roof just in time.

"Still not feeling any better?" he asked me as he wandered, stark naked, into the bedroom after showering.

I tried to keep my eyes on his face. "No."

He pulled on a pair of black joggers and came and sat next to me on the chaise-lounge.

"It's cooler out there now," he said. "A walk will help."

Typical doctor. They all believed exercise was a cure-all.

I wrinkled my nose in distaste but rose groggily off the seat with an unenthusiastic "Okay."

As it happened, the wind was quite soothing, but I still didn't feel like a walk, preferring instead to sit down on the sand a few meters from the incoming tide. Nate kneeled behind me and gently massaged the muscles in my neck and shoulders.

"I don't remember the storms being this bad before," he said.

He was right. Out at sea, an angry tempest brewed. Each summer, the thunder and lightning seemed to grow more and more intense.

"Maybe mother Earth is trying to fix the climate now the humans are gone," I answered.

I heard Nate sigh. "Good on her."

"Do you think if we got the chance again, we'd do it differently?" I asked him.

It was a few seconds before he replied. "Yes. I do."

These days, we lived more harmoniously with nature, but it wasn't out of choice. Life was easier with cars and nuclear power and all that other jazz. Would we willingly renounce modern life in favor of a more simplistic existence, one that respected mother earth instead of destroying her? I knew Nate would. And I would too. But I couldn't see Rebecca passing up the opportunity to go back to the way things were—she'd told me repeatedly that she wasn't meant for provincial living.

Rebecca. It was never going to be an easy subject to bring up but now seemed as good a time as any.

"Nate, I have to go home."

"You are home," he replied.

"To my aunt's, I mean."

Nate's entire body stiffened against mine. "No," he said flatly.

I shimmied around to face him. "No?"

His tone came off slightly angry, but more confused and panicked. "You said you'd stay. I don't understand. I thought you loved me."

"I do love you. And *I will* stay with you. But I can't leave Rebecca on her own any longer. It isn't fair."

Nate frowned. "Then we'll go together. You can't expect me to let you go off by yourself. It'd drive me mad, not knowing when I'd see you again or if—"

I rolled my eyes and cupped his face in my hands, kissing him quickly. "I meant for you to come with me, Nate. I don't want to be apart from you either."

He tutted but grinned. "You could've said that first."

"Sorry."

He relaxed. "We could bring her back here?"

"Maybe." Truthfully, I hadn't thought that far ahead.

"We could set up one of the caravans for her," Nate added. "That was always my plan if more people ever turned up."

His expression became a little distressed, so I leaned in and kissed him again.

"How did you do it?" I said after finally pulling away from him. "How did you cope with being on your own for so long?"

He flashed me a broad grin, "Cold showers."

"Not what I meant."

He sighed and looked past me to the shoreline. "I don't know, Halley. I don't think I *coped* very well at all. At first, it wasn't so bad. I was sure survivors would come here. Or that I'd find someone."

He cleared his throat, still firmly directing his gaze away from mine. "As time went by, I started having bad days. I'd sleep all the time or get drunk, but I'd always pick myself up again and carry on."

With a strained breath, he interlocked his hands with mine, his grip so tight my fingers throbbed. "I'd stored all my parents' belongings under the cabin. I don't know why. I just couldn't bring myself to chuck it out. One night, I got totally wasted and lit a fire on the beach. I burned it all. Everything. That's when I found a bottle of my dad's heart medication—he had an arrhythmia. I knew if I took too much, I'd fall asleep and not wake up."

"I set a date. If no one came, I would take the pills, and that would be it," he continued. "Three times I made that deadline, but I couldn't go through with it. But the day before you came I—"

He shuddered. "I was in a bad state. I'd been drinking for a week straight. I just didn't want to be here anymore. So, the next morning, I took the pills and fell asleep."

"Oh, Nate." My heart broke for him all over again. I wished I hadn't asked the question at all, although maybe it'd do him some good to talk about it, in the same way that I'd needed to talk about my stepfather. For me, it'd been a purge of sorts—a way to get the bad stuff out so it couldn't hurt me as much anymore.

Wriggling my numb fingers free of his clasp, I locked them around his neck instead. "I'm so sorry."

Why hadn't I left home sooner? Why couldn't I have been braver?

I tried hard to keep my tears at bay, but a few broke free and rolled down my face.

"You've nothing to be sorry for," Nate whispered and gently wiped away the droplets on my cheek with his thumb.

He tried to smile. "Thing is, even as I swallowed down the pills, I kept hoping someone would come and stop me."

He looked into my eyes. "Halley, I wished for you.

I wished for you, and you came to me."

I raised my eyebrows and sat back. No wonder he'd believed me to be a figment of his imagination. It was a miracle I'd found him without seeing his signs, let alone finding him *in time* to stop the pills from killing him. As someone who didn't believe divine intervention, I still couldn't help but wonder what'd led me here. Was it luck? Or something more inexplicable?

"I think I wished for you too," I said, before aggressively pushing him back onto the sand and smothering him in unrelenting kisses while untying the drawstring on his sweatpants.

Sex wasn't going to make all the bad memories and the unanswered questions go away, but it served as one hell of an effective distraction.

****

Before…

My aunt's cottage was fairly secluded, surrounded by woods and farmland. Our closest neighbor lived about five minutes' walk away, down the lane. Since moving in with Rebecca, I'd only seen him once in passing.

One morning, he came knocking at our side door while we ate breakfast in the kitchen. We'd just managed to microwave some stodgy porridge before the power cut out again.

"Don't let him in!" Rebecca said in a hushed voice. I went to the door where he stood with his face pressed up against the grubby glazing, peering in.

He was about the same age as my aunt, tall and well-built with thick muscular arms. If he'd wanted to get in, he wouldn't have found it much of a challenge.

"Rebecca," he called. "Let me in!"

She hovered behind me, an uneasy expression on her face. "What do you want, Will?" she answered him, arms crossed, biting her nails.

"I need to talk to you, please. I'm not sick," Will replied.

I turned to her. "What should we do?"

"Don't open the door," she said.

"C'mon Becca," Will pleaded. No one had ever called her 'Becca' that I was aware of. Not even my mother.

"My wife phoned. She told me that Oliver…"

Rebecca moved in front of me, concern flooding her face. "Oliver is what?"

Will covered his mouth with his hand as his eyes began to glisten. "He didn't make it, Becca. My boy is gone."

She stood there for a moment, breathing heavily through clenched teeth. Then she unlocked the door and stepped outside, leading Will away from the cottage and down the side path to the front gate. I went into the lounge so I could watch them through the net curtains without being seen.

Will was crying. Rebecca had a hand on his shoulder, her own eyes now a little red and watery. I watched her mouth move, unable to make out what she was saying. Somehow, it turned into an argument. Even though their voices were both raised, I still couldn't hear their conversation other than a few words: 'our fault,' 'stupid,' 'blame me.' While their interaction was heated, there were also fleeting moments of tenderness between them—a reassuring touch, a sorrowful glance, a brief clasp of hands.

Clearly, she knew him far better than she made out.

Eventually, Will left, charging off angrily down the lane. I thought Rebecca might go after him, but she didn't.

We never saw Will again—not alive, at least.

A month later, when our supplies dwindled, we went over to his house. We knocked and knocked on the door of his cottage, but there was no response.

Just as I was about to suggest breaking a window, Rebecca produced a key and unlocked the front door. She insisted I stay in the hall while she looked around first—downstairs and then upstairs.

After a minute or two, she hurried back down the stairs with a crestfallen expression on her face. "He's dead."

We emptied his cupboards of food and took anything else we could use; tools from the garage, several bottles of whiskey and vodka, and the small trailer parked on his drive.

As we left, Rebecca took hold of the vodka and stuffed a washing-up cloth into the neck of the bottle. She lit it on fire and then smashed the bottle against the hallway wall.

With old timber beams and a thatch roof, the cottage caught fire easily.

Later that night, sat at our kitchen table, Rebecca and I downed a few shots of the twenty-five-year-old whiskey she'd taken from Will's house.

"His favorite," she told me, after pouring herself another glass.

Tonight, she was distinctly melancholic, her eyes glistening as though on the verge of weeping.

"We slept together a few times, while he was still married. His wife found out and took their son," she said. "I'm not proud of what we did."

I didn't respond with anything comforting, although I probably should've. Sometimes, *I wanted* her to feel bad. *I wanted* her to hurt, for not fighting harder to get me away from Andrew. For leaving me there.

I knew it was stupid to feel the way I did. The past couldn't be altered. It was pointless being mad at her now.

Not when there were far more awful, terrible things to be angry about.

Chapter Ten

After...

Leaving the cabin behind, even for a short time, was more problematic than I'd initially considered.

Firstly, we'd have to eat the chickens because we'd be gone too long and there'd be no one here to feed or water them. Secondly, the vast majority of the plants—and thus our source of fresh vegetables—would most likely dry out with no one to tend to them.

Guilt quickly to assailed me. "Maybe going alone *would* be easier. I wouldn't be gone for more than a few weeks. It's so much upheaval otherwise."

"There's no way I'm letting you go alone. We'll just have to live off tinned food until we can re-plant," Nate said in a stern tone.

The discussion ended there.

I still felt bad about the chickens though, no matter how succulent and tasty they were.

Nate decided we would leave in a few days, and I agreed, even though a part of me didn't want to leave at all.

Trouble was, I felt very conflicted. Not only was my mind on Rebecca, but I also thought about the other people that'd survived the virus. Where were they? From the news, I knew they existed, but were they still alive now? Were there others we hadn't heard about?

As I helped Nate pack our clothes into a large

camping rucksack, I said, "Maybe we could go to Bristol on the way back to Rebecca's?"

He stopped and glared at me. "It's not on the way. And why Bristol?"

I shrugged. "It's what I planned originally. To see if anyone was there."

Nate rubbed the back of his neck. "There's no one there." It was a flat, definitive response.

"Further north then? Or London?"

He tensed. "You said you needed to get back to Rebecca."

"I know but—"

He cut me off. "It's awful out there near the cities, Halley."

"But, if there *were* people out there, that's where they'd be?"

"I don't know!" he snapped, his tone catching me off guard, causing me to shrink back a little.

He immediately noted my uneasiness and took me in his arms. "Sorry."

"Shouldn't we, at least, try?"

He clenched his jaw. "Halley, I want to find others as much as you do, but you don't know what it's like out there."

I couldn't disagree with him, knowing he'd seen the worst of it, *before* and *after*. The thought of facing all that death again clearly unsettled him.

With a heavy sigh, he stepped away from me and went over to his chest of drawers. Opening the bottom drawer, he pushed a bunch of t-shirts aside and pulled out a collection of papers. As he unfolded them, I realized it was a large map. He spread it out on the bed, smoothing down the creases until it resembled the lower half of England. It was covered in hand-written notes, with large areas circled red and marked with hundreds of X's.

I kneeled on the mattress to inspect it more closely. "What *is* this?"

Nate sat next to me. "This is a map of everywhere I went."

"What are the X's?" I ran a finger over one of the little black criss-cross markings.

"The X's are where I left messages—I spray painted instructions on where to find me, on bridges and roads, anywhere people would see. The main roads toward London were a nightmare by car, so I covered the southwest first and then headed a bit further North. That's when the fuel went bad, and my car wouldn't run anymore. I'd intended to go to London, but it was too far to walk with things already set up here. It was difficult to leave for more than a few days at a time," he explained.

With my index finger, I traced the coastal route I'd taken to get here, realizing I'd only just missed a few of his messages. "So close."

My finger drifted further right toward Exeter and then on to Plymouth—Nate had marked X's by these places too.

My aunt had been to both cities for supplies, more than once. Had could she have *not* seen the signs? How could other people have *not* seen them?

The truth was obvious. Either Nate's messages had gone unseen—or ignored—by people passing by them, or, *no people* were passing by at all.

The thought of it all made me nauseous.

Nate took hold of my hand. "What's wrong with it

just being us?"

My stomach churned. I needed air, or I was going to throw up. I moved away from him and told him I was going for a walk. He looked completely dejected but said nothing, letting me slip from his grasp.

****

The peaceful motion of the waves slinking back and forth down the beach did nothing to ease the deep, unsettling feeling in my chest, although I managed to suppress the urge to vomit.

My mind was addled. What if there were no other people? Not just here, but everywhere. What if the human race now only consisted of three people?

No. We couldn't be all that was left.

There were other survivors in the beginning. There *had* to be others out there somewhere. But what if they were so far away from us that they were beyond our reach? Across the sea even? Sailing large distances was problematic without diesel to run an engine, and finding a boat intact was another issue entirely.

I.D.R.I.S had ordered the army to burn or sink most of the ocean-going vehicles in an attempt to stop people from spreading the virus to other countries. Not that it'd done any good.

What's wrong with it just being us? Nate's words came back to me as I considered the reality of us being together.

What *was* wrong with that exactly?

Nothing. There was nothing wrong with that. I'd be perfectly content to grow old here with Nate and let the memory of humanity die with us. But first, I had to at least *try* to find other survivors. If I didn't, I'd always wonder if there was someone else out there, alone and desperate, like Nate, that we could've helped. Someone we could've saved but didn't.

The awful thing was, I knew Nate felt the same way. He'd tried so hard to find people after the apocalypse because that's who he was. He saved people. He helped people.

So, why didn't he want to look for people anymore?

The answer was simple. All the while he *didn't* go out there looking, he could hold onto the hope there *were* still people alive out there. What if we searched and found no one? Would it be better to have hope than to know we truly were the only ones left?

He'd already lost all hope once, and maybe he knew how easy it'd be to slip back into the darkness again.

But things were different now—he had me by his side to help him through it, to keep him from doing something stupid again.

Perhaps, though, I wasn't enough for him. I certainly hadn't been enough to stop my mother from slitting her wrists in the bathtub, so why on Earth would I think I'd be a good enough reason to stop Nate from going over the edge again? I hadn't magically fixed him. He'd never be fixed. Neither would I. It was selfish of me to have pushed him, and then I'd just walked out without a thought as to how he felt.

I hated that he was in so much pain, and *I hated* that, this time, I was the cause of it.

I hated that I'd lacked the courage to leave my aunt's sooner.

I hated that she'd stopped me every time I'd tried to leave.

I hated knowing she'd clearly *not* been looking for other survivors all this time, for whatever reason.

I hated my mother for leaving me. *I hated* Andrew. *I hated* the apocalypse.

The anger and resentment bubbled away inside me until I let out an ear-shattering scream at the sea. I picked up a piece of driftwood and threw it furiously into the water. Finding some other bits of flotsam, I did the same until the muscles in my arm began to pinch. It made me feel slightly better and distracted me long enough for my wraith to dissipate to a level where it was safe to be around another human again.

Of course, *that human* had been watching me the whole time. In the distance, I saw him, leaning against a tree on the edge of the beach, arms and legs crossed casually.

He was still afraid I'd disappear.

I started to walk back to him but quickened my pace until I broke into a run. As soon as I reached him, I jumped up and wrapped my legs around his waist, kissing him in short, urgent bursts.

"It's okay if it's just us," I said, stroking his face.

He looked at me. "Yes, it is. But, you're right."

"Am I?"

He exhaled deeply and kissed my forehead. "We need to know. We need to do this."

"What if we don't find anyone?"

"Then, we don't."

Despite the determined expression on his face, I still felt unsure. "But—"

He touched his finger to my lips. "*You* are the only thing I need. As long as I have you, nothing else matters."

More than anything, I hoped that was true.

****

Before…

Three months had passed since the outbreak.

The power had been off now for several days, leaving us nothing to listen to for information other than a battery-powered radio which only picked up two stations—the emergency broadcast frequency and some foreign station that played jazz music on a loop.

I'd always loathed jazz music; this really was hell on Earth.

Rebecca had taken to going to bed early with the assistance of sleeping pills and diazepam for her anxiety, wiping her out for twelve hours straight, sometimes longer.

I envied her ability to slumber her way through the end of the world because I hardly slept.

Morning saw me get up early to boil some water on the camping stove for my breakfast sachet of artificially flavored porridge. Hovering close to it, I warmed my hands on the fire.

We'd been blessed with a mild winter so far, although early mornings still brought a bitter frost. The cottage had an open fire, but we only lit it when absolutely necessary, so we wouldn't use too much of the wood we'd chopped and stockpiled.

I'd just finished stirring the dry porridge flakes into the pot when I heard a car pull up outside the front. The sound of an unfamiliar engine surprised me. I.D.R.I.S had warned people to stay home and to avoid the major roads as they were gridlocked or closed. The army now manned roadblocks on every motorway in an effort to slow the spread of the virus, checking the passengers of each vehicle for signs of illness before being allowed through the barriers.

Not many people made it past. Instead, they were escorted off to make-shift roadside hospitals. Some people refused and quickly had their keys confiscated—often by force—while their vehicles got towed to the nearest embankment. A few desperate souls had tried their luck on the hard shoulder, building up speed to ram the barriers. It never ended well. Either their tires got shot out, or the driver's brains were blown out over the dashboard, depending on how close they got to the barricade.

The media was fairly critical of these incidents, imploring the prime minister to take back control of the army from I.D.R.I.S, but it never happened. They were the ones in charge now, and they took no prisoners.

Curious, I turned off the stove and went out the side door, making my way down the iced-over path leading out to our driveway.

The sight of Andrew's car in front of our garage instantly rendered me paralyzed, sending a cold sweat over my body.

How dare he come here! *Why* would he come here?

As he squared up on the driveway, his fingers lifted from the steering wheel in a gesture of acknowledgment when he saw me watching.

I steadied myself and tried to think calmly. Should I run back inside and lock all the doors? Or would he smash his way inside anyway? Calling the police wasn't an option either because no one would come. *Shit*. What the hell did he want?

"I just want to talk," Andrew said as he flicked the engine off and got out the car.

He didn't look too good. His skin was white and gleaming with perspiration, his voice gruff when he spoke. "Please, Halley. I'm sick."

I swallowed hard. "How did you get past the roadblocks?"

He shrugged. "The army left. It's pointless. Everyone's sick. We just have to be with the people we love now."

I glared at him. It was almost funny. "Why the hell did you come here then?"

Andrew gave me a pleading look. "I was devastated when you left. You're the only family I have, Halley."

A laugh left my lips. "I am *not* your family. You need to go."

He sighed. "Go where?"

"I don't care!" I spat.

"Don't say that. You don't mean it."

"Go away, Andrew. You aren't welcome here."

His expression turned indignant. "After everything I've done for you, this is how you repay me?"

"Yes," I said hotly, anger matching my fear. "This is exactly what you deserve."

He shook his head solemnly and started toward me with his hand out. "Please."

As he edged closer, panic set in, and it was enough to get my body moving again. I quickly bolted past him and down the lane, away from the cottage. With Andrew, the only thing I'd ever been able to do was run away.

Once I made it to the crossroads leading to the main road, I stopped to catch my breath, my eyes searching for somewhere to hide. When I heard his car approaching, I started sprinting again, as fast as I could.

Of course, he quickly caught up, his car screeching to a halt just meters in front of me.

"Halley, love. Please," he pleaded again as he slid from the driver's seat. "I don't want to be alone. I'm sick."

For a second, *one tiny second*, I felt bad for him. But then, I remembered. My mind went back to that day in the car when he…

"Then hurry up and die!" I cried.

"Don't be like this! I—" he whimpered, but a coughing fit stopped him from saying anything else.

A large splatter of blood quickly formed on his shirt, and he began to wheeze. He bent over with his hands on his knees and retched until a dark red, clotted mass spilled out of his mouth and showered down onto the asphalt.

I recoiled, horrified.

He managed to stand upright again and stumble toward me, gargling each time he sucked in a breath of air.

"Please," he begged. "Help me!"

He unexpectedly lunged forward to grab my hand before his knees buckled and he fell face down on the ground with a heavy thud. I quickly yanked my hand from his sweaty, bloody grasp, and then backed away until the hedgerow swallowed me up.

I knew Andrew was dead when a thick pool of blood mushroomed out from his head and spread out across the road. A few streams of crimson oozed over to where I stood, stopping only inches from my trainers.

Still, I waited to see if he got up again. For a long while, all I could do was stand immobile, shivering as the blood puddle frosted over.

Eventually, when the cold wind was too much to bear any longer, I turned and hurried back to the cottage.

My aunt was up and making her breakfast in the kitchen when I returned.

"What have you done to yourself?" she asked, motioning to my hand.

I looked down to see Andrew's blood on my skin. "I...slipped," I stammered, trying to keep my voice even despite the tightness in my chest.

I quickly went into the bathroom and poured bleach over my hand, scrubbing off the dried blood with a nail brush until my skin stung. After tipping a pitcher of cold water over my arm, I examined my flesh closely for any traces of blood I might've missed.

"Be more careful," Rebecca said when I reappeared.

I nodded. "I might go back to bed for a bit."

"Still not sleeping?"

"No," I replied and headed to my bedroom.

I wasn't feeling well. Perhaps it was just the shock of coming face to face with Andrew and then watching him suffer a horrible death. But, a few hours later, my skin dripped in sweat, and a painful ache gnawed at my bones. When my ribcage burned with every breath I took, I began to cry, knowing I'd finally caught the virus. And from Andrew of all people.

Because of him, in less than twelve hours, I'd be dead.

Chapter Eleven

After…

London. We'd go to London.

Nate spent a few days plotting our course on his map and marking places to avoid. He said there were bad *things* he didn't want me to see, although he never disclosed what those *things* were. I told him he couldn't possibly shelter me from it all. Besides, he'd no idea what to expect the closer to London we got as he'd never managed to travel that far.

I guessed he would rather not see those *things* either.

London was almost two-hundred-and-fifty kilometers from 'Siren Bay,' and Nate estimated we'd cover around thirty kilometers a day. By the time we left, it'd be September, a little cooler than the last few months, making the heat less of a problem. Even now, when the sun went down, a slight chill hung in the air, and I found myself reaching for one of Nate's hoodies when we took our evening walks.

We'd both have to carry full rucksacks now, which would slow us down, but he suggested that we loot bicycles from somewhere if it became an issue. Unfortunately, the more *southeast* we went, the more *uphill* everything would become, making bikes of limited use.

I'd begun to think this journey was a bad idea, but

Nate actually developed some enthusiasm for the trip, whereas my keenness had wavered. The thought of walking so far made me feel lethargic just thinking about it. I wasn't sleeping very well either, one thing or another kept me awake at night—I worried about Rebecca, but I worried even more about Nate's state of mind. How would seeing all that death again affect him?

Last night, I'd tossed and turned well into the early hours of the morning until my anxiety became so unbearable that I threw up repeatedly, leaving me with a perpetual headache that wouldn't dissipate. Somehow, I'd have to find a way to put my anxieties aside before I drove myself mad.

We packed everything we'd feasibly need, keeping food provisions to a minimum. Nate didn't seem to think there'd be too much of a problem finding something to eat each day—if we couldn't loot something, he'd catch us a fish or a rabbit for dinner. He approached each potential problem with a cool, logical head, offering reassurance whenever I looked apprehensive. I guessed it was the doctor in him.

"We'll go to London," he'd said, with a grin. "At the very least, we'll do a little sightseeing. Then we'll head to Rebecca's."

Sure, why not? I'd always wanted to see the houses of parliament.

The evening before we were due to depart, I sat on the veranda, on a blanket, and watched the sun go down, taking mental photographs as though I was never going to see this place again—which was ridiculous—but, I still couldn't shake the unease off.

I was grateful when Nate came outside with a

bottle of expensive-looking champagne and sat down beside me. He popped the cork and then poured us a large glass each. A rush of bubbles tickled the back of my throat as I took a sip. I wasn't a massive fan of champagne but figured it might help me relax enough to get some sleep.

"I don't want to go."

He gave me a dimpled grin. "Yes, you do."

"I do, and I don't."

He laughed. "We'll be back soon enough, and then we'll have winter to look forward to. Trust me, it can get a little bleak here when it's cold—not so picturesque. It's not the paradise you think it is."

"I didn't come here for the scenery," I said, giving him a wink.

He threw his head back. "What can I say to that? I hope you give me a favorable review online."

"Four and a half gold stars," I chuckled.

He frowned. "Why not five? I've kept up with your sexual demands, haven't I?"

I almost spat out my champagne. "*My* demands?"

He licked his lips and smirked. "I blame myself entirely. I've created a monster."

"Whatever," I said, rolling my eyes, and he kissed me before I could throw any more sarcastic comments his way. Minutes later, we were making love on the veranda.

This time it felt different. Perhaps because we were leaving tomorrow, and it'd be a while before we could do this again here. I'd really miss this place, but as long as Nate and I were together, we'd be okay. *He* was my home. Being with him reminded me that the world wasn't all bad and we *could* still be happy, despite everything.

As though he savored every second, Nate moved his body in a way that felt like he was tempting me, drawing out each movement to the very edge and then gradually, deeply, bringing us together again. When it became impossible to hold back any longer, I moaned and held onto him as tightly as I could. Flushed and breathless, we fell away from each other.

"Nicely done," I said.

He rolled over onto his side to face me and propped his head up with his hand. "*Now* do I get five stars?"

I glowered at him in mock indignation. "Fine."

****

Reluctantly, we left the cabin behind.

A fine drizzle had begun to fall from an ominous gray sky just as Nate turned off the electricity and locked up. I dragged my feet a little as we walked through the wood, past the other caravans, but Nate took my hand and squeezed it in the reassuring way that he often did.

Feeling more positive, I put it down to Nate's mood, which remained upbeat despite my misgivings. Maybe he *did* need to do this as much as I did.

"I *would* like to know what happened to them," Nate said.

"What?" Lost in contemplation, I'd not heard much of the conversation.

"The other people who survived the virus," he repeated, "I'd like to know what happened to them."

"Didn't you say there was a survivor at your hospital?" I asked.

Nate nodded. "Yeh. A woman. Right at the

beginning, when we were still allowed to treat the infected."

The Infected. Sounded very much like a zombie horror to me, only there were no ravenous, brain-eating monsters in this B-movie. Thank Christ.

Once the hospitals had become over-run with *the infected*, they'd been forced to shut their doors while they dealt with their current patients—or rather, while they moved the corpses taking up bed space. Nate had previously explained to me that once the virus was discovered to be airborne, I.D.R.I.S had stepped in and ordered the hospitals to deny admittance to anyone with the virus. Despite the extra precautions though, most of the medical staff got sick soon after, Nate included.

"An ambulance brought her and her kids in—three boys, all under five years old," he continued. "She was the only one that pulled through. I had to tell her."

"Bloody hell," was all I could respond with.

Occasionally, Nate would come out with something truly harrowing. He really *had* seen the worst of it. Although, as a doctor, it probably wasn't the first time he'd been the bearer of awful news or witnessed terrible tragedy. Maybe it was the very reason he'd been able to remain strong for so long.

"What happened to her?" I asked.

"I.D.R.I.S moved her to an army hospital somewhere. I fought them on it though. She was too weak to be transported anywhere. They took her anyway."

A chill traveled up my spine. "That seems wrong."

"They were desperate to find out how to stop the virus," Nate said, "But, yes, it seemed strange to me, her being spirited away like that. I tried to find out how she was doing, being my patient and all, but they wouldn't tell me anything."

I frowned. "But, if she survived, where is she?"

His tone was ominous. "Exactly."

What had been done with—and to—the survivors? What lengths had I.D.R.I.S gone to for a cure? I wasn't sure I wanted to know.

As we started up the slope leading to the cliff top, Nate shifted his backpack into a more comfortable position, the perspiration already forming on his forehead from carrying the heaviest bag.

"I heard rumors, you know," he continued.

I cocked my head. "Rumors?"

"The hospital coordinator was a friend of mine. I dated his sister in college, and sometimes we'd all meet up for drinks after work. Brett Franklin, his name was." Nate smirked as if he remembered something pleasant for a change. "Couldn't hold his drink."

"Anyway, it was his job to liaise with I.D.R.I.S. We had to send all our test results and blood samples off to them. As things got worse, we were all exhausted from working round the clock. One night, I found him in his office with a bottle of vodka; he was wasted. I tried to sober him up with some coffee, but then he started ranting. He said I.D.R.I.S had a cure but weren't going to use it. I thought it was bull at the time—the drunken ramblings of a man stressed to his limits. But the more I thought about it, the more it made sense."

I stopped abruptly, my mouth agape. "If they had a cure, why wouldn't they use it?"

"That's exactly what I asked him. Apparently, he'd overheard a conversation between one of the army commanders stationed at the hospital and an I.D.R.I.S rep. The commander was questioning why 'certain plans' had been delayed."

"What plans?"

"Brett seemed to think I.D.R.I.S intended to infect the population with a survivable strain of the virus. He surmised that the virus had mutated in survivors, and infecting people with this strain was the only way to save them."

I stared at him in disbelief, but in the back of my mind, it made perfect sense. We'd all been promised a vaccine was only days away from being distributed, but then…nothing. Was it a lie to placate the people? Or had something gone wrong?

I shook my head. "If a cure existed, they'd have given it to us."

Nate shrugged. "Not if the cost was too high."

"What do you mean?"

"Infecting everyone with a different strain of the virus isn't exactly a cure. There would still be fatalities in people who weren't physically able to survive the *effects* of having the virus—same as those people who die from the flu. And what about the side effects? Like making everyone infertile? No way would the government let I.D.R.I.S distribute such a vaccine."

"But, even so, more people would be alive now if they had," I growled.

Nate gave a solemn nod. "I did wonder, when it got *really* bad, why they didn't use it anyway. Like you said, at least people would've *lived*."

I sighed. "Maybe it was too late by then."

"Or maybe there was another reason."

"Like?"

Nate scratched his head. "No idea. I guess we'll

never know."

"Guess not," I mumbled, puffing as the slope inclined.

We soon reached the cliff-top and headed over to the group of vehicles I'd seen parked here when I first arrived. Nate had mentioned earlier needing to get something from his car, although he didn't say *what,* and I couldn't imagine where he'd put it, given how jam-packed our rucksacks were.

Nate turned to me with a grin as he approached the cars. "Only one of these is mine. The rest I stole from a dealership in the village. It was easier to drive cars with full tanks of fuel, rather than filling up at petrol stations. Plus, when the power went off, the fuel pumps locked off too. And who knew fuel had such a short use-by date?"

Indeed, there was a long list of things that would've been useful to know before the world ended.

Our previous conversation suddenly got me wondering, had the media lied to us about the virus? Or had they been lied *to* by I.D.R.I.S?

When people started getting sick, we were told it was nothing to panic over. Everyone carried on with life as if none of it was really happening. They kept on going to work, and they did their Christmas shopping as they did every year, stocking up on the champagne for New Year's too. They did everything the television and the news had told them to do—keep calm and carry on. Only when a few thousand deaths turned into one billion, did people start to panic. Until that point, we'd all just waited around for the cure, eyes glued to our televisions for a good news announcement.

I still couldn't quite let go of my anger, even

though none of this stuff mattered anymore. Dwelling on the past would do me no good, especially when the present was so much more appealing.

Here I was, walking hand in hand with the man I loved. Ironic as it was, taking an apocalypse for me to find true happiness.

"You okay?" Nate asked.

Turning my attention back to him, I leaned in to kiss his cheek. "I'm good."

Nate flashed me a smile and then went around to the rear of an expensive-looking silver hatchback and lifted the boot. He rummaged around for a bit while I drew a smiley face in the dirt on the passenger window. Like all the other vehicles, the paintwork had begun to peel and crack from the constant battering of the elements up here, and the sea air was slowly rusting the metal on the door creases. Despite the heavy rain over the last few weeks, the years of grime build-up remained ingrained on the windows and around the lower half of the car. I continued drawing little patterns with my index finger until I saw Nate throw a small rifle over his shoulder.

"A gun?" I shot him an unsure look.

"It's mostly for shooting rabbits," he said.

Mostly. I thought about the wolf I'd encountered on the way here, and despite my dislike of guns, it seemed sensible to carry a weapon capable of packing more punch than a crowbar.

Nate continued rummaging in the boot, eventually pulling out a box of bullets which he slipped into the side pocket of his rucksack, and then he produced a hunting knife which got clipped onto the belt of his jeans. Oddly, I found it a little bit sexy.

Wandering round to the rear of the car to where he stood, I peeked into the boot, shocked to see it contained a neatly organized collection of weaponry and hunting accessories.

"Is that a crossbow?" I asked, leaning forward to examine a weapon wrapped partially in a small blanket.

"Yes," he said. "Overkill for hunting bunnies, though. I'm also an appalling shot."

I frowned. "It's quite an arsenal you have here."

"Well, when I looted all this stuff, I had no idea what to use and how to use it," he explained.

"So, you're a self-taught serial killer?" I chuckled, but he shot me an intensely disapproving glare.

"Actually, I hate it. It's why I don't keep any of it in the cabin."

I put an arm around his waist and laid my head on his shoulder. "I understand."

He kissed the top of my head and then shut the boot down. That's when I caught sight of the number plate, my eyes flicking repeatedly over the last three letters—*NMR*.

Silver car. *NMR.*

No, it couldn't be.

"NMR," I whispered.

Nate looked at me. "Personalized plate. Bit ostentatious, I know. *Nathanial Mark Reynolds.*"

I'd never asked his full name before. I swallowed hard and leaned back against the car, my head swimming.

Nate frowned. He put his hands up to my face and tilted my chin up to look at him. "What? What's wrong?"

Dazed, I finally managed to speak. "I'm…so

sorry."

He paled a little. "For what?"

I blinked. "I saw you."

"When?"

My voice grew hoarse, my heart thumping in anguish. "In Cornwall. Near Liskeard. You were there, weren't you?"

In my mind, the image of his map flashed before me. All of those little marks he'd made had been so near to us at the cottage.

"Uh, I don't know. Early on, I guess. But it's pretty rural there, and I just passed through," Nate answered.

Nodding soberly, I buried my head in his chest, gripping his t-shirt in my hands. "I saw you."

He shook his head in disbelief.

"I saw you," I whispered again. "And I let you go."

****

Before…

Somehow, I survived.

Rebecca, unlike me, didn't contract the virus, despite staying by my bedside while the infection seared through my body.

I couldn't recall very much after the fever started; other than the moments I woke up in pain. A searing heat in my veins so excruciating that I wished for death. Thankfully, after a minute or two of anguish, I passed out.

As the pain inside my body eased, my skin burned instead, like I'd caught on fire. I remembered screaming, and Rebecca holding me down—nothing like what I'd seen happen to Andrew, who'd perished quickly after developing the fever.

Five months had passed since the outbreak, and our

supplies began to dwindle again. Rebecca and I argued for days over who should be the one to go into town, but she hid her car keys and refused point-blank to let me go alone or to accompany her, claiming it'd be safer for me to stay here.

"Safer than what?" I snapped.

"We don't know who, *or what,* is out there!" she snapped back.

"What are you afraid of? Flesh-eating zombies?"

"No," she said. "It's the human monsters that I worry about."

Like Andrew, I thought.

The night before she left, I struggled to sleep, alternating between a fear of being alone and worrying something terrible would happen to her while she was gone. It amounted to the same thing really.

I got up just after sunrise and walked through the empty village until I reached the edge of the A390, which was about as far as I'd ventured recently.

Andrew had died here. This was the exact spot where I'd left his body to rot, and I didn't care to see what remained of him. This time, however, I plucked up enough courage to go beyond the invisible barrier I'd created and out onto the highway.

His body wasn't there, although a faint bloodstain still discolored the asphalt. For one horrible second, I panicked, thinking he might not really be dead, but his car was still in the same place on the hard shoulder. It was far more likely that some hungry animal had dragged his carcass away somewhere and dined on it. The notion of him being eaten up brought a smile to my lips, followed by a pang of remorse for even thinking such a horrid thing. Still, a fitting end to such a vile human, in my opinion.

Standing on the grassy curb, I looked up and down the road, my eyes sweeping over the fields and out to the horizon. I wasn't sure what I was looking for, but I lingered there for a long while before heading back.

The lane back to the cottage was long and narrow, lined by an ancient, hawthorn hedgerow obscuring anything beyond it. At first, I thought I was hearing things, but as it came closer, I recognized the sound of a car engine and the whir of tires on asphalt. I spun around and ran back up to the main road, my heart beating hard against my ribcage. Before I managed to reach the end of the little country lane, the vehicle passed by in a flash of silver. I darted out onto the highway about ten seconds later and sprinted after the car as it sped along, oblivious to my presence. All I could make out were the bold, black letters on the yellow number plate, shrinking as the car moved further and further away.

Something... 7... 2... NMR.

I raced down the middle of the road, screaming until my throat was sore and waving like a castaway on a desert island upon seeing a ship.

It was no use, though, because the car was out of sight in a matter of seconds.

Undeterred, I ran back to the cottage and roused my aunt from sleep by shaking her awake.

"I saw someone!" I panted. "In a car. Just now. If we hurry, we might catch them!"

Rebecca simply glared at me.

"I tried to stop them, but they didn't see me," I added.

"That was stupid!" she barked. "What the hell were

you thinking?"

I was taken back by her anger. "What?"

She huffed and swung her legs out of her bed. "Halley, I told you, it isn't safe! We don't know who those people are or what they might do!"

Her statement left me gobsmacked. "But, we…"

She raised her palm to silence me. "I mean it! It's not safe."

My blood boiled. If she'd wanted to protect me from harm, it was a little too fucking late. Frustrated, I left her bedroom with clenched fists and an overwhelming urge to punch something.

I thought about the silver car for the rest of the day, lingering around by the highway in the hope they'd come back.

Each morning, I walked down to where I'd seen it. Sometimes, I'd go in the evenings too.

Every day. For six months.

In the end, I told myself they were probably dead now.

Whoever it was, they were long gone and out of my reach.

Chapter Twelve

After…

Nate said nothing; he simply held me. The tears came anyway, despite trying hard not to cry.

But the tears weren't for me. They were for him.

If I'd fought harder, maybe Rebecca would've gone after him, and then he wouldn't have spent the last four-and-a-half years alone. But, no, instead of standing up to my aunt, I'd kept my mouth shut and behaved. Like a good girl.

Okay, maybe some of these tears were for me too—the ones that fell out of self-loathing. Because of my weakness, Nate had suffered, alone and despairing.

I stepped back away from him, sure he'd be angry once he realized what I'd done—or rather, what I'd *not* done. After drawing in a long breath, I told him everything, unable to look him in the eye as I spoke. I simply stared down at the dusty ground, thumbing away the tears from my eyes before they fell.

"She wouldn't go after the car. After *you*. I could've done something. You were alone all this time, and you didn't have to be. I knew you were out here, and I did nothing."

After an awkward moment of silence, I forced myself to look at him again. There was a sorrowful look in his dark eyes, but it wasn't angry like I expected.

He sighed and rubbed his forehead. "Halley," he

said, unpeeling a strand of my hair from my tear-drenched cheek. "It's not your fault. It's not Rebecca's fault either. She was just trying to protect you."

"First time for everything!" I spat, crossly, kicking at the dirt in frustration. "You know that she ignored your messages, right? She must have! There's no way she couldn't have seen them."

Nate clenched his jaw and breathed deeply. "Maybe."

"Maybe? Why aren't you angry?" I shouted.

His refusal to acknowledge my failings—and Rebecca's—made me want to scream. Without thinking, I rushed forward and pushed him hard. "You should be angry!"

He caught hold of my wrists tightly as I was about to do it again and shoved me back onto the boot of the car.

"Stop it!" he snapped at me.

His sudden shift startled me, but I didn't back off.

"You want me to be angry at you?" he snarled.

"Yes!"

Nate glared at me for a few seconds before his expression turned to one of pure exasperation. "For Christ's sake, Halley. Stop. None of this is your fault. I'm not angry. I *won't* be angry at you, no matter how much you think you deserve it."

"But I should've—"

He let go of my wrists and put his hands gently around my face. "People do what they need to survive. They might steal, or kill, if they have to...or..." He let his words trail off. "Two women alone? Your aunt was right to be cautious."

I took a moment to consider what he'd said. Maybe

I'd judged myself—and Rebecca—a little too harshly.

My fury faded a little. "We still should've come after you. At some point, you just have to trust in basic human goodness."

"I agree, but your aunt was trying to keep you safe the best way she knew how."

"You're too *fucking* nice!" I growled.

He raised his brow with a smirk. "That's the first time I've heard you use the *f-word,* Halley. It's kind of sexy."

A smirk crossed my lips. "Well, what can I say? You're rubbing off on me."

Nate swore so often it was like he used cuss words as sentence enhancers. And, yes, it was kind of sexy.

We *really* were both so incredibly messed up.

****

Nate's planned route sent us down the coast, apart from a few diversions through nearby towns he'd visited before. We made it to the first of them within a few hours.

Though a fairly large town, it still had a quaint quality to it. The main high street housed less of the well-known chain stores and more of the craft-artisan-new-age-type of shops. The entire long and winding road was lined both sides with the remnants of bunting and streamers, strung up along the lampposts and weaved into the metal railings.

A few needle-less dried-out pine trees dotted the pavement and jutted out of the shopfronts, most of which were adorned with all manner of Christmas décor. Faded, dusty Santa's sat in nearly every window, giving us rosy-cheeked smiles as we walked by.

A little unnerved, I stayed close to Nate. When we

passed by a bakery displaying an array of moldy piles of greenish slop, a wave of nausea caught me by surprise, and I puked violently over a storm drain for a good few minutes.

After my stomach was finally empty, I swilled my mouth out with water and toothpaste while Nate put his palm to my forehead and told me I was a little too warm for his liking.

"I'm fine!" I told him, fighting the urge to retch again.

"You're really hot."

"Thanks," I joked.

Nate screwed up his face. "I can't help it if I worry about you."

"I know."

We carried on walking until late afternoon when we reached the open countryside. It came as a relief when Nate suggested we call it a day and pitch the tent. He found a patch of grass on the edge of some woodland and set up camp while I slumped down cross-legged onto the ground and pulled off my trainers. I peeled my socks from my red, sweaty feet to let the open air soothe my skin, and then I lay back in the cool grass.

"Need any help?" My tone was unenthusiastic, and I made no attempt to hide it, knowing it was going to be a while before I'd summoned enough energy to move again.

"Nah," he said. "You should rest anyway."

"Yes, Doctor Reynolds."

He chuckled. "You know, I don't know your full name? Considering I know everything else about you."

The smile fell from my face briefly before I forced

it to return. Truth was, he didn't know everything. Not yet. I still hadn't spoken about how my mother really died.

"Halley Clarke," I answered quickly. "I went by my mum's maiden name."

"What was your mother's name?" he asked.

"Natalie. Let's not talk about her though," I said flatly.

Nate nodded, giving me one of his concerned smiles. After putting the tent up, he muttered something about looking for sticks to make a fire and then disappeared into the woods. I closed my eyes and tried to zen-away the headache gnawing at my temples since I vomited. At some point, I drifted off. When I woke up, Nate had lit a fire and was slowly turning a skinned rabbit around on a stick over the flames.

"Feel better?" he asked me as I stretched out lazily.

I sat up and ruffled my hair, certain that a few creepy crawlies had taken up residence while I slumbered. My stomach lurched with a ravenous hunger.

"You've been busy."

"I managed to shoot a rabbit as it came out of its burrow." The pride in his voice was obvious.

My nose wrinkled in distaste. Given the choice, I would *not* have eaten anything I'd once owned as a pet. But I was hungry, and it smelled so good.

I shimmied over to hug him and watched the embers shoot up out of the fire as the carcass roasted. Once the rabbit was cooked, I wolfed down my share and then licked each one of my fingers, thoroughly satisfied.

"Good?" Nate asked.

"Amazing."

Nate insisted on cleaning up by himself. He took the rabbit bones down the road and buried them, in case the smell attracted predators to the camp. He then set out our water canisters ready to catch any rain that fell. I could already feel moisture in the air, and the fire began to sizzle periodically as the raindrops hit the hot kindling.

Nate was far better at this survival lark than me. Thinking back, I'd been extremely lucky the wolf hadn't killed me. Or that I hadn't died of thirst. And, of course, finding Nate was pretty miraculous too. Maybe someone—or something—*had* been looking out for me. For us.

And what about the irresistible magnetism that drew us together? Had I felt *the pull* that morning I went down to the highway? Why *that* day? Especially when I'd avoided it so zealously since the day Andrew died. Had Nate felt something too? Had he taken *that* particular highway on *that* particular day for a reason?

These kinds of burning questions were enough to drive a person mad. The answer was unknowable, like most questions of a spiritual nature. It came down to faith and what a person chose to believe. Honestly, I didn't know what to believe—my mind was too addled by a million other things to start pondering life, the universe, and everything else.

It was what it was.

When Nate returned, yawning, he motioned for us to go into the tent. We kissed and fooled around for a while until he reluctantly admitted defeat and let himself fall asleep. I stayed awake a little longer, listening to the raindrops hitting the tent fabric, but it wasn't long before the sound lulled me to sleep as well.

I'd only been asleep a few hours when I sat up, startled, my head still pounding. A noise outside the tent must've woken me, but now there was only the sound of rustling branches and the distant hoot of an owl.

I shimmied out of Nate's arms and unzipped the tent. The air was decidedly chilly, but refreshing, nonetheless. The rain was light, so I clambered outside and took some deep, shaky breaths. I was incredibly thirsty. I downed one of the canisters of rainwater that had refilled in the downpour. The clouds had dispersed enough to see the moon, and it was bright enough to illuminate the field and the surrounding trees.

Every now and then, a flash of movement caught my eye, until a fox darted out from between two clumps of wild rye near the roadside. His eyes glinted as he edged a little closer, meandering across the field. When he was no more than a few meters away, he sniffed the air and crept further forward.

Without thinking, I held my hand out to him. He took another cautious step toward me, stretched his body out, and touched his dewy nose to my fingertips. After a brief threat assessment, he turned away and then bolted. Perhaps, he'd remembered that humans weren't to be trusted. Or maybe, he'd never seen a human before at all.

Sighing, I crawled back into the tent and snuggled up to Nate.

****

We'd manage to avoid any major scenes of mass-mortality until we reached the main road that led to Brighton. We passed a sign for a ferry terminal about eight kilometers back, but it wasn't until we got closer that we came across an army barricade and a few thousand cars queuing in every lane of the motorway, headed to the port turn-off.

Nate grew increasingly agitated, and I found myself overcome with dread. *This* was what my Aunt had described to me, the very scenes she'd tried so hard to keep me from witnessing. Now, I knew why.

On the sloping embankment, an army truck was parked askew, its olive-green soft-top covering flapping about in the wind, intermittently revealing a pile of plastic-wrapped bodies with bright yellow biohazard stickers stuck to them. I averted my eyes as we hurried along the hard shoulder, Nate pulling me a little faster than I could comfortably walk. Out of morbid curiosity though, I occasionally glanced inside the vehicles we passed, although most of the windows were whited-out with paint and marked with huge red X's. It was how the army identified the dead—the people who'd never made it to their intended destinations, back to their family, or wherever home was. Or anywhere but here.

"Nate!" I called out, stumbling to keep up with him.

He stopped and waited for me to catch my breath.

"Sorry," he mumbled.

I reached into the side pocket of my rucksack for my water bottle and took a swig. "Are you...all right?"

Nate frowned and gestured to our surroundings. "Not really."

Instantly, the gnawing feeling of guilt returned, coupled with my qualms about suggesting we do this in the first place. Just the look on Nate's face was enough to wrench my gut and insist we turn back. However, I knew that he'd refuse such a notion. The only thing I could do was distract him. Pulling him close to me, I leaned in and pushed my lips onto his in a hungry and frenzied kiss.

After a few minutes, he pulled away and raised an eyebrow, smirking. "You're not the kind of person that finds horror and gore erotic, are you?"

The scowl I gave him in response wiped the grin from his face.

The exit was thankfully only a few kilometers further, and I was more than happy to be off the motorway. The plan was to spend the night just outside of Brighton before heading north to London the next day.

A slow build-up of wind during the day had turned into a gale by sunset, making it impossible to put the tent up, so I reluctantly picked a house at random for us to take shelter in.

Although the idea of sleeping on a nice comfy mattress was extremely appealing, neither of us liked the idea of sharing a house with corpses. Since most people had died in their own homes, the chances of finding bodies inside were high. *Needs must when the devil drives*—this saying was becoming my go-to catchphrase these days.

The front door was unlocked. Nate went in first, brandishing a torch, and slowly edged down the hall to the living room, giving it a quick scan. Nothing there, aside from a community of silverfish inhabiting the moldy baseboard under the bay window. The room smelled strongly of mildew and dust, having been shut up for so many years.

I whimpered when a large, hairy wolf-spider

scurried up the side of the flat-screen television and disappeared into a mass of cobwebs. I shuddered and promptly backed out, shutting the door. We headed further along the hall into the kitchen, also devoid of any human remains.

"I'll go check upstairs," Nate mumbled, his expression ill at ease.

If there were any corpses in here, the bedrooms were the most likely location—sick people stayed in bed, after all.

While Nate headed to the stairs, I slipped my rucksack off, setting it down on the countertop. Nate had packed some tealight candles in my bag to save the torch batteries. I pulled a few out of their cardboard box and lit them with a matchstick.

It wasn't late enough to be completely dark yet, but the cloud cover had hastened the onset of night.

Using candlelight, I began to search through the kitchen cupboards for edible food, finding a couple of tins of beans, fruit salad, spaghetti, and a half-dozen bottles of water. I also came across a half-opened packet of rice infested with weevils and something green and ominous in a clear jam jar, which I quickly chucked into an empty pedal bin.

I stacked the rest of my finds on the counter and listened to the creaking of the floorboards above my head as Nate moved about upstairs. No shrieks of horror as yet.

Just then, some movement in the kitchen window drew my eye into the garden. It strained my vision to separate objects from their shadows, but I managed to make out a large tree at the end of the garden. For a moment, I thought it was the swaying of a loose branch in the wind that'd caught my attention, but as my sight adjusted, I saw it wasn't a branch at all.

A partial skeleton hung from a rope lashed to one of the thickest and highest boughs. In the strong wind, it blew from side to side, its singular remaining arm and leg swinging in harmonious union.

As Nate came back downstairs, I closed the blinds.

"There's no one here," he said, visibly relieved.

I cleared my throat. "Great."

We ate in the kitchen before heading upstairs with the candles and the water. As Nate went into the master bedroom at the front of the house, I quickly darted into the box room at the back to close the curtains on the window overlooking the back garden, shutting out the unpleasant view in case he came in here.

The master bedroom was dusty and smelled stale, so I cracked open a window ever-so-slightly and hunted down some fresh bed sheets, finally finding them stowed away in an ottoman at the foot of the king-sized, leather, sleigh bed. On the dresser, I sniffed at a dozen bottles of expensive perfume until I found one I liked and then sprayed it around for good measure. It didn't take long to make the room cozy, and it distracted my mind from conjuring up the image of the former occupant hanging outside from their tree.

During my impromptu spring clean, Nate went into the en-suite bathroom to freshen up. He managed to shave and wash himself with one of the bottles of water and then suggested I do the same, although it seemed like a waste of fresh water to me. But, since we'd had no trouble finding supplies on our route so far, I decided to take his suggestion, not knowing when I'd get another opportunity.

Of course, the fact that so many of the shops were un-plundered meant only one thing; nobody else was around to loot them. Even though most of them had been securely locked up, it was nothing a bit of perseverance and a crowbar—or a bullet—couldn't remedy. If someone wanted to get inside, it wasn't particularly difficult to do so. Despite all the signs, though, I hadn't given up hope of finding someone. Our journey wasn't over yet.

In the bathroom, I washed thoroughly and even shaved my legs and armpits before shampooing my hair. I used the toilet after filling it with bleach and then rummaged through the bathroom cabinet, hoping to find a band to tie my wet hair up with. All I found were a box of tampons and a pregnancy test, none of which were of any use to me, not having had a period since catching the virus. I supposed it was something to do with the infertility issue, but I.D.R.I.S hadn't ever discussed it, in any detail, on television.

It'd never really bothered me before—not having children—but, ever since Nate had told me about wanting to be a dad and have a family, I'd felt a little down about it. Probably because, for the first time in a long time, I could picture a future for myself. One that I never thought possible—a content existence spent with the man I loved.

That said, even if we could've had children together, was this really the kind of world we wanted to bring a child into? Especially when it would probably suffer the same fate as the rest of humanity and die of the virus.

Eurgh. *Talk about depressing*. What the hell was wrong with me? What good did it do to let such dark—

and completely redundant—thoughts enter my mind?

Crossly shutting the mirrored cabinet doors, I glared staunchly at my reflection. "C'mon Halley. Buck up. Don't let it get to you."

In truth, everything I'd witnessed today left me feeling quite disturbed and melancholic, the scene in the garden troubling me the most. It made me think of my mother and how miserable she must've been to take her own life. And, of course, I thought of Nate.

"Halley?"

I jumped.

He leaned casually on the bathroom door frame and shot me a concerned frown. "Everything okay?"

"Yes. No. I don't know."

He exhaled deeply and took hold of my hand, leading me out of the bathroom and back into the bedroom. Motioning for me to sit down on the bed, he kneeled between my legs and sat up so that we were eye level with each other.

"It's okay not to be okay, Halley," he said. "Do you understand now why your aunt didn't want you to see it?"

Yes, I understood. But it still wasn't right to keep me secreted away at the cottage for the rest of my life either.

As I huffed and let out an obstinate growl, he reached out and twirled a strand of my hair between his fingers. "Believe me, it used to be much worse out there. Back when the people still looked like people and not just piles of bones. For a long time, I thought I was actually *in hell*. All the death and despair finally got to me."

Not a topic I particularly wanted to discuss before

bed, but it seemed to be something he needed to get off his chest. Perhaps he wanted me to know what'd truly impelled him to swallow all those pills.

Facing the demise of humanity up close had somehow opened a door in my mind that hadn't been there before, an opening which allowed the *really* bad thoughts to slip inside. The kind of despairing notions that, if left unchecked, were powerful enough to push a person over the edge.

"It eats away at you until you're consumed by it," he added sorrowfully, his eyes boring into mine. "But I won't let that happen to you, Halley."

"How do you stop them?"

He smiled. "You brought me back. You reminded me of what it's like to be *alive*. Even amongst so much death."

Giving him a warm smile, I took the opportunity to lighten the mood with my usual retort of mockery. "You found vodka, didn't you?"

"No," he sniggered. "But there *is* a copy of Monopoly downstairs."

I groaned and flopped back onto the mattress. "And I thought things couldn't get any worse."

He laughed and climbed onto the bed, positioning himself over me. He leaned down and started kissing my neck, the tip of his tongue lightly connecting with my skin each time his lips parted. My fingers fumbled with the towel wrapped around his waist, untwisting the knot until it slid from his hips and fell to the floor. In response, he yanked off my towel in one expertly coordinated maneuver, leaving me with a slight friction burn on my bottom.

"Ouch!"

He mumbled an apology but carried on exploring my naked body with his mouth, causing a static wave to ripple pleasantly over my body. In these moments, I could only think of Nate and nothing else.

No guilt.

No darkness.

No death.

No wonder I was so addicted to him.

****

Before…

Rebecca had been gone for almost a week—the longest she'd ever been away looting. The car had broken down a few weeks ago, kangarooing to a stop just outside the village as she'd set off. At first, she thought it was the engine, but after trying a dozen other vehicles, she realized it was the fuel. We searched every garage and shed in the village for petrol, hoping to find some in a sealed container that hadn't been exposed to the air, but only managed to scavenge up a few jerry cans' worth, not enough to be of use.

Reduced to cycling with a small trailer in tow, Rebecca stuck to her planned route anyway, leaving me behind as usual. This time, however, she wasn't in search of food supplies.

Mindful of our need to survive another winter, she decided to scour the caravan parks of North Cornwall for butane canisters—any the army hadn't seized. In the weeks leading up to the *beginning of the end*, they'd come knocking on every door with a compulsory surrender order for cooking and heating fuels to keep the army fed and warm on the wintry motorway battlefields. No more BBQ's for us this summer.

"I'll be back soon, my darling. We'll grill a few

carrots to celebrate," she'd laughed, bidding me farewell as she rode away from the cottage.

Sometimes, I think she saw her little excursions as holidays; breaks from reality. I imagined her cycling around the holiday parks, down to the beaches, like the apocalypse never happened.

More than anything right now, I wanted to be with her, not confined to this small village, walking the same roads, past the same houses and shops, over and over, like a hamster in a wheel.

Lonely and bored, I jogged down to the children's playground and sat down on one of the narrow, rubber swing seats. I dug my feet firmly into the mulchy wood chips to push back on the swing as hard as possible, going as high as the chains would let me, and leaning back, so the only thing I saw was the endless blue-gray sky.

Eventually, making myself feel rather dizzy, I skidded to an abrupt stop and hopped off, heading across the road to the village shop.

This was one of the first places my aunt and I had looted for food. We'd smashed the glass entry door with Will's hammer to get inside and then made several trips back and forth to the cottage until everything of use was safely packed away in Rebecca's garage. It was like she thought someone else would steal it if we didn't grab it first.

Now, the racks were completely empty.

I stepped inside the shop and picked up one of the wire hand baskets stacked by the door. I looped it around my arm and began wandering down aisle one, trying to remember what'd been kept on these shelves—cereals, biscuits, and hot drinks if memory served. After a few moments of indecision, I picked up an invisible box of sugary flakes and placed it in the basket along with an imaginary jar of coffee and a packet of non-existent chocolate biscuits. Drifting up and down each aisle, I continued doing my intangible shopping until it was time to pay. Making my way to the till, I stared at the empty space where the cashier would sit before lifting the basket onto the motionless conveyer belt.

"Nice day, isn't it?" I said to the ghost of server Karen—the check-out girl who never smiled and always looked hungover.

Karen didn't answer. Not unusual for her.

"I know what you're thinking, Karen," I said. "You think I've gone mad, don't you?"

Again, no response.

"Well," I huffed. "I haven't. I know you're not real. So, I can't possibly be crazy, can I?"

Not yet, anyway. Bored, definitely, but not crazy. Karen could bugger off with her baseless allegations.

I batted the wire basket off the checkout, sending it spinning to the floor, and then laughed out loud, my voice echoing down the aisles of the barren shop.

I needed to get out of here. Now. Somehow, I'd have to find a way to stay sane while Rebecca was away, or I'd end up with a whole group of imaginary friends before long.

"Goodbye, Karen," I muttered, quickly exiting the store. "I sincerely hope we never talk again."

I'd never liked Karen anyway.

Chapter Thirteen

After…

London was silent. I'd only ever been here once before on a school trip, and I remembered being in awe of the gleaming, city landscape. It was a strange integration of old and new architecture, spanning the previous millennium to the present one. A thousand years of human ingenuity in one place, from gothic cathedrals to impossibly high skyscrapers. No matter which direction you looked in, the vista told a different historical story; often brutal, sometimes beautiful.

Various shades of green dominated the urban landscape now. Most of the buildings wore a covering of moss on the windows, along with a vast smattering of bird shite. Ivy had snaked its way into the city from the suburban gardens and quickly smothered the columns and lampposts. Sapling trees grew up through cracks in the concrete pavement while asphalt volcano-mounds littered the roads and pathways, spewing dandelions and all kinds of colorful wildflowers from their crumbling mouths.

We walked carefully, searching for signs that someone might've been here recently—something written somewhere, or the remnants of a campfire. Anything.

We passed by a designer clothing store with the entire glass shopfront smashed to smithereens, the tiny shards sparkling in the sun like diamonds. Judging by the tire marks on the pavement, a car had rammed it.

Nate inspected the debris and then stepped cautiously into the store. It'd definitely been looted at some point as the rails were sparse, if not entirely bare.

"Do you think this place got raided recently?" I asked.

He looked down at the floor and made a line in the thick dirt with his foot.

"Not sure," he replied pensively.

Hope flickered within me.

We left the store and pressed on, finding a half-dozen more shopfronts in a similar state; another clothing store, a health food shop, a liquor store, a pharmacy, a sports shop, and a furniture store, all thoroughly cleared out. All the other establishments in the high street remained locked up and untouched.

"What do you think?"

Nate's brows knit into a quizzical frown as he glanced up and down the road. "It looks like someone was stocking up," he said, "For a group of people, I think, unless whoever did this was a compulsive hoarder."

"Or a kleptomaniac."

"Exactly," he chuckled. "But the question is, *when*?"

Four years or four months ago? There was no way to know right now.

"We should get to higher ground," he suggested. "Get a better view."

It was nearly dark when we found a multi-story car park with a decent panoramic view of the city from the roof. By the time we climbed to the top, there was little to see without a light source. We'd have to wait till morning.

Deciding it was a good place to camp for the night, we laid out our sleeping bag in the back of an abandoned pick-up truck and stared up at the stars, tracing patterns out with our fingers, trying to remember the names of the constellations.

I found Canis Major and Orion's Belt easily enough but couldn't identify any others. "Where do you think the virus came from?" I asked Nate as I sketched out the shape of the celestial archer with my thumb.

Nate swiveled his head to look at me. "I don't know. Why? You think it was from space?"

I laughed and shrugged my shoulders. "No. Maybe. I don't think they ever said, did they?"

"No, they didn't," he answered. "It was all very mysterious. The outbreak pattern was unusual in itself—it happened in several major cities at the same time. Generally, these things start off in one place, not in cities separated by thousands of miles."

"Meaning?"

"Biological weapon, maybe."

"What else?" I asked.

He sighed. "A contaminated specimen of some kind. Passed from one research laboratory to another for analysis."

His comment made me sit up. "Like a meteorite?"

"Could be anything. In recent years, we've gone deeper into the oceans, further into space than ever thought possible, and drilled down into the polar ice caps...the virus could've been hiding anywhere. Dormant. Undiscovered."

I shivered, disliking the idea of the human race

being wiped out by something that'd lived here all along, lurking under the surface and waiting to strike. And the possibility of it coming from space? It was all a bit too *out there*. Bioterrorism was a less fantastical pill to swallow.

"I'd bet on it being a biological weapon. Or an engineered plague designed to curb our relentless breeding habits. Only, it got out of hand."

He raised one shoulder in a half-shrug. "Possibly, but the only people who know for sure are dead, so I guess it's another one of those things we'll never find the answer to."

"I think we're better off not knowing," I said, laying back again.

Nate grinned. "As a pursuer of knowledge, I disagree."

He patted the space next to him and beckoned for me to join him in the sleeping bag. I obliged, snuggling up to his body and resting my head on his chest. I'd gotten used to falling asleep with his steady heartbeat in my ear, drumming like a gentle lullaby.

He slid his arm around my waist and drew me even closer to him. "Sweet dreams," he mumbled, kissing my temple.

"You too."

But my dreams weren't sweet at all.

I find myself back in the red wasteland again, walking along a path of lush, green grass. Everything else around me is covered in a thick layer of ash, falling like snow from a slate-colored sky. The path winds and twists across the desert, and I follow it until I see something up ahead; a lake. The water shimmers and sparkles as if sunlight shines onto its surface, but there is no sun in the sky here. When I look into the lake though, the reflection is beautiful. There is a bright blue sky dotted with bulbous white clouds above a blooming green field of flowers. I reach out and touch my own reflection, causing the water to distort in concentric circles and fan out across the whole lake.

"Halley..." I hear a voice which sounds like it's coming from the lake, like the water can speak. It whispers again, but I struggle to make out the words.

River...the river...something...

Leaning closer, my ear presses lightly against the cool liquid.

River...

I don't see the shadow looming beneath me in the water until it reaches out and grabs hold of my shoulders. It pulls me down into the lake, down...down...where the voice is louder.

Not one voice, but many. Thousands of whispers.

"Follow the river," they say.

****

I woke, whimpering and gasping for air, only to find Nate leaning over me, stroking my face and softly calling my name.

"Just another bad dream," he said soothingly.

I wiped the beads of sweat from my forehead. "Another?"

He shrugged and flicked on his torch. "You have them most nights, Halley."

"I do? I don't remember them."

He nodded. "Probably for the best."

"Sorry," I muttered.

He brushed a few tendrils of my hair away from my face and kissed me. "You don't need to apologize."

"Do you ever have nightmares?" I asked him.

Considering the things he'd witnessed, Nate had far more reason than me to have bad dreams.

"Used to," he sighed. "Not so much now. I had this one recurring dream all the time—"

I blinked. "Wasn't in the desert, was it?"

"No," he answered, frowning. "It was always the same, though. I'd be in the cabin, and then I'd hear someone knocking on the front door. I'd try and open it but I couldn't. No matter how hard I tried, the door would never open. The windows too. I was always stuck inside, never able to reach the person on the outside."

A chill snaked up my spine. "When I *do* remember my dreams, I'm always in a red desert and…it's weird."

"Weird how?"

I shrugged. "Like I've been there before."

He tried to reassure me. "It's just your brain trying to find meaning from random electrical signals fired off during R.E.M sleep."

My uneasiness faded, and I grinned. "Is that the medical definition, doctor?"

"Not exactly," Nate replied. "Actually, no one's ever figured out the precise reason we dream."

Another one of life's mysteries that would never be solved.

I settled back down, letting him wrap his arms around me in a protective swaddle, and squeezed my eyes closed, hoping I'd fall back asleep quickly.

****

As if it was some kind of cosmic joke, we got up to a very foggy, very damp morning. The visibility from the top of the car park was practically zero, so we decided to walk further into the center of the city, toward Westminster.

If anywhere in London hosted a secret bunker, this was the most likely place. Under the houses of parliament maybe, where a select few government types had concealed themselves. Perhaps, the royal family were all down there too, feasting on out-of-date baked beans and washing them down with a bottle of vintage champagne.

The thought of it made me smile to myself, as far-fetched and unlikely as it was.

There probably wasn't a bunker.

The Queen was probably long dead.

We were probably just indulging in a bit of post-apocalyptic sightseeing.

By the time we reached Tower Bridge, the fog had lifted a little, but the vapors of mist still draped over the stony turrets and embrasures of the towers, curling around the blue suspension arms and cables. The river Thames flowed serenely beneath its algae smothered foundations, sporadically disturbed by the splash of a fish tail.

We crossed the bridge and carried on, passing by each legendary building or monument and exploring them briefly before moving on.

"I really expected the queues to be longer," Nate quipped, breaking a moment of prolonged silence.

Sometimes, his sense of humor was a little dark. I hid a snigger.

At midday, he used a net to catch a couple of trout. It didn't take long as the Thames appeared to be teeming with them. We carried them to a nearby park where he lit a campfire under the long, drooping branches of a weeping willow. It provided good shelter from the fine drizzle in the air, and the ground was dry enough to sit on.

We immediately attracted the attention of a few hundred ducks that swarmed toward us and encircled our camp, waddling and quacking as they inspected us curiously. Still, they kept a safe distance away, though a few loners came a little too close to the fire once or twice, lured by the smell of fish.

"What I wouldn't give for some plum sauce right now," Nate said, eyeing a plump looking mallard.

"Poor things. Run!" I shooed the ducks away. "Save yourselves!"

Nate shook his head at me, laughing, and carried on grilling the fish.

"So," I said, "When do we give up and go home?"

"To your aunt's, you mean?"

It was at least four hundred kilometers back to the cottage. Getting there would take weeks.

How long had I been gone now? Two and a half months? I'd left Rebecca by herself for all that time. Not my fault. She could've come with me. In any case, a few months alone was nothing compared to the years Nate had spent by himself. Rebecca *would be* okay, although she'd be thoroughly *pissed* at me for being gone so long. Would she be happy I'd found Nate? I hoped so.

I nodded. "Yes, how long before we call it quits and head to Rebecca's?"

He considered the question. "I don't know. The city is a big place. A few more days, at least. Before we go, I'll leave messages, just in case."

"Good plan."

"Maybe I should spray paint '*Nate woz ere*' on the side of Buckingham Palace," he snickered. "What do you think?"

I cracked up with laughter. "Go for it!"

He served the fish with a side of tinned ratatouille we'd looted earlier from a posh health food shop. The meal tasted good but wasn't quite enough to sate my hunger, so I munched on a few packets of stale crisps throughout the remainder of the afternoon.

The night fell too soon, and as another day faded, so did my hope of finding other survivors. We camped out in the lobby of a museum, watched over by two dueling dinosaur skeletons, surrounded by fossil and bone displays from various eras throughout pre-history.

Nate found it quite wondrous and fired facts and anecdotes at me as he roamed around the exhibits, like my own personal tour guide.

Growing up in London, his parents brought him here often, until he grew out of his dinosaur obsession at thirteen and moved on to other pursuits—like girls, and death metal.

"When did you know you wanted to be a doctor?" I asked.

"When I was fourteen, my parents took me on holiday to the beach. It rained the entire time," he laughed. "I went swimming anyway. Suddenly, I see this kid in the water. Drowning. I dragged her out of the water and performed CPR until she started breathing again. That's when I knew."

I looked at him in awe. "You wanted to save people."

"Yes. Later, I became fascinated by the human brain. All the complexities of it. The hidden mysteries.

The search for consciousness. I wanted to know everything there was to know—" he must've mistaken my enthralled expression for tedium because he abruptly ended his sentence and turned to me with a chuckle. "I'm boring you, aren't I?"

"No," I smiled. He really wasn't. He spoke with such passion that I couldn't help but find myself captivated. I also found his intelligence incredibly alluring—he could probably enchant me with any subject he chose to speak about; brains, dinosaurs…cucumbers. Whatever.

"What were *you* into as a kid?" he asked.

"I read a lot. I read everything I could."

"Favorite book?"

"Alice's Adventures in Wonderland," I replied quickly. "It was my mum's favorite book."

He hooked his arms around my waist and maneuvered me over to a collection of gemstones. "You still don't say much about her."

"Sore subject," I sighed, plucking a lump of smooth, waxy amber from its display stand and rolling it between my thumb and forefinger, surprised at how light it was. "I just find it hard to talk about her."

Nate kissed the top of my head. "I get it. But it's not good to keep things bottled up."

"I know," I replied, faking a yawn. "We should get some sleep."

After lighting some candles, we pushed together two vinyl padded, wooden benches and laid down on them, our bodies interlocked inside our sleeping bag.

The ceiling in this room had been painted to resemble a prehistoric sunset, with a few terrifying-looking pterodactyls added in for dramatic effect. The flicker of the tea-light candles caused strange shapes to dance about on the walls, playing havoc with the shadows of the bony beasts around us. I must've fallen asleep watching the pseudo shadow-puppet show because the next thing I knew, Nate had shaken me awake.

Drowsy, I sat up. "Was I dreaming again?"

"No," Nate whispered as he got up and grabbed his torch. All but one of the candles had burned out. "I heard something."

I rubbed my eyes. "Like what? An animal?"

He stared down the long room to the revolving glass door that we'd come in through and then pulled his trainers on. He snuffed out the remaining flame, plunging the room into total darkness. "No. It sounded like voices. Human voices."

The statement quickly roused me from my fuzzy-headed state. 'What? Are you sure?'

We stayed perfectly still for the longest time, listening and waiting, before Nate sighed and switched his torch back on, shooting me an apologetic smile.

"Sorry," he breathed, "But, I was sure I—"

Then, I heard it.

We both did.

A scream. A loud, human scream.

I quickly slipped my shoes on, my heart thumping hard, and went and stood by Nate, who'd already flung his rifle over his shoulder. We edged slowly over to the revolving doors, my hands anxiously kneading the fabric hem of Nate's hoodie as he moved in front of me and flashed the torchlight out into the street.

There was nothing out there, only darkness.

It was raining hard now. A mixture of fear and

anticipation welled in my chest.

Suddenly, a figure darted out from between two buildings. It ran in our direction until it became aware of the torchlight and then skidded to a halt.

It was a woman. I could just about make out the shape of her body before she fled down a side road.

"Wait!" I yelled, impulsively tearing after her.

"Halley! Stop!" Nate shouted as he ran to catch up with me. He caught my arm and stopped me just as I turned into the side road.

"We need to be careful," he whispered.

He shone the torch down the street, from one side of the road to the other. There were a hundred different places to hide—in between parked cars or in shadowy doorways.

A loud clatter sounded a few streets away, like the sound of something heavy and metal hitting the ground hard. I thought I heard hushed voices too, but the wind was whistling just enough to convince me I'd conjured it in my head.

"Hello?" I called.

Nate instantly covered my mouth with his free hand and shot me a pleading look.

"We don't know who—or what—is out here," he muttered, barely audible.

He was right. I hadn't thought it through before dashing off. Why had she screamed? What had scared her? Why was she running?

Nate lowered the torch and covered it with his hand, leaving a small amount of light leaking from it, just enough to see us safely into the dark arch doorway of a London-themed souvenir shop. He then turned it off, plunging us into such a void of darkness I couldn't even see my hand in front of my face. I clung tightly to him, his breathing just as fast as mine as we stood silently, listening. As the clouds moved above us, the thinnest slice of moonlight managed to brighten a portion of the dark street.

In the near vicinity, I heard footsteps on wet tarmac—definitely *not* my imagination. The woman suddenly sprinted out from behind the back of a car and bolted toward us, careening into me as she tried to make herself invisible in the shadowed nook. Her eyes were wild as she looked at me and placed a finger to her lips, beseeching our continued silence.

She was younger than me, in her teens still, with long blonde hair soaking wet and plastered to her pale face.

When the footsteps became louder, she stiffened and whimpered. A bright beam of light flashed into the street then, from one side to the other.

"Claire?" It was a man's voice, gruff but gentle. "C'mon, Claire-bear, talk to us."

The torchlight found us.

The girl—Claire—stared at me, shivering. "I shouldn't have run!" she croaked. "Or…was I was *supposed* to run? I can't remember!"

She hit the side of her head a few times with her fist in an act of frustration and then, just like that, she stepped back out into the road and waved at whoever was pursuing her.

"I'm sorry!" she yelled at them, clutching her head. "Don't make me sleep, please."

My fingertips dug deeply into Nate's arm as I gripped it hard, reeling from the inexplicable scene that played out before us.

Two men, both of them tall and stocky, edged toward her slowly like she was a startled deer who might scarper from them any minute. She held her hands up, her chest rising and falling rapidly.

"I'm sorry," she sniveled again and then swung her arm out in our direction. "But, look at what I found!"

She pointed to us with a trembling finger and then turned back to the two men. "Don't put me to sleep though, yeh?"

The man on the right glanced at us. "Well done, Claire-bear," he said.

His hand went under his jacket, producing a dark object which he then pointed at the girl.

It was a gun.

Nate instinctively lunged forward and aimed his rifle at the man, who didn't even flinch. In fact, a low chuckle escaped from his throat.

"Calm down. It's just a tranquilizer gun. See?"

He then turned from us abruptly and shot Claire in the chest.

She screeched but didn't fall.

Nate stepped forward again, his finger curling around the trigger of the rifle. "What the hell is going on here?"

Gulping down my fear, I managed to will my shuddering legs to move into a position beside Nate.

"Stay back, Halley!" he snapped, but I stayed where I was.

The man with the dart gun re-aimed it toward Nate. "Put the rifle down, mate, and we'll talk about this, yeh?"

At that moment, Claire stumbled forward and lowered herself to the ground, dizzily. The second man went over to her and propped her up against one of the cars.

"Sleep tight," he muttered, pulling something off his belt and holding it up to his mouth. It was a walkie-talkie. "Need some help here, we're on Brompton," he said into it as it crackled and whined.

"Be there in two," came the muffled reply.

More people. We'd soon be outnumbered, which felt like an extraordinary thing to be, considering only half-hour ago we thought were the only two people on the southeast coast.

Nate held the rifle steady. "Put yours down first," he called out.

The man with the dart gun nodded in compliance, but instead of lowering his weapon, he suddenly leaped sideways and fired it. The dart caught Nate in his left shoulder and forced him to drop the rifle to the ground. He pulled the dart from his skin and clutched the area where he'd gotten hit. I desperately tried to hold him up, but there was nothing I could do to stop him from falling to his knees.

The man casually walked over to us; the gun now aimed at me.

"Please," Nate mumbled, 'Don't...hurt...her.' His voice faltered until he lapsed into unconsciousness.

I kneeled next to Nate's limp body and cradled his head, shock rushing over my body and rendering me completely numb.

I couldn't speak. I couldn't move. I couldn't think.

The gun clicked as it fired again.

A sharp, burning pain seared across my collarbone as the dart's metal tip pierced my skin. I fought hard against the sedative, holding onto Nate as tightly as I could until the effect of the tranquilizer sent my head into a fog and I passed out.

****

Before…

The leaves on the trees had only just begun to turn to their fiery autumnal shades when Rebecca began hanging up Christmas decorations. The cottage ceiling was adorned with shiny metallic stars and lanterns, spinning on their strings every time the slightest draft wafted through. Each day, at least one of them fell and had to be stuck up again with an even bigger blob of tac than before.

Insisting we hand-make paper chains, I spent several days cutting out strips of paper and then haphazardly applying glue and glitter until it was a suitable level of tacky.

Sometimes, I spelled out swear words with sticky gems—a passive-aggressive demonstration against the art project I'd been forced to participate in. It was childish and stupid, but it made me smile.

Although October by Rebecca's calendar, this was to be our first Christmas, post-apocalypse, almost a year since the outbreak began. Not that it mattered to me what day or month it was because every day was mostly the same.

Wake up, have breakfast, clean, feed the chickens, make lunch, read, nap, walk, make dinner, sleep, and repeat.

Repeat.

Repeat.

Luckily, I had the ability to completely disappear into a novel.

Rebecca now made monthly looting trips to the

closest towns where she picked up a half-dozen books for me every time. So many titles were now stacked in piles around my bedroom that we burned the not-so-good ones for kindling. I kept the better ones in my bookcase in order of ranking; in an emergency, the bottom shelf would be offered first as a sacrifice to the open fire in the lounge, but the top shelf was precious. It would've had to be pretty bloody cold before I considered burning those.

I preferred to immerse myself in fantasy worlds rather than anything based on real life, but I read everything Rebecca brought me, even the vapid, D-list celebrity autobiographies. They caught fire super-quick.

As well as cooking a passable Christmas roast dinner, my aunt also managed to make a Christmas pudding, although she swathed in so much brandy it made my mouth burn. Probably to hide her rather eccentric choice of substitute ingredients.

She'd also got me presents and wrapped them, placing them under a potted fir tree she'd dragged in from the garden. Being stuck here all the time, I'd had to be more resourceful, resorting to making something of my own creation. I painted her a portrait of her favorite actor, which looked nothing remotely like the handsome man on the magazine cover I'd copied it from. In fact, it was like Picasso had drawn it, drunk and blindfolded.

When Rebecca unwrapped it on the date that she designated as Christmas day, it took her a good few minutes to figure out who it was, and then we fell about laughing until we cried. She hung it proudly in her bedroom, and for several weeks after, I heard her laugh whenever she walked in there.

Ironically, it was the best Christmas in a *very* long time.

Chapter Fourteen

After…

When I finally managed to peel my eyelids apart, I blinked and flinched from the painful brightness suddenly piercing my pupils. Dusty beams of sunlight streamed into the room, where I lay immobile, and nauseated from the sensation of being on a carousel.

After a massive effort, I managed to roll over onto my side and dry retch, breathing deeply between heaves until the dizziness wore off and my surroundings became clearer.

The room was square and off-white, with areas where the paint peeled back to plaster. There were two windows covered with metal shuttering—the kind that concertinaed out of the way if you wanted to open the window, though a chunky iron padlock hung at the end where the catch was. I lay atop a single mattress that was covered with a creaseless yellow sheet. I'd been provided with a pillow too, freshly laundered and smelling of berries.

On another mattress on the opposite side of the room, was Claire, still out cold and snoring lightly with her face buried in her pillow. It was at least an hour before she finally stirred.

As I started retching again, she stretched and yawned. "Hey."

She crawled over to me and put her hand on my

205

back, giving my spine a gentle rub. A momentary wave of static prickled between us. She quickly withdrew her hand and frowned, flexing her fingers briefly before she took hold of my arm and helped me sit up. Her pale face was racked with concern as she pushed my hair back behind my shoulders and then sat cross-legged next to me.

"You all right?" she asked, staring at me out of chocolate brown eyes. They were ringed with red like mine and Nate's. She was a survivor.

"No," I snapped.

My thoughts went to Nate. I needed to be with him. *The pull* tugged at me, along with a feeling of homesickness fused with longing. *Where was he?*

"I have to find Nate," I muttered.

"That the man you were with?" Claire asked. "He's probably in one of the other cells—sorry, *holding* rooms. Not supposed to call them cells."

Cells. Seemed like an accurate description to me, and I was willing to bet the door was locked so we couldn't escape.

"Where are we?" I quizzed her, still too weak to get up and look out the window. Were we still in London? We had to be. They couldn't have carried us very far on foot.

"This used to be a boarding school. These were classrooms," she answered.

I glanced around again. In my haze, I hadn't noticed the bottles of water placed at the foot end of our mattresses. I leaned forward and grabbed one, sucking down the water until there was less than an inch left in the bottom.

She watched me curiously. She didn't seem to be

as affected by the tranquilizer as I was. Maybe it wasn't the first time she'd been darted? Hadn't she begged them not to '*put her to sleep*?'

"There are dormitories in the west wing. I have a room there. You'll get a room too," she added.

"I don't want a room," I snapped. "I want to find Nate and go home."

She frowned and shook her head. "You can't go home! I was sent to find you, so now you *have* to stay."

There was something very peculiar about her. A childishness to her manner and the way she spoke. Seeing her features in the daylight reinforced my estimation of her age—fifteen or sixteen at the most. Her long hair was curly now it was dry, with tight ringlets springing from her temples, framing her oval face. Her thin lips were a little crooked, becoming more apparent when she smiled, but it suited her.

Confused by her statement, I growled and kneaded my temples roughly with my fingers. "*Who* sent you, Claire?"

She flopped back against the wall next to me and cast her eyes downward, shrugging. "*They* did. *They* told me to run and *where* to go."

She stared blankly at me for a moment, as if she'd lost her train of thought, almost like someone had pressed her pause button. Finally, though, she blinked, and her vacant expression vanished.

"I got confused. I *always* get confused. Too many voices telling me what to do. I don't know which ones I'm supposed to be listening too!" She sighed defeatedly, hugging her knees against her chest and rocking a little. "I didn't want to go into the water. But I know I must."

Clearly, she wasn't entirely sound, but given she would've been around ten years old when the virus hit, it was really no surprise.

"Who told you to run?" I asked, deciding to humor her.

"I don't think I should tell you," she murmured. "You'll think I'm mad. Mostly everyone thinks I'm mad."

Yes, I bet they did. "I promise I won't think that."

I kept my tone as reassuring and gentle as I could. The last thing I wanted to do was upset her, in case she was also prone to being a little volatile. We *were* locked in a room together, after all.

She continued to look down at the floor, huddling tighter into her fetal position. "I used to…take pills, because sometimes…I heard…*things* in my head." She faltered as she spoke, and it was clearly a subject that made her uncomfortable. "There were these…voices. They said such horrible things. The pills made them go away, though. Then everyone got sick and left. I got sick too, but I didn't leave."

Then everyone got sick and left. I assumed this was her own unique way of explaining how everyone had died. Still, it was an odd choice of words—*they left*, as though the human race had all just gone off on holiday.

Casting my mind back to my psychology classes at college, we'd only just touched on mental disorders, but she seemed to fit the profile for schizophrenia.

"I stopped taking the pills, and then the nasty voices came back," she continued. "This time, there were also…new voices. Actually, they aren't voices— not really—but it's the only way I can describe them."

She finally lifted her head to look at me. "*They* told

me to wait and that someone would come for us. Me and Peter."

This conversation was making my head thump more than it already was. "Peter?"

She beamed. "My little brother."

Little brother? Shit. She must've had to look after him, alone. How on earth had she managed to stay alive?

"We hid out in a shopping center near Dartford and waited," she said, still smiling. Her affection for Peter was obvious. Maybe the end of the world was a little easier when you had someone to look after. *Easier* was probably the wrong word. *Bearable* was more apt.

"Where is Peter now?"

She shrugged. "He's here somewhere."

It sounded like Peter had probably fared better than Claire after the apocalypse. Little kids had a way of bouncing back better than older ones and adults. At least, I hoped that was the case.

"Did someone come for you?"

I needed to know more about the people here and, more importantly, what the hell was going on. Why were we being kept in these cells? And by whom? There were so many questions, but I didn't want Claire to feel interrogated. I had to tread carefully.

"Yes. We waited, and waited, and waited," she replied, her tone puerile as if to emphasize how bored she'd been. "Then, Eve came."

Her last sentence took me by surprise. I'd expected her to mention one of the men from last night, but *Eve* was an entirely new entity. How many people were there here?

"Eve?"

She beamed again. "Yes. Eve finds people. That's what she does. That's what the voices tell her to do."

"Do they?"

I'd hoped that this *Eve* might be more rational than Claire, but it didn't sound very promising. Although Claire probably wasn't the best source of information.

Feeling a little stronger, I pushed myself up off the mattress and got to my feet. My legs were like lead weights, but I managed to stagger over to the window. The cell—or classroom, or whatever she'd called the room we were in—was one floor up from the ground, looking directly over a large courtyard. It was paved, free of weeds, and bordered by a dozen or so neatly pruned rose bushes of pink and red. In the center of the courtyard was a big stone fountain with a mermaid in the middle. Her algae-covered tail rose up out of the water as she held a conch shell to her ear and stroked her long moss-strewn hair. A tall red-brick wall surrounded the courtyard and clutched a set of immense wrought iron gates at the far end, each emblazoned with a heraldry shield—probably the school crest.

My breath caught when I spied people—five of them—coming out onto the courtyard to sit on the edge of the fountain. They began to chat animatedly, one of them puffing away on a cigarette as he sipped from a steaming cup.

Although I hadn't wanted to keep pressing her, I turned to Claire and said, "How many people are there here?"

"Twenty or so," she said matter-of-factly.

My shock was evident from my sudden gasp. "Twenty?"

Twenty people. My heart leaped. I never imagined

there'd be so many people in one place.

"Or so," she repeated. "There's more, but Eve can't get to them. It's why they came to London, to be closer to the tunnel. The one to France."

"How long have they been in London?"

She scratched her head in pensive contemplation. "A year, I think. They were somewhere in Scotland before. In the bad place."

Bad place? My mouth opened to ask her another question, but I was silenced by the rattling of the cell door. The clanking noise of a bolt sliding across its bracket confirmed my suspicion about being locked in.

It was the man from last night, the one who'd shot us. He stood in the doorway and glanced back and forth between Claire and me.

"Morning," he muttered. He wore a blue polo shirt, snug enough to be able to see the outline of a gun tucked into his belt. In his hand, he had a carrier bag which he chucked down onto Claire's mattress. The contents spilled out a little to reveal a few packets of snack food and more water.

"Eat," he ordered gruffly. His eyes were tired and a tad bloodshot. I could see by the ring around his blue irises that he was another survivor like us.

His gaze settled on me. "You must be Halley?"

He was no less intimidating in the cold light of day. His head almost touched the top of the door frame as he moved into the room, blocking out the fluorescent lighting from the corridor behind him with his bulky frame and broad shoulders. His neck was thick, his larynx protruding prominently from behind a fine dusting of stubble that reached his jawline. His eyes flickered over me in a way that made me feel like I was being intimately scrutinized.

"How do you know my name?" I asked him.

He scratched his head and ruffled his sandy-brown hair. "Your boyfriend keeps asking for you."

Swallowing hard, I moved forward. "Is he okay?"

"Oh, yeh. He's peachy," he said, and despite his upbeat choice of words, he was distinctly impassive.

"Can I see him?"

"After."

"After what?"

"After Eve has spoken to you. She'll be along soon," he added. "Either of you ladies need to use the bathroom?"

Claire shook her head. "I'm fine, thank you, Ben."

My thoughts were so consumed by Nate, I simply shook my head in a mechanical, indifferent manner.

"Sure?" Ben asked, his query directed solely at me. "We've got hot running water, ain't that clever?"

"And power. And running cars," Claire piped up.

Her comment was significant enough to rouse me from my dazed state. Ben glowered at her, making it clear he didn't want me knowing too much.

"Cars? How?" I asked.

Ben licked his lips and looked me up and down once again. For a moment, I thought he wasn't going to answer me, but he did.

"One of the survivors here is a mechanic. He got a few old diesels to run on vegetable oil."

I didn't know it was even possible to run cars on anything other than the commonly used fuels. Vegetable oil? Not too difficult to get hold of. My aunt had a dozen bottles stashed in the garage back home.

Getting hold of an older diesel car might be more

problematic since the British government banned them from road use for being too damaging to the environment. We could scour scrap yards maybe. A running car would be an invaluable asset.

"I see."

Ben continued to stare at me for a few seconds more before turning to leave. "I'll be going then. See you tonight, Claire-bear."

Claire gave him an unsure look.

"No running this time though, okay?" Ben added before shutting the door. He spoke in a soothing tone of voice, the same way you would reassure a child getting a tooth pulled out at the dentist.

To me, it sounded distinctly unnerving, like something very bad was about to happen to Claire.

"What's happening tonight?" I asked her, after he'd gone.

Her forehead wrinkled as a distraught look crossed her face. "I have to go back into the water. I must be brave."

"Why? Why must you go into the water?"

Her eyes lit up. "It'll make me better."

This was making no sense at all. "Is it...magic water?"

She tossed her head back and laughed loudly. "Don't be daft. Of course it isn't magic water!"

My frustration was only exacerbated by her response. What was so important about going into the damn water? "Is it more like a baptism, then?"

She pursed her lips thoughtfully. "Yes, I suppose it is a bit like that. But when I come back out of the water, the bad voices will be gone. Forever."

Maybe there wasn't anything macabre going on

here after all. In all likelihood, this was simply some religious thing. Just because a plague had wiped out humanity didn't mean people couldn't adhere to their faith.

Perhaps they'd even invented a whole *new* faith?

The word *cult* suddenly sprung to mind and notched my anxiety up another level. I had to find Nate and get out of here.

"You should eat," Claire said as she got up and began delving into the carrier bag that Ben had brought in.

"Not hungry."

She tossed me a packet of crisps anyway. "Eat. She needs you to be strong."

"What?"

Her expression became perplexed. I repeated her statement back to her, but she simply cocked her head as though I'd spoken in a different language.

"It's loud in my head today," was all she said.

****

My eyes only closed for a second, but somehow, I slipped into several hours of deep sleep. It was probably due to the effects of the tranquilizer still wearing off. Upon waking, I was surprised to see that Claire had changed into a long, white, bohemian-style dress, and was chewing on the contents of a packet of jelly sweets, reading a magazine that rested on her knees.

"Hey," she said, only looking up for a second.

I *really* needed to use the bathroom now. "Is someone coming back? I need to use the ladies."

Claire stood and went over to the door and thumped on it heavily. "Need to pee!" she yelled.

The door unlocked and opened.

This time it was a woman who stood before me.

She stretched out her arms with an audible crack and then beckoned for me to leave the cell.

By my reckoning, she was in her late forties and reminded me of one of those fifties pin-up girls with a tiny waist and impossibly long legs. Her blonde hair was cut into a long choppy bob, and her full lips were smothered in bright red lipstick. A quick glance over her tightly fitting pencil dress told me she wasn't concealing a gun on her person, but her icy glare was enough to convince me not to make any sudden moves.

"Follow me," she said, a note of irritation in her voice.

As I left the room, I noticed a plastic chair across the hall. A collection of magazines and sweet wrappers were haphazardly discarded onto the floor beside it, along with several empty mugs of what smelled like coffee. This woman had obviously been posted outside our door since we'd been brought in.

She began to lead me down the long corridor, but I stopped abruptly outside of one of the other classroom doors.

There was a plastic chair outside of this one too, but no guard.

"He's not in there," the woman said.

I didn't believe her. I felt like a magnet had suddenly latched onto me, drawing me toward the door. There was no doubt in my mind that Nate was in there. Besides, the bolt on the door had been pulled across—why would they lock the door if there wasn't anyone in there?

But what could I do?

The woman's stony facade softened a little. "He's

okay. We just had to give him a little something to take the edge off."

My stomach knotted. "Why?"

Her impeccably crafted eyebrows knitted into a frown. "He tried to attack Ben."

With that, she put her hand on my back and ushered me away from the door. "He—Nate, is it?—he really is just fine. You don't need to worry."

Really? I wasn't about to take her word on that.

She offered me a forced, crimson-lipped smile. "Ben won't take it personally. We've all tried to punch him in the face at some point."

Was she trying to be funny? If so, her humor was misplaced, although I imagined what she'd said about Ben was probably true.

For lack of any other choice, I reluctantly let her lead me further down the corridor until she stopped by a set of male and female toilets—the kind you'd typically find in a school. I went into the female restroom while the woman stood outside.

The walls were an insipid shade of yellow and decorated with several famous paintings far too upmarket to be hanging in a school toilet. A floral chaise-lounge sat in the corner next to an elaborate bronze side table adorned with various pillar candles and a scented reed diffuser. The sweet smell was so overpowering, I covered my nose and swallowed down the urge to retch.

I picked a stall at random and relieved myself before lingering at the sink for a few minutes to splash my face with hot water and soap. I hoped it might banish the residual sedative-induced brain fog.

The woman poked her head around the door to

check on me after some time had passed. "Everything okay?"

No, it wasn't.

Biting my lips together angrily, I left the bathroom. "Fine."

The woman set her pace beside me as we headed back up the corridor. "Halley? Is that your name?" she asked. "Like the comet?"

I wasn't in the mood to be sociable, but at least she wasn't staring daggers at me anymore. Perhaps, she'd expected me to cause trouble. Like Nate.

"Yes," I said flatly.

"Laura," she said, motioning to herself.

As we passed by, the desire to linger at Nate's cell door struck me again, but Laura pre-emptively placed a firm hand on my back and steered me back into my own cell.

Claire was gazing out of the window when I returned. There were people in the courtyard again. One woman scattered rose petals into the fountain, and another set up a row of pillar candles. Two men were going back and forth with buckets of water, topping up the water level in the fountain.

"They like to make a big deal out it," Claire mumbled.

The fountain was obviously where this 'baptism' would be taking place.

She still looked unsettled, so I gently put my arm around her. The static prickled again the moment my palm touched her shoulder.

"What is *that*?"

The question was rhetorical, and I certainly hadn't expected an edifying response from her.

"The little shock thingies? They help us connect," she said.

"Have you felt them before?"

She nodded. "Sometimes, with the others."

"What do you mean *they help us connect*?" I demanded.

She laughed. "Are you sure you want to be asking *me* that question? I'm mad, after all."

She made a valid point. Why did I think that she had the answer when, by her own admission, she was nuts?

"I want to know."

She gave me one of her faraway looks before her eyes refocused on mine. "You're trying to tell me something. Or *they* are. Or both, probably."

Right. I shouldn't have asked. My eyes rolled involuntarily before I could stop them.

"I told you you'd think I was mad," she responded with a grin.

My psychology teacher had once told me that *truly* crazy people didn't know they were crazy. Conversely, Claire *knew* she was *away with the fairies*—a saying my mother had used often to describe her own state of mind, like it was a fun pastime. But Claire was nothing like my mother. She wasn't sad and melancholic, although she probably had good reason to be. Instead, she exuded a kind of innocent optimism.

There was something else too…something about her I couldn't quite define.

"I think we're all mad, Claire," I muttered.

She returned her gaze to the courtyard with a broad smile. "All the best people are."

Instantly, I stiffened. "That's from Alice's

Adventures in Wonderland."

Claire shrugged. "Is it? I've never read it."

"Then, how do you know the quote?"

Quite frankly, I felt like I was on the edge of the rabbit hole myself, about to descend into a trippy, alternate dimension.

"Just popped into my head," she replied absently, her attention on the people below us.

Sure. It just popped into her head, just as I'd thought about my mother, who'd read 'Alice's Adventures in Wonderland' to me every night before bed when I was little.

I wasn't on *the edge* of the rabbit hole at all. I'd fallen in. Plummeting down and down and down.

To Wonderland.

****

Before...

Rebecca and I only celebrated New Year's Eve once, post-apocalypse. And only because there were five bottles of Irish cream in the larder about to expire. We started on the drink late afternoon and were sloshed well before midnight.

My aunt, her inhibitions lowered, began to talk about subjects that were normally off-limits—her childhood, for example.

My grandfather had served in the Navy for most of his youth, and so they'd moved around constantly, rarely staying anywhere for more than a year. When my mother was born, ten years after Rebecca, he left the service and took a normal nine to five job at a library.

"I felt like he'd missed most of my childhood. I hardly knew him,' she told me. "As soon as I was old enough to rebel against him, I did. I was a total brat."

Her confession made me laugh. It was hard to imagine Rebecca as a rebellious teenager.

"I left home at eighteen, and we barely spoke. When he got diagnosed with cancer, I came home, and we made up. I'm glad I got the opportunity, but I wish we'd had longer, you know?"

Too tipsy to add anything to the conversation, I simply nodded.

"Your mother was seventeen then. I hardly recognized Natalie when I came home. She was head over heels in love with this man she'd met at a party. He was at university, a little older and more mature than her previous boyfriends."

My mother had never mentioned any of this to me, never spoken about how she'd met my father, or even what he looked like.

"I did something terrible, you know," Rebecca said, her words slurry and slow. "I never forgave myself."

Licking my lips, I gulped down another glass of Baileys. I wasn't clear-headed enough for heartfelt confessions, so I figured I'd just get more sozzled and then hopefully if it was anything too bad, I'd have forgotten about it by morning.

"I slept with him. She never knew. He broke up with her to be with me, but I didn't love him. I didn't care about him at all."

My mouth fell open.

Rebecca stared solemnly into her drink. "It was jealousy. I envied her relationship with our father. She was the favorite. I wanted what she had."

She glanced up at me then. "If it weren't for me, you might've gotten to know your father."

A tear formed in the corner of her eye and ran down her cheek. I'd never seen her cry before.

I managed to articulate a response. "He cheated on my mother, with you, her sister. He doesn't sound like the kind of man I'd want to know."

Rebecca reached across the table and grabbed my hand. "I had no idea she was pregnant with you at the time. I really didn't. I'm sorry, Halley. Forgive me, please."

When I didn't reply, she let go of my fingers and poured herself another drink. My mouth twitched as a comforting sentiment formed on my tongue, but I stayed silent, pursing my lips together tightly. If she wanted forgiveness, she should've sought it from my mother while she was still alive.

"It doesn't matter now," I said finally.

With another drink downed and one in hand, I left the kitchen and stumbled into my bedroom.

When I woke the next morning, I greeted Rebecca with a warm smile and grumbled about my hangover.

"It's such a blur," I lied. "We must've had fun."

"Yes," she replied hoarsely. "I suppose we did."

Maybe she wanted to forget about it, as I did.

It was better this way. My aunt's betrayal was not a story I wanted to remember.

Chapter Fifteen

After…

Eve wasn't what I expected. As Ben predicted, she finally made an appearance just after sundown.

The moment she waltzed into the room, it was clear that she was in charge by the way she held herself, exuding confidence and supremacy. She wasn't much taller than me, but her big round eyes were the most vibrant shade of green I'd ever seen and clashed with both the red ring around her irises, and the fiery curls cascading down to her shoulders. She was probably in her early thirties but had the kind of pearly luminescent skin that redheads often did, making them look younger than they actually were.

She was followed into our cell by a man she introduced as Daniel.

"Halley, nice to finally meet you," he said, standing by Eve's side. "Apologies for the delay, it's been a busy day for us."

His accent had the slightest tinge of welsh in it, but it was only just detectable. He was taller than Eve and a little older—early forties at a guess. His eyes were such a deep shade of brown that his pupils were indistinguishable at a distance, and it made him look downright fiendish. The rest of his appearance embodied the term 'dark and brooding' with a head of thick black hair and an artfully trimmed goatee beard.

"Are you ready to go?" he asked, his attention turning to Claire. It wasn't really a question, though.

Claire smiled half-heartedly and then gave me a little wave. "See you on the other side."

In a matter of seconds, Daniel had ushered her from the room, his hand clutching her forearm so tightly his fingers left indents in her flesh.

I didn't want her to go, and I couldn't shake the feeling of doom building in my gut.

"I hope that Claire kept you company?" Eve asked, leaning back against the wall opposite me with her arms crossed. "Did she tell you much about us?"

"A little."

Eve smiled. "She can be…muddled, at times."

In no mood for small-talk, I breathed deeply through gritted teeth. "I need to see Nate."

"Of course," she said, coolly. "I just wanted to come and talk with you first."

My growing irritation channeled its way into my hands where it made balls of my fists. It took me a good few seconds to settle myself enough to respond as impassively as possible.

"Fine."

She moved toward me. "To be honest, we don't normally do things this way. It's been *messy*, to say the least."

My next response was far from unemotional and came out far more curtly than I'd intended.

"You don't normally lock people up then?"

"No, we don't," Eve replied. "Not unless we have to."

My composure fractured there and then. "You didn't *have* to lock *us* up!"

"*You* had a gun and threatened one of *us*," Eve countered.

"We thought *you* were going to hurt Claire," I snapped, copying her turn of phrase.

She said nothing until her lips finally curled into a sneer. "Like I said, *messy*."

She walked over to the window and peered out onto the courtyard. "I have to protect the people of this community. You understand that?"

I watched her carefully, but she gave nothing away other than what she chose to convey; *concern* for her people, *regret* for the way things had happened. Right now, she was trying to take the moral high ground.

A swell of guilt rose in my stomach and forced me to suppress the urge to apologize. This mess was *not* our fault. Were they right to distrust Nate and I? Yes, of course they were, but we had just as much reason to distrust them.

"Yes," I snapped. "I understand that."

She turned back to face me. "In any case, once we all get to know each other, I'm sure you and Nate will fit right in."

My fingernails dug painfully into my palms as my fists flexed. "What makes you think we'd want to stay here?" The words tumbled from my mouth before I could stop them. Pissing off Eve wasn't going to do me any favors, and I wanted—needed—to see Nate.

She smiled again, seemingly unaffected by my remark. "Well, we were hoping you would stay for a little while, at least."

Whether she was truly attempting to be reasonable or simply stringing me along, I couldn't decide. My only choice was to play her game. "Why is that?"

"This is where we're all meant to be, Halley," she answered, matter-of-factly. "Besides, a doctor would be very useful to us.'"

I shot her a quizzical look. "How did you know Nate was a doctor?"

Eve shifted a little closer to me. "Because he was *my* doctor."

"What?"

Eve slinked further forward until she was directly under the bare light bulb hanging from the ceiling in the center of the room. The light brought out the flame-like highlights winding through the coils of her auburn hair. It was almost ethereal.

"When I got sick with the virus, he was there at the hospital," she clarified.

Was this woman the survivor Nate had mentioned? The one who'd pulled through only to be told that her three little boys hadn't made it?

"In Bristol? That was you?"

Eve dipped her head in response. "He stayed with me, day and night," she said, exhaling heavily. Her cool repose was broken momentarily by a flicker of something in her eyes that was gone before I could define it.

Her unruffled demeanor returned, "I recognized him straight away. What are the odds of that? If it isn't fate, then I don't know what is."

I still wasn't sure if I believed in such things, but the chances of running into someone you knew in a world where only the most minuscule percentage of the population had survived were infinitesimally small. No wonder she wanted us to stay. If Eve *was* a believer in something divine, then having Nate show up would have strengthened her conviction tenfold.

The hairs on the back of my neck tingled uncomfortably and only added to the sense of uneasiness I felt.

"He tried to stop those bastards from taking me too," she added. "He was a good man."

I didn't like her talking about him in the past tense like he wasn't here anymore. "He still *is* a good man."

Talking about Nate triggered a feeling of utter desperation to rise in my chest. It was *physically* hurting now, turning into a constant ache deep in my bones, like I was coming apart. This was the first time I'd ever wished our connection wasn't so intense—not because of the pain so much, but more so because it was making it hard to think clearly. If we were going to get out of here, I needed my wits sharp.

"Eve, please, can I see Nate?"

She opened her mouth to answer me, but we were interrupted by a knock on the door.

"Eve? Are you coming?" a voice said from the corridor.

"I have to go," she said, flashing me an apologetic smile. "You'll see Nate tomorrow, I promise."

After she left, I fell back against the wall with my head in my hands.

Tomorrow. Tomorrow. Tomorrow.

I wanted to scream—loud, in the hope he might hear me. I wanted him to know I was still here, and I'd find a way to be with him again.

Somehow.

****

Hearing the low murmur of voices echoing up from the courtyard, I moved sluggishly to the window and pressed my face against the metal shutters.

The pillar candles were all alight now, flickering gently in the breeze. Further back against the perimeter wall, a dozen solar lamps burned brightly.

A crowd of at least fifteen people gathered around the concrete bowl of the fountain, some sitting on the edge while others stood well back. I caught sight of Daniel and Laura then, standing off to one side, both wearing the same subdued facial expressions. When I glanced back to the fountain, someone was in the water, leaning casually against the frolicking mermaid. I was sure it was the other man who'd chased Claire, but I could only catch brief glimpses of him when he moved into the light. He was bare-chested and wore jeans rolled to the knee, although the water in the fountain reached his mid-thigh.

It wasn't long before Eve appeared, followed closely by Ben, who had a firm grip on Claire. A few of the onlookers gave her a clap, and one even rushed forward to hug her. She smiled politely at them, but her body remained rigid in the embrace.

Ben helped Claire climb into the fountain and then got in beside her. She still wore the white dress she'd changed into earlier, the pretty ruffles fanning out in the water as the two men lowered her backward until she was floating.

For a ceremony intended to be tranquil and calm, most of the onlookers shifted uncomfortably now, their heads turning from the scene in front of them. Even Daniel looked away, casting his glance downward with one hand flattened over his mouth, while his free hand interlocked with Eve's as she came to stand next to him.

The moment she nodded at Ben, a cold shiver ran down my spine.

Putting his hands flatly on Claire's ribcage, he pushed her down under the water and held her there.

Seconds passed—too many seconds.

Let her go. Let her go.

When Claire began to struggle and kick out, the other man grabbed hold of her legs to stop her thrashing. A scream ripped from my throat, and my fists pounded hard against the shutters.

"Let her up!"

Claire's body jerked and twisted, until eventually, she grew still, her arms floating up to the surface, bobbing limply beside her.

Hooking my fingers around the shutters, I rattled them as forcefully as I could. It was more out of rage than anything else—no way anyone would hear me from up here, no chance of me being able to pry the shutters away from the wall either.

Exhausted from it all, my forehead slumped against the cold metal. Unable to sever my attention from the scene unfolding before me, I continued to watch, helpless, in the same way I'd watched the news in the early days of the apocalypse.

Finally, the men released their grip on Claire's body, leaving her to float serenely on the surface of the water for a moment until Ben lifted her out. The crowd dispersed quickly, including Daniel, who marched from the courtyard at some speed, leaving Eve and Laura as remaining bystanders. Laura walked forward and placed two fingers on Claire's neck, presumably to feel for a pulse. She shook her head and then motioned for Ben to follow her back inside the building.

Obediently, he carried away Claire's lifeless body.

Eve lingered in the courtyard, pursing her lips close to each candle before blowing out the flame. When she was done snuffing out the lights, she headed back into the school, pausing momentarily to glance up at my window. There was a distraught, unhappy expression on her face as our eyes met.

Seconds later, she walked away, disappearing completely from my view.

****

I didn't see anyone again until morning when Laura brought me food and took me to use the bathroom. She was friendly at first, but when I refused to converse with her, she got the hint and didn't bother to speak to me again.

In the bathroom, I spent at least half an hour throwing up, despite having barely eaten. Weary and utterly sapped of energy, I slumped down next to the toilet and hugged the porcelain bowl. Not one of my finest moments. At some point, I must've passed out because the next thing I knew, Laura was beside me. Her blond hair fell over my face as she slipped her arms around me in an attempt to prop me up against the cubicle door. The sound of her shrill voice as she yelled into a walkie talkie for help, roused me further from my daze.

The call was answered by Daniel, whose voice I instantly recognized despite the crackly response. He got to us in less than a minute, panting as he crashed into the bathroom.

"What's wrong with her?" He threw one of my limp arms around his neck and then scooped me up off the floor.

"I don't know, Daniel. I'm a vet, not a bloody doctor," Laura snapped.

Daniel let out a vexed huff. "Yeh, well, *the doctor* is still out of it. How much did you give him, Laura?"

"He was uncontrollable, Daniel! I panicked!"

"Ben tells me she won't eat. She's probably exhausted."

"What do you want me to do?' Laura spat. "I can't force her!"

"This whole thing has turned into a complete fucking mess!"

As I became more aware, I kept my eyes closed, listening to them bicker as they took me back to my cell, hoping to hear something of use. At least now I knew Nate was alive, albeit heavily sedated.

"Well, that's what happens when you let Ben have a gun!" Laura countered. "He didn't need to dart them."

"Really? Do you think they'd have come here willingly after seeing him chase down Claire like that?"

Laura grunted. "My point exactly."

They went quiet while Laura tried to make me comfortable on the mattress. She placed her palm against my forehead and then dug two fingers into my wrist, searching for a pulse.

"I could put her on a drip, get some fluids into her," she suggested.

"There's no point. She'll be going in the water tonight."

My breaths grew unsteady as an icy surge of fear wracked my body.

I was going in the water tonight.

It all made sense now. Nate was the one they really wanted—the doctor. They probably had limited resources and killed off anyone who wasn't of use. Eve had simply lied to placate me.

"Just give her something to make her sleep till then," Daniel barked.

No. No. No. If they made me sleep, there was no way I could get out of here.

Too late. The vein in my left arm suddenly stung from the insertion of a needle tip.

They were going to drown me.

But, not Nate. He'd be okay. He'd live. They needed him. He was safe.

"As long as I have you, nothing else matters."

Shit. He wouldn't be okay, though. They were going to break him all over again. He would end up back in the dark place. No hope. No reason to…

My head spun as the need to sleep scattered my train of thought. "Nate."

Laura leaned close to me and whispered in my ear. "Sleep now, honey. You'll see him tonight."

What? What did *that* mean? Would they make him watch me die?

Don't make him watch. Please, God. Don't let him see. *Don't let him see…*

My prayer went unfinished as the world faded to black.

****

Before…

Despite my willingness to bury my emotions in the deepest hole I could dig, the relationship between Rebecca and I became increasingly strained. While I carried on as usual, she was easily riled and snappy.

What did she want from me? It felt like she was angry at me for *not* being angry, like she wanted me to scream and shout at her until all her sins were absolved. Perhaps my refusal to fight with her was a worse punishment than not talking about it all, which I found difficult to reconcile. Part of me *did* want to punish her, not only for what she'd done to my mother, but also for leaving me with Andrew. She could've fought harder, taken him to court, maybe.

Anything instead of just walking away.

After a bad storm one night, the chicken coup took a serious battering, suffering a partial collapse of the hen house and fencing damage. Rebecca and I worked together, quickly making repairs before the chickens escaped or predators got to them. The rain was cold and brutal as we hammered together a new enclosure around the old one, removing and replacing sections as we went. By the time we'd finished, our hands were scratched to shreds by the sharp ends of the wire mesh we'd nailed to the fence posts, and our clothes were thoroughly sodden.

We congratulated ourselves on a job well done and, just like that, the tension lifted.

Later that night, Rebecca became unwell but assured me it was just a cold. Before long though, she was running a high temperature and wheezing with every breath.

"I'm fine, Halley. Don't fuss," she said, as I brought her the traditional honey and lemon concoction, and a hot water bottle.

Still, her temperature rose higher. I found myself in a state of abject panic, convinced she'd finally caught the virus and would die. Night after night, I watched over her, monitoring her breathing and checking her fever.

Please don't leave me. Please don't die.

After a week, since no other signs of the virus made an appearance, I relaxed a little, chalking it up to a bad cold like she'd said it was. Her cough, however, worsened. When she began to choke up blood, my anxiety went into overdrive.

"I just need antibiotics. There are some in the medicine box," Rebecca said, still unconcerned.

Finding nothing of use, I hurried into the village and smashed the window of the chemists. After rifling through the contents of the shopfront and storeroom, I managed to find a box of penicillin specifically for chest infections. They were well out-of-date, but I hoped for the best.

It took a fortnight for the color to return to her cheeks and a full month before she was her old self again.

The fear of almost having lost her kept me awake at night, despite her assertion that I'd over-reacted. Sure, I'd been quick to think the worst, but what about next time? What about when the pills didn't work anymore?

How long would it be before I was left alone here, forever?

Chapter Sixteen

After...

The sedative wore off much quicker than last time, and I was fully alert when they came for me. It was Ben who appeared at my cell door, while Laura waited in the corridor behind him. With no possible way to overpower them, I resorted to pleading.

"Laura, you don't have to do this!" I whispered to her as Ben took me by the shoulders and escorted me out of the room.

Laura avoided making eye contact with me. "Just don't struggle."

As we passed Nate's door, I noticed it was open slightly. Impulsively, I jumped back out of Ben's grasp and slammed into the door, which swung open with a bang as it hit the wall behind it.

"Nate!" I choked out as Ben hooked his fingers painfully around my forearm.

The room was empty. There was only a mattress on the floor and empty bottles of water lined up against the wall next to it.

My heart sank. Where was he? Were they really going to make him watch?

Ben adjusted his hold on me so that I couldn't make any more sudden moves, his arms so tight across my ribs that I strained to breathe as he carried me down the remainder of the corridor. Laura scurried ahead to open a set of double doors leading to a stairwell, which Ben descended quickly as if the weight of lifting me was no effort at all. At the base of the stairs were another set of double doors and a corridor almost identical to the one upstairs. The entrance to the courtyard was mid-way along, preceded by a massive stone arch and a set of heavy oak doors that were already wide open.

As Ben lugged me outside, he let me slip down a little. I dug my feet down into the gravel, carving out long lines in the path as he dragged me into the courtyard.

Eve, Daniel, and three other men stood in a row in front of the fountain—not quite the crowd that'd been here last night. Perhaps they'd all lost their appetite for senseless murder.

Only Eve turned to look at me as Ben hauled me forward. He stopped abruptly behind her and said, "Let's just get this over with," but made no further move toward the fountain.

Laura caught up with us and stood next to Ben with her arms crossed. "I thought you said *she* wanted to be here."

It was Daniel who responded, the same forlorn expression on his face as last night. "Tobias is bringing her down in a minute."

She who?

"Well, if you wait much longer, the good doctor will need another shot," Laura snapped.

Nate?

I twisted about in Ben's grip until I could see past Eve. The courtyard was mostly in darkness aside from the solar lights—no candles or pretty petals for me, it would seem.

Daniel stepped forward slightly, producing a torch from his jacket pocket. He cast the beam across the gravel and settled it on the fountain, lighting up the stony mermaid in her tranquil loll.

My eyes took a moment to adjust. There was someone else in the water already, flanked by two men who held the figure firmly in position.

"Fine," Eve sighed, turning her attention back to the fountain. "Go ahead, Max."

As the torchlight reached the face of the captive in the fountain, I screamed.

It was Nate. *Nate was in the water*.

I elbowed Ben hard in the ribs, causing him to cough and hunch forward, and managed to wriggle down enough to duck under his arms. Before I could get anywhere, he caught my wrist and twisted it up behind my back until I shrieked, feeling my shoulder muscles crunch.

Ben quickly wrapped his other arm around my neck, constricting my throat, while his right leg hooked around mine, stopping me from kicking back at him. In seconds, he'd rendered me completely unable to move.

Nate shouted then, struggling with his captors as they forced him down onto his knees.

"Eve! You said you needed him!" I croaked out, my vocal cords compressed by Ben's lumpy bicep.

Eve didn't acknowledge me, but I continued to beg her. "Please, don't…"

"Halley!" Nate shouted my name as the men struggled to keep hold of him, but I could tell his strength was failing, still battling against the effects of the sedative. He managed to twist his head to look at me, and then he just stopped moving, like he knew it was a fight he couldn't win. There was a swollen bruise around his right eye and a little trickle of blood spilling from his top lip. He blinked slowly and mouthed "I love you" before they gripped the back of his neck and pushed him roughly down under the water.

I squeezed my eyes shut and bowed my head to the floor, unable to watch. The frenzied splashing and the distorted sound of Nate's voice permeating through the water was enough to fill me with more despair than I'd ever felt.

Then, there was silence.

Nate became still. And, just like that, he was gone.

My soul left my body, leaving me empty and paralyzed. As my knees gave out, my body lapsed back against Ben, who barely managed to keep me from hitting the floor.

An age seemed to go by before they eventually lifted Nate out of the water and laid his body down on the gravel next to the fountain. No one said a word or moved, they just stood frozen, eyes on the lifeless body before them.

Laura was the first to break the silence when she cleared her throat and walked over to Nate. She bent down and took his pulse the same way she had done with Claire and then glanced over to the man called Max.

"Take him away," she said, her expression stricken. There was an undertone of anger in her voice, maybe a touch of remorse too. Not that it mattered. It was too late.

Her eyes briefly flashed to me before she turned back to Nate and gently closed his eyes with her fingers.

Suddenly, she let out a muffled yelp and fell backward.

Nate *breathed*.

It was a sharp, deep intake of air that lifted his chest and shoulders. Seconds later, his eyes snapped opened and he rolled onto his side, coughing out water and gasping for oxygen.

I got to my feet, but Ben still wouldn't let me go. He tightened his grasp on me again and held me firmly against his sweat-drenched chest.

"Well," he whispered, so close to the side of my face that I felt his hot breath in my ear. "Looks like your boyfriend didn't need our help, after all."

What the hell did that mean?

As Nate slowly crawled to his knees and tried to stand up, I tried calling out for him, but I choked beneath Ben's stranglehold.

"Get him upstairs!" Daniel barked.

Max and the other man quickly rushed to Nate and grabbed hold of him. He tried to pull away from them, but he was dazed and just ended up falling against Max.

"Laura, go with them!"

She shot Daniel a look of fierce indignation. "This isn't what I signed up for!" she growled as she barged past him to follow the men back into the school.

Daniel ignored her. "Get Halley into the water," he ordered Ben, the mention of my name jarring me back to a state of semi-awareness.

My limbs were lead weights as Ben picked me up and carried me to the fountain.

For Christ's sake! Fight!

The cold water enveloped my body as Ben

clutched my shoulders and pushed me back into the water.

Fight!

At that moment, another figure appeared by the fountain and leaned over the rim.

It was Claire.

Claire.

Claire, who'd died yesterday.

She loomed over me, smiling. "Don't be scared."

I reeled. "Claire? How are you alive?"

"We didn't know about Nate," she whispered, ignoring my question. "If we'd known, we wouldn't have put him in the water."

"Known what? Claire?"

She smiled again and rested her hands softly on my chest. There was an unexpected burst of static under her palms when her skin made contact with mine, so intense she staggered back with a screech. Her brows knitted in together in a pained expression as she inspected her hands.

"I—I don't think we should do this," she stuttered, twirling round to face Eve.

Ben groaned. "Oh, for Christ's sake. What now?"

"No. We can't. We can't!"

Then, suddenly, Claire screamed out in agony and covered her ears.

Eve ran to her side. "Claire? Honey, look at me. What's wrong?"

Claire thumped her ears and then covered them again. "So loud. Screaming. We have to stop! We aren't supposed to do this. *Not to her!*"

"Claire—"

"You're not listening!"

239

Claire yelled into Eve's face so vehemently that she stepped back, her emerald eyes wide with astonishment.

Ben shook his head. "Screw it!"

With that, he used his knee to pin my legs while wrapping his hands around my neck. As the cold water rushed over my face, I clawed at Ben's hands with my fingernails, but he pushed me down deeper until the back of my head hit the concrete bottom. My chest burned from the lack of oxygen as I resisted the urge to let the water fill my lungs. Above me, through the cold murk, warping outlines of people took shape. For a second, I thought it was my imagination when the ripples turned red, but I recognized the way the red tendrils curled through the water—it was blood.

I was abruptly released.

And Eve was pulling me up.

I sucked in air and coughed out the stale water that sat in the back of my throat. My sodden hair was plastered to my face, and it wasn't until I scraped it out of my eyes, that I saw Ben laying on the ground, his body jerking violently. His white t-shirt was now saturated in the blood that poured out his mouth and dribbled down from the corners of his eyes.

I gaped, unable to comprehend what'd happened.

Daniel glared at me. "What did you do?"

Claire stopped hyperventilating and let her hands slide slowly from her ears. "It wasn't her," she said sternly, staring Daniel down. "It was *them*."

****

Before…

The fear of ending up alone in this hell lingered constantly in the back of my mind. Every day, at some random moment, a vision of Rebecca lying dead in her bed would force its way into my consciousness, and nothing I did made it go away.

To add to my anxiety, being unwell had really taken it out of Rebecca. At least once a day, I'd find her dozing on the couch or slumped over the dining table asleep. She was more tired now than she was before she'd gotten sick. I thought maybe she'd become anemic or deficient in one vitamin or another, and so I badgered her into taking a supplement.

However, not before I'd found her sleeping in the garden against the chicken coup.

"Fine, I'll take the damn vitamins," she said, as I insisted on putting her to bed for the afternoon. "On the condition that you stop worrying about me catching the virus."

"Okay."

"I'm probably immune. Otherwise, I'd have gotten sick by now."

I shrugged and threw her duvet over her legs. "If that's true, you can't be the only one."

"Maybe."

"I remember watching the news and hearing about a few people in America who were immune," I said. "There might be people here in Britain that are immune too."

"I doubt it," Rebecca responded flatly.

Did I dare broach the subject of survivors again? Even though it was always met with the same categorical rebuff.

"We could look together. We don't have to stay here forever, Rebecca. We could move around."

"Halley—"

"Remember the car that I saw? What if they were immune, like you? Or, a survivor, like me?"

"I told you that I looked, Halley. There was no one," she growled, the veins in her neck throbbing with irritation.

"But we could go further North, or...wherever. Please say you'll think about it."

Rebecca stared at me, a fleeting expression of sympathy crossing her face. "Fine. I'll think about it," she sighed. "But, not now. We'll see how things are when the weather warms up."

For the next few months, I waited eagerly for the daffodils and bluebells to appear, wishing away Winter so that, maybe, we could finally leave this place.

Chapter Seventeen

After…

Still in a trauma-induced haze, I remembered nothing of how I ended up in a little office on the ground floor of the school. As my brain fog cleared, I found myself sat on a well-worn leather armchair, wrapped in a thick fleece blanket. Claire was in here too, behind a large oak desk, spinning idly on a swivel office chair, clockwise and then anticlockwise, muttering something indecipherable under her breath.

I'd never taken any hallucinogenic drugs of any sort in my life, but I imagined this was what a bad trip felt like. Reality had left the building, taking common sense and sanity with it. Now I knew how Alice felt when she fell down the rabbit hole into Wonderland.

Daniel and Eve were just outside the door, whispering to each other in a hushed, yet heated exchange. When they finally entered the room, Daniel went straight to Claire, without so much as a glance in my direction. He held her shoulders to stop her spinning and then clicked his fingers in front of her face to try and garner her attention. Claire merely stared at him, expressionless and vacant.

"I thought she was supposed to be better now," Daniel snapped at Eve.

"She *is* better. But her bond with *it*—*them*—is stronger than mine." She let out a long sigh and leaned back wearily against the faded paisley-papered wall. "I don't expect you to understand."

Daniel let go of Claire, who returned to her incessant swiveling. "Well, I'm tired of being kept in the dark! And I'm not the only one!" he snarled. "I'm going to check on Ben."

He stormed out, slamming the door shut as he left.

Claire immediately ceased her spinning. "He's so moody. I don't know how you put up with him, Eve."

I almost laughed. Clearly, she hadn't been catatonic at all.

Eve glared at her. "Claire, what's going on? What happened to Ben?"

Claire stretched and then leaned forward, sliding her elbows onto the desk, knitting her fingers together to rest her chin on them.

"I warned him to stop," she said. "He didn't listen. So *they* stopped him."

They was a term Claire seemed to use a lot. Who t*hey* were exactly was not clear, but Eve—and probably the others too—seemed to put a lot of stock in what Claire and the voices had to say. Any logical person would assume Claire was mad, but something told me that she wasn't mad at all.

No, I didn't hear voices in my head, but I did *feel* things that I couldn't explain—like the connection I had with Nate and how I'd found him in the cabin, on the edge of nowhere.

We were meant to find each other. Had we also been led here? Did it have something to do with the strange dreams I'd been having?

"Will he be okay?" Eve asked her.

I didn't care about Ben in the slightest, but I didn't

want him to die either. And I certainly didn't want the people here to think I was somehow responsible for it.

"Depends," Claire said, glancing over to me with a concerned frown. "We have to protect Halley. She can't go back in the water. *They* won't allow it!"

Eve slowly shook her head from side to side. "I don't understand. Why not her?"

Claire sighed. "That's what I've been trying to find out."

"And?" Eve said, a little curtly. It was easy to see she was becoming increasingly frustrated. Coaxing any sense out of Claire proved a slow process.

After a minute of staring into space, Claire finally responded. "It would be very bad."

"Bad for Halley?" Eve pressed.

"No," Claire replied. "It would be bad for the baby."

Eve gave an exasperated groan. "What baby? What are you talking about?"

"Halley and Nate's baby."

My mouth dropped open as a tingle of static prickled against my spine and lifted the hairs on the back of my neck. "What?"

Eve whirled to face me. Her forehead knitted in confusion. "You...you're pregnant?"

"No," I snapped. "Of course I'm not! It's not possible."

No way. It really *was* absolutely impossible.

Claire grinned. "Sometimes, I've believed as many as six impossible things before breakfast."

Another line from 'Alice's Adventures in Wonderland.'

Of course, another impossible thing was that Claire

was alive after I'd seen her drown. Nate too.

I shivered in my wet clothes and huddled further into the blanket. This was all too much.

"Claire, why don't you go to your room and get some rest?" Eve said. She'd flipped back to using her composed, pacifying voice. "I'm going to get Halley some dry clothes."

Claire pulled a face. "Fine."

She slid off her swivel chair and quickly threw her arms around me in a clumsy hug before she left.

The idea of being alone with Eve set me on edge, but it wasn't like I had any choice.

She led me down the corridor, which led to another corridor and then another, like a maze. The building was enormous, with a mixture of old and modern features. Most likely, it'd started off as a stately home and later been converted into a school by sectioning off the bigger rooms with stud walls.

Some of the doors to the classrooms downstairs were wide open; a few rooms were lined with dark wood paneling and ornate picture rails while others were plain and devoid of character. They were all being used for storage, stacked high with cardboard boxes or full of jumbled furniture, such as bed frames and desks.

Eve directed me into one of the larger classrooms. This one contained row after row of clothing racks and stacks of shoeboxes piled as high as they could go without toppling.

"Help yourself," she told me after taking a perch upon a pile of clear plastic storage boxes.

Shivering, I hesitantly drifted over to a rack of casual women's clothing and picked out a black, velour tracksuit. It looked warm. I also found a vest top and, thankfully, new underwear, although it was lacier and more delicate than I'd normally wear.

Each item still had the price tags attached—the underwear set cost more than three times my monthly wage waitressing. *Somebody* had obviously looted more of the upmarket, trendy London stores. And why not? It would only sit gathering dust otherwise.

Eve turned her back as I kicked off my water-logged trainers and dumped my wet clothes in a pile on the floor. Once dressed, I hunted down a pair of socks and pulled them on over my cold, puckered toes. Lastly, I found some trainers in my size.

"Where is Nate?" I asked Eve. "I want to see him."

"Do a test," she replied, turning back around to face me.

I gave her the most incensed glare I could muster. "There's no point!"

"Humor me," she said. "I'll take you straight to Nate as soon as we're done."

Was this a negotiation? "What if I say no?"

Her jaw clenched. "I really think we need to know, don't we?"

We? This was none of Eve's business. But she *had* offered me a deal, and if I agreed to her terms, she'd take me to Nate. Right now, he was all I cared about.

"Fine."

She nodded. "I think I saw some test kits in the school nurse's office when we were clearing it out. It's on the way."

We headed back in the direction we'd just come from and ended up in a small room across the hall from the office.

A few faded medical advice posters were still taped

247

to the walls, torn on the ends and rolled up slightly where they'd become unstuck. One displayed a detailed description of how to perform CPR, while the poster next to it had a dire warning about the dangers of drug use slapped across it. Various flyers filled the gaps between the posters, all featuring an image of a handsome teenage boy with the phrase *'Do I look like I have Chlamydia?'* on his t-shirt.

Screwing my nose up, I sat down on a leather examination table while Eve searched through an array of boxes all marked 'dump.' She ignored the 'keep' boxes. I guess they'd thrown out all the pregnancy tests, along with the contraceptives, being of no use to anyone anymore. Clearly, no one else in this community had ever gotten themselves pregnant.

This strange community where people came back from the dead.

"How is Claire alive?"

Eve paused momentarily to look at me then went back to rifling through the boxes. "I wondered when you were going to ask *that*."

"What *is* going on here, Eve?"

She groaned when another box didn't contain what she was looking for. Part of me hoped her search would come up empty.

"It's hard to explain. We help people…evolve."

"Evolve?"

"Yes."

"By drowning people?"

Eve sighed. "Until you experience it yourself, you won't understand."

"I might."

She gave another frustrated growl and started

emptying the contents of the boxes onto the floor. Before long, there were files and assorted bits of stationery everywhere, along with pamphlets on every topic a school nurse might dish out to her adolescent patients. And condoms. Hundreds of condoms.

She briefly paused her ransacking to blow a ringlet of red hair from her face. "After I recovered from the virus, I was taken to an army base in Scotland. What they did to us there was—" she stopped midsentence and gave me a glassy-eyed look. "It still keeps me awake at night, Halley. I used to think that most humans were good people, but it's not true. We'll do anything to survive. No matter how abhorrent or immoral. The army was supposed to protect us, but instead, they let I.D.R.I.S torture us."

She pulled another box toward her. "In doing so, they made a discovery. We aren't the people we used to be. We've changed, Halley. The virus has done something inexplicable to us.'

Eve's revelation should've come as a shock, but it didn't—I already had my suspicions.

"Like what? What has it done to us?"

She hunched her shoulders. "We don't know exactly. That's the problem. We don't even know what the virus really is," she answered. "We only know that the virus just sits dormant in us…until we die. Then, somehow, it comes *alive*. It makes us *better*."

"Better how?"

"We heal faster. We age slower. We don't get ill anymore. No colds. No diseases. It's very hard to kill us, although I.D.R.I.S found a few ways. Some of those ways were permanent. I've died more times than I can count, but I came back. Others weren't so lucky."

It sounded like a plot right out of a horror movie. "I thought they were supposed to be looking for a cure?"

"At first, yes. They told us we could help them develop a vaccine. We trusted them. But then it all changed. They brought in this man—Doctor Lawson. He saw us as nothing but lab rats."

Imagining all the awful things that might've happened to her turned my stomach. How many people in this community had been subjected to the experiments? I almost couldn't bear to think about it.

She stared at me, a look of anguish in her chartreuse eyes. "It's why we need Nate, Halley. We have questions that need answering."

Unexpectedly, I found myself warming to her a little. Or maybe Stockholm Syndrome had kicked in.

"And what about Claire? What's up with her?"

"Claire has been with us for a few weeks now. I don't know for sure what her mental health issues were before the virus, but she seems to be able to—" Eve considered her choice of words. "She's more receptive than the rest of us. Sometimes, I hear *them,* but not like she does. She can communicate with *them*—the virus, I mean—or whatever it really is."

"You're saying Claire's…a conduit?"

"Yes. A conduit."

"This is madness," I muttered, shaking my head.

Eve raised her hands, palms up, in a *who knows* gesture. "You don't know the half of it. Wait, what's this? A-ha!"

At the bottom of the very last box, she found what she was looking for. In her hand was a pretty purple packet with the image of a giggling baby on the front.

I felt nauseous just thinking about it. "You know

this is ridiculous, don't you?"

She shot me a knowing smile. "Is it?"

I couldn't respond.

****

Before…

I despaired when the snow fell.

It covered the spring flowers in such a thick blanket of white there was no trace of them left. Everything froze. The rainwater inside the butts became a solid cylinder of ice, and it was so cold that Rebecca brought the chickens into the house and let them wander around freely in the kitchen.

We weren't going anywhere anytime soon.

Most days, I stayed in bed, cocooned in a sleeping bag with a duvet wrapped around me. When I wasn't asleep, I read, my gloved hands struggling to turn the pages as my hot breath coalesced with the cold air and fogged my view.

Rebecca asked me, more than once, if I was depressed, but I denied it.

In truth, I was miserable. But, what right did I have to feel that way? I was alive when everybody else had died. I was lucky, wasn't I?

I found myself thinking about my mother a lot, wondering if this was how she'd felt on the bad days when she couldn't get out of bed or leave the house. As a child, I hadn't been able to understand her depression—I was resentful of it because I wanted my mother to be like the other mothers. I wanted her to bake cakes for the school fair and run in the parent races on sports day, but she didn't. Couldn't.

"Take some of these, you'll feel better soon," Rebecca said, handing me a packet of pills.

Diazepam.

"No, thanks." I tossed them back at her. "I'm fine."

But I wasn't fine. After a few weeks, I knew I had to do something to get me out of the black hole I'd fallen into.

I needed a friend.

In a chest, under my bed, I kept the letters that Lizzie had sent me after I'd moved in with Rebecca. She totally begrudged having to write to me by hand, but the cottage lacked two things; broadband and a reliable phone signal. Sometimes, her texts would reach me, but more often than not, they'd get lost in the ether. On average, she wrote twice a month. The last letter I'd received came a few days before the outbreak.

Slowly, I read through them all, laughing at all the shenanigans Lizzie got herself involved in and reminding myself of what life used to be like…and how it could be again if we ever managed to find other people. I began to remember what hope felt like.

Lizzie's final letter to me was my favorite, even though it was the last.

Halley,

I'm writing this letter from Terminal B of Gatwick airport! Can you believe that? We're finally here after a year of planning this trip! Wish you could've come with us, but if it makes you feel any better, it's been a disaster so far. Our plane was delayed for four hours, so we all went to the bar for a few drinks. Bad idea. My boyfriend got absolutely hammered. We had to pretend to be sober so they'd let us board the plane.

It was all good till he tripped and smashed his face going through the walkway thing. What an idiot! He had to go to the hospital to have stitches! Now we have to sleep at the airport and catch a different plane tomorrow.

With any luck, he'll manage to survive until then, and we'll be off on our adventures.

I know what you're thinking...that I'm going to hate slumming it in hostels and shared bathrooms...and you're completely right, but I'm hoping the scenery makes up for it.

Anyway, I miss you loads, and I really would rather be going with you than with my idiot boyfriend— I do love him really, but you know I love you more!! Ha-ha.

Love always and forever,

Lizzie.

I smiled. Lizzie had always been an optimist, even when faced with the direst of circumstances. She'd never let anything get her down. She'd never let anyone, or anything, stop her from doing what she wanted. If somehow Lizzie survived the apocalypse, she'd be kicking its ass right now.

She wouldn't have given up.

And neither would I.

I'd find a way to leave this place, and if there were survivors out there, I'd find them.

No matter how long it took or how far I had to go.

With or without Rebecca.

Chapter Eighteen

After…

I was getting closer to Nate. I could feel him nearby as we sat in the restroom down the hall from the cells.

I'd done as Eve asked, and now we had to wait the obligatory two minutes for the results.

Perched on the edge of the sink counter, Eve read over the instructions while I laid back on the pretty pink and gold chaise-lounge, taking deep, controlled breaths to stave off the panic attack building in my gut.

As I clutched the little plastic stick against my chest, I distracted myself with thoughts of Nate to stop me from peeking at the results too early. If Eve kept up her end of the bargain, I would see him soon.

"Ben said something to me when we were outside. He said that Nate *didn't need help after all*. What did he mean?" I asked, unsure if I wanted to know the answer.

Eve looked up. "Nate's already *evolved*. We didn't need to put him in the fountain after all."

"Not sure I understand."

Eve seemed hesitant to respond. She chewed at her lip a little before speaking again. "It normally takes hours, or sometimes days, to come back. But Nate returned almost immediately. That's because…he's already died and come back to life."

"No. That's crazy. Wouldn't a person know if

they'd died?"

She shrugged. "Possibly not."

No. It couldn't be true. Nate was alive when I found him at the cabin. It'd been a close call, but I'd brought him back. I'd saved him, hadn't I?

"When I first found Nate, he'd—" I stopped. This wasn't my secret to tell.

"He'd what?" Eve pressed.

Shaking my head, I looked away. "Never mind."

A few seconds later, I heard her sigh and slide down off the countertop. She repositioned herself on the end of the chaise-lounge and put a hand on my knee.

"He was alone before you found him?" she asked.

"Yes."

The entire scene played out again in my head—the moment I'd seen him, the faintest trace of a pulse under my fingertips, the crackle of static as our lips connected.

But it wasn't me that'd brought him back to life. The virus had.

"He'd taken some pills," I muttered.

When I finally looked up again at Eve, she gave me a weak smile. "Desperate times, Halley."

We fell into a depressive silence until the timer on her watch beeped, shaking me out of my contemplation.

Sitting up, I sucked in a deep breath and turned the test around in my fingers.

Not possible.

But there they were; two dark pink lines indicating a positive result.

Eve quickly plucked the stick out of my hand, her eyes darting from the instructions and back to the test several times.

"Congratulations."

"How is this possible? I don't understand."

She let out a gleeful laugh. "I don't know, Halley. But you are! Do you realize what this means? We have hope now!"

Her words barely registered with me. My brain burned with questions I didn't even know how to articulate.

"You're in shock," she said softly.

I blinked. "You think?"

She lowered her head, a contrite frown on her brow. "This has been a lot for you to deal with. We've handled things badly and—"

"I need to see Nate. Now," I demanded. Eve could apologize later if that's what she was trying to do. Right now, it was time for her to come good on her promise.

She nodded. "Of course."

She slipped the test back into the packet and pocketed it. I didn't ask what she planned to do with it, but instinct told me Daniel would be the next person to hear the good news. As we left the bathroom and walked toward Nate's cell, the need to be with him became all-encompassing, pushing all of my fear and worry to one side.

Feeling brave all of a sudden, I sought to use Eve's good mood in my favor.

"Eve? Can you do something for me? Can we keep the baby thing between us, for now? I need time to get my head around all of this."

She opened her mouth to reply, but I cut her off. "Please. You help me, and I'll help you."

Eve widened her eyes a little and cocked her head

to one side. "Okay."

Her quick response left me somewhat surprised, but I thanked her and managed to put a sincere smile on my face, despite feeling like I might've just made a deal with the devil.

When we reached Nate's cell, she released the bolt on the door and opened it, motioning for me to go in first.

This had better not be some kind of trick.

But there he was, sprawled out on the floor, unconscious.

I rushed to him, sliding to my knees so that I could hold him. "Nate?"

He was breathing, but he was out of it. His clothing was cold and soaking wet from being in the water.

"He's freezing!" There was no hiding the disdain in my voice.

Eve crouched down beside us. "I'm sorry. Laura must have doped him and then gone straight to deal with Ben." She unclipped the walkie talkie from her belt and turned the top dial round. "Tobias? You there?"

"Yep," came the reply.

"I need you to bring some blankets up to me. And some clothes."

"For the doc?"

"Yes," she answered.

"Okay. Give me five minutes."

She set the handset to one side and then motioned for me to help her roll Nate over onto his back. "Help me take his clothes off."

Not a situation I ever thought I'd find myself in, but here we were, undressing my undead boyfriend while he slept.

We managed to peel off Nate's jeans and t-shirt, but left his boxer shorts on, although for a second, I thought Eve was going to insist we take those off too. Nate would *not* appreciate waking up without his underwear, of that I was certain.

It didn't take long for Tobias to show up. He tossed the blankets onto the edge of the mattress and set the clothes down neatly on a plastic chair, which he pulled in from the corridor outside.

"Howdy," he said to me, with a wink. "How we doing?"

His accent was Irish, soft and distinctly southern. He wasn't overly tall but still fairly brawny. His hair was a hundred different shades of dark blond, tinged with red, which matched the five o'clock shadow under his nose and around his jaw.

He helped Eve lift Nate off the floor and get him into a more comfortable position on the mattress. Nate, still totally comatose, didn't stir once.

"Thanks," I muttered, grabbing the blankets and covering him over.

Eve handed me her walkie talkie. "If you need anything, just radio for Tobias."

I gave an incredulous scoff at her sudden hospitality.

"We aren't the monsters you think we are," she said.

Tobias sniggered. "Well, Eve is. But the rest of us aren't."

If looks could kill, she would've murdered Tobias with the frosty glare she sent his way.

"We'll talk tomorrow," she said to me. Then she

left.

Tobias waited till Eve's footsteps died away. "I'll be sleeping with one eye open tonight," he grinned.

I liked him already.

"Holler if you need anything," he told me as he left the room.

He pulled the door closed, but I didn't hear the bolt slide across. Either Tobias was forgetful, or we were no longer considered a threat. We weren't going to be making a daring escape either, considering Nate's condition.

Wearily, I crawled onto the mattress and got under the blankets with him, huddling as close to him as I possibly could. He was so cold. But he was alive. Slowly, the painful, wretched ache in my body began to fade, and a sense of relief washed over me. I leaned in and kissed him, feeling his breath on my lips. For several hours, I watched him until my over-adrenalized nerves began to settle, and exhaustion kicked in. Reluctantly, I closed my eyes.

****

Someone whispered my name.

I prized my eyelids open to see Nate staring down at me, his eyes tired and dull. He put a hand up to my face and stroked my cheek. "Halley."

My lips went to his. "I'm here."

He glanced around, confusedly, and then lifted the blanket to survey his mostly naked body.

"I took your clothes off," I said quickly. "They were wet."

He propped himself up on his elbows. "Yes, I remember being in the water." His face dropped, full of concern. "What did they do to you, Halley?"

"Nothing," I told him. "I'm fine." It wasn't a lie.

His darkened eyes narrowed beneath his taught forehead. It was clear he didn't believe me. And right now, I probably *did* look like I'd just returned from the dead.

"How do *you* feel? What do you remember?" I asked, running my fingers through his hair.

Nate shuddered in my arms. "I remember them holding me under the water until I…" As his voice trailed off, he swallowed a lump in his throat, his expression distraught.

He needed to know the truth, and it was better to hear it from me as opposed to Eve.

First, I told him about Claire and then attempted to explain the rest of it, recalling as much as I could about everything up until his resurrection. I omitted the part where they'd tried to drown me and why they hadn't. Telling him about the baby could wait—I'd dropped a big enough bombshell on him as it was. As a medical doctor, I wasn't sure what he'd make of the dead coming back to life, but he listened to everything without saying a word, although the expression on his face alarmed me. It wasn't disbelief. It was acceptance.

Nate sat up, bringing his knees to his chest and stared down at the floor. When I tried to put my arms around him, he tensed and shied away from me.

"What's wrong?" A stupid question, given the content of the conversation.

"I'm not *me* anymore."

I wasn't exactly myself either. The only thing that made us different was that I hadn't evolved. Yet. "You're the only version of *you* I've ever known."

Nate looked at me with sad eyes but didn't

respond.

Just then, fear washed over my body. "Do you feel differently about *me* now?"

He exhaled deeply. "I couldn't change the way I feel about you even if I wanted to."

I wasn't sure how to take that. "*Would* you want to?"

"What do *you* think?" he replied, a smirk forming on his lips.

"Shut up, then." Snaking an arm around his waist, I leaned my face close to his, planting a light kiss on his temple. He turned slightly, his lips catching mine in an intense, hungry moment of desire. The *pull* suddenly hit me like a bolt of lightning, and I couldn't stop or disengage from him. He didn't seem to be able to stop either because I was undressed to my underwear in a matter of seconds. This was completely the wrong place and the wrong time, but it was happening anyway.

The light above us flickered as a static hum suffused the air, tickling my skin and lifting my hair. His name tore from my throat as he brought me to a rapid, yet powerful climax. A second later, the light bulb hissed and then shattered, plunging the room into complete darkness.

"Well," Nate said, breathlessly. "That's new."

A piece of the hot filament dropped down onto my head. Yelping, I quickly flicked it away.

"I'm sure it was purely coincidental."

He carefully brushed a few shards of glass from the mattress and collapsed down beside me, panting.

"Fine," he said. "We'll go with that."

****

Leaving Nate to dress in the clothes Tobias had

brought, I crept down the corridor to the bathroom. The lights were off, but the sun had begun to come up, casting enough light into the hall for me to see where I was going. Aside from a few distant voices drifting in through an open window, there wasn't anyone else around.

No guards. Not a single soul.

It wasn't until I caught sight of the little, blinking, red light in the shadows that I realized we were being watched. A camera. All the exits were probably still secured by guards, ready to dart us again if we tried to escape. There was one thing that was of *some* comfort, though—they didn't want us dead. Not permanently, at least.

In the restroom, I used the toilet, then filled the sink with hot water and freshened up as best I could. I felt nauseous but not enough to make me throw up.

How long had I felt sick for? With no menstruation dates to help me figure out how far along I was, I had to look at the other possible symptoms. The first time I'd felt a little off was about three weeks after I'd arrived at the cabin. Headaches too, but I assumed it was all down to other causes, like the heat or stress or…too much sex, maybe. So, exactly *how* pregnant was I? Ten weeks, at most? Still pretty early. What if I told Nate about the baby and then something awful happened? He'd be devastated. I couldn't put him through that because he'd already lost too much. Perhaps it was better not to tell Nate. For now.

My hand fell to my lower stomach.

How? How had this even happened when we were all infertile? And what about the virus? What would happen to the baby?

Shit. There were so many unanswered questions circling in my mind. I was scared. Not because I didn't want it, but because I did. Despite the negative scenarios running through my head citing a list of reasons to not go through with this, I was actually *happy* about it. Really happy. As shocked as I was, I knew immediately that I wanted it.

Nate's baby. Our baby.

I just prayed, to whoever or whatever was running the show now, that *it* would somehow be okay. That *all* of this would somehow be okay.

When I left the bathroom, a figure stood in the corridor waiting for me. I balked out of surprise and drew in a sharp gasp.

"Didn't mean to startle you."

Hand on heart, I frowned at the middle-aged man before me. "Well, you did."

He gave a low, raspy chuckle. "Apologies."

Giving his appearance a fleeting once-over, his attire seemed overly formal. He was dressed in smart black trousers paired with a silky, crimson shirt worn underneath a black, tailored coat.

He held his hand out to me. "I noticed you were up already and came to introduce myself," he said. "I'm Gabriel."

Ignoring his gesture, I motioned to the cameras. "Yes. I did have a distinct feeling I was being watched."

Gabriel laughed. "For security purposes, you understand. Not much of a voyeur myself. That's Max's job. I've been away. I only arrived back a few hours ago."

"Right."

He smiled. "Congratulations by the way."

Had Eve already gone back on our deal? "Eve said she wouldn't say anything."

"She didn't. I've got my own sources."

I tilted my head to one side. "Is it in the newspapers already, or do you hear the voices too?"

He smirked. "Actually, I ran into Claire. Don't worry, I asked her not to speak of it to anyone else. Your secret is safe."

With one hand placed on my spine, he shepherded me back down the corridor, the tiniest, almost imperceptible fizzle of electric fluttered under his fingertips.

"Let's walk." His voice was gravelly but gentle, with a slight cockney lilt. Gabriel was a Londoner to be sure. He ran a hand over his head and scratched wearily at the receding hairline of his fringe.

"Sounds like I missed all the fun while I was gone. That'll teach me to leave Eve and Daniel to their own devices. I should've known that chaos would ensue."

"I thought Eve was in charge around here?"

He smirked again. "Depends who you ask, I suppose."

"I see."

"Eve thinks her magic powers make her a more suitable leader. She has a sixth sense when it comes to finding people. Her range is limited, though. Don't tell her I said that."

"My lips are sealed," I muttered, hiding a smile.

He continued. "I've just returned from Scotland, transporting down the last generator from the bunker. The well-being of this community is our priority right now. *That* and finding other survivors."

I snorted. "And when you find them, do you mention that they'll be imprisoned and drowned as soon as they arrive?"

He turned to me with a grin. "Obviously not."

He seemed unaffected by my indignation. If anything, it appeared to amuse him.

"Besides, that's not generally how we do things. And just so you know, the fountain was never my idea. I'm not one for ceremony. I'd much rather give people the choice of whether to evolve or not," he added, a hint of irritation in his tone. "Or shoot them. It's quicker."

I didn't know what to make of Gabriel or what the point of this conversation was. Why was he telling me all of this? As a newcomer and *not* part of this community, why on earth would he be sharing his misgivings with me?

"I thought the voices *wanted* you to *evolve* people?"

He sighed. "So Eve says. But there was no specific memo about how to do that," he replied. "I know there's a better way than drowning people. Until Claire came along, none of our conduits were *in tune* enough to start asking questions. Not even Eve has a strong enough connection to *them*."

There was that word again. *Conduit*.

"I think Claire might be able to give us the answer. I just need time to talk with her."

My pace slowed to a complete halt. "What has this got to do with me?"

He massaged his stubbly chin with his fingertips. "Eve and Daniel want something from you and Nate. I want you to ask for something in return."

"Like?"

"A room with a view of the Thames. More chocolate chips in the canteen cookies. A boycott of the fountain."

Right. He wanted me to ask Eve and Daniel to stop drowning people in return for our help—or rather, Nate's help. I couldn't see how I'd personally be of any use to them.

"Why do you need me to stop them? Why can't you do it?"

He gave a defeated shrug. "Majority rules, I'm afraid."

Although I doubted Eve and Daniel would agree to my—our—terms, I nodded. "I'll try."

His mouth stretched into a broad, toothy smile. "Good. Let me know if there's anything I can do for you."

I'd only been here for a few days, and somehow, I'd unwittingly entered into a mutually beneficial, back-scratching pact with two of the community's supremos. Cloak and dagger wasn't something I was good at or comfortable with, and I disliked having to do it. But perhaps it was time I learned.

"Oh, and this conversation never happened," he added. "We've not met, got it?"

My index finger pointed toward the ceiling. "What about the cameras? Isn't someone watching?"

"Yes, but nobody who doesn't owe me a favor."

Interesting. "Fine."

He winked as he turned around and strolled off back down the corridor, his shiny leather brogues tapping on the floor as he went.

Nate was agitated when I returned to the room.

"I was just coming to look for you," he said,

slipping his arms tightly around my waist.

"Got held up."

As I told him about my encounter with Gabriel, Nate listened intently, a troubled shadow in his eyes.

"So, what do we do?" he asked me.

"Find the canteen. There are cookies."

He glowered, despite the slight smile that briefly crossed his lips. "This is serious."

I shrugged. "We listen to what they have to say."

Nate nodded and then rested his chin on the top of my head. "Anything that keeps you safe."

"Keeps *us* safe," I corrected.

He didn't know I meant the *three* of us.

****

Before...

The weather warmed.

I asked Rebecca again about going to look for survivors. Sometimes she was willing to discuss it, and sometimes she wasn't. She was purposefully stalling me.

Knowing there was a good chance I'd be leaving without her, I quietly made plans and drew up a list of supplies I'd need to take. I already had a decent sized backpack, which I kept hidden under my bed. Every time I found something useful, I'd pack it and hope she wouldn't notice it'd gone missing.

Early one morning, while Rebecca was still in bed sound asleep, I went into the garage to look for more supplies. We kept our tinned and packet foods in here, along with anything we didn't need close to hand. I shoved a few packets of dried, flavored pasta and noodles into a carrier bag and anything edible light enough to carry.

Under a tarpaulin, tucked away in the back behind a stack of boxes, I discovered an old bicycle Rebecca no longer used. She'd acquired a brand new, sturdy mountain bike for her looting trips, which she kept in the shed out the back.

This bicycle was vintage, though, with a shiny red frame and little white flowers painted on the stem. After plucking dead spiders out of the spokes and dusting the cobwebs from the handlebars, some soapy water and a light scrub made it sparkle. The rear tire had deflated to a pancake, but there was a puncture repair kit and a pump in the shed. An easy fix.

I continued searching the garage, finding a rusty crowbar and a small, wind-up pocket torch. The crowbar would be a tight fit but essential for looting purposes as I'd have to find the majority of my food from stores along the way.

Just as I was about to call it a day on the foraging, I spied something colorful tucked beneath a dust sheet in the corner of the garage. Curiously, I lifted the sheet away and pulled out the little floral box that'd captured my attention. Immediately, I recognized it as my mother's. I flipped it open and examined the contents gingerly, lifting out an old photograph of my mother as a small child, pigtailed with a face full of ice cream. There were also a few items of inexpensive costume jewelry, including a watch and a string of plastic pearls. At the bottom of the box was a book—a well-worn copy of 'Wuthering Heights,' my mother's second favorite book.

I'd never had the opportunity to read it as she always carried it with her, stowed away in the bottom of her handbag, or secreted within the deep pocket of her favorite raincoat. When I'd searched for it after the funeral, it'd disappeared. Assuming it was one of the many things Andrew had purged from the flat, I gave up hope of ever seeing it again.

But here it was. Rebecca had it all along. She must've rescued a few of my mother's personal items and brought them back home with her.

Why leave them out here in the cold to gather dust?

Pressing the book to my septum, my nostrils took in the familiar scent of old print and binding glue. To me, it was the best smell in all the world.

I opened the book up and leafed through the first few pages, which contained a short biography on Emily Bronte. Before the main story began, there was a blank page that someone had written on.

Natalie,
Saw this book and thought of you.
Stay wild!
Love, Sam.

The words on the page left me dumbstruck.

Sam was my father's name. This book had been a gift from him.

Why would my mother keep hold of the book when she rarely spoke of him and cringed at the mere mention of his name?

Yet here was her treasured copy of 'Wuthering Heights,' a book that she'd read many times over, with a big painful reminder of my father scrawled in it.

I closed the lid down on the box but dropped the book into the carrier bag. When I got back to my room, I slipped it into the top shelf of my bookcase between two other classics.

One day, I'd read it, but not now. There was no

room in my backpack for anything else, especially after stuffing the crowbar and the torch inside. Thankfully, although the bag was heavier than I anticipated, I could still carry it comfortably.

It was almost time for me to venture out into the new world.

To be wild.

Chapter Nineteen

After...

An uncomfortable silence lingered in the air after all the introductions were made. We'd been taken downstairs to the office where Nate and I now sat, in front of the big oak desk, while Eve, Daniel and Gabriel sat behind it.

Eve was the first to break the silence, which didn't surprise me. "Nate, I will never forget what you did for me in the hospital. I want you to know that."

He responded with a nod and a brief, labored smile. Perceptibly tense, he gripped my hand tightly and squeezed it in a token of reassurance.

"What did Halley tell you about us?" Daniel asked, leaning forward.

Nate's answer was brusque. "Everything."

Eve's eyes flickered to me, and I gave her the faintest of head shakes—she wanted to know if I'd told him about the baby yet.

"Then you know what we want from you?"

"You want me to help you understand the virus," Nate replied.

Daniel pushed back on his chair and casually swung his feet up on the desk. He let a few long seconds of silence tick by before he sucked in a sigh and spoke again.

"After surviving the virus, we were all taken to an

army facility in Scotland," he began. "It was a bunker of sorts, set up for disaster scenarios. We were kept in a section of it that functioned as a hospital—or so we thought. It wasn't long before we realized it was more of a research laboratory and that we were nothing but test subjects to them."

Daniel touched his palms together, making a steeple with his fingers. "We were wholly expendable in the search for a cure. They believed survivors carried a different strain of the virus. One that was survivable. We think they planned to infect the rest of the population with it, but when they discovered the infertility issue, they brought in a doctor by the name of Lawson. He—"

"Thomas Lawson?" Nate cut in.

"Yes? You've heard of him?"

"I've read some of his published papers. He's a geneticist—*was* a geneticist," Nate said, "And his wife—Kara Strahovski—was a pioneer in reproductive endocrinology. They wrote some pretty controversial articles on eugenics together."

Eve sat up. "Strahovski was there too, for a while. But Lawson sent her away when the virus got into the bunker. After that, they began dropping like flies." The vehemence in her voice was palpable. "Lawson was a monster. He was the one who figured out the virus had changed us. From that point on…well, there were eight survivors to begin with, and only five of us got out of there alive. Lucky, that bastard Lawson and his minions all died off, or we wouldn't have made it either."

"Who was in the bunker with you?" I asked.

"Daniel, Tobias, Laura, and Ben," Eve answered.

I glanced at Gabriel. "What about you?"

"I was working in Aberdeen when the virus hit. I ran into this lot about six months later."

"And how did *you* evolve?"

Gabriel sneered. "I had a running car. Someone else wanted it. I got my throat slit for it. Aren't humans wonderful?"

If he was traumatized by it, he certainly didn't show it. In fact, he seemed to have a permanent smirk painted to his face as if he found it all a little bit amusing.

Daniel continued. "We stayed in the bunker for the next four years, searching for survivors and trying to build a community. A year ago, we decided to relocate to London and focus our search on the south of the country, as well as the possibility of venturing into Europe through the tunnel. We brought the research with us—laptops, files, reports. It's all here. Some of it we've been able to make sense of, but the only person here with a medical background is Laura. And she's a vet."

Nate ran his tongue across his bottom lip, shaking his head. "Be that as it may, I think you might be overestimating my abilities."

Eve smiled. "Not at all. Something tells me that you're the one we've been looking for."

It was an ominous statement. Christ only knew what she was implying.

Nate raised an eyebrow. "What's *that* supposed to mean?"

Gabriel waved a hand at Eve before she could share her insight. "Look, Nate. I'll be honest with you. Despite our new state of being, the human race is still doomed unless we fix the big issue. If we don't start reproducing soon, our species is done for."

Nate let out a disbelieving laugh. "You think I can find a way to cure the infertility when the experts couldn't?"

Eve gave me a knowing glance and then smiled at Nate. "I have complete faith in you. Besides, I believe Strahovski was close to figuring it out. Her notes on it were comprehensive, but only partially written in English. Don't suppose you speak Polish?"

Nate sighed. "Fluently. My mother was Polish."

He'd never mentioned that before.

"Well then," Eve said, "More proof that you're meant to be here. Both of you."

Nate shifted uncomfortably and squeezed my hand again.

Eve was clearly convinced we were here by divine influence—if *divine* was even the right word. Epidemiologic intervention?

I saw my opportunity. "If we agree to stay, you have to stop drowning people."

Daniel crossed his arms in a gesture of defiance. "There are worse ways to die, believe me."

"I don't care. It stops."

"Done," Eve replied. Daniel shot her a disapproving frown.

"And we can leave anytime we want," I added.

"Give us six months," Gabriel responded. "After that, if you choose to leave, we won't stop you."

"Three months. That's all you get," I countered. On the outside, I feigned a stern resolve, but on the inside, my chest tightened painfully with anxiety.

"Done," Gabriel agreed.

Both Eve and Daniel glared at him then, but he just

snickered, pleased with the terms of our arrangement. He evidently enjoyed dissenting against them.

Eve stood. "We have already set up a room for you."

Presumptuous much? Not that it was any great surprise. I'd known before coming in here that we weren't going to be allowed to leave without a fight, and it wasn't a fight we were in any position to win. Staying, for now, was the only option.

****

The old school dormitories were in the west wing of the building, set out over two floors. The corridors were dark with small arch windows, framed by heavy velvet curtains. Mahogany paneling stretched from floor to ceiling, apart from a few sections of wall, papered with lines of jacquard fleur-de-lis and Tudor roses. The floorboards groaned and cracked as we walked on them, and I imagined the former students trying to creep into each other's rooms in the dead of night, caught out by the noise their footsteps made.

It was eerily quiet too when it should have been filled with the sounds of school children, going from class to class, chatting and laughing. Now, there was nothing but the creak of wood and the sporadic whoosh of the wind as it blew through the windows and struck the curtains.

A dark, sobering thought crossed my mind then.

Assuming an infant managed to survive the virus somewhere, the youngest person on the planet would now be almost five years old. In no time at all, the last child on earth would grow up, and that would be it. *Unless* the little life growing inside me survived, and then the very last child on earth would be *my* child.

What would it be like to be the only one? Would she be lonely without other children to play with? Not that she would know any different.

She? Why did I think it was a girl?

"This is it," Eve said, stopping outside of the only room with an open door. "Get yourselves settled and then come and see me—I'm three doors down. I'll show you where the canteen is. There's a small, en-suite bathroom in your room, but the water pressure up here isn't great. There are more showers downstairs."

Nate mumbled a thank you, and then we shut the door on her.

I was surprised to see a little key in the lock, which I turned until it clicked, and then twisted the knob to check it *was* actually locked. It appeared we'd been afforded some privacy, presuming there were no hidden cameras anywhere.

The room was big and much brighter than the oppressive corridor outside. The walls were a soft, powder blue—I could still smell the odor of fresh paint—and the scuffed floorboards had been covered with a large, plush, silvery-gray rug. An ornate, wrought metal, double bed sat in the corner next to an empty, oak-veneer bookcase and a glass-topped writing desk. The window in here was huge, with blinds instead of curtains, and overlooked a playground. I peered out, pressing my forehead to the glazing, my breath fogging up the glass.

Directly beneath us was a net-less, rusted basketball hoop, and I could still just about make out the faded blue lines that marked out the sections of the court. Much further off to the right, was a sparse, grassy area with dozens of sapling trees, and one massive, gnarled and ancient sycamore beside them.

Nate came up behind me and locked his arms around my waist. "Do you really think they'll let us go after three months?"

Sighing, I leaned my head back on his chest. "I don't know."

"What do we do about Rebecca?" he asked.

My stomach lurched as the guilt immediately came flooding back. What *could* we do?

"She'll have to wait," I said.

At this rate, by the time we finally got to the cottage, I'd be showing, presuming nothing bad happened before then. There'd be questions from Rebecca. Lots and lots of questions.

But maybe we wouldn't have to walk there.

"They *do* have working cars here. I wonder if we could borrow one?"

He lifted an eyebrow. "Borrow?"

Borrow. Or steal, if need be.

Moving away from the window and pulling him with me, I slumped down on the bed. Weary and tired, it would've been easy to sleep right now. Possibly for several days straight, given the chance.

"Are you okay?" he asked. He put his arm around me and kissed my temple. "I know that's probably a stupid question."

"I'm just tired," I responded. "And stressed. I never *ever* want to go through anything like this again. I can't. It hurt. I watched you die, Nate."

He hugged me closer to him. "I don't remember much. The sedative they gave me knocked me out but, whenever I did wake up, there was only pain. Deep in my bones, like being infected with the virus all over again."

I tilted my head up to look at him as he spoke.

"It was excruciating. I knew the only way to stop it was to find you and get you away from here. I thought something terrible was going to happen to you."

Did he hear the voices too? Were they trying to tell him I was in danger?

My eyes moved from his and down to the floor. "I think they planned on drowning me too, but when you came back to life, they changed their minds. I don't know why. I didn't ask too many questions."

The lie fell proficiently from my tongue.

He kissed my temple again. "This thing with us…it just seems to get more mysterious, doesn't it?"

"Does it worry you? That something else might be controlling us?" I asked him. It was unsettling to think some unknown entity was acting as puppeteer. "What if what we feel for each other isn't real?"

He looked wounded. "How can you think that?"

"I just think if it weren't for the apocalypse, someone like *you* would never have been attracted to someone like *me*."

He leaned away from me. "What?"

Twisting to lean back against the bedhead, I crossed my arms. "C'mon Nate. Would you—a thirty-five-year-old, intelligent, handsome doctor—have ever looked twice at an inexperienced waitress in her mid-twenties with emotional issues?"

He laughed. "Yes."

"Liar!"

He huffed, cocking his head to the side. He crawled up the bed and then hooked his arm around my waist, sliding me down so that I lay flat.

"I'd have come into where you worked and ordered breakfast." He swung his leg over me and straddled my knees.

"Bit of a long way to come for breakfast," I pointed out.

"I might've been on holiday." He leaned down and kissed me quickly. "Anyway, I'd have seen you and thought 'wow, she's beautiful' and then I would've said something witty to make you laugh. I'd have come in every day and talked to you."

After a few more fleeting kisses, he continued. "Eventually, I would've asked you to come for a drink with me."

"I would've said *no*."

"I'd have charmed you into saying *yes*."

I rolled my eyes. He really could be very smooth-talking when he wanted to be. It was almost believable.

"We'd have gone out and talked more. I would've found out how funny, and clever, and compassionate you are."

"Would we have kissed on our first date?"

He winked at me. "Yes."

"Is that all?" I asked. "Or would you have expected more?"

His body tensed as he replied, his words coming out snappy. "Despite what you might think, I do have *some* self-control! I would never have pushed you, Halley! Christ, do you know me at all?"

I growled. "Of course, I do! I'm sorry. I know you wouldn't have pushed me. This is a stupid conversation!"

He relaxed a little and sighed, shaking his head. "I'm not Andrew, Halley. Not *now* and not *before*."

The mere mention of his name made me feel sick. "I know."

Nate climbed off me and rolled onto his back. "What is *really* bothering you? I feel like there's something you aren't telling me."

"Nate, I—" Now was *not* the time to announce our impending parenthood. He needed time to digest everything he'd heard today. As did I. "I need to know what you feel for me is real and of your own free will."

A canny misdirection, but still a question I wanted answering.

He shifted onto his side. "If we have been thrust together—poor choice of words—*brought together* by some mysterious force, it's *only* a physical thing. It doesn't have any control over my heart."

I tutted in mock annoyance. "Good answer."

He smirked. "Anyway, I could ask you the same thing. How do I know whether *you* truly love *me*?"

Rolling toward him, I pressed my body against his and smiled. "Because there's no way in hell I'd let you touch me if I didn't feel something real for you."

"Good answer."

As he planted a soft kiss on my bottom lip, my hands snaked up the front of his t-shirt and lightly brushed over the contours of his skin. In response, he began undoing the drawstring of my trousers.

"Hey,' I whispered, batting his hand away. "No time for that."

"Fine," he grinned, but then stared at me for a few moments, seemingly deep in thought. "I suppose we've got all the time in the world now, considering not even death can tear us apart."

As mad—and romantic—as that sounded, it was

true.

"We could be stuck with each other for a really long time," he added, with a smirk.

It sounded like a pretty good outcome to me. "Yes, but unless I let Eve drown me, I'll carry on aging while you'll still be in your prime."

He chuckled, but then gave me a more serious look. "I agree with Gabriel. If we *are* meant to die to evolve, there has to be a better way. If there isn't…well, maybe I could find some more humane way to kill you."

I laughed. "Oh, be still my beating heart."

"Exactly."

****

Eve didn't give us much time to 'settle in' before knocking on our door to tell us that lunch had been served in the canteen. The hunger pangs churning in my stomach had begun to make me lightheaded, and I couldn't get to the food quick enough.

The canteen was on the ground floor of the east wing, but the smell of food was detectable the moment we entered the stairwell and headed down. Eve led the way, introducing us to any people we passed. I tried to remember their names, but my brain seemed to have reached the point where any new information refused to be absorbed.

The canteen was huge, divided into two halves. One side had tables and chairs with an open kitchen running alongside, while the other half was being used for food storage with rack upon rack of tinned and dried foods. There appeared to be some organization to it— the racks were color-coded with red, blue, and green tape. The goods on the red taped racks had 'off-limits' signs stuck to them, whereas the blue and green racks had 'help yourself' signs.

"So many people," Nate muttered under his breath.

Perhaps it was the gnawing pain of an empty gut that distracted me, but it took me a while to notice the crowd. In stunned silence, I mentally performed a quick headcount.

Claire had told me that there were twenty or so other survivors here, but it hadn't sunk in until now as I watched them interact with one another, laughing and talking.

Eve replied to Nate. "Yeh, it's a full house today. A couple of looting parties returned last night," she said, and then pointed to a table of five people. "That's Erik—he's a tech genius. He keeps the water pumps and the hydrogen generators running. We brought one down with us from the bunker in Scotland, but we've just retrieved another two. More people mean we need more power."

Her finger moved from the tall blonde man she'd identified as Erik and went to others that I recognized. "That's Tobias, Max..." she stopped. "Sorry, you must be starving. We'll get you some food before any more introductions."

She ushered us toward the kitchen where the food was all laid out on a long silver counter, along with tubs of cutlery and stacks of multicolored plastic trays—probably what the school would've used. As I perused the food, somewhat bedazzled, my nose detected the heavenly scent of curry.

I was immediately drawn to the four large slow cookers at the end of the counter, all bubbling away in a cloud of steam, flanked by dishes of baked potatoes, chips, and rice. My mouth practically filled with drool just thinking about it.

"Help yourself," Eve said. "Most days, they serve the same stuff—vegetable chili, rabbit curry, rabbit stew, rabbit pie. Luckily, the rabbits are still at it like…well, rabbits. On Fridays, they cook battered fish. Carlos makes his own flour from the wheat we grow here."

I ladled some curry onto a baked potato and then piled on some chips and a generous dollop of rice. Nate wasn't quite so indulgent but still heaped a good amount of food onto his tray.

"Are all of the people here survivors from Britain?" he asked Eve.

"No. Erik and five others came over from Iceland by boat about four months after the outbreak—they'd heard there was a safe zone in Scotland. Of course, there wasn't. We think I.D.R.I.S put out a call on the radio to lure more survivors to the bunker. Erik and his group just happened to pick up the broadcast.

"We also have a survivor from the Faroe Islands— by luck, he was picked up by Erik's group en-route. Tobias and Ben were both living in Ireland at the time of the outbreak but were flown to Scotland like Daniel and I were. Laura was flown over from Italy—she was born here in London, her family moved to Venice when she was a kid.

"Based on those numbers, we think there could be a few hundred survivors worldwide. Whether those people are still alive or not, we don't know. We suspect Scotland wasn't the only facility testing on survivors."

It was a lot of information to absorb. "What about people who were immune to the virus?"

Eve shrugged. "We've never come across any. I wouldn't put it past the government to invent such a notion."

Nate and I exchanged furtive glances, both thinking of Rebecca.

We followed Eve to a table and sat down. A few people began to notice our presence, throwing curious glances in our direction, along with some hushed murmuring behind their hands. It made me feel a little uncomfortable. Not to mention, it'd been such a long time since so many new faces surrounded me.

From the corner of my eye, I saw Ben enter the canteen with Laura. He appeared to have recovered well from our last encounter, although he scowled at me when our eyes met. To my surprise, he purposefully passed by our table on his way to get food.

"What do you want, Ben?" Eve said as he stopped beside my chair.

"Just to welcome our new friends." He glanced down at me with a snicker. "Oh and, in case you were worried, I've stopped bleeding out of my eyes now!"

Eve groaned as her eyes rolled. "We weren't worried. Move along now, Benjamin. The adults are talking."

Ben huffed and raised his middle finger. Still, he did as instructed.

"What happened to him?" Nate asked me.

This was the part of the story I'd omitted. It invited questions I didn't have the answers to and a secret I wasn't ready to divulge.

I took a bite of a chip and focused my attention on the food in front of me. "You punched him. Don't you remember?"

Not a lie, technically.

Nate widened his eyes. "Vaguely," he said. "How *hard* did I hit him?"

Eve cleared her throat, and when I looked up at her, she had a hand over her mouth, hiding a smile.

"Really, really hard," I replied.

I decided, there and then, this would be the last time I ever lied to Nate.

****

Before...

Packed and ready to go, the only thing stopping me now was the rain. For three days, it fell torrentially and unrelenting. So, I waited.

What would a few more days matter after years of waiting?

"I supposed it's good for the grass," Rebecca muttered, staring out of the kitchen window.

Her mood had been low the last few days, and I noticed several bottles of whiskey had disappeared from the drink cabinet. These days, Rebecca seemed more inclined toward spirits and other liquors, rather her usual bottle of red. Apparently, the vino wasn't taking the edge off anymore.

Who could blame her? Under normal circumstances, everyone was prone to spells of depression, but these weren't normal times. They were often lonely and difficult and gloomy.

This in mind, I found it even harder to understand why she wouldn't leave this place. Why not go out and look for other survivors? There was nothing left to lose anymore. Literally nothing.

"I noticed you repaired the tire on the bike in the garage."

I froze. "Yes. I thought I'd go for a ride when the weather was better."

"Ride where?" Rebecca asked.

Retrieving a sharp knife from the block on the counter, I sat down at the kitchen table. It was one of my daily chores to prepare dinner, so I began by peeling some baby turnips for tonight's stew.

"Anywhere," I shrugged, avoiding her gaze.

Rebecca began to pat dry some asparagus she'd just washed. "Just around the village?"

"I don't know yet."

She dropped the long green shoots onto the table next to the turnips and poured herself a tumbler of whiskey. "You won't go far though, will you?"

The knife caught the flesh on the side of my thumb, and I hissed, sticking the bloody digit in my mouth to stop it from dripping on the vegetables. "I won't go far."

The tumbler in Rebecca's hand was soon empty and refilled again. "You won't like what you find out there."

Ignoring her, I began chopping the turnips again.

"I don't think I could stand being here alone," she said.

The irony of her comment made me laugh. "But you leave me here by myself all the time."

"Because I know you're safe here. I know where you are."

I pursed my lips together angrily. Funny how my safety hadn't been more of a concern to her after my mother had died. As it turned out, living with Andrew had been far more dangerous for me than the apocalypse, so far. But I couldn't tell her about that.

Instead, I lied. "I won't go far, Rebecca."

She smiled and gulped down another drink. "You'll think me awful for saying this, but sometimes I think they were the lucky ones."

"What?"

She looked at me, her eyelids drooping from the inebriation. "It's always worse for the ones left behind."

"Are you saying we'd be better off dead?"

Rebecca shrugged and stared at me. "No," she muttered after a long pause. "But, sometimes, I wonder—" Then she laughed. "What do I wonder? I don't know."

She was quite clearly drunk now, and it irritated me. "Why don't you go and lay down? I'll cook dinner."

She nodded and swiped the whiskey bottle off the table, putting it under her arm. She kissed the top of my forehead and then shuffled off to her room.

When she was gone, I turned back to the turnip in front of me and stabbed it repeatedly with the knife, my knuckles white from gripping the handle so hard.

After the tenth or so lunge, I felt a little less angry.

Chapter Twenty

After…

Every file, folder, and laptop from the bunker got taken to one of the old science classrooms. Nate spent over a week reading through report after report and making lists of equipment he needed, including medical books and journals. Daniel said he would get a looting party together so they could scour the local hospitals, but Nate insisted we go with them. Daniel was reluctant, but Gabriel won him over by pointing out to him that we weren't prisoners here, and he trusted us not to go back on our agreement.

Frankly, I wasn't sure we wouldn't just run off at some point, but for now, we intended to keep up our end of the bargain. Plus, I couldn't deny that fish and chips Friday was one of the best things to happen since the apocalypse.

Continuously hungry, and slightly less nauseous, I visited the canteen several times a day in between the main mealtimes. Someone I'd not met yet would usually stop me to introduce themselves and invite me to sit with them. Then we'd spend an hour or so talking and eating. Living among so many different humans felt like a novelty, and I never grew tired of hearing them speak about their lives.

A slight swelling in my lower stomach meant that my size ten trousers were starting to feel uncomfortably tight. Eve insisted I must be nearing the twelve-week mark after finding me some more drawstring trousers in the next size up. I couldn't be sure how far along I was or that my slight weight gain wasn't down to anything other than all the chips I'd been scoffing over the last two weeks.

She and I had developed a routine of going down to the canteen together at lunch, to eat and meet with others in the community. Nate would stay in the classroom reading, and I'd bring him up a plate of something later after we'd finished.

I learned quickly that when he focused on something, it was best to leave him to get on with it as he was too distracted to hold even the shortest of conversations. Still, most of the time, I stayed in the science room with him, reading books I'd picked up from the school library and fetching him coffee every now and then.

At dinner, I dragged him down to the canteen to coax him out of his academical trance for the night. He needed the break, even though he was reluctant to take it. If he resisted, I resorted to other, more physical measures to bring him back to reality. Our need for each other hadn't waned despite his new distraction, though I'd worried it would, given his previous admission of being a workaholic.

"Halley, this is Priya," Eve said as a coffee-colored goddess plonked herself down on a chair at our table.

She was stunning. Tall, yet curvy, with long, wavy black hair and deep brown eyes. She wore a sleeveless black churidar suit with gold and pink embroidered flowers running asymmetrically down the length of the dress, combined with bright pink leggings and matching heels.

"So good to finally meet you," she said, smiling a dazzling smile with her glossy fuchsia lips. Too absorbed in her visage, it took me a few seconds to realize she was speaking to me.

"You too," I mumbled, still somewhat mesmerized.

Eve chuckled and leaned in close to my ear. "It's all right. Priya has that effect on everyone. Even when we see her in jeans and a t-shirt, she has us all weak at the knees."

I frowned. "That's kind of weird."

Priya scoffed. "Tell me about it. I was never this admired *before* I died."

"So, it's your superpower then?"

"Being adored? I sincerely hope not," she laughed.

Eve leaned forward and rested her chin on her knuckles, batting her eyelids at Priya in a mock dreamy-eyed gesture. "Priya effects the people around her. Calms us when we're angry. Lifts us when we're sad. She can also read emotions. We just don't know exactly *why* she has these abilities."

Priya sighed. "Yes. It would be nice to know what *they* have planned for me."

Wouldn't we all. "Maybe you're a doula or someone like that?"

Eve sat up. "Isn't that like a midwife?"

"It can be, but not always," I said. "My friend Lizzie wanted to be a doula for people with dementia. And dogs. She was a bit eccentric, to be honest."

Thinking of Lizzie broke my heart a little. The anguish must've shown on my face because Priya gave me a warm smile and laid her hand over mine. The static surge from the connection caused me to jerk back, almost tipping over the chair I sat on. From out of nowhere, a fleeting sense of euphoria undulated over me.

Priya shook herself and blew out an unsteady breath. "That's never happened be——" She stopped mid-word and blinked at me. "Oh my—you're—"

I quickly cut her off. "Not telling anyone right now!"

Priya puckered her lips as if she needed to physically stop the rest of her sentence from coming out of her mouth. After a moment of composure though, she smiled.

"Bloody hell," she whispered.

Eve, totally unfazed, gave Priya one of her stern glares. "Not a word to anyone until Halley is ready. Nate doesn't know yet."

"Why haven't you told him?" she asked me. "I know how scared you are. I feel it. It would scare me too. If you ever want to talk to me about it—about your mother—we can. Anytime."

"How did you know——" *Stupid question.* The virus had told her when we touched, along with announcing my pregnancy. I wondered why the same thing hadn't happened with Nate, given our bond.

In any case, I didn't want to talk about it. Time to change the subject. "What do you do here, Priya?"

Eve had already filled me in on the inner workings of the community. Everyone here had a specific job, depending on where their talents lay.

Priya was taken aback by my sudden redirection but quickly adapted, flashing me a sympathetic smile before she answered. "I'm a teacher. But, as you might imagine, the class sizes are rather small."

Eve interjected. "Erik spoke English already, but the others in his group weren't as fluent, so Priya taught them."

Priya grinned at me. "I learned to speak Icelandic in return."

Beautiful, psychic, *and* smart. I couldn't help but feel intimidated.

"Priya is also going to be teaching Claire soon," Eve added.

It made sense. Claire would've lost out on a huge chunk of her schooling because of the apocalypse. Just because the world ended didn't mean the end of fractions and long division. Sadly.

"What about her brother?"

Eve and Priya exchanged troubled glances.

I sat up. "What? Did something happen to him?"

Eve sighed. "He's gone."

I certainly hadn't seen anyone younger than Claire around. "Gone where?"

"Peter isn't real," Priya said. "And he seems to have gone for good since Claire evolved."

When Claire spoke about him, he seemed so real. It never even occurred to me that he might be a figment of her imagination.

"Claire was ten when the outbreak started, and then she was alone for four years until we found her. She created Peter for company," Eve explained.

Priya shook her head sadly. "I spent almost two years alone. That was bad enough. Imagine what it must've been like for a child."

My gaze shifted to Eve, who had the most wretched expression on her face.

"We should've headed down this way sooner," she

muttered.

Guilt. It was self-blame that caused Eve to look so tormented. I knew the feeling well. My entire life was filled with things I *should* have done.

"That's awful."

Eve nodded. "This is why we have to keep looking for people."

Yes. Nobody should have to be alone, I thought, my regretful conscience conjuring up an image of Rebecca sitting abandoned at the kitchen table, waiting for me to return.

After finishing our food, Priya suggested some fresh air.

We chose to sit under the old sycamore tree I'd seen from the bedroom window. The morning's mist had cleared completely now, giving way to a sunny day with clear skies, although the grass around the tree was still dewy in patches where the sun hadn't touched it yet.

We found a dry area to spread out on, beneath the shade of a rickety wooden pergola where Eve kicked off her shoes off and lay down with her knees up, her head resting on her knitted fingers. Priya and I chose to sit cross-legged, leaning back against one of the horizontal beams of the pergola, the timber beneath barely visible through the twisted vines of a bushy, purple wisteria plant.

"Surely, finding people is easier with running cars though," I said.

I wondered how many vehicles they had here and whether it would affect them badly if one were to go missing.

"Short distances. Yes," Eve said. "But, running

them on vegetable oil isn't ideal. And we'll run out eventually. We have some electric cars, but charging them is problematic, given the output of the generators we have. Not to mention, they only go about two-hundred-and-fifty miles on a full charge. It's not feasible for long-distance journeys. As for LPG, supplies stopped being imported to Britain about a month after the outbreak, so we're out of luck there too."

Priya frowned. "So, what's the answer?"

"Damned if I know," Eve shrugged. "We're hoping Erik can figure something out. A solar car or a boat, maybe."

"I always fancied learning to sail," Priya said.

"I mean, the other option would be to get people to come to us. But we'd need a radio transmitter with a wider range and more power." Eve growled in frustration. "We didn't know how easy we had it before the outbreak."

"Can't argue that," I mumbled.

"Isn't it kinda nice to have a clean slate though? We have an opportunity to do things differently this time. We can work *with* nature instead of against it," Priya mused.

Eve sighed. "All irrelevant if we can't repopulate."

Priya turned her head to me. "Tobias and I would love to have children."

I'd no idea they were a couple. "Wouldn't you be afraid the baby would catch the virus?"

"Yes, I—"

"That's what we need Nate for. He's going to help us. He will figure out the risk, if there is one," Eve said quickly.

"*If* there is one?"

Eve sat up, brushing the grass from her arms. "I don't believe the virus—or *they*—would allow you to conceive if the baby was at risk from the virus. It wouldn't make sense. I truly believe something is happening here. Something important."

I admired Eve's conviction. "Maybe."

Priya crossed her arms. "Part of me believes you're right, Eve. But the cynical human part of me needs a more *professional* opinion on it. Let's face it, there's a good chance we're all simply delusional, and you're just talking bollocks."

I laughed. "Maybe one of us is in a coma, and this is just some drug-induced dream."

Eve narrowed her eyes at us. "Heathens."

Priya grinned. "Anyway, what about you, Eve? Do you want children?"

Eve looked away, choosing to focus her attention on the game currently being played on the basketball court. Did Priya know about Eve's past? About the children she'd lost to the virus?

"Of course," she replied, but there was nothing in her voice to suggest it was the truth, despite her impassioned mission to save the human race.

For Eve's sake, I changed the subject again.

****

"Halley, I'm not sure you should come with us."

Just as I swung one leg up into the passenger footwell of an old Range Rover, Nate put his hand on my shoulder, a concerned frown over his eyes.

"Tough. I'm coming."

In reality, the notion of venturing anywhere near a hospital sent me into a cold sweat. The highways were bad enough, but a hospital would be a hundred times worse, jam-packed with the rotting corpses of the infected.

He leaned forward and kissed my forehead. "You can be very stubborn at times, Halley."

It surprised me this realization had only just dawned on him. It was a trait I shared with Rebecca, although I'd always give in first because her pig-headedness far exceeded mine.

Tobias, our appointed designated driver, sat behind the wheel of the vehicle, turning the keys repeatedly to get the engine started. A few times, he thumped down hard on the dashboard with his fist and swore while pumping the clutch pedal. Parked beside us, Ben and Laura sat in an open back pick-up truck, engine purring and raring to go.

Eve finally appeared and climbed into the front passenger seat, informing us that Daniel wasn't coming after all—despite the fuss he'd kicked up about letting us come along in the first place.

"Thought he wanted to keep an eye on the captives," Tobias smirked, gesturing back to us.

Eve snarled at him. "He's helping to get the generators set up."

Tobias shrunk a little but gave us a sly grin when her attention was focused on doing up her seatbelt.

After a few more attempts at getting the engine started, it coughed and roared, the smell of charred oil wafting in through the vents prompting me to cover my mouth and nose.

As we set off, Eve twisted around to face us both, although her question was directed at Nate.

"So, is any of the research making sense yet?"

Nate shrugged. "Well, sort of. I've only caught up on what everyone else knows already."

We hadn't talked about his research efforts so far, and I hadn't asked. Part of me didn't want to know. There was something to be said for the perks of being blissfully ignorant. Any major revelations would most likely send me into an agonizing panic about the baby. Still, it was cowardly and ultimately avoiding the inevitable.

"Anything I need to know?"

Nate reached over and took my hand. "Yes, but that doesn't mean I *want* to tell you."

I winced. "Just tell me."

"Maybe Nate doesn't want you to worry about it, Halley," Eve cut in.

"Just tell me." I also didn't want to be sheltered from it anymore.

Nate set his jaw, apprehensively, but after a brief moment of consideration, he spoke. "The virus isn't a virus."

It wasn't the first time I'd heard this. From my recollection of watching the news at the time, such rumors had been circulated by some members of the British Press, but quickly dismissed as ridiculous by I.D.R.I.S.

I swallowed deeply, my heart fluttering with anxiety. "Then what is it?"

"They weren't sure. It behaves like a virus, but it also has some of the attributes of an intelligent organism," he said.

No great surprise there since it'd been trying to communicate with us.

Nate continued. "It invades a host and immediately

begins to replicate itself, cloning every cell in the host's body. It then seems to integrate its own genetic information into the new cell. The old cells are recycled for energy, which is pretty clever."

It almost made me laugh out loud. "Cloning?"

Nate nodded. "That part is a rather bitter pill to swallow."

I set that particular piece of information aside for now. "If it's so clever, why did so many people die?"

"The incompatibility of the human brain."

The apprehensive look on his face had been replaced by the wide-eyed expression of wonder he donned whenever he spoke about a subject that interested him.

"The virus can't copy brain cells because the electrical impulses in our brains interfere with the cloning process. The new brain cells it creates are faulty, which—to cut a long story short—quickly results in complete organ failure."

This made no sense. "Then how did *we* survive?"

"It's complicated, but essentially, in a small proportion of people, the virus behaved differently. At first, they thought it was a mutation, and that a cure could be developed from the new strain. But there was no mutation, not one they could identify anyway."

"So, if it wasn't a mutation, then what was it?"

"Not sure. Maybe it *learned* instead," Nate replied.

"Learned what?"

"Not to copy our brain cells while the electrical impulses are still firing," he said. "From what I can gather, it goes dormant until we die. As soon as the electrical impulses stop firing, it finishes the cloning process and then activates itself in every cell and disables or alters the genetic traits in us it doesn't like."

Intriguing. "What traits?"

"Susceptibility to illness, the aging process, the speed at which we heal."

Okay. Fine. *Not so bad.* I could deal with that. Probably. "Clones though?"

Tobias glanced back over his shoulder at me. "There's a bright side, you know. For me, at least."

"Oh?"

"I was in Ibiza on a stag-do for my best mate's wedding, right before the outbreak. I got so drunk that I ended up in a tattoo parlor. I woke up the next day with this awful piece of art on my arse. It's gone now. No trace it was ever there."

I raised an eyebrow. "It's gone?"

"The virus doesn't replicate things like scars or tattoos," Nate explained.

As I attempted to take in this new information, the car fell silent. It wasn't until we ran over something bulky on the road, that I spoke again as my head collided with the roof.

"Ouch."

Tobias grimaced. "Corpse. Shit. Didn't see it."

Eve turned to him, her nose screwed up in distaste. "I am *not* scraping *that* off the bumper."

The hospital wasn't far from the school and took about twenty minutes without the delay of London traffic to slow us down. We drove down the ambulance lane, avoiding the few thousand vehicles that spilled out from the massive car park and onto every curb and verge in the near vicinity. Even the ambulance lane was lined with cars, although we had just about enough room to pass by without bumping wing mirrors. We stopped outside the entrance to the accident and emergency department and reluctantly got out.

The building itself reached twelve stories at its highest point and looked far more like a swanky office block than a hospital. The lower part of the building was brick with ultra-modern, geometric paneling covering the outside of the ground floor wall. The automatic, glass double doors to A&E were locked shut.

Ben ordered us all to stand aside before getting back into the pick-up truck, reversing it as far as he could down the lane, and then ramming it into the doors that cracked and shattered without any resistance. Instantly, a massive dust cloud mushroomed up and billowed out in all directions, bringing with it a sickening, sulfur-like odor. The smell of my freshly laundered t-shirt was just about enough to stop me gagging once I'd pulled it up over my nose.

Ben got back out of the truck and knocked down any remaining glass shards with a hammer and then gestured for us to go inside.

"Not my first rodeo," he mumbled to Nate and me as we passed him. Clearly, it was Ben who'd been responsible for all the smashed, looted shops we'd seen after arriving in London. By the smug look on his face, the destruction appealed to him.

As the dust cleared, the death and decay became visible. It was everywhere.

Bodies lined the corridors and filled every seat in the waiting area of the A&E department. They were on the floor, sprawled out in the positions they'd died in, and some were even still standing against the walls or leaning against the snack machines. The smell was much worse, the closer we got.

We followed the corridor down until we ended up in the main lobby of the hospital. There were bodies in here too, but only on the leather chairs that made up the coffee shop seating. A barista in a green apron was slumped over the service counter, his bony index finger still wrapped around the handle of a coffee mug, a brown stain on the linoleum floor below it.

Why anyone would still go to work in the midst of a pandemic, to one of the most likely places to catch it, was beyond me. The doctors and nurses, I could understand, given they had a duty to take care of sick people, but a coffee shop worker?

"They sure are running a skeleton staff today," Ben mumbled as he passed by the ex-barista, swiping a cereal bar from the display in front of the till. "Hey, Tobias. What did the zombie do after he dumped his girlfriend?"

"No idea."

"He wiped his arse!"

Tobias snickered. "You're a sick man, and you need help."

"Ben, if you don't shut up, I'm going to *kick* your arse," Eve snapped as she looked over a huge map of the hospital stuck up on the lobby wall. Nate perused it too and then pulled a piece of paper from his jeans pocket. He tore off a section of it and handed it to Eve.

"The medical archives are on the fourth floor, next to the consultant's offices. This is a list of the books and journals I want. Find as many as you can and then wait for us outside." He turned to me with an austere expression. "Go with Eve, Halley."

It was an instruction that left no room for

argument.

Eve and I headed to the main stairwell and began our ascent. After two minutes of stair-climbing, the stench of the dead burned my nostrils so vehemently that nothing could block it out. It took everything I had not to spew my breakfast over the linoleum.

"Go back to the car, Halley."

My teeth ground together in an effort to stop gagging, and with a quick shake of my head, I quickly carried on up the stairs.

Fortunately, the fourth floor was corpse-free and far less pungent than the ground level and stairwell. Some kind soul had left a window open, and a fresh breeze blew through the corridor, providing enough ventilation for me to breathe without retching.

The archive was basically a library; a large room with shelf after shelf of books and a few computers on desks against the far wall.

There were five books on Nate's list—one of which was authored by Kara Strahovski and entitled '*Factors of reproduction.*' I wasn't sure whether to look under S for Strahovski or 'F' for the book title.

Eventually, we located it in a section dedicated to fertility research.

Kara's book was a thick hardback, and judging by the state of the outer sleeve, very well-read. The back cover included her bio and a small photograph. She was a pretty blond in her early forties with black-rimmed spectacles and thin lips. She didn't look at all like a mad scientist.

I tucked the book under my arm and began looking for another of the titles on Nate's list. Eve made faster progress than me and had the other three titles in hand before I'd even located the section with '*The evolutionary history of vertebrate RNA.*'

She came to lean casually against one of the shelves next to the section I'd begun to rummage in. "Why haven't you told Nate yet?"

I ran my index finger down the spines of a row of medical encyclopedias. "I told you I needed time."

She sighed. "Time for what? Doesn't he want children? Are you afraid of what he'll say?"

"Yes, he wants children." My reply was abrupt. "But it's early still, right? Something could go wrong."

"So, what? You'd rather he didn't know?"

"Yes. If something bad happened, I'd rather he never found out about it."

A look of shock registered on her face. "But—"

I cut her off. "He's seen so much death, Eve. He's lost so much. I'd rather save him the heartache."

She simply glared at me, huffed and shook her head crossly. "You have no right to keep this from him. What are you afraid of?"

Ignoring her, I sidestepped over to another shelf of books. The huge tome I'd been searching for was here, nestled amongst other gigantic works. As it slowly wiggled out of its slot, she appeared beside me and slapped her hand across the book to stop me from pulling it out any further.

"You're afraid if you lose the baby, he'll do something stupid."

With an indignant glare aimed directly at her, I batted her hand away and dug my fingernails into the book's spine to get a better grip on it. "I *will not* let him go back to the dark place he was in when I found him."

Suddenly, she became incensed. "Are you bloody

kidding me?" She grabbed my wrist. "I've seen the way he looks at you. Nate would never do that to you. No matter what happens. You're an idiot if you think otherwise. He loves you."

"Sometimes, love isn't enough!" I recoiled and yanked my wrist from her grasp. The book, along with a few other volumes, dropped to the floor in a series of heavy thuds that echoed throughout the room.

"Priya mentioned your mother." Eve's stare was penetrating, but not so condemnatory. "Did something happen to her?"

"Yes!" I snapped, not thinking.

Did I really want to talk about this now? With Eve?

My mother's suicide had gnawed at me for the last ten years. A long time to hold onto the belief that I'd not been *enough* to keep my mother from killing herself. From slitting her wrists in the bathtub and leaving me with Andrew. Hadn't I loved her and behaved like a good girl? Or was there something more I could've done?

Exhaling, I let my body slump back against the bookshelf. "She left me, Eve," I muttered. "She took a bath, slit her wrists…and she left me."

****

Before…

The night before my planned departure, I snuck my backpack into the garage and dropped it down next to the bicycle, ready to go.

After wolfing down breakfast, I informed Rebecca that I'd be going out for a while.

"Don't be too long," she said.

Not wanting to leave her with a lie on my lips, I simply nodded. As far as she was concerned, I was only going to cycle around the village.

With the backpack on my shoulders and my fingers wrapped tightly around the handlebars, I pushed the bike out of the garage and down the path. As soon as the ground leveled, I hopped onto the seat and began to ride.

In no time at all, the highway loomed into view, and once the bike was traveling along the hard shoulder, it coasted easily without me having to pedal. It felt good to have the breeze in my hair and the pre-summer sun on my skin.

Half an hour later, a roadside sign informed me it was twenty kilometers to Saltash. From there, the coast was only a short distance away, and my expedition could properly begin.

Thirsty, I stopped to take a swig of water from the bottle clipped to the bicycle frame and wiped the sweat from my forehead with a cloth I'd stowed away in the front basket.

Looking around at the acres of overgrown farmland, my attention was caught by some movement in a field off in the distance. Cows. Only a dozen, grazing idly on the long grass, where large herds used to roam.

The cows had mostly starved or died from illness. The remaining ones moved constantly from pasture to pasture in groups, mainly to deter foxes from attacking the weaker members of the herd. As they munched and meandered, my gaze followed them until they disappeared from sight.

Survival was easier in groups; that was a fact.

And yet, here I was, all alone in the outside world. It didn't frighten me, although perhaps it should have.

My worry was for Rebecca.

Without me, she'd be vulnerable, especially in the state she was in. I hadn't even told her I was leaving.

"Fuck!" My frustrated scream echoed across the silent landscape.

A few moments later, I steered the bike around and cycled back to the cottage.

Chapter Twenty-One

After...

Speaking about my mother's death had lifted a weight from my shoulders, although it was strange to have finally shared it with Eve, of all people. She'd sympathized with my fears but made it abundantly clear she disapproved of my decision to keep the pregnancy a secret—for the sake of my sanity.

She also pointed out that Nate was far more impervious to death now than before he evolved, but I wasn't reassured—if someone really wanted to find a way to end their life, they would. Eve's last comment on the matter was to tell me I was more screwed up than she thought, but she would continue to keep my secret for the time being.

Outside the hospital, Tobias and Ben had just finished loading a big, expensive-looking piece of equipment into the back of the pick-up when we returned. Ben secured it with a strap, alongside a heavy-duty microscope, and then covered it all with a dust sheet.

Unable to hold it in any longer, I vomited onto the rear wheel of an abandoned police car. Eve rushed to my aid, holding back my hair and giving my back a gentle rub as my violent retching reached its peak. After swilling out my mouth and downing a bottle of water, I started to go back inside the hospital to help Nate, but

Tobias stopped me.

"Don't!" he warned. "Just stay here, we won't be much longer."

Ben jumped down from the back of the pick-up. "Yeh, it ain't pretty in the basement."

From the map, I'd gleaned that the laboratories—where Nate had gone to get the equipment from—were on the lower levels, next to the mortuary.

I grimaced, not wanting to think about it.

Eve turned to me. "We'll wait in the car."

Despite my reluctance to abandon Nate to the horrors of the hospital basement, I knew that if I went back in there again, the puking would recommence, and I'd be no help at all.

With a sigh, I climbed back into the Range Rover and shut the door, pulling the neck of my t-shirt up over my nose again, and rested my forehead against the cool glass of the passenger door window. I closed my eyes, picturing one of my favorite old movies in my mind to distract me from the putrid smell outside. Finally, the ache in my stomach muscles eased enough for me to relax.

In no time at all, the fatigue in my body pulled me down into a deep sleep, only rousing for a few seconds to acknowledge Nate when I heard the car door open. I felt his hand brush gently against my cheek as he shifted me into a more comfortable sleeping position, with my head on his lap.

"She's been kinda tired recently."

"Oh?"

"She has nightmares."

The voices sounded a million miles away. The rest of their conversation was lost to me as I sank into a deeper slumber.

Once again, I find myself in the red desert. It looks more like the images beamed to Earth by the Mars rover than any place on my own planet.

I sit beside the lake, leaning back, with my feet dangling in the water as though I'm basking in the sunlight of a hot summer's day. The reflection in the water is of a blue sky again, although the sky above me here is the same dismal gray it always is.

Someone is swimming in the lake, and as he floats closer, I recognize Nate. He smiles at me, then walks out of the water as if there are invisible steps I cannot see. We both bask on the shore, soaking in rays from an absent sun.

After a while, he turns to me and gently kisses my lips. "I know it's going to hurt, but you must remember what I told you the first time we met."

I frown. "When you were lying on the sofa in the cabin?"

Nate shakes his head. "No, before that."

Before I can reply, lightning flashes and blinds me. When I'm finally able to see again, Nate is gone, as is the lake.

There is nothing here now but endless dunes of dry, red sand, as far as the eye can see.

I am alone.

****

It took me a while to get my bearings, but I eventually managed to sit up straight and focus.

The car had stopped at an awkward angle, and a thin trail of smoke was wafting out of the dashboard, above the steering wheel. It stunk of burnt plastic and quickly filled the car in a thick gray fog.

My lungs burned as I pressed my palm to my mouth and stifled a cough. "What happened?"

Nate unbuckled my seatbelt quickly and pulled on the door handle. He then gave it a hard kick with his foot, and it swung open with a defiant squeal. "Halley, get out!"

I quickly slid off the seat and stepped out onto the pavement.

We weren't far from the school, but somehow the Range Rover had mounted the curb and plowed into some railings, trapping Nate and Eve on the passenger side. As Nate jumped out onto the street, Eve clambered over the center console and onto the back seat. She wasted no time exiting the vehicle.

"Christ," Tobias swore from behind me. He was already out, jumping up and down, shaking and flexing his hands.

"What happened?" I asked again.

A few orange flames began to lick at the edges of the bonnet, charring and bubbling the paintwork as it spread downwards toward the grill.

Eve stared at me. "You were having some kind of nightmare and then—" She stopped and threw both hands into the air.

Nate cut in. "The engine cut out, then Tobias lost control."

Eve took hold of my shoulders and looked me up and down. "Are you okay?"

We couldn't have been traveling very fast, especially given the state of the roads. Still, the panic rocketed in my chest when my thoughts turned to the baby.

Nate answered for me. "She's fine. She slept

through the whole thing." He put his arm around me and moved me a little further away from the car, gesturing for the others to do the same.

Tobias huffed. *"I'm* not fine! I got electrocuted!"

Eve rolled her eyes at him. "Don't be so dramatic. You'll heal." She turned back to me. "Has this ever happened to you before?"

I shot her a confused look. "What do you mean?"

"There was…a surge. It came from *you!"* Eve's eyes were unblinking and wild. "Halley. I think *you* did this."

"What?" I couldn't help but laugh.

Sure, there'd been the incident with the light bulb that one time, but this couldn't possibly be anything to do with me. Could it?

Nate pulled me aside. "There was static, Halley. It was all over you, I could feel it," he muttered, under his breath.

"How? How could I have done this?"

My mind spun. Someone could've gotten seriously hurt. Because of me. And because of something I couldn't control.

Eve pulled out her walkie talkie. "Daniel…?" She paused abruptly when she realized the radio wasn't making the crackling noise it usually did. She fiddled with the controls and bashed it, but it was dead. Tobias tutted and unclipped his radio from his belt. "Dead," he said, after a few attempts of trying to contact the school.

They both looked at me curiously. It felt as though I were an exhibit in a freak show, the star attraction, scrutinized by onlookers captivated by my abnormalities.

An irate growl left my throat, and with a shake of

my head, I stomped away toward the school. I was in no mood to stand around ruminating—there was only one person who might be able to help me understand this. Claire.

If this *was* my fault, I needed to get it under control.

"Halley—" Nate caught up with my swift stride. I looked back to see Tobias rescuing the books from the boot of the Range Rover, while Eve followed us, although she kept a good few meters behind.

Nate took hold of my hand rather forcefully. "Don't shut me out!"

His eyes filled with apprehension. Was he worried about me? Or was he scared of what I might blow up next?

We stopped under the dilapidated canopy of an old pawn shop where I leaned against the metal security shuttering with my arms crossed.

"I'm not," I snapped, and then sighed.

Wearily, I stepped forward, taking his hand in mine, giving it a firm squeeze as I kissed his cheek. This wasn't his fault. "I need to speak to Claire."

"You think she can ask *them* what's going on?" Nate asked.

"Maybe."

Nate held the back of my hand up to his lips and kissed it. "Fine. Just don't keep things from me. Whatever's going on with you, I want to know."

I glanced up at him, feeling instantly guilty. "What if I'm not ready to tell you?"

Nate shrugged. "Then I'll wait."

****

When we arrived back at the school, Daniel was at

the gate with Ben, pacing.

"Where have you been?" Daniel shot an icy glare in our direction, before putting an arm around Eve. "I knew I should've come with you."

He clearly thought we'd tried to run, and his distrust of us was evident in his suspicious expression.

"We broke down," Eve said quickly.

Tobias appeared behind us, the books piled in his arms, stacked high enough to hide his conspiratorial smirk from Daniel. He was loyally sticking to Eve's version of events.

"The Range Rover is caput," he muttered as he passed through the gates.

Mumbling an excuse to leave, I hurriedly left Nate and the others to unload the pick-up and headed to the library. Claire had started her daily lessons with Priya today, so I knew that's where she'd be. Curiously, the library was empty, but after running into Priya in the stairwell to the dormitories, she informed me Claire had gone back to her room to study.

Good, I thought. We could talk privately.

Claire's room was next to Eve's. I knocked gently until I heard her invite me in. She was sprawled on her bed with a book, looking thoroughly bored. Her room was smaller than mine but made even smaller by the amount of stuff she had everywhere.

In her short time here, she'd managed to accumulate quite a collection; mainly stuffed unicorns and other mythical creatures. The walls were the same pale blue as in my room, but I could barely see the color past the posters of dragons and winged horses she'd stuck up everywhere.

Claire looked up at me with a smile. "Hello! They

said you were coming."

Of course *they* did.

She waved her book at me with a disgruntled expression on her face. "Priya wants me to read this...King Lear! It's boring and I can't make out what anyone is saying."

She chucked it on the floor and patted her sequined mermaid duvet, motioning for me to sit.

"Yeh, that pretty much sums it up," I chuckled, slumping down beside her. "So, what else did *they* say?"

She ruffled her hair and sighed. "That if you want to know something, you should ask *them* yourself."

"How am I supposed to do that?" My head fell into my hands with a growl of frustration.

She put her arms around me and rested her head on my shoulder. "Don't be sad!" she whispered in a soothing voice. "Your connection with them is even stronger than mine, talking to them won't be as hard as you think."

My connection? "I doubt that."

She grabbed my wrists and pulled my hands away from my face. "Why do you think they chose *you* in the first place?"

"Chose me for what?"

She smiled, making a gesture of zipping up her lips and throwing away an invisible key.

"Stop being afraid of your dreams and listen to them. Invite *them* in."

Right. Not sure I wanted to do that. "Why do they need an invitation?"

She frowned. "Human brains are complicated. We have...barriers that *they* can't pass through very easily.

Most survivors can hear *them*, in some way, but not like *we* can. We're different. You, me, Eve and Priya."

"What makes us different?"

She tapped her head. "We've always been broken."

"What does that mean?"

She threw her hands up. "Dunno."

With a shake of my head, I got up and headed to the door, but stopped abruptly before reaching for the handle. "Claire?"

"Mm?" she responded.

"After what happened in the fountain, you said *they* were protecting me?"

She nodded. "And the baby, yes."

"And *they* were the ones that hurt Ben, right?"

A sheepish grin spread across her face. "That's what I told Eve, but I lied."

Before a response left my lips, she slid off the bed and gave me another one of her all-encompassing hugs. "A half-lie. It was *you* and *them*."

With what Nate said about the virus cloning our cells and then integrating itself with us, was it possible that my—our—relationship with the virus was somewhat symbiotic? Maybe, there wasn't a *them* at all, only an *us*.

The entire concept left me with a mounting ache in my temples. This was more Nate's thing.

"Okay," I said, squirming out of her embrace.

I left her room and headed to ours, eager to climb into bed and sleep off my headache. As my fingers reached out for the doorknob, a hand closed over mine and lifted it away.

"I've been looking for you," Nate said, his eyes racked with worry again.

"I spoke to Claire," I muttered.

"And?"

Glancing up and down the corridor, I put my index finger to my lips and motioned for us to recommence this conversation in our room, lest we be overheard.

Once inside, I flopped down wearily onto our bed, making a starfish shape with my limbs.

"Are you afraid of me, Nate?"

He laughed. "No."

Maybe it was an overreaction. After all, I hadn't killed anyone. *Yet*.

"Honestly, I'm more curious than anything," Nate added. "I mean, we've both felt the static before, but why's it stronger now?"

An excellent question. Never once, in all my time at the cottage, after the apocalypse, had I ever encountered it before meeting Nate. And it'd only gone into over-drive since being here at the school. Also, the red desert dreams were far more lucid now than they'd ever been.

"Maybe it's something to do with being around other survivors," I answered.

Was it possible that the virus had led us here because it needed us *all* to be together for some as-yet-unknown purpose?

There were too many questions and only one apparent way to get answers.

I had to *invite them in*. Whatever that meant.

****

Before going to sleep each night, I silently invoked *them* to communicate with me, but ironically, my sleep was completely undisturbed for the next two weeks. According to Nate, with none of my nightmare induced fretting waking him up, he'd slept like a log.

By accepting the dreams, they'd stopped altogether, or so it seemed. Perhaps I'd tried too hard to force them, instead of letting them come naturally. Defeated for the time being, I gave up and concentrated on helping Nate research the virus instead.

One afternoon, however, I'd dozed off on a desk in the science lab after attempting to read one of the books we'd brought back from the hospital. 'The evolutionary history of RNA' had failed to grip me, so I'd used its thick bulk as a pillow instead.

The lab was stiflingly hot as we'd had a few days of summery weather, despite the onset of what was usually a chilly and rainy October. The stuffiness of the room combined with my hormonally induced predilection for napping meant that no matter how uncomfortable I was, I quickly slipped into a deep sleep.

The red desert has changed, finally becoming the world that's always reflected in the lake. The sky is cloudless and blue, and a golden sun beams down on the lush, green valley that contains the lake.

There are people here, but they aren't solid. They wander about as blurry shapes, all apart from one that approaches me slowly from way off in the distance.

It is a woman with long, blonde hair and vivid green eyes. She's exactly how I remember her—it is Lizzie. She stops a few meters away and smiles, her hair blowing wildly in the wind.

"Lizzie?"

I run to her and wrap her in my arms, even though it can't really be her. I've missed her so much. Fake-Lizzie's hug feels the same as always, and her hair smells pleasantly of coconut and fresh limes. It reminds me of Pina Coladas and tropical beaches. If it isn't Lizzie, how do they know what her shampoo smells like? Are they reading my thoughts?

Lizzie pulls away from me and strokes my hair. "I'm so glad you aren't afraid anymore, Halley," she says. "It's so hard for us to reach you—all of you. The human brain is like nothing we've ever encountered. Its complexities have confounded us at times."

She smells like Lizzie but doesn't sound like Lizzie.

"What have you been trying to tell me?" I ask.

Fake-Lizzie smiles. "Only what you need to know at this moment in time. Which is a difficulty for us—the passage of time is not the same for us as it is for you. We do not occupy your dimension. The virus is our link to you, although only a part of it resides in your universe."

Definitely not Lizzie. "Who are you?"

"I'm your friend." Lizzie laughs, then beckons for me to follow her.

We walk along the lakeside, weaving in and out of the shadow people. "For so long, we were trying to send you where you needed to be, but you couldn't hear us."

"Well, I can hear you now."

Lizzie nods, but then she frowns and strokes my hair again. "Your connection to us is strengthening. It will become even stronger once you know the truth."

Quite the conundrum. No wonder Claire struggles to make sense of what she hears.

"And what is the truth exactly?"

Lizzie takes a deep breath and frowns. "I can't tell you. Human minds are fragile. But when you're ready to know the truth, you'll remember everything. Make no mistake, the truth will hurt your heart. That's why you resist it."

"Can you give me a clue?" *I asked, somewhat flippantly.*

With a grin and a quick roll of her eyes, Lizzie shakes her head incredulously. *"Nate told you something very important before you met."*

"That doesn't make sense."

"It will."

"You speak in riddles!" *I snapped.*

Lizzie shrugs. *"It won't always feel like that. Have faith, Halley, you're on the right path now."*

I exhale deeply and grunt out of frustration. *"The path you chose for me, you mean?"*

"One of the many. The past is set. The present is volatile. And the future is a tree with over a billion branches. We can only steer you to where you need to be."

"We still have free will then?"

Lizzie smirks. *"Unfortunately."*

Her answer is comforting. We walk in silence for a little while until she says, *"Did you have a question for us?"*

"How long have you got?"

Lizzie laughs. *"Coming here is tiring for us both. If you have a question, ask it quickly."*

"Am I dangerous?"

"Highly, should you choose to be."

"I can't control it."

Lizzie reaches out and flattens her palm against my heart. I feel the static building beneath her hand. *"Influencing the static is easier than you think. The static is not the beginning of something, but the end. It is a product of the virus and can be channeled and directed."*

Her touch begins to burn a little. Then it burns a lot. My heart skips a few beats as the static sears through my chest.

"Lizzie," I whisper, now lightheaded and overcome by exhaustion.

There are more questions I want to ask, but I'm so tired.

I fall to the ground, and everything goes dark.

I sat up quickly, painfully peeling the plastic dust cover of the book from my sweaty cheek. Nate hadn't moved from his spot at the desk opposite where he peered intently into the eyepiece of a microscope. The fluorescent lights above me dimmed a few times, almost imperceptibly; the only sign I'd been dreaming. I happily considered it a victory.

****

Before...

The years passed by. I watched each season turn to the next without knowing—or caring—what day or month it was. I'd ceased all talk of finding other survivors, although, on my darkest days, I cycled to the highway and spent a few hours watching and listening for the car I'd seen that'd never returned. Each time I gazed at the long road in front of me, the desire to leave became stronger and stronger, like I was space debris on the edge of a black hole, resisting the inevitable dive into oblivion.

At home, Rebecca seemed content with her daily routines and our fleeting interactions. Some days, I rarely spoke to her, although I smiled and nodded when

I needed to, pretending to be as content as she was. I found it better not to think about life outside of the little bubble we'd created for ourselves. But I was suffocating, and all I wanted to do was stick a pin in it and breathe deeply again.

Occasionally, she would ask me if I was okay. I'd give her the same mechanical smile each time because my reply was irrelevant—nothing would change.

I wondered how long I could carry on like this before I finally broke down.

What would happen then?

What would I do?

What was I truly capable of?

Chapter Twenty-Two

After...

"What are you looking at?"

Yawning and stretching, I stood up and shuffled around to Nate's desk, sliding my arms around his waist and kissing his cheek. He looked up from the microscope and smiled wryly at me.

"A sample of semen," he said.

My nose wrinkled in distaste. "Glad I asked."

He laughed. "Take a look." He slid his chair back and made a space for me to look into the microscope.

"I'd rather not."

"Would it make you feel any better if I told you it was mine?" he grinned.

"Not really."

Out of morbid curiosity, I looked anyway. All I could see were hundreds of shadowy round blobs with spindly tales twitching and wriggling about.

"What's wrong with them?" I asked, still observing the slide, oddly mesmerized.

"Nothing's wrong. The sample is completely normal."

I snapped my head up. "What?"

Normal? It was half the mystery solved, at least.

He reached over to another table and grabbed one of the notepads he'd been scribbling on. A few times, I'd attempted to read his scrawling to no avail. His handwriting—in typical doctor fashion—was dire.

"On one of the laptops, I found an email written by Kara Strahovski. It included a report on the infertility problem. She'd sent it off to a few other doctors in her field asking for their opinion," Nate explained. "It would appear that once the virus infiltrates the male reproductive system, it destroys all the sperm and halts the production of new sperm. In women, it destroys their entire supply of ova."

"Why?"

He flicked through a few pages of his notes. "I have a theory. I think the virus disables our ability to reproduce, so we can't pass on inferior genes. At least, until we die and evolve. It wasn't until I found an autopsy report on a man named Simon James that I discovered that—post evolution—his sperm count had returned to normal."

"Simon James? Was he one of the people in the bunker with Eve?" I asked.

He nodded. "It's a pretty harrowing read."

"Tell me everything."

"Sure?" he asked me, concern knitting his eyebrows together.

"Tell me."

After a hesitant start, he finally gave me all the gruesome details.

Simon James had been flown to the bunker in Scotland from Australia. He was the first survivor I.D.R.I.S experimented on. Initially, they injected him with a lethal overdose of Pentobarbital, which induced Simon into a coma state. Then, an hour later, he died. The doctors planned to dissect his organs to get a better understanding of what the virus had done to the survivors and, if possible, synthesize a vaccine. Six hours later, however, he'd awoken, right as rain.

"Everything changed at that point," he said with a solemn bow of his head. "It gets worse. In the end, they removed his liver and kidneys in order to see how the virus would adapt. He lasted a week, far longer than any normal human would."

My mouth opened in shock. I couldn't imagine the suffering Simon James had endured at the hands of the people that'd promised to save mankind, but it didn't surprise me, given what we knew some humans were capable of. Especially in such desperate times.

Eve and the others held at the bunker may not have met such a brutal end as Simon, but they'd still been tested on and tortured. I wondered how such an experience might affect a person long term.

"But he *did* die? Permanently, I mean."

"Yeh, the virus has its limits. It can't grow new body parts; it can only repair them."

Hearing this was somewhat of a relief. To me, it meant we *were* still mostly human. The ability to regrow vital organs was far too alien a concept.

"Anyway, Simon's autopsy report was bizarre, to say the least, but they did find his reproductive function had returned to normal," Nate continued. "Which makes sense if you think about it. After we evolve, the inferior genes are erased or disabled, leaving only the new and improved ones."

I looked at him. "So, why no babies?"

He shrugged. "I have another theory, but it's not good news."

"Go on…"

"I think the virus made a mistake," Nate said.

"When it destroyed the women's supply of ova, it was unaware that, unlike sperm, the female body cannot produce more."

I knew from a distant memory of a school biology lesson that women were already born with all of the eggs they needed to reproduce. Once those eggs were used up, that was it.

It made me wonder if maybe, by some miracle, the virus hadn't destroyed all of mine, making conception still possible. It was obvious though, by the four-year absence of periods, that my reproductive system wasn't functioning as it should.

In any case, would *they*, or the virus, really make such a massive mistake? From what I'd learned about them, it seemed highly unlikely.

"It's just a theory, though," he added. "An explanation to offer Eve and Daniel."

"They want more than just an explanation, Nate. They want a solution."

He pursed his lips. "There's a chance I may have found one."

My eyes grew wide as he rubbed his stubble and shot me a grin. "There's a drug called ABVD, used for chemotherapy. Before the virus, a version of it was being trialed as a fertility drug. As an unexpected side-effect of Cancer treatment, doctors discovered it had the ability to trigger the production of new ova. It was re-branded as 'Restova' and sent out for more clinical trials right before the outbreak. If we could get hold of some, there's a chance it could work."

Intelligence was *such* a turn on. "You're a genius, do you know that?"

He laughed, putting his thumb and index finger

together. He made a small space between them and said, "It's a small chance."

"A chance, nonetheless."

He sighed. "If it doesn't work, I'm out of ideas," he said. "I'll also need volunteers to take the drug. Maybe Eve can find some women here who'd be prepared to take it."

I kissed his cheek. "I don't think it'll be a problem. I get the impression there are a few couples here who want a baby."

"Yeh, I thought that was probably the case."

My lips moved to his jawline, where I kissed him in soft intervals until I reached his lips.

"Halley," he groaned, but pulled away. "You've been distant this past week—"

A ravenous kiss was enough to stop the rest of his sentence from leaving his mouth.

It wasn't something I wanted to talk about. When he said *distant*, he meant that I'd been avoiding sex. Not any easy thing to do, given our connection.

It was killing me not to be intimate with him, but I was sure that if he saw me naked, he would figure out I was pregnant. He'd know it wasn't just the chips. Chips didn't increase bra cup sizes.

I'd hoped to be able to tell him in a few weeks' time—to be on the safer side—but, realistically, it'd have to be sooner than that.

For the moment though, my kiss was enough to distract him completely. He stood and lifted me up onto the desk next to his, swatting a pile of notebooks onto the floor.

Positioning himself between my legs, he pushed my dress up around my waist and then moved his hands slowly over my thighs until he reached my underwear, which he promptly tore off. My head fell back with a gasp in response to the sound of ripping lace.

As we kissed, deeply and hungrily, he pushed me back onto my elbows, and moments later, with my legs wrapped around his hips, we made love.

I hoped to god no one found a good reason to visit the science lab right now.

The fluorescent tubes above us pulsed and dimmed, but there was no explosion. Not from the lights, anyway. As the heat built up inside me, my legs embraced him tighter, bringing him as close as possible before a stifled whimper escaped my throat. Seconds later, he gave a husky moan and slowed his pace, breathing heavily against my neck.

"Halley, can I ask you something?"

I slid down from the desk. "What?"

He straightened up and raised the zip on his jeans. "If it worked, would *you* take the drug?"

His question took me by surprise, and I simply stared blankly at him.

"Do you want to have children?" he asked, taking my hand.

"Why? Do you?"

He shrugged and smiled. "Yes."

Anxiously, I wedged my bottom lip between my teeth. "Wouldn't you be worried that something would happen? It might not survive like we did."

Nate sighed, dropping my hand, and sat down on the stool in front of his desk. "I've thought about that a lot. I couldn't, in good conscience, allow anyone here to conceive if the risk was too great."

Too late. "And?"

"I found something in Strahovski's notes. She'd also considered the use of ABVD to stimulate fertility, but she was also concerned about the effect of the virus on a developing embryo."

My stomach lurched. "Oh?"

"She and her husband—Doctor Lawson—had discussed various scenarios given the information they'd gleaned from their study of the virus."

As anxiety turned my legs to jelly, I pulled up a stool in front of him. "Go on."

"If conception was successful, there were two possible outcomes," he continued. "It's a bit similar to how some women with rare blood types miscarry because their immune system attacks any fetus with a different blood type to that of the mother."

"The virus, they believed, would do the same. A developing fetus, susceptible to the virus, wouldn't survive. But a fetus formed from human cells, already integrated with the virus, wouldn't be at risk from it."

"Even if the mother hadn't evolved?"

"I don't see how it would make a difference. Especially since it's only the brain cells that have yet to be cloned and integrated. The risk might be a little higher, perhaps."

"How much higher? How would I—the mother, I mean—know if her baby wasn't going to make it?"

He frowned. "The pregnancy would result in early miscarriage."

"I see." Using the desk for support, I stood abruptly and moved toward the door. "I need to think about this."

My panicked brain struggled to make sense of everything Nate had said, and of everything I already knew. The risk of losing my baby was higher but at the same time, *they* were protecting her. Did it mean she was safe?

He followed me down the corridor and grabbed my hand, stopping me from going any further. "I'm sorry. I shouldn't have said anything."

"It's fine. I'm fine. It's just all a bit overwhelming."

"I know. I'm sorry," he whispered, holding me so tightly I could barely breathe. I didn't attempt to move out of his arms because he was the only thing keeping me from sinking to the floor. For the sake of my sanity, he needed to know about the baby. I was done trying to deal with this alone, despite my fears for *his* sanity should something go wrong.

"Nate, I really need to tell you—"

My confession, like a tense movie cliff-hanger, was interrupted by the sound of the double doors swinging open at the end of the corridor. It was Ben, and he was in a rush.

"Hey. Sorry to break up this tender moment, but you both need to go to Daniel's office. Now."

"Why?" I asked him, feeling like Nate and I had just been caught kissing behind the bike sheds and ordered to the headmaster's office for a severe reprimand.

"Medical emergency," was all Ben would say.

****

Gabriel was outside Daniel's office when we got there. He flashed me a crooked smile as I went past him.

"Sit," Daniel ordered. He was leaning back against the wall, arms crossed and looking decidedly tense.

329

Nate and I sat obediently and exchanged apprehensive glances. I had no idea what we'd been summoned for or what constituted a medical emergency around here, in a group full of semi-immortals.

Eve was the last to turn up, in a dressing gown and slippers, her hair soaking wet with a towel around her shoulders,

"You couldn't have given me ten minutes, *Gary*?" she sneered.

Gabriel closed the door and gave her a vengeful glare. "No, I couldn't, *Evelyn*."

I laughed much louder than I'd intended to. Gary? Gabriel's real name was Gary?

Daniel huffed. "Eve, this is important."

The grin disappeared from Eve's face—clearly, she'd no idea why she was here either.

"We've had a radio transmission from a group of survivors," Gabriel began.

"They're close by I take it?" Eve asked, rubbing her sodden red curls on the towel.

"Folkestone," Gabriel replied. "But it's not good news. They've come through the tunnel from France, but it appears one of the southern nuclear power stations there wasn't shut down properly after the outbreak and has now broken containment."

As humanity dwindled, most of the governments worldwide had ordered the nuclear plants to be shut down and made as safe as possible. Given the short amount of time they'd had to complete such a massive task, it seemed inevitable that one or more of them would eventually cause a problem.

"They're all suffering the effects of radiation sickness," Daniel interjected. "We need to pick them up and bring them here as soon as possible." He turned to Nate, "We need you to do as much as you can to make them comfortable until we can…make them well again."

My blood boiled. "You're going to drown them!"

Gabriel held his hands up. "No one said that. Well, no one apart from Daniel."

Daniel's nostrils flared. "Well, what else do you suggest we do?"

"I suggest," Gabriel snapped, "That we pick them up and take it from there."

"Fine," Daniel responded in a flat tone.

"Nate, Halley, Eve, Ben, and I will go," Gabriel added.

Daniel shook his head. "I never agreed to Halley going. She's not evolved, won't this be dangerous for her?"

Gabriel rolled his eyes. "She'll be fine. I asked Erik if we were in any danger from the leak, given that it's relatively close to us. He said it was far enough away not to pose a threat to anyone—evolved or unevolved. For the time being, at least. However, he did suggest we decontaminate the survivors before bringing them back."

Nate nodded. "So, we take clean water for them to wash in and give them fresh clothes."

"Exactly," Gabriel agreed.

Daniel shook his head again. "Halley stays."

Eve put a hand on Daniel's shoulder. She whispered something into his ear, and he relaxed a little, giving me a half-smile.

"Fine," he conceded, his voice turning to a low mumble. "Just look after her."

He knew about the baby. It should've been obvious, given his reluctance to let me go and his sudden concern for my well-being. I couldn't be angry; Eve had kept my secret for far longer than I'd expected her to.

"When do we leave?" Nate asked.

Gabriel stood, his expression stern. "In an hour."

****

While Nate and Ben made a quick run back to the hospital for some medications and other supplies, I showered and found something warmer to wear—the nights were cold down by the coast this time of year. Nate suggested we clear out two of the classrooms adjacent to the science lab and set them up as a makeshift ward. Eve asked me to meet her there as soon as I'd finished dressing.

The smell of bleach was detectable from the stairwell and became even more pungent in the corridor by the lab. Tobias and Max barely noticed my arrival as they were busy assembling some metal bed frames. Claire gave me a nod as she unenthusiastically mopped the floor around them. Laura and Eve showed up a few minutes later, wheeling in the expensive-looking piece of equipment we'd looted from the hospital on the first pillaging trip.

"What *is* that for?" I asked.

"It's an ultrasound machine," Laura replied. "It's the simplest way to look inside our bodies to see what changes the virus has made."

Claire looked up. "And to look at babies. I saw Peter on one of those before he was born."

She gave me a quick wink and then returned to her cleaning duties.

Laura scoffed, her hands going to her hips. "Thanks for that useless bit of trivia, Claire."

"Not useless," Claire muttered without taking her eyes off the mop.

"It is since no one here is pregnant nor ever likely to be," Laura replied.

Eve chided in, her eyebrows rutting into a disapproving smirk. "Ye of little faith."

"What can I say? I'm cynical. I'm supposed to believe that somehow, Nate can miraculously fix the infertility issue when the experts couldn't. He must have *some* magic wand!"

Claire snorted with laughter while Eve firmly pressed her lips together. I retreated into the corridor, with hot cheeks and a smile hidden under my palm.

"Maybe he does have a magic wand, it might explain a few things," Eve muttered under her breath as she followed me out.

"Do you need me for anything else?" Laura sniped. "If not, I'm going to find some *adults* to converse with!"

"You do that," Eve replied, still smirking.

Unable to stomach the smell of chlorine a moment longer, I excused myself and headed down to the courtyard for some much-needed fresh air. The pick-up truck was ready and waiting, although Erik had his head under the bonnet, checking the oil from what I could see.

It wasn't long before Nate and Ben returned—in a red Volvo estate I hadn't seen before—and once all the designated travelers were present, we set off for Folkestone.

It wasn't a long drive from London, but our

progress was hindered several times by cars blocking our route. The motorway was mostly devoid of other vehicles until we were about three miles from a turn-off housing an army barricade. To pass by, we had to clear a space big enough for our cars to squeeze through, which took over two hours.

It involved the rather unpleasant job of removing the corpse-driver from behind the wheel of each car and then letting the handbrake off to steer them to the left or right, leaving a just-about-big-enough gap in the center of the road for us to drive down. All in all, a one-hour journey took almost four hours, though at least we knew it'd be quicker coming back.

The survivors had told Gabriel they'd be waiting in a hotel not far from the channel tunnel, but by the time we found the place, it was close to midnight and pitch black. Ben went to the boot of the Volvo and handed us each a torch—Eve and Gabriel also carried dart guns. To my surprise, Ben had brought Nate's rifle along, which he slung over his shoulder with a grin.

Nate didn't look at all impressed. Ben simply laughed and said, "Better to have it and not need it than to need it and not have it."

A part of me couldn't disagree with his statement, but before we even got inside the hotel, a man appeared in the entrance doorway, hands in the air, looking terrified.

"P—please, we have no weapons," he stuttered. He spoke with a French accent.

Nate stepped forward. "I'm a doctor," he said softly. "I can help you."

The man slowly lowered his hands and beckoned for us all to follow him inside. He led us through the hotel lobby and into a dining area lit with dozens of candles.

"My name is Luc," he said, his voice strained. "And this—" He gestured to a man slumped up against the wall, a blanket over his legs. "Is Phillipe."

Phillipe's breathing was labored, and he barely managed to raise a hand in acknowledgment as we approached.

Phillipe was *not* a survivor. As my torchlight found his face, I noticed instantly that his eyes were *not ringed* with red. I turned back to Luc, but he'd moved away to the bar area. He waved his hand to someone who was hiding behind the long, black, glass counter.

"*Tout va bien, sortez.*"

Ben impulsively went for his rifle, but Eve quickly slapped a hand across his chest and stood in front of him. "Down boy."

Two figures crawled out from behind the bar. The first was a young girl with long, mahogany-brown hair, no older than ten years old.

"Isabelle," Luc said.

When he motioned for her to go toward us, she got to her feet and walked forward, although it clearly took effort. The other figure was smaller and younger than Isabelle. He had a head of blonde, curly hair and a round, dimpled face.

"Sebastian," Luc mumbled, helping him stand.

As they all moved closer toward us, I identified the red ring in both Luc and Isabelle, but Sebastian's bright blue eyes were untouched by the mark of the virus.

Not good news.

My eyes flickered to Nate. By the stricken look on his face as he observed the little boy, it was obvious he'd come to the same conclusion that I had. Not everyone here was going to make it.

Our fears soon came to pass. Less than half an hour later, Phillipe was dead.

****

Before…

One morning, I awoke to discover it was my birthday. For once, the weather was about right to be March, so I reluctantly accepted being another year older, despite my disinclination to celebrate.

Rebecca had risen early to decorate the living room with streamers and a home-made banner that had 'Twenty-four' painted across it in big, pink writing. Looking at those two numbers was a jarring reminder of how much time had passed since the outbreak—more than four years.

She came in from the garden and beamed me a broad smile. "Happy birthday," she said and then threw her arms tightly around my neck.

I returned the hug but couldn't force a smile onto my face.

"I got you a present," she said, rushing into her room.

After a moment, she hurried back with a neatly wrapped, rectangular parcel in her hands. It would be a book because Rebecca always bought me books.

I unwrapped it carefully, crunching the wrapping paper up in my hand, making a fist.

"Alice's Adventures in Wonderland."

"I know that you left your mother's copy back at the flat, and I finally found the same edition in a charity shop last year!" she smiled, entwining her fingers together in glee.

My fingers trailed over the faded red cover, tracing around the gold image of Alice in the center. I lifted the book to my nose and sniffed it. This one smelled slightly of mold and furniture polish, not like my copy, which carried the scent of my mother's favorite perfume.

"Thank you."

She nodded and told me to sit down while she cooked breakfast. I went into my room and slid the book onto the bottom shelf of my bookcase.

I'd read 'Alice' so many times, I knew the story off by heart. I didn't need the book in front of me to immerse myself in Wonderland.

She meant well with her gift, but she didn't understand. She would never understand.

Sitting on my bed and gazing around my room, the four walls seemed to be closing in on me little by little as each day passed. I'd stared at them for so long over the past few years that I knew every tiny smudge on the lilac paintwork and noticed each new crack that appeared.

I couldn't do this anymore.

I couldn't let another year go by without knowing if there was anyone else out there.

She wouldn't stop me this time.

Back in the kitchen, the smell of onions and eggs filled the air as she fried an omelet in a pan over the camping stove. She scooped it out onto a plate and handed it to me.

"I'm leaving, Rebecca," I said, my hands shaking as I gripped the edges of the floral dish.

She gave me a sad nod. "I know."

Chapter Twenty-Three

After…

Eve helped Luc wash the children down with fresh water and gave them new clothes to wear, although nothing we'd brought with us fit them. No one had been told there were children here. In the end, Isabelle and Sebastian just ended up in t-shirts, and after Luc had been adequately decontaminated, all three of them sat in the back of the Volvo estate with blankets and pillows. Isabelle cried softly from time to time, muttering in French about Phillipe and burying her head into Luc's chest.

"*Ne pleure pas, mon petit enfant,*" he whispered to her.

Sebastian slept the entire way back to school after Nate gave him some pain relief and a few other tablets, making him instantly drowsy.

"Are they *your* children?" I asked Luc.

"They may as well be," Luc answered. His English was very good.

He was a man in his early forties with short, black hair and the beginnings of a reddish beard on his chin. His face was thin, but attractive, with pale, blue eyes and thick bushy eyebrows.

He hugged Isabelle closer to him. "Before the virus, I was a pastor. I often visited an orphanage just outside of Nice. When the children became sick, I went there to help them," he said. "I got sick, but I survived. Isabelle was only five at the time, but by some miracle, she made it too. Bastian, I suppose, is immune."

"And Phillipe?" I asked.

He swallowed hard. "We found Phillipe about a year after. He became a dear friend to me and the children."

I gave him a half-smile and turned my attention back to the road. Nate, who sat beside me on the back passenger seat, watched Sebastian closely, monitoring his every breath.

It was almost three A.M when we arrived back at the school. The only light emanated from Daniel's office, where he and Laura waited up for us to return. They were both in the courtyard before we'd even parked up.

The first thing Eve did when she got out of the car, was throw her arms around Daniel and bury her head in the opening of his cardigan. Luc slid from the open tailgate with Sebastian curled up in his arms, but he was too weak to carry him any further. Nate quickly came to his aid, gently putting Sebastian over his shoulder. Isabelle insisted on walking unaided, but as soon as we reached the stairwell, she began to struggle, breathing hard.

"It's okay princess, I got you," Ben said, swooping her up onto his hip.

It was a tender side of Ben I hadn't seen before, and I wondered if he'd been a father before the outbreak.

I helped Luc on the stairs, but he was breathless by the time we reached the first floor. He paused before the double-doors to steady himself and get his bearings.

"We didn't know about the radiation until Phillipe got ill. I thought it was the virus, but then Bastian and Isabelle—" He coughed and covered his mouth. There was a trace of blood on his bottom lip before he wiped it away.

"You need to rest," I said, ushering him down the corridor and into the treatment room.

The children had already been tucked into the beds while Nate and Laura set up intravenous drips for them.

"Can you be brave for me?" Laura asked Isabelle as she was about to insert a cannula into a vein on the back of Isabelle's hand.

Luc shuffled over to Isabelle's bed and muttered something reassuring to her. I found him a chair to sit on and gave him some water to drink, but there wasn't much more I could do to help.

"Halley, go to bed," Nate said, flashing me a quick smile.

"No, I want to help."

"There's nothing you can do right now," he whispered. "I'm going to administer some morphine for their pain and then get my head down for a few hours too. Get some rest, Halley."

Reluctantly, I left, making my way back the dormitories in darkness, relying on moonlight to show me the way. To save power, most of the corridor lights were turned off around midnight by whoever was on duty. Tobias or Ben normally took it in turns to patrol, but tonight—or rather, this morning—Erik was the one protecting our perimeter.

From what I'd gathered, the biggest threat to our safety came from wild animals who sometimes dug in under the fences, searching for food. I ran into Erik just as I entered the west wing. He and a woman by the name of Disa were canoodling in the stairwell, and both gasped in surprise when I came through the double doors.

"How is everyone?" Erik asked, looking sheepish.

Disa stepped forward and clutched my forearm. I hadn't seen much of her since I'd arrived as she usually had her head under an engine or deep in the innards of one of the generators. An Egyptian-born engineer and self-professed nerd, Mandisa and tech-head Erik had hit it off immediately, according to Priya. Their romance was currently the talk of the community. It was heart-warming to see them together.

I knew some of Disa's story from things Priya had told me. Mandisa and her husband had been working in Canada at the time of the outbreak but tried to get home to Aswan by boarding a flight, before all the airport closures began. They'd been diverted to Manchester and quarantined, where they'd both caught the virus. Disa survived but her husband didn't. Priya had eventually followed her sixth sense and found Disa living alone in an old football stadium. Later, they'd headed to Scotland—again guided by Priya's intuition.

"How are the children?" Disa asked me. News of our new arrivals traveled fast, it seemed.

"Stable for now," I replied.

She shook her head. "Poor babies. My father went to Fukushima after the disaster there. He saw people with radiation sickness, and it gave him nightmares. I pray the children can be saved. And their dear *baba,* of course."

Erik gave a heavy sigh. "We'll hope for a miracle."

Hope and *miracle* were two words used a lot

around here. "Yes," I replied flatly, then smiled. "I'm off to bed. As you were."

Erik gave me another coy grin before I ascended the stairs, my footsteps muffling the sound of Disa's breathy giggling.

Eve and Daniel's bedroom door was ajar when I entered the dormitory corridor. Lingering a few feet away, hidden in the shadowy folds of one of the heavy curtains, my ears pricked to the sound of their muffled voices.

"Eve," Daniel said, in a low, soothing voice. "Please…"

"I can't help it, Daniel," Eve replied. Her voice was raspy, and I heard her sniff. "They're kids."

"I know. I know," Daniel replied.

Eve began to cry softly. Seeing the children so ill must have stirred up more than a few unpleasant memories for her. Despite her strong and cool facade, she clearly still grieved deeply for the children she'd lost. I couldn't imagine a worse pain and hoped never to experience anything like it myself.

Absently, my hand dropped to my lower belly, and I stroked it gently. It was a strange feeling to love someone I hadn't met yet. Even worse, to fear losing them before having the chance to hold them in my arms.

Poor Eve. Poor everyone. We'd all experienced enough death to last a thousand lifetimes. To lose another—especially a child so young as Sebastian—would be devastating. But, what could Nate do? Sebastian was immune, and if Nate couldn't save him, the little boy wouldn't be coming back to life.

I moved away from Eve's door, slowly tiptoeing

along to my room, trying not to disturb the floorboards as my weight shifted from one foot to another. Apart from a few inaudible creaks, I reached my door and managed to open it without making a sound. The last thing I wanted was to disturb Eve and Daniel, then get accused of eavesdropping. In a matter of minutes, my clothes were piled neatly on the floor next to our bed, and my body was comfortably wrapped up in the cozy duvet.

"Goodnight," I whispered, placing my hand back on my belly, feeling the faintest of flutters just below my navel. I wondered if it was my imagination or maybe a nerve, but the fluttering moved left and right and then a little further down.

My baby was moving.

I intended to stay awake awhile, to observe more of the nudges and bubbling, finding the sensation both wondrous and reassuring, but my weary body had other ideas.

****

My eyes didn't reopen again until just after midday. By the lack of disheveled sheets on Nate's side of the bed, he hadn't come to bed at all, so I headed straight for the canteen to get him something to eat and a strong coffee before heading to the science classrooms.

Upon returning, I found Nate sound asleep on one of the spare beds. Loathed to wake him, I gave the coffee to Eve, who sat by Sebastian, watching him as he slept.

"Where's Luc?" I whispered to her.

"He's in the room next door. He's pretty sick and didn't want the children to see," she said, not taking her eyes away from Sebastian's pale face.

"How are they doing?" I asked, glancing across the room to Isabelle, who snored softly as she slept. In the daylight, her illness was painfully obvious. Her skin was yellowing while her lips showed a blueish tinge. The shadows beneath her eyes leached all the way down to her sunken, sallow cheeks.

"There's nothing Nate can do for them," she whispered. "Daniel wants to evolve Isabelle and Luc, but Nate asked for a little more time. Daniel has given him till tonight."

While I disliked the idea of drowning Luc and Isabelle—a child, for Christ's sake—in the fountain, it was the lesser of two evils in comparison to a slow and painful death by radiation poisoning. They would live.

Sebastian, on the other hand, would not.

An impossible situation with no solution. Shaking my head sorrowfully, I slumped down into the chair beside Isabelle's bed and took her hand in mine. She squeezed my fingers but didn't open her eyes. An hour later, Luc came in, flanked on either side by Ben and Laura, who helped him to walk. He'd diminished significantly in the eight hours since I'd last seen him, although his dilated pupils gave me the impression he'd been heavily medicated. This probably contributed to his inability to walk unaided.

I stood to let him take my seat next to Isabelle. As I leaned in close to kiss her forehead, I realized something was wrong. Still and silent, Isabelle had stopped breathing.

"Nate!" I shrieked.

He was up and by my side in seconds, a hand immediately on her neck, feeling for a pulse.

His voice was hoarse. "She's gone into cardiac arrest!"

"My Isabelle!" Luc bellowed.

Nate kneeled awkwardly on the side of the bed and knitted his fingers together, placing his hands firmly on Isabelle's diaphragm. After muttering a count-down with each compression, he breathed into her mouth in short bursts. As a doctor, letting Isabelle slip away went against every constitution he stood for, but in this case, it was the preferable outcome.

I gently pried his interlocked fingers away from Isabelle's heart and held them tightly while the seconds ticked by.

"What are you doing?" Luc shouted. "Do something!"

Nate grit his teeth together but didn't move, staring into my eyes with an anguish-ridden intensity, as if our locked gaze was the only thing keeping him from trying to resuscitate Isabelle again.

"She'll be all right," Ben said.

Luc pulled out of his grasp, a seething expression darkening his face. "What the hell are you talking about? She's dying! Do something!"

"No," Ben said firmly.

Luc, of course, didn't know the things that *we* knew. He was certain that his daughter was about to die—for good—and from all appearances, it looked as though we were happy to let it happen.

He must've used every last ounce of his strength to lunge forward and drag Nate off the bed. He rammed him up against the wall, his fist slamming hard into the side of his face. Ben was on Luc before he got the opportunity to throw another punch, twisting his arm up behind his back and forcing him down onto the ground, face first. Luc didn't have the fight in him to resist, especially after Laura stuck him with a needle, promptly knocking him out.

I rushed around the bed to Nate and threw my arms around him. "You did everything you could," I whispered. My hand went to the red welt on his cheek and he winced back with a hiss.

"Sorry."

"I'll live."

He held me for a few moments longer and then went over to Sebastian's bed. Eve hadn't moved from his side, despite the commotion, her focus solely on the little boy.

"I wish there were something I could do for him," Nate said, brushing one of Sebastian's cherub curls aside to lay his hand on his forehead. Judging by the moisture on his skin and the redness in his cheeks, Sebastian was running a fever.

A lump formed in my throat. It was getting harder and harder to watch the little boy suffer, and it would only get worse from here on in.

There had to be a way to save him. "What if you could infect him with the virus?"

Eve's gaze finally shifted from Sebastian to give me a stark and stony glare. "He'd die!"

"With the version of the virus that learned not to kill its host, I mean."

Nate shook his head. "Even if I knew a way of doing that, I can't. He's resistant to it. Somehow, his body can fight off the virus. I need more time, but—" he stopped when his voice became hoarse, his eyes glistening as he glanced at Eve.

Her face instantly contorted with sorrow. "How long?"

He bowed his head. "In a few hours, his pain will be unbearable."

Eve's eyes filled with tears, but she wiped them away quickly with the sleeve of her cardigan. "We can't let him suffer. There must be something you can give him to…end it before that happens."

He glared at her. "I can't Eve…"

"Just tell me what to give him. I'll do it," Eve said, her jaw tensed resolutely.

He looked to me for counsel. I simply nodded and said, "Eve's right. We can't let him suffer."

"Christ," he whispered and covered his face with his hands. "Okay. I'll…get…it ready."

Eve turned to me. "Halley, can you find Daniel for me? He'll probably be in his office."

My heart felt so heavy; I could hardly move. It took all of my willpower to leave the room and walk along the corridor.

As it happened, on my way down, Daniel and I collided on the stairwell. He barely acknowledged me as he passed, ascending each stair as if the effort exhausted him. From the bottle-shaped bulge in his jacket pocket and the eye-watering stench of alcohol on his breath, he'd been drinking heavily for the past few hours.

"Eve needs you," I said softly.

Daniel rubbed his face. "Yes, Ben told me about Sebastian." He leaned back against the metal handrail and lowered his head.

In my time here, I'd found Daniel the most perplexing, but only because he rarely did anything that gave away any feelings of deep emotion. He generally maintained a stern façade, but occasionally, with Eve, he relaxed and was able to laugh a little.

"She's upset."

Daniel kept his attention fixed on the floor. "I don't know how to help her."

Reaching out a hand, I gave his arm an awkward pat. "You can't help her. She just needs you to be with her."

Daniel's mouth opened to respond but fell silent when Gabriel, red-faced and wild-eyed, came rushing up the stairs. His fists clenched around the fabric of Daniel's jacket as he swung him around and pinned him against the stairwell wall.

"What the hell, Daniel?" he yelled.

Daniel didn't look surprised by the sudden intrusion, and he did not attempt to fight Gabriel off. "It's for the best."

Confused, I stepped away, my eyes darting between the two men.

Gabriel shook his head. "I asked you to let me speak to him first! To try and explain—" he spat.

Daniel shrugged off his grip and straightened the creases in his jacket left by the imprint of Gabriel's sweaty palms. "What's the point? He won't understand. They never do."

As he watched Daniel climb the stairs, Gabriel glowered at his disappearing shadow and muttered a string of swear words.

"Bastard," Gabriel snarled. He hurried back down the stairs without so much as a glimpse in my direction.

"What's going on?" I asked, following him.

"Ben has taken Luc to the fountain. On Daniel's

orders. I wanted a chance to explain everything to him first."

Out in the courtyard, the rain fell heavily from a thick swell of gray clouds, making everything so much darker than it should've been for mid-afternoon. Ben and Laura were stood by the fountain, either side of Luc, who lay on the gravel slumped limply against the concrete basin. He stared ahead blankly, his face full of confusion and shock.

At the sight of Gabriel stomping toward him, Ben adopted a determined stance, like a bull about to charge. "I'm just following orders, Gabe."

While the two men exchanged heated words, I dropped down onto the gravel next to Luc and took hold of his hand. The rain had soaked him to the bone, and he shivered so violently my fingers struggled to keep a grip on him.

"I'm so sorry."

"Isabelle?" Luc mumbled, but he didn't look at me when he spoke. A thin trickle of blood seeped from the corner of his left eye and ran down his cheek, instantly washed away by the deluge of rain. A scaly red rash had begun to form on his forehead, spreading into his hairline. In parts, the skin had begun to lift and blacken, exposing raw muscle.

If we didn't drown him now, his death would be an excruciating one.

"Isabelle will be all right, Luc. I promise," I said, using my index finger to push his sodden fringe away from his eyes.

His head rolled back as he looked at me, blinking slowly. He didn't understand that Isabelle wasn't really dead, and he was no state to be educated on the subject.

If he even believed it.

As loathe as I was to admit it, Daniel was right—there was no other way. If we did this now, Sebastian might still be alive when Luc woke up, and he'd be able to say goodbye to his son.

Sebastian. I wanted to scream. This was all so unfair. All of it.

I closed my eyes and thought of the red desert, silently imploring *them* for help. I might've even uttered a prayer out loud, but not to any deity. My prayers were to *them*. In the blackness behind my closed eyes, I suddenly saw myself standing in front of Lizzie, her hand over my heart, blue bursts of static emanating from her palm.

And then I knew what to do.

I unbuttoned the top few buttons of Luc's shirt and placed my hand on his chest. It took only a matter of seconds for the static buzz to build and spread out in waves like ripples in a pond.

Luc's body arched and shook for a moment before his eyes rolled back in his head, and he dropped sideways onto the gravel.

"What the—" Laura screeched, dropping to her knees. She felt for a pulse on his neck, and then on his wrist. "He's dead."

Having just killed a man, I promptly upchucked and then blacked out. The last thing I remembered was the sharp, wet gravel digging into the side of my face as I collided with the ground.

Lizzie waits for me.

She stands in a field of long grass and cow parsley; the little white flowers tickle my knees as I brush past.

Lizzie smiles. "I knew you could do it. He was right

about you."

I sigh. "Who was? I don't understand."

"You will soon, I promise. There is someone here with us who has a story to tell you, but not right now," she says. "Just know that both you and Nate are very important to us. As is your daughter. Trust in us."

Easier said than done.

Lizzie turns to walk away, but I grab her shoulder. "Tell me how to save Sebastian!" I demand. "Tell me if there's a way to infect him with the virus and live. Please? Your virus accidentally killed seven-and-a-half-billion people. We've seen enough death. Please help us."

Lizzie frowns. "What makes you think it was an accident?"

"Nate said...he thought the virus made a mistake..." I shake my head in disbelief. "You murdered seven and a half billion people on purpose?"

Lizzie takes a deep breath and gives me a solemn look. "Do you know what would've become of humanity if you'd all carried on as you were?"

A lump sticks in my throat.

"Humanity's end was a brutal one. More violent and devastating than you could possibly imagine. A thousand times worse than our virus," Lizzie tells me, with an indignant glare. "But because of our intervention, those souls live on. Every life the virus takes—and will ever take—is here. Trillions upon trillions of souls."

My eyes grow wide. I have many questions, but no time to ask them. "What about Sebastian? He doesn't have the virus! He's dying."

Lizzie smiles. "Do you choose him to be one of

you?"

I nod. "Of course! Yes."

"Then give him our blood," she answers.

"Will that save him?" I ask.

Lizzie raises an eyebrow. "Do you trust us?"

"Yes," I answer, resolutely. What choice did I have?

Lizzie gives me a doubtful look, but chuckles. "Our blood is the key. Tell Nate, and he'll know what to do."

Before I have the chance to thank her, she shimmers like heat rising from a hot pavement, and disappears. For a few seconds, I watch the empty space that Lizzie's body had occupied, feeling a strange sense of loss. It isn't long before I shimmer and disappear too.

****

Before…

"I know that you've not been happy, but are you sure you want to do this?" Rebecca asked me as I made my preparations to leave.

"I have to."

She nodded and looked out of the kitchen window at the heavy gray clouds about to burst and deliver a torrent of rain upon us. "Fine. I won't stop you, but do something for me?"

I looked up from the map I'd spread across the kitchen table. "What?"

Rebecca pulled up a chair next to me. "Wait till cold weather has passed. It might still snow—"

"No," I cut her off.

She grunted angrily. "Freezing to death for the sake of waiting a few months tells me you aren't as sensible as I think you are."

I'd assumed it was another ploy to make me stay, but her logic was sound. Having to pack for wintry conditions meant carrying extra clothing and supplies. If the weather did turn icy or snowy, I really didn't want to be stuck out in it with no guarantee of finding a warm place to sleep.

"Okay," I said dejectedly.

"Thank you," she replied. "I'll help you and make sure that you have everything you need."

Would she really help me, or would she would change her mind again and beg me not to go?

"Why don't you come with me?" I asked her. I'd do it alone if need be, but I'd rather not leave her by herself if there was any chance she might accompany me.

She shook her head. "No. I've seen everything I needed to see."

I sighed. "You're sure there's no one alive out there?"

She considered my question for a moment. "The only thing you'll find out there is death."

I turned away from her.

"Besides, even if you *did* find someone, how do you know they'd be...all right?" she added.

"What do you mean?"

She shrugged. "Desperate, lonely people do dark and desperate things."

A chill ran up my spine. It wasn't like the thought hadn't crossed my mind.

"I *am* a little worried about stumbling across a community of cannibals," I answered her, with a grin.

She gave me a stern look. "I'm glad my worry for you is amusing."

Taking hold of her hand, I gave her a reassuring smile. "I'll be fine. You've been out there plenty of times and come back in one piece."

"I know," she huffed. "But you'll probably end up going further than I ever did. I know you, Halley. You won't give up easily."

She was probably right. "I won't be gone long. I promise."

Her expression was skeptical. "We'll see."

Chapter Twenty-Four

After…

What felt like hours, lasted only minutes. I awoke to find myself slumped over Ben's shoulder as he carried me down the corridor, toward the stairwell. As I dangled limply down his back, the blood rushing to my head filled my ears with a throbbing, thunderous roar, prompting me to slide awkwardly from Ben's grasp.

"Luc will be awake in a few hours," I muttered. "You should get him somewhere comfortable."

"It usually takes longer than that," Ben answered.

"Not this time."

"How would you know that?"

I shrugged. "I just do."

Ben snickered, although there was a shadow of uneasiness in his eyes.

"I have to see Nate. Now"

I ran, my wet shoes squeaking and slipping on the smooth floor tiles as my feet hit the stairs, taking two at a time.

"I know how to help Sebastian," I panted, bursting in through the door of the treatment room.

Eve and Daniel were sat together on the far side of Sebastian's bed, arms around each other as Eve cried onto Daniel's shoulder. Nate stood next to the intravenous drip trolley, about to inject a syringe of something into the clear tube attached to Sebastian's hand. He spun to look at me as I stood shivering in the doorway, a puddle forming at my feet.

"What *happened* to you?" Nate asked, aghast. He grabbed a blanket from one of the other beds and threw it around my shoulders.

"Long story. Not much time," I breathed. "You have to give Sebastian our blood."

He stared at me for a moment and then turned back to the little sleeping boy. "Like a transfusion, you mean?"

"Maybe. I don't know. *They* said it would make him like us—a survivor. The virus won't kill him. *They* said you'd know what to do."

He started rummaging through one of the boxes of supplies he and Ben had brought back from the hospital yesterday.

Daniel stood. "What good will giving him a blood transfusion do?"

Nate tipped the box upside down onto one of the empty beds. "It will bombard his body with the virus. It might just be enough to stop his immune system from resisting it. Especially in his weakened condition."

Daniel regarded Sebastian, a pensive frown wrinkling his forehead. "We infect him, and then we evolve him so that his body can heal?"

Eve suddenly came-to from her distracted grief state, a horrified look on her face. "We can't do that to a child, can we?"

I went to tell her that we didn't have to drown people anymore, but Nate spoke first.

"We might not have to evolve him, not straight away at least," he said. "Think about how the virus works. Every cell in his body will be replaced and thus no longer affected by the radiation exposure. Apart from his brain cells, anyway. They will still be irradiated, but I may be able to treat him with potassium iodide in the short term. In any case, if it works, it'll buy us some time."

"*If* it works," Daniel added.

My eyes drifted to Eve who's reddened, tear strewn eyes began to look hopeful.

"It *will* work," I said, mostly to her.

"Do it," she replied.

Nate gathered together everything he needed and then radioed for Laura to come back to the treatment room. As soon as she stepped through the door, he ordered her to set everything up.

"Eve, what's your blood type?" Nate asked.

Eve hunched her shoulders. "I don't know!"

He directed the same question to Daniel.

"O positive," he replied.

"Perfect," Nate said. "Roll up your sleeve."

To get out of the way, I went and sat on the spare bed. Eve came and sat beside me after being asked by Laura, somewhat brusquely, to move. I put my arm around her, not knowing what else to do.

"How did you know how to help him? Did Claire speak with *them*?" she asked, after ten minutes of silently observing everything that was happening.

"No," I said. "*They* told *me*."

Both Laura and Nate glanced over to me briefly then. Nate smiled in a supportive kind of way, but Laura was obviously unsettled. The look she gave me was the same look people gave to Claire when she came out with her nonsensical utterings.

"How?"

"In my dreams."

If my revelation surprised Eve, she certainly didn't show it. In fact, she gave me a slow nod and a knowing smile, like she'd seen it coming. "You sound like Claire."

"I know."

"*They* tell you anything else?" Daniel asked, wincing as Laura jabbed a needle into a vein in his arm.

I wanted to be honest about my communication. "The virus did exactly as it was supposed to. It meant to wipe us out. There was no mistake."

Nate snapped his head up, anger flashing in his eyes. "They purposefully committed mass genocide?"

Was this the appropriate time to be making such revelations? Somehow I doubted there would ever be a good time to explain it.

"They don't see it that way." I went on to describe my encounter with Lizzie and what she'd told me about how every soul they killed with their virus was now with them, wherever that was.

"They're not gone?" Eve asked me, the hope in her eyes growing exponentially. She took great comfort in my statement, and the others would too.

"It's a kind of *afterlife*, I think," I mused.

Everyone fell silent then, in quiet contemplation. The word *afterlife* had ramifications. Perhaps I should've chosen a different term to explain it, but something told me I'd described it perfectly.

"And who are *they*, exactly?" Nate asked, finally.

There was no way to respond to that question. Were they Gods? Angels? Aliens? None of those appellations seemed correct. Whatever *they* were, it was a term we didn't have in our human vocabulary. *Yet.*

Giving a shrug and a palms-up gesture, I stood. "I need to get out these wet clothes."

Nate moved close to me and whispered in my ear. "You okay?"

I nodded. "Yeh, we'll talk more later."

Back in our bedroom, I hurriedly shed my wet clothing and got into the shower. The water was hotter than usual, the blissful heat quickly taking the chill off. After spending so long under the shower that my fingertips puckered, I got out and dried myself off, before deciding to rest a little before heading back to see how Sebastian was doing.

Of course, once my body was warm and cozy under the soft duvet, not even an earthquake could have stopped me from falling asleep. The dreams that entered my mind were the nonsensical variety, not a red desert in sight.

The sound of the shower running finally roused me again, whether it was minutes or hours later, I couldn't tell. Nate appeared, naked and wet, toweling himself down, as I stretched and yawned.

"How long was I asleep?"

He smiled and then climbed in under the covers with me. "About six hours."

Obviously not the brief cat nap I'd intended it to be. "How's Sebastian?"

"Stable. I took the opportunity to check in on you and take a shower."

"Will he make it?"

"Yes. Thanks to you."

He slid his hand up my thigh and around to my back, pulling me into him for a long, hungry kiss. I swung my leg over his pelvis and then pushed myself up on top of him, kissing his lips forcefully while my hand guided him into the space between my legs. He groaned as my body met his, my hips finding a leisurely rhythm that rapidly generated a pleasant tingle within me.

When my pace increased, and my breathing quickened, he swore and grabbed hold of my waist, controlling my movements in such a way that, seconds later, I trembled from the sweet release, feeling him pulse with gratification at the same moment.

"Nate," I whispered, after collapsing down onto his chest. "I need to tell you something."

He stroked my hair and kissed the top of my head. "What is it?"

The butterflies of anxiety instantly began to dart about in my chest. I rolled back onto the bed and sat upright, wrapping myself up in the duvet.

He sighed. "I know something isn't right with you," he said, sitting up and swinging his legs out of bed. He got up and walked over to our dresser, pulling out some jeans and a fresh pair of boxers. He dressed and then stood nervously in the center of the room with his arms crossed.

His expression became serious. "Whatever it is, just tell me."

Sliding off the bed, I shuffled over to the dresser and dropped the duvet once I'd pulled on a long, baggy t-shirt dress.

"There are a few things I need to tell you," I said, moving in front of him and putting my arms around his waist. "But I've been too scared to say anything. I thought if something bad happened, it would be better if you never found out."

"What?"

"You told me once that you couldn't lose anyone else that you cared about," I said. "I thought by not telling you, I could protect you."

He shook his head, flustered. "From what? Halley, you're scaring me!"

I breathed deeply and cast my glance toward the window, watching the dribbles of rain meander down the glass against the backdrop of a dark night. "My head is messed up."

"I already knew that."

"My mum didn't die of a heart attack, Nate." The words almost choked me. "She killed herself."

He exhaled and rubbed his face. "Oh, Halley. I'm so sorry."

I kept my eyes fixed on the winding raindrops. "I loved her, but it wasn't enough."

Nate drew in a sharp breath and stood beside me. His fingers gently nudged against my chin, slowly bringing my head around to face him. "No matter how bad things might get, I swear that all the while you live and breathe, you're stuck with me."

I laughed but took another deep, shaky breath before continuing. "I needed you to know how I felt because it's the reason I've been keeping things from you. I wanted to make sure everything was going to be okay before I told you. But, the truth is, I don't know if it's going to be okay. I mean, I think it is—"

The worried frown reappeared on his brow as he cut me off. He'd clearly had enough of my ambiguous rambling. "Just tell me!"

"I'm—you're—" I stammered. "You're going to be a father, Nate."

He stared at me and then laughed. "What?"

"I'm pregnant, Nate."

He stiffened and let his hands drop to his sides. "No, you can't be."

"I took a test."

"Tests can be wrong," he said, matter-of-factly.

A nervous laugh left my lips. He didn't believe me. "It wasn't wrong."

"It's also not possible for you to be pregnant."

His reaction had me at a loss. Aside from asking him to confirm it with a blood test, I didn't know how else to convince him.

I grabbed his hand and placed it on my stomach. "I know it's probably too early for you to be able to feel anything, but she's moving around."

He snatched his hand back. "This is madness! You are *not* pregnant!"

A growl of exasperation rattled in my throat as I forced his hand back on my lower abdomen.

Then, from somewhere in my poor, addled brain, I heard a whisper.

"*Show him.*"

I put my hand over his and moved his palm down to where I felt the bubbling sensation.

"Close your eyes."

"Halley—"

"Shut up and close them," I snapped.

"Fine."

In the same way as I'd done with Luc, I concentrated on forming the static in between our touched hands.

Claire was right when she told me the static could be used to send a message—just as the electrical impulses in our brains formed thoughts and memories—and, as I focused on trying to make him feel what I felt, the static warmed and prickled under my palm.

He suddenly gasped. "How are you doing that? I— I can feel it. She's moving—wait, she?" His eyes flew open, and he looked at me. "It's a girl?"

"I think so." Keeping the static going was making me lightheaded. I let go of his hand and put my arms around his neck.

"It's not...I don't understand how..." he stammered.

"Me either, but since you're the doctor, you'll have to figure it out."

He put his forehead against mine. "How far along do you think you are? If you can feel her moving, then you must be at least—"

"Fifteen weeks, almost. I think." I let out a long, weary sigh. "I should've told you sooner. I totally understand if you're pissed at me."

He shook his head. "I'm not pissed at you. Well, maybe a little, but I'll get over it. Once the shock wears off."

Then he kissed me with one of his urgent, dizzying kisses.

"I take it that you're okay with this?" I asked.

"What do *you* think?" he responded, with a grin. "Although there is one thing that kinda worries me."

"Only *one* thing? Lucky you." About a billion worries were circulating in my mind right now. "What is it?"

"What will Rebecca say?"

I laughed. "Oh, she's going to kick your arse, for sure. But she'll get over it." I parroted his previous words back to him. "Once the shock wears off."

****

Isabelle was up and walking around when we returned to the treatment room. She stood by the window, closely holding onto Eve as they both peered up at a bright, orange-tinted moon.

"We were just coming to find you," Eve said, smiling as she turned. She gestured to Sebastian, who was sat up in bed, eyes open with a wide, toothy grin as Laura spooned jelly into his mouth. He still looked a little pale and washed out. It'd be a while until he was back to a normal, precocious seven-year-old.

I walked over to him and looked into his eyes. His sky-blue irises were now ringed with red, and I never thought I'd be so happy to see the mark of the virus on someone. Nate did a quick check on Sebastian's vitals and then gave the boy a broad smile as he ruffled his blonde curls playfully. "He's a fighter. We'll see how he responds to the iodine before making a decision about further options."

Laura's mouth twitched into a labored smile. "Hasn't Halley told you, Nate? Evolution just *evolved*."

"We'll discuss that later," Eve said to Laura, throwing a disapproving glance her way. Laura must've reported back to her already on the incident with Luc in the courtyard earlier. With everything else going on, I'd forgotten to tell Nate about it. Frankly, he'd already had his fair share of surprises today and didn't need another one.

He looked at me. "You have something else you need to tell me?"

"Not right now," I sighed. "Later, okay?"

He nodded and smiled, turning his attention to

Isabelle. Now she'd evolved, there was probably no need to fuss over her, but he still made a point of looking into her ears with an otoscope and getting her to stick her tongue out and say 'ah.'

"Perfect! All better."

She giggled shyly, seeming to understand him, a reassured grin on her face.

Our brief moment of harmony was abruptly broken by the sound of a gunshot resounding in the corridor outside. We all recoiled instinctively, although Nate rushed swiftly to the doorway, glancing tentatively from left to right. When his face blanched and his hands went up beside his head, panic gripped my diaphragm, forcing the air from my lungs.

Without a second thought, I ran to Nate, positioning myself in front of him like a shield.

"Get back!" he muttered, using his body to try and maneuver me out the way.

I turned to see Luc at the far end of the corridor, Nate's rifle rested on his shoulder as he moved slowly toward us.

How the hell had he gotten hold of the gun?

"Where are my children?" Luc demanded.

At that moment, Ben and Daniel came thundering up the stairwell, crashing through the double doors and into the corridor, shock registering on their faces as Luc swung around and pointed the gun in their direction instead.

"Put it down, Luc," Daniel said to him in a stern and composed voice. "Put it down, and you can see your children."

Luc screwed up his nose as tears streaked his reddened cheeks. "My children are dead!"

"That's not true. They're alive and well."

He tensed. "Liar!"

Behind us, Eve slowly edged out of the treatment room, holding onto Isabelle's hand, keeping her firmly pressed to her hip, away from Luc's line of sight.

"Papa!" Isabelle called out to him.

Luc wheeled around, the rifle leveled at us again, although it sank a little upon hearing his daughter's voice. "Isabelle?"

She emerged from behind Eve and smiled sadly at him.

"You're alive?" Luc stuttered, an expression of astonishment on his face. He let the rifle slip from his shoulder as he charged readily toward us.

Ben, in his wisdom, used the distraction to lunge forward, hooking an arm around Luc's waist with the intent to tackle him down. Instead, Luc stumbled forward and fell to his knees, the rifle butt slamming hard onto the floor, triggering it to fire. The bang resounded throughout the corridor.

Daniel and Ben immediately piled onto Luc, pinning him flat to the floor with his arms forced behind his back. Isabelle screamed and ran toward her papa, Eve sprinting after her.

"Halley, are you—" Nate didn't finish his sentence.

When I looked up at him, his fraught expression became one of despair.

An intense, searing agony hit me then, radiating from the left, upper side of my chest. My vision blurred as I raised my right hand to my wound, feeling warm liquid flow like running water through the gaps in my fingers.

Nate caught me as I fell backward, lowering me

down onto the cold floor while yelling for help.

"No. No. No." He pushed down tightly on my wound to stop the bleeding as Laura fell to her knees and covered his hand with hers to add more pressure.

The pain grew more and more intense until it became a white-hot burning heat, sending me into a state of half-consciousness. Before the darkness covered me like a blanket, I felt Nate's breath against my cheek.

"Stay with me, Halley," was the last thing I heard him say.

****

Before…

The days became warmer and the nights became shorter, so I knew it was time to go.

Rebecca insisted on cooking a three-course meal for dinner the night before I left, promising an all-the-trimmings breakfast the next morning too. She was a little sad but supportive nonetheless, smiling whenever tears welled in her eyes and reminding me of anything I might have forgotten to pack. Her mood had lifted significantly since she'd gone back on her anti-depressants.

"You can still come with me," I said as she served up a spicy carrot and coriander soup—she'd managed to follow one of my recipes but had added a little too much chili powder. It was tasty, despite the fire burning in my mouth.

She poured herself a glass of red wine and then filled my glass to the brim. "No. I'll wait here and keep everything going, like you always did for me when I went away."

I wouldn't ask again. She'd made her decision and,

like it or not, this was to be a solitary quest.

By the time we finished eating, my stomach was full to bursting, and my head swam a little from the wine. Still, I offered to help clean up, but she said she'd do it in the morning.

"Get an early night," she said, not realizing it was gone ten o'clock already.

I nodded and stood up. "Thank you, Rebecca."

She got up and rounded the table to wrap me in a tight hug. "I love you, Halley. I wish you didn't have to go."

Was she about to beg me not to go?

She quickly kissed my cheek. "I'll wake you at nine for breakfast."

Smiling, I went to my bedroom and sat down on my bed, setting my battery-powered alarm clock for seven-thirty A.M. I had no intention of staying for breakfast and planned to sneak out early, leaving a note for her saying goodbye. I'd already written the letter and tucked it away in the drawer in my bedside cabinet. I'd written it so many times now, I could recite it from memory.

Rebecca,

I'm sorry that I left without saying goodbye. I'll miss you every day, but I promise not to be gone long. I'll find someone out there, I know it.

Love always,

Halley.

A cowardly way to leave, but if I'd said goodbye to her in person, there was a good chance my guilt would've forced me to stay.

Hoping the night would pass swiftly, I pulled the quilt up over me and laid back on my pillow.

Chapter Twenty-Five

After…

Drowsy and confused, I pried my eyelids apart with all the effort I could muster and groaned when the bright lights of the treatment room burned into my pupils.

"Halley," someone whispered. A women's voice—Eve, I think.

I turned my head slowly to see her sat next to me, holding onto my hand, which was attached to an intravenous drip of clear liquid. When I tried to sit up, a sharp pain stabbed at an area of muscle next to my collar bone, and I instantly grew weary, flopping back on the bed with a hiss.

"Take it easy!" Eve commanded in a tone that was somehow both soothing and imposing. Her shirt was splattered in blood, and smudges of red dotted her neck and jawline.

A feeling of dread sent me into a cold sweat. "Whose blood is that? Where's Nate?"

She tutted but then flashed me a smile. "I made him go shower and get something to eat. He's fine. It's *you* that had us all worried."

My mind slowly sharpened.

The gunshot. Luc. Pain. Panic.

"Eve! The baby? Is she—"

"You need to stay calm," she replied, cutting me

off.

I shook my head. "I can't calm down. I need to know if she's okay!"

"You need to rest. You lost a lot of blood, and Nate had to give you some of his. The bullet went right through your shoulder, but it nicked an artery."

Nate entered the room then, looking thoroughly exhausted and distraught. "Oh, thank Christ, you're awake!"

Eve stood and moved out of the way so he could sit next to me. As he rushed to my side and leaned over me to plant a kiss on my forehead, I noticed how raw and bloodshot his eyes were.

"Don't ever scare me like that again. Ever," he muttered, his lips touching mine briefly.

"I need to know if our baby's okay, Nate."

There were no little flutters in my stomach right now, which left me feeling more agitated with each passing minute, but it was the grim look on his face that sent me into a complete spiral.

"You lost *a lot* of blood, Halley."

I couldn't breathe. "What does *that* mean?"

"I tried to find the baby's heartbeat earlier with a Doppler," he began, but then paused.

"And?"

He bit his lip. "It might just mean it's too early to pick it up."

No heartbeat. This couldn't be happening.

No. She *had* to be okay. *They* were protecting her, right? That's why they didn't want me drowned in the fountain—it would harm her.

My mind raced. "I need to know."

He nodded. "We'll do an ultrasound. Now. But

Halley—"

"It's fine, Nate," I said, interrupting him, "I understand."

I knew what he was about to say—that whatever the outcome, he loved me and everything would be okay.

Not what I wanted to hear right now. It wouldn't be okay.

Eve came and sat back down beside me and tried to make small talk while Nate got the ultrasound machine ready and handed me a bottle of water to drink. He said having a full bladder would make the image clearer.

"Daniel and I moved Isabelle and Sebastian to our room for the time being," Eve said. "Until Luc is...better. Gabriel has been talking to him, trying to explain all this."

I nodded mechanically, not wanting to think about Luc. Even though he hadn't intended to shoot me, this *was* his fault.

He wheeled the ultrasound machine up to the left side of the bed and pushed my legs aside a little so that he could sit down. He gave me a blanket to cover up my naked, upper body as he pulled down the sheet covering me, gently tucking it into the hem of my pants.

I looked down at my wound. The bandage wrapped tightly across my left breast and shoulder had a two-inch round pool of blood staining it, just below my clavicle. He gave it a quick visual appraisal but seemed unconcerned. From that, I gathered the bleeding had stopped.

"This will be a little cold," he said, smearing something onto my stomach from a plastic bottle. He then turned the ultrasound machine screen away from me so I couldn't see it. When he put the sensor wand against my skin, his hand shook. I watched him closely as he ran the probe over the lower part of my belly, tapping on the ultrasound keyboard once he had located what he was looking for.

I held my breath until he smiled.

Eve immediately leaned over the bed so she could see the screen, practically crushing my shin with her elbow. She smiled too.

"For Christ's sake!" I snapped, exasperated, after a few long seconds of silence.

Nate broke out of his temporary trance to turn the screen around to face me.

It was just a jumble of black and gray shapes. "Where am I supposed to be looking?"

He grinned and ran his index finger around a shape on the screen. "Our baby."

Before pointing out a little flickering smudge in the middle of the screen, he quickly tapped a button on the keyboard in front of him. The speakers on the side of the screen crackled and began making a rhythmical drumming noise.

"Is that the sound of her heartbeat?"

He nodded to me without taking his eyes off the monitor.

"It sounds too fast," I said, feeling anxious again.

Eve laughed. "It's how they always sound."

He began to move the wand around again, and the noise stopped. "I just need to take a few measurements," he mumbled, flitting from worried father back to doctor mode.

"Does she look healthy, though?" I asked.

He smiled. "It all seems to be in the right place

from what I remember, but I'm going to have to refresh my memory on obstetrics for the next scan."

He clicked around on the keyboard a few more times. "Baby is fifteen weeks from conception."

We stared at the screen a little longer until he turned the machine off and pushed it aside. Eve congratulated us and announced she was going to shower and go to bed. She left after giving us both a quick hug.

Nate shook his head. "It's all a bit surreal, isn't it?"

"You think?"

He let out a sigh and rubbed his eyes. "You nearly died, Halley. You lost so much blood. I know from the I.D.R.I.S autopsy reports that the virus can't fix everything. If I couldn't save you, I'd lose you." He put his head in his hands and shuddered. "And the baby."

"She's strong. Stronger than us."

My gut feeling told me our baby was a little different than we were—still *ours*, but with a little piece of *them*. This knowledge probably should've scared me, but it didn't. In fact, I felt relieved. That *little piece of them* made her safer.

In this new world, she would thrive.

****

As October came to a close, it was time to leave. I *had* to get home to Rebecca.

"You think they'll let us go?" Nate asked me.

We were in bed, lingering under the covers to stay warm as the heating in the school had broken down, leaving the entire building distinctly chilly.

I shrugged, wincing as a sharp pain shot through my shoulder. Weeks on from the shooting incident, I was mainly just sore, but occasionally an awkward movement of my muscles made it sting and remind me of the entire ordeal.

"I'll talk to Eve later," I said.

"Good luck," Nate replied.

He leaned over to kiss my neck, placing his palm on my belly, which was now—at eighteen weeks—too prominent to hide.

Last week, at the monthly community meeting, Eve had made a lengthy speech, much to my dismay, informing everybody of the good news. Each day now, somebody would seek me out wherever I was, ask me how I was doing and if I needed anything, and bring me a gift. Our bedroom quickly grew cluttered, and whenever there was a knock on our door, I half expected the three wise men to turn up.

This time, however, the knock came from Claire.

"Hey, it's me," she shouted. "Let me in."

Nate sighed, realizing our lie-in was over and got up to unlock the door.

Claire bounded in excitedly and launched herself onto Nate's side of the bed.

"Morning!" she grinned and patted my tummy gently. "Eve sent me to get you. She promised Isabelle and Sebastian we'd all carve pumpkins for the Halloween party tomorrow night."

Eve spent most of her time with the children, doting on them as if she were their mother. Priya had begun to teach them English and the basics of a few other subjects. I rarely saw Luc, except on occasions when he joined in with their lessons in the library.

He stayed in his room most of the time. Eve said he was struggling with everything he'd been told about the virus. Who could blame him? As a former man of the church, he'd begun to question his faith.

I also suspected that he was trying to avoid everyone, especially me.

It'd taken me a while to let go of the niggling anger I felt toward Luc for shooting me and putting the baby at risk, but I knew I would need to speak to him about it soon.

"Is Luc carving pumpkins too?" I asked.

She shook her head.

"I'll go talk to him."

I got dressed out of my pajamas and told Nate I'd meet him in the courtyard before heading to Luc's room. He'd been given an old classroom to utilize as a bedroom, not far from the science lab. It was big enough to comfortably accommodate him and the children, although Sebastian and Isabelle took turns to stay with Eve and Daniel.

I knocked on his door and entered when he invited me in.

"Halley." He was clearly surprised to see me.

The room was still fairly bare on his side of the room, but on the children's side, there were already dozens of stuffed toys, various board games, and a wardrobe full of newly looted, designer kidswear.

I walked a little way into the room and flashed him an awkward smile. "Can we talk a minute?"

Luc nodded nervously. "Of course."

It was still an effort to look him in the eye. "I meant to come and see you a while ago, but I didn't know what to say."

"You don't need to say anything, Halley," he said, giving me a wretched look.

I moved closer to him. "I want you to be a part of

this community, Luc, and you can't do that hiding in here."

Luc shrugged. "I don't deserve to be a part of this community."

"Of course, you do," I said softly, leaning forward to touch his arm. "What happened was an accident, and you didn't mean to hurt me."

His eyes glistened. "No, but I still stole the gun, and I *did mean* to threaten you all with it," he replied, his voice cracking as he spoke. "I almost killed you...and your baby."

Shortly after I'd static-shocked Luc to death in the courtyard, Ben had taken him to one of the cells to recover. Max was left to guard him but, upon waking, Luc had overpowered him and escaped.

He'd sneaked down to the front of the school where the cars were still parked, and then smashed the back window of the Volvo to get the rifle, having seen Ben chuck it into the boot the night we'd brought them back to the school. Daniel and Ben had seen Luc from the office window and given chase as he'd entered the stairwell. After firing a warning shot at them, Luc had headed our way to find his children.

"I'm fine, and so is my baby," I told him.

His miserable expression didn't change. Any remnant of anger I harbored toward him, completely dissipated when I saw how utterly remorseful and dejected he was. He needed my forgiveness, but I suspected it wouldn't be enough for him—right now, he had no faith to offer him the absolution he so desperately wanted.

"It was an accident, Luc," I said, wrapping my arms around him. "I forgive you."

He shook a little in my arms but held me tight for a few seconds before pulling away.

"Thank you, Halley," he sniffed. "But I will never forgive myself."

I sighed. "Give yourself a break, Luc. You were chosen to be here just like we all were. You have a purpose. Your belief may have been tested, but you're still the same person. Mostly. We need someone like you, I think. Someone to confide in. Someone to give us counsel."

The words spilled from my mouth before I'd even given them any conscious thought. It seemed to be happening a lot lately—little whispers in the back of my mind, guiding my voice and actions.

Luc breathed deeply, considering what I'd said. It seemed to resonate with him because, after a few moments, he attempted a smile.

"Okay," he murmured. "Where do I start?"

****

The courtyard was already adorned with over a dozen pumpkins and decorated with various spooky paraphernalia. I almost tripped over a polystyrene headstone as I made my way over to the fountain, where everyone was busy carving pumpkins.

Luc followed me, somewhat apprehensively, but was greeted enthusiastically by Isabelle and Sebastian. Both of them were already covered in pumpkin entrails, their clothing stained orange and dotted with seeds. Claire, Nate, Tobias, and Priya sat on the brim of the fountain basin, intently working on their art.

Eve, who was down on the gravel in amongst buckets of pumpkin guts, got to her feet and wiped her hands down her apron. She then untied it and chucked it at Luc.

"Your turn," she chuckled.

"Merci," Luc replied.

Priya growled and let her pumpkin fall to the floor. "I'm no good at this!"

Tobias picked it up and looked at it with a frown. "What's it supposed to be?"

Priya pouted. "A cat."

Tobias spun the pumpkin around to show Isabelle and Sebastian. "Does this look like a cat to you, kids?'

Luc turned to them. "*C'est un chat*?"

Sebastian shook his head, laughing uncontrollably. "*C'est un chaussure!*"

Luc grinned. "He says it looks like a shoe."

Tobias snorted as Priya rolled her eyes. She got up and turned to Nate. "May we borrow you for a moment?"

Nate, absorbed in his creation, looked up, confused. "Huh? Oh yeh, sure."

He got up and handed me his pumpkin. The design he'd carved looked like a large hole next to something vaguely resembled a bat.

"Is that meant to be a full moon?"

He gave me a wounded look. "I think it's pretty good."

I laughed. "Well, you tried your best, and that's all that matters."

Nate kissed me and then gave me a sly wink. "Can't be good at *everything,* can I?"

"Eurgh!"

Priya touched my arm. "Won't keep him long," she said, and then she headed back into the school with Tobias and Nate.

I turned to Eve. "Where's Gabriel and Daniel?"

"Canteen, why?"

"I need to talk to you all about something."

We made our way to the canteen, where we found Gabriel, Daniel, and Ben standing around a table, examining a map of the southwest of England. It seemed fairly apt considering what I was about to ask them.

Gabriel glanced up at me. "Hi there. We were just talking about you."

I cocked my head to one side. "Oh?"

Gabriel handed me a pen and gestured toward the map. "Where were you and Nate hiding out?"

I leaned down and marked an X by the location of 'Siren Bay,' and then, after a moment of hesitation, I drew an X next to Liskeard.

"Is that where you lived before you found Nate?" Eve asked me.

"Yes. Actually, that's what I want to talk to you all about."

Pulling a chair out from under the table, I sat down on it, resting my elbows on the map over the Orkney Islands. Eve and Gabriel sat too, but Daniel continued to stand, arms crossed with a suspicious look on his face.

"My Aunt is alive. I lived with her before I found Nate, and now we need to go get her."

Gabriel pursed his lips together. "What do you want from us?"

"A car."

"We can leave today," Daniel replied. "Shouldn't take more than five or six hours to get there, right?"

I nodded. "Yes. But it's something we'd prefer to

do…alone. I've got a lot of explaining to do, lots to tell her, and it would be better if I could do that in my own time."

Daniel shook his head and laughed incredulously. "You want us to give you a car and trust that you'll come back?"

"Yes."

"No way," Daniel snapped. "Not happening."

Gabriel grinned and reached into the pockets of his jeans. He produced a set of keys and chucked them at me. "Take the truck."

Daniel ground his teeth and glared at Eve as if he expected her to support his view.

She gave him a shrug and said, "They aren't prisoners here, Daniel."

Her reaction surprised me. "We'll be back in a few days," I said.

It wasn't a lie either. We *would* be back. After everything that'd happened, I could honestly call Eve my friend. And many of the others here too. Even Laura and I had grown a little closer, despite her initial frostiness toward me. Daniel remained a mystery, and I didn't care much for Ben, but the others I would sorely miss.

Eve sighed. "I'll get the truck fueled and pack up some provisions for you."

"Thank you."

I stood and gave Gabriel a half-hug. He didn't seem to enjoy public displays of affection, often embraced against his will by Claire. He always looked thoroughly uncomfortable.

Ben, who'd stayed silent during our conversation— probably because he couldn't care less whether we stayed or left—shot me a quick smirk and said, "Where's my hug?"

"Next time, maybe."

He shrugged in mock disappointment. "Whatever."

An hour later, the truck was packed and ready to go. A few people came to wave us off, including Claire, who wore a miserable expression as she kicked aimlessly at the gravel.

"We won't be gone long," I told her.

She pouted. "I know. I just don't want you to be sad when you remember."

Her words sounded ominous, to say the least, but there was no point asking her what she meant. Even if she understood, she wouldn't tell me.

I hugged her goodbye and got into the truck. Nate started the engine, and we drove down to the school gates that'd been left open for us. As we left, I watched the school slowly disappear in the rear-view mirror, feeling a little pang of melancholy.

But, finally, I was making good on my promise and heading home.

****

Before…

As the sun rose, I woke with a start, my nightclothes drenched in sweat, my heart pounding rapidly.

I only knew the dream had been terrifying but remembered nothing of it.

The battery-powered alarm clock atop my bedside cabinet informed me it was five A.M.

It wasn't quite time for me to get up, but with the remnant adrenalin of the nightmare still coursing through me, there was no point trying to go back to sleep again. Rising wearily, I stretched my arms wide, my spine cracking as though I hadn't moved my body in days. After a brief massage of my neck muscles to soothe the painful crick, I made my bed and dressed quickly.

Before leaving the room, I reached into the top drawer of the cabinet and retrieved a small white envelope with the name 'Rebecca' written neatly across it. My fingers traced the lettering as a wave of sadness caused my heartbeat to falter. I swallowed down my emotion and clutched the letter close to my chest.

You can do this, I told myself, repetitively chanting it like a mantra in my head.

Taking one last glance around my bedroom, I shut the door as quietly as I could and then crept across the lounge and into the kitchen.

The remnants of our last meal together were still on the dining table, so I set the letter down against a wine bottle where I was sure she would find it.

Rebecca.

On tiptoes, I slipped back into the lounge and toward Rebecca's bedroom. The door was ajar enough for me to poke my head through the gap and look in on her. She was soundly asleep, so swaddled up in her duvet that all I could see were the long tendrils of her dark hair spread out over her pillow.

I blew her a silent kiss. "Goodbye, Rebecca."

Outside, the sun rose higher into a cloud-strewn, pink and orange sky. As the rays broke through the cloud and touched my skin, I tilted my head back and closed my eyes, savoring the warmth.

The twittering of a sparrow brought me out of my reverie. The little bird sat on the thickest branch of a nearby apple tree, flexing its mottled black and brown feathers as it chirped and sang. It gave me a brief glance before it took off and flew southwards, to the ocean.

As I made my way around to the garage to collect my backpack and bike, the worries and doubts began to circulate in my mind again. My hand hovered uncertainly over the door lever for a few seconds before I took a deep breath and twisted the handle.

You *can* do this.

I conjured up an image of the ocean and closed my eyes, trying to recall the sounds of the tide coming ashore—the roaring whoosh of the surf, and the clank of rolling pebbles as the sea dragged them into its belly.

You can do this.

I lifted up the garage door just enough to duck under it and then walked the bike down the path through the front garden, resting it against the fence while I returned quickly to close the heavy metal door. If it were open for more than a few minutes, an opportunistic squirrel would get in and wreak havoc on the packets of dried food stored in there.

Once I mounted the bike, I let it coast down the lane toward the highway. At the main road, my feet found the peddles, cycling fast and hard until my thighs cramped, and I couldn't ride anymore. Then I got off and walked, covering as much distance as possible before sunset, by which time my aching legs were like jelly.

Tomorrow, I would head along the coast.

Finding an old bus stop to sleep in, I huddled down into my sleeping bag with a contented smile on my face, knowing I'd traveled too far to turn around and go back home.

Chapter Twenty-Six

After…

After three hours on the road, Nate pulled the truck over by a petrol station to stretch his legs. I took the opportunity to use the bathroom situated in a small building on the far edge of the car park. The women's bathroom stank of stale urine and mold. I managed to pee quickly and hurry back outside without retching.

Nate went into the kiosk to see if there was anything worth looting. The glazing in the entrance door was smashed, though the little shards of glass had been cleared to one side of the floor, leaving a clear path inside.

When he came out, he seemed a little unsettled. "I've been here before."

"What do you mean?"

"I looted this place years ago."

He took hold of my hand and led me around the building to the side that faced the motorway heading south. In big, black spray-painted letters on the whitewashed wall of the kiosk, Nate had written a message.

SURVIVORS COME TO SIREN BAY was there for all to see, and just below it was a map of the lower half of England, hand-painted and a little crude, but easy to follow. One red dot marked the location of the petrol station, and one red X marked the location of

Nate's cabin.

I moved closer, tracing the X with my fingers. "Good thing I didn't need a map to find you."

"Guess not." He wrapped his arms around me and rested his hands on my stomach. "Want to know some hot gossip?"

"Always."

He laughed. "Actually, it isn't *really* gossip because they said I could tell you. I'm not breaking patient-doctor confidentially or anything."

I wheeled to face him, hand on hips, shooting him a demanding frown. "*What* are you talking about?"

"Priya is pregnant."

"What?"

"That's what she and Tobias wanted to talk to me about. Priya suspected but wasn't sure, so they asked me to confirm it."

I blinked. "The drug worked?"

"I hadn't started her on it."

It took me a moment to process the information, but it still didn't make sense. "Then, how?"

He shrugged. "I don't know. I have a few theories, but nothing I can prove right now. I originally assumed the virus had made a mistake and hadn't been able to re-start the female reproductive system after destroying all the ova, but that doesn't seem to be the case now. Besides, *they* don't make mistakes, do they? I think reproduction just works differently now."

"Different how?"

"What if an egg is created and released exactly when it's needed rather than every month? It's a far more efficient means of population control, especially in a population that will age slower and live longer?"

"That only explains the absence of good old 'auntie flow' though," I replied.

He chuckled and threw his hands in the air. "Exactly. It doesn't explain why it took nearly five years for someone to conceive a child, or how you—an unevolved human—managed to conceive in the first place."

"Maybe *they* decide when we get to have children."

He shook his head. "Maybe, but I think it's more about community. Ultimately, we all need each other. Survival is easier in groups. Perhaps we all just needed to be together first."

I smirked. "Fine. We'll go with that."

We walked back to the truck and recommenced our journey, veering away from the main roads as much as possible to avoid getting stuck behind roadblocks or traffic jams. Mostly we were able to drive through the countryside, only having to reverse once or twice to find another route after coming across fallen trees or potholes so large they'd become swimming pools. The truck was efficient at plowing through overgrown bramble, but the windscreen suffered a crack when an overhanging vine smacked so hard against the glass, I instinctively ducked.

It forced us to slow down significantly, and it was dark when the truck headlights finally fell upon Rebecca's cottage as we pulled into the driveway.

No light came from inside, no sign that anyone lived here at all. Not that it was unusual for my Aunt to be in bed by this time of night, although I did wonder if she'd left home and come after me since I'd been away so long.

If so, where the hell was she now?

Nate grabbed a couple of torches from the glove compartment—part of the provisions packed by Eve—and we both slid out of the truck, somewhat apprehensively. The night was eerily silent except for the occasional hoot of an owl and the sound of our footsteps on the concrete pathway.

When we reached the side door, I opened it cautiously, waving the beam of my torch around the kitchen. A smell of something decaying and rotten imbued the air around me and burnt my nostrils, prompting me to use my sleeve to cover my mouth and nose to prevent me from gagging.

The smell was familiar. It was the same sickly odor that had filled the corridors and wards of the hospital. There was death here too.

Ignoring the sinking feeling in my gut, we moved forward through the kitchen and into the lounge. It was cold in here; no glowing embers in the fire, no recently expunged candle wicks. So cold.

Nate stopped me as I reached my hand out to Rebecca's bedroom door.

"Don't," he whispered.

My hand dropped to my side, and I stepped back so he could move in front of me. He pushed the door open slowly and shone his torch around the room.

"Stay there," he commanded me as he walked forward. He paused briefly to cough and cover his nose before he disappeared from my view.

I wanted to follow him, but I couldn't. An overwhelming sense of foreboding kept my feet from stepping through the doorway, much like the time I stood outside of the bathroom in my mother's flat while she lay dead in the bathtub.

Nate reappeared after a minute and firmly closed the bedroom door behind him.

He took hold of my shoulders. "I'm sorry, Halley."

Rebecca was dead.

"How?"

"It looks like she died in her sleep," Nate whispered

"When? How? I don't understand."

I pulled away from his grasp and went back into the kitchen to stand by the open door. The stench was worse by Rebecca's bedroom, and if I didn't get some air, I'd throw up.

When my torchlight fell onto the kitchen table, I spied my letter to Rebecca exactly where I'd left it, unopened and propped up against the mostly empty bottle of wine. The blood iced in my veins as I grabbed the letter and turned it over in my hands. The envelope was still sealed.

"She didn't read my letter," I muttered as Nate surveyed the mess on the kitchen table. All the plates from our last meal together were still there, moldy from the remnants of food we hadn't managed to finish.

"Rebecca was alive when you left her?" he asked me, picking up the wine bottle and sniffing the neck.

"Yes. I checked on her before I left. She was asleep. I think." The stink of decomposing flesh and putrid food began to make me feel lightheaded. "I...I don't know."

He took the wine bottle over to the kitchen counter and poured the dregs into a glass tumbler. For a second, I thought he was going to drink it, but instead, he held it up to his torch and swilled the red liquid around, peering closely at it. I moved to his side, watching a strange, powdery film form on the surface of the wine.

"What is it?"

He frowned and dropped the glass into the sink. His eyes darted around the kitchen until he spied the bin. He stood on the pedal to open the lid and then used a wooden ladle to turn the contents over. Suddenly, he stopped and reached his hand inside, pulling out a small box.

"Diazepam," he muttered.

My Aunt's pills.

He ripped open the box and slid out the foil blister packets, which contained the pills. Each one of the packets were empty.

He looked at me, his eyes full of sadness and pity. "I think Rebecca overdosed, Halley. She crushed up the pills and put them in her drink."

"But why would she do that? Why put them in the wine? I drank it too, Nate."

He blinked. "That many pills…you'd have been able to taste it," he replied and then looked at all the pots and pans on the countertop. "Who cooked dinner?"

There was that horrid sinking feeling again. "She did."

He picked up one of the saucepans and ran his finger over the lip finding a small trace of the white powder.

My jaw clenched involuntarily as grief turned to anger. "She put it in the food."

Unable to stomach being inside the cottage anymore, I ran outside and vomited violently onto the pathway. Nate was behind me in seconds, arms around me and holding my head against his chest as I sank to my knees.

"I would know, wouldn't I?" I whispered. "I would know if I'd died?"

But Nate hadn't known. He'd simply taken the pills and fallen asleep, waking up none the wiser.

I thought back to the last night that I'd spent here. It'd been fine, hadn't it? No obvious indication that she intended to kill us both with a fatal overdose. Had I remembered it wrong?

Suddenly, as I searched my mind for answers, a floodgate opened, and the truth came pouring in.

"You can still come with me," I'd said as Rebecca had served up a spicy carrot and coriander soup. Too much chilli powder. Spiced up to conceal the bitter taste of Diazepam.

She had poured herself a large glass of red wine and then filled my glass to the brim.

"No," she'd said. "I'll wait here and keep everything going, like you always did for me when I had to go away."

Halfway through the main course, I'd begun to feel tired. Really tired. But it'd been a long, exhausting day, checking I'd packed everything and then re-packing. I'd also deep cleaned the chicken pen so that Rebecca wouldn't have to do it for a while.

I'd declined a second glass of wine when she tried to fill my glass again. "Oh, just one more."

Dessert had been steamed fruit and sweet honey. Sickly sweet.

"Get an early night," she'd said. Then, we'd hugged. "I love you, Halley. I wish you didn't have to go." She'd kissed my cheek, and I remembered feeling something wet against my skin. When I'd looked back at her, there'd been tears in the corners of her eyes.

Once in my bedroom, I'd practically fallen onto my bed, just managing to set the alarm clock before my eyes grew so heavy I couldn't keep them open any longer.

For a long time, I remembered there being nothing but darkness and the faintest of whisperings in my head.

Until the dream came.

****

Before…

I am in a barren desert. I am alone, surrounded by mountains of reddish-brown, their peaks covered by gray ash. I walk forward because there is nowhere else to go, pressing on for what seems like hours until eventually, I reach the base of one of the mountains. There is a lake here, spanning as far as the eye can see and, in the middle of it, is a wooden structure.

A cabin.

The water of the lake is black and reflects nothing but the miserable gray sky. I look around for a way across, but there isn't one. My only option is to swim.

The deep, dark water terrifies me, but I wade in until the black oily liquid reaches my waist. The water is warm and feels like treacle against my skin, which makes it hard to swim in, but I force my body through the water, and just as I think my arms and legs are about to seize, my feet find something hard to stand on.

There are wooden steps beneath the lake, and I clamber up each one until I am out of the water and standing on the wooden veranda that encircles the cabin.

Exhausted and breathing hard, I walk slowly to the front door. It is open, although I cannot see what's inside because the doorway is blocked by something dark, shimmering and rippling like a rectangle of upright water. I linger there frustrated, until I pluck up the courage to plunge my hand into the rippling pool and then propel the rest of my body through after it.

The world inside the cabin is very different; it is warm and cozy, lit by the glow of a dozen candles. A man sits on the floor with his back to me, holding a small child, maybe a year old, on his knee. He is reading 'Alice's Adventures in Wonderland' to her.

The child looks up at me with the most beautiful blue-gray eyes I've ever seen, even though they're ringed with the red of the virus. The man gently slides the child off his knee and onto the carpet before getting to his feet. He turns around and smiles at me.

"She has your eyes," he says.

He has beautiful eyes too, dark and a little sad, but also full of love.

"Where am I?" I ask.

"Home," he replies.

He steps forward and kisses me. I should pull away from this strange man, but I don't. When his lips finally leave mine, he smiles again and gestures to the child on the floor.

"See, she's perfect. She's safe from the virus. All the children will be safe. I need you to remember that, Halley. It's important. Tell the others."

I shake my head, confused. "There are no others."

"You don't believe that. That's why you came here," he replies.

"Who are you?"

The man grins. "I'm someone you trust."

I laugh in disbelief. "I don't trust anyone!"

"You trust me," he says.

"I don't know you!"

The man leans forward and kisses me again. I don't resist this time either.

"You will. You just have to find me. Find us."

I blink, and he is gone.

Everything is gone.

I am standing back where I started, all alone again.

"No," I shout, spinning around, my eyes searching the horizon in the hope that I'll find the cabin again.

But it isn't there.

I scream.

****

Now...

The cottage burned like old, dry newspaper. Once the flames began to lick the roof, the thatch caught quickly, sending thick black smoke up into the night air. When the heat of the fire on my cheeks grew too hot to bear, I climbed into the truck and continued to watch the destruction from the comfort of the passenger seat.

In the footwell was my mother's copy of *Wuthering Heights* and Lizzie's letters. They were the only things I'd taken from the cottage before asking Nate to burn it to the ground.

As he slid into the driver's seat, I shuffled over a little to lay my head on his shoulder. We hadn't said a word to each other in over an hour—neither of us knew *what* to say. No words of comfort could quell the swirling storm of anger and guilt and grief within me.

Finally, though, when the cottage was almost nothing but a mass of shrinking bonfires, I cleared my throat and spoke.

"Why would she do this? Do you think it was my fault for wanting to leave?"

Nate stroked my hair and sighed. "No. This isn't your fault. I can only make a guess as to why she did this, given my own struggle with the darkness."

"And?"

"She went mad, Halley."

It was almost funny. I tilted my head to look up at him. "You knew, didn't you?"

He arched an eyebrow. "Knew what?"

"That I was already dead."

He inhaled deeply and leaned back against the headrest. Truth was, he hadn't looked remotely surprised by any of this.

"I wasn't sure," he said. "I became suspicious when your wound healed so quickly, much faster than that type of injury normally would. But I also thought it might've been because I gave you *my* blood. That it somehow sped up the healing process."

"I see."

"Not to mention, the process of death is what fully activates the virus within us. It's like a reboot. I don't think conception is possible in an unevolved survivor," he added.

I managed a smile in order to mock him. "Must be nice to know all the answers."

He rolled his eyes. "Not even close, Halley. I still don't know why you were the first to conceive."

"They chose us," I said, matter-of-factly.

"Why us? Chosen for what?"

My hand went to my belly, giving it a soft pat. "Chose us to be her parents, Nate. She's a little different from us, though. I can feel it. Not in a bad way—in a good way. *They* sent me to you so that we could make her."

"Did *they?*"

I nodded. "The night I died was the first time I dreamed of the red desert. I just didn't remember it until now. It was awful. Horrible. You were there, and then you just disappeared."

He hugged me a little tighter. "You probably blocked everything out. It was probably too traumatic for you to remember until you came back here, and it triggered the memory."

I recalled what Lizzie had told me in one of my dreams. *"I'm sorry, Halley. It's going to hurt you, but you really must remember."*

Quite an understatement, in truth.

"What did I do in this dream?" Nate asked.

"You gave me a message and told me not to forget. Which I did, until now. You said the children would be safe from the virus. All the children. Then you told me to find you."

"So, they pretended to be me to give you this message?"

I bit my lip. "No. It *was* you."

Nate closed one eye, skeptically. "I'll have to give that concept some serious thought."

"I wouldn't bother. I'm sure *they'll* explain things eventually. Besides, we have more important things to focus on."

Nate nodded. "So, back to London then?"

I took one last look at the remnants of the cottage. "Not yet."

Epilogue

I needed to go home.

Although I considered London to be our home now too, Nate's cabin was more than that. It was our sanctuary and exactly where I wanted to be more than anywhere else right now.

I dozed a little on the way but woke when the truck's engine coughed to a halt at the top of the steep road that led to 'Siren Bay.' We headed down, just as the sun rose amidst a light rain.

The moment I saw the cabin, my heart lifted, and the sound of the sea filled me with a sense of calm I hadn't felt in a long time.

While Nate quickly went around back to turn the power back on, I waited on the front porch, watching the sky turn from a deep blue, streaked with pink, to a stormy gray. My nose savored the salty air as I closed my eyes and listened to the seagulls squawk, and the gentle tapping of raindrops falling onto the wooden veranda.

When I heard Nate's footsteps behind me, I opened my eyes again and leaned back against him as his arms went around me.

"How long are we staying?"

I sighed. "Forever?"

Nate chuckled. "Tempting."

I swiveled around and put my arms around his

neck, pulling his head toward me so that I could kiss him. "We'll stay a few days, then head back to London."

He nodded and yawned. "Okay. What do you want to do now?"

"Go to bed."

Nate grinned.

"To sleep," I added, with a smile.

He feigned disappointment. "And after that?"

"I don't know, what did *you* have in mind?" I asked him.

His expression became sheepish. "Monopoly?"

I tutted and rolled my eyes. "Thought you wanted to cheer me up?"

"I'll let you win again."

My mouth dropped open. "You did not *let* me win!"

He laughed. "C'mon Halley, everyone knows you buy Mayfair as soon as you get the chance!"

I shook my head and playfully slapped his arm. "Fine. A rematch it is."

As the rain began to fall with a greater intensity, a low growl of thunder emanated from a cluster of charcoal-tinted clouds out to sea.

Taking hold of Nate's hand, I led him into the cabin and closed the door firmly on the oncoming storm.

A word from the author...

My inspiration for this book came from a strange dream I had one night. I put it down to eating too much cheese before bedtime, but the story stayed with me, and so, en-route to a comic-con in Birmingham, I began to write it down. The story isn't finished yet—although this part of Halley and Nate's tale is over, there are so many questions that still need answering. All I can say is; stick around, you're going to love it.

As for the real world, I am a mum residing in the southeast of England. Geek to the core, I am often found at comic-cons dressed as my favorite characters—usually from fantasy or science fiction—while indulging in a bit of celebrity stalking. I also enjoy napping with my dog.

Lightning Source UK Ltd.
Milton Keynes UK
UKHW020955081219
354991UK00015B/526/P